Catherine Mangan grew up in Ireland and studied languages at University College Cork. Shortly after graduation she moved to Italy, which was the beginning of a life-long love affair with the country. Under another name, Catherine is an award-winning Irish entrepreneur. She now divides her time between Ireland and the USA.

Also by Catherine Mangan

The Italian Escape

Catherine Mangan

One Italian Summer

Cath Mangan

SPHERE

SPHERE

First published in Great Britain in 2022 by Sphere

1 3 5 7 9 10 8 6 4 2

A CIP catalogue record for this book
is available from the British Library.

ISBN 978-0-7515-7987-1

Typeset in Baskerville by M Rules
Printed and bound in Great Britain by
Clays Ltd, Elcograf S.p.A.

Papers used by Sphere are from well-managed forests
and other responsible sources.

Sphere
An imprint of
Little, Brown Book Group
Carmelite House
50 Victoria Embankment
London EC4Y 0DZ

An Hachette UK Company
www.hachette.co.uk

www.littlebrown.co.uk

For Alex and Luca.
My biggest and littlest fans.

Chapter One

Lily Ryan weaved her way through the glamorous, post-work crowd, waving excitedly when she spotted her best friend Dee already seated on a high stool at the bar.

'You really need to work on your entry, you know. That wave was far too energetic,' Dee said with a sarcastic eye roll.

'I know, sorry. I'm just glad it's Friday,' Lily said, wrapping her friend in a big hug. 'My boss caught me on the phone to my sister in Dublin at lunchtime and was totally passive-aggressive with me all afternoon, *and* she said I'm short one vacation day for the Italian trip so she's docking my wages. I swear to God she's on a personal crusade to ruin my life. She's such a miserable cow.'

Lily sat heavily on the stool alongside Dee, hanging her bag on a hook directly underneath the bar. They had arranged to meet at the Monkey Bar, a retro-chic cocktail bar and restaurant in the high-profile East 54th Street neighbourhood of Manhattan. The Monkey Bar had long been a favourite of publishing and entertainment executives, but a feature in the hugely successful *Sex and the City* sitcom brought it to the attention of the younger, up-and-coming executive crowd.

'You're looking very glam,' Dee said, raising her glass of wine to her lips. 'What's that all about?'

'Are you joking? I have to make an effort when you pick a place like this, and unlike you I'm not dressed in a power suit with sharp edges and fancy jewellery all day. God, it's so swanky, isn't it? Look at these people,' Lily said, turning to scan the well-heeled crowd.

'Yep, you can smell the money. All these powerful mid-town types. Honestly, these chicks spend more on their outfits than I do on my monthly mortgage payment,' Dee said, glancing around the crowded, dimly lit bar. 'It's not really my thing,' she shrugged, 'but it's close to the office, so it takes less time to get to my first post-work drink.'

'I think it's fabulous! I can pretend to be glamorous and sophisticated for a couple of hours, before I head home, put on my PJs and order Thai food online.' Lily grinned. 'But not tonight – I'm meeting Peter for dinner after this at Marea.'

Dee raised an eyebrow in mock disdain. 'Swankier still!'

The bartender placed a monogrammed coaster on the bar in front of Lily.

'What will it be, ma'am?' he asked, with a friendly smile.

'I'll have a vodka Martini, please.'

'How would you like it?'

'Sorry? Oh right, yeah. Um ... dry, please, and um ... with a twist. Thanks,' she replied, feeling her cheeks flush.

'Coming right up.'

Jesus, Lily ... Vodka Martini, dry with a twist. How hard is it to say that all in one go? she said to herself with a loud sigh.

'Since when do you drink Martinis?'

'I've been practising.'

'How do you practise drinking a Martini? I mean, what is there to practise?'

'I had to get out of my pink drink phase,' Lily said, nudging her stool closer to the bar. 'It just reeks of girly drinks. Peter drinks Martinis, so I thought I'd see if I could like them.'

She cringed inwardly as she heard the words come out of her mouth. The look of disapproval from Dee was instant and unmistakable.

'Eh . . . since when do you drink what Peter drinks?' Dee asked, frowning slightly.

'I don't!' Lily said defensively. 'I just like the glasses. Don't go all "women's rights" on me. I just needed a more grown-up drink to go with my new life as a successful copy-writer. Cheers!'

'Ah, that's right. Cheers to that. New job, new man, new drink of choice. Got it. So, are you still madly in love?' Dee asked, referring to Lily's boyfriend of six months, Peter.

'Yes, but it's costing me a fortune in lingerie. I had to dump my entire underwear drawer. Nothing matched any more. So now I think I'm contributing significantly to Victoria Secret's EBITDA this quarter.'

'Okay, first of all, you do know you can wash and re-wear your knickers, right? You don't have to don new undies every time you see the man. Second, since when do you know or care about EBITDA?'

'Oh, I had to learn all this new financial language at work. I'm attending the senior team meetings now and I felt like a total dope when they started talking about finances.

So, I paid one of the junior finance guys to teach me what I'd need to know in order to survive the senior team meetings. I paid for drinks a couple of nights a week for three weeks and now I sound smart!' she said, proudly. 'Man, this Martini is good!'

'You're sounding more American by the day,' Dee laughed.

'So, did you get your tux?' Lily asked, her eyes not leaving her Martini glass as she raised it slowly to her lips.

Dee rolled her eyes. 'No, they screwed up the order. I really don't want to talk about it, I'll just get into a rage in my head again. Anyway, they're a bunch of imbeciles. I should have known better than go to a department store in the first place,' she said, shaking her head.

'*What?*' Lily screeched. 'So, what are you going to do now? You're getting married in a few weeks.'

'Yeah, don't remind me. Why did I ever let Morgan talk me into a fancy wedding in Italy? We should have just gone to City Hall and buggered off afterwards to Bora Bora, or something like that ... Hang on a second,' she said, placing her right hand on Lily's arm. 'Excuse me!' she said, signalling the waiter. 'Can I have another one of these, please?'

'Coming right up, ma'am,' he said with a nod.

'So, what are you going to do now?'

'Oh, Morgan has stepped in.'

'Uh-oh. Is she displeased with you?' Lily asked, with a grin.

Morgan, Dee's soon-to-be wife, had a notoriously short fuse and a wicked temper. She was used to the finer things in life and would stand for nothing short of exceptional service. Morgan was sophisticated, successful and loyal to a point, but incompetence and sloppiness were easy triggers for her rage.

'No, she has just sworn off said department store for life. She took the matter in hand and went directly to her stylist at Tom Ford.'

'Tom FORD?' Lily shrieked. 'Tom Ford is like, a thousand dollars for a pair of pants!'

'It could be more actually, and yes, the tuxedo is costing four thousand dollars. But apparently that is okay because a) it is my wedding, and b) it's a bargain because it's off the rack.'

'Sweet Jesus, that's two months' rent.'

'Trust me, it's easier to spend the money than listen to Morgan.'

'I suppose so,' Lily said, her eyebrows raised in disbelief. 'Right, so what other details do we need to finalise? I haven't had to do anything as your maid of honour yet.'

'This is why people go to the registry office.' Dee grimaced. 'All this wedding crap. I never wanted any of it.'

'Yeah, well we both know you don't have a say in the matter.' Lily laughed. 'Should I get a second one of these, or would that be bad?'

'Eh, sorry, excuse me? Since when do you question having a second drink? I hope this man isn't changing you too much, Lily Ryan!' Dee said in her thick Dublin accent. Turning to catch the barman's eye, she motioned to the two glasses. 'We'll take another round when you have a chance, please.'

The barman gave a wink in their direction. 'Sure thing, ladies. Settling in for the night?'

'Could be.' Dee nodded. 'Do you have any nuts or anything?'

'I've got popcorn. I'll get some right over to you.'

'Awesome, thanks.'

'And you say that I'm the one sounding more American?'

'Listen, I've been here twenty years. That's one year longer than I lived in Dublin, so I'm allowed say "awesome".' Dee laughed. 'Christ, do we have to talk about this wedding? It's all we talk about at home.'

'Well, if you want me to help, then yes, we do.'

'Okay, so I have to finalise the ceremony details. Morgan wants nothing to do with that part. She's taking care of the resort, music, food, all that stuff. I'm doing the wine – there's no way I was letting her choose the wine. We'd be flying in some reserve bottles from France if she had her way.'

'God, yes, she'd lose her mind altogether with that,' Lily said, as the barman placed another round of drinks and a bowl of warm popcorn in front of them.

'No, we're going Italian and we're going local. I put my foot down.'

'Wow, how did that feel?' Lily asked with a frown, as she carefully lifted her second Martini glass.

'Terrifying,' Dee said, throwing her had back with her signature raucous laugh. 'Anyway, I have to do the ceremony and I don't actually know what's involved. I googled foreign weddings but all I get is all this soppy crap and hymns. I'm looking for the basic requirements here to actually get out the other side of this.'

'Um, I'm not sure if I'm allowed ask this question, but why is this the first time I'm hearing about this? Have you done *anything* for the ceremony yet?'

'Don't start. We just had a disastrous quarter and I had to claw back forty million dollars from our budget, so I'm really unpopular at work and given the state of the economy, fintech in general is screwed right now. My life's a mess.' She shook her head. 'I really don't have the head space for any of this ceremony shit so yes, I need your help.'

Dee was chief financial officer for Paratee Financial, a publicly traded financial technology platform, and so was ultimately responsible for the finances of the 200 million-dollar company.

'Funny, I always think of shark costumes when I hear "fintech",' Lily said, grinning.

'Not helping, Lily!'

'No, I know, sorry. Okay, so what can I do? I could find some not-too-soppy readings or verses, or whatever they're called. Ooh, what about music? I could google some songs for the violinist to play. You booked a violinist, didn't you?'

'No, she has since been replaced with a string quartet, and that's Morgan's remit so I'm not messing with that. Can you just find some readings that are not too vomit-inducing? I don't want any of that perfect love stuff. Just some normal love stuff.'

'Normal love stuff. Got it.' Lily nodded in support.

'Right. I've got to head. I'm meeting Morgan at Nobu.'

'Okay, me too. I'm meeting Peter in twenty minutes,' Lily said, her face brightening into a wide smile.

Peter was older than her by twelve years and divorced with two sons whom he rarely saw. He ran his own head-hunting company, which was massively successful, and was very well connected in the New York social scene, as connections were imperative for his business. While Lily wasn't easily impressed by money, she had to admit that the past few months had been a fun rollercoaster ride of great restaurants, fine wines and some lovely pieces of jewellery.

'So, are you wearing new underwear for your date?'

'Yep! Teal green. He says it brings out my eyes.'

'But you don't have green eyes.' Dee frowned.

'Yeah, I know, I think he might be colour-blind, but I don't want to ask. I like the compliments, even if they're for eyes of a different colour. I don't want to put him off!' Lily giggled.

'That's not weird at all ... Okay, so do you want to meet for brunch tomorrow or are you fleeing to the Hamptons?' Dee asked, signalling for the bill.

'Can't, I have that goddamn baby shower tomorrow.'

'Christ, do people still have those? I thought they went out with the nineties?'

'I wish. Nothing worse than sitting in a room full of new mothers all congratulating each other on how clever their babies are, and my favourite part is when they give me a sympathetic smile and tell me that my time will come too,' Lily said, rolling her eyes. 'I think I've caught your eye-roll habit.'

'Condescending bitches. Just because they've got a sprog stuck to their hip they assume that every other woman on the planet wants the same thing.'

'So, you don't fancy coming with me then?' Lily joked.

'I'd rather shove chopsticks under my nails.'

'So, that's a "no"?'

They both laughed.

'I've got this,' Lily said, pushing Dee back and handing her card to the barman. 'I think I've been a crap maid of honour so far, so at least let me pay for the drinks.'

'Okay, just make sure you find some half-decent poems or whatever,' Dee said, picking up her purse and making way for the four well-heeled women hustling to land on her bar stool first. 'Try not to drop any babies tomorrow. Doesn't look good on a résumé.'

'I told you, I have my perfect job now!' Lily said with a proud smile.

'Oh, that's right. I keep forgetting that you are no longer my normal, scatty friend, but you are now successful, in love and on the path to true happiness. What's that like?' she said, grinning, as they reached the door of the Monkey Bar.

'I'm living my best life!' Lily joked, waving over her shoulder at her friend. She turned the corner and made her way down Madison Avenue.

Chapter Two

Lily arrived at the front door of Marea, an elegant seafood restaurant on West 59th Street, just before seven o'clock. Summer in New York brought searing waves of humidity that sat like a heavy cloud between the tall skyscrapers flanking both sides of every street. It only took a few blocks to go from being perfectly made up to looking like a hot, sweaty mess. Pushing through the double doors, Lily made her way through the vast lobby, keeping to the right so she wouldn't be seen from the bar – a firm favourite of the glamorous midtown set. Elegantly dressed women air-kissed each other as friends and colleagues met for pre-dinner drinks.

'How come none of them have moisturiser rolling down their faces?' Lily muttered as she pushed open the solid oak door of the bathroom.

'You're a shiny mess, Lily,' she proclaimed, as she patted her face with a tissue, grimacing at her reflection in the mirror.

It was the kind of establishment that considered paper towels too commonplace and instead displayed baskets of neatly rolled, miniature cloth towels. Lily soaked one under the cold tap and, reaching under her dress, dabbed under her arms, and under her bra, letting out a sigh as the cold towel touched her skin. A click behind her alerted her to the fact that an older lady in a pinstripe skirt suit had stepped out from a cubicle. In horror, Lily realised that she was flashing her underwear in the mirror as she dabbed sweat from her underwired bra.

'Oh God, sorry! So hot out, isn't it?' she said, faking a smile.

The lady dropped her gaze to the floor and raised an eyebrow as she quickly rinsed her hands and breezed past Lily without uttering a word.

'Please don't be sitting at the table next to me at dinner,' Lily whispered, this time under her breath, as she flipped open her purse and pulled out several pieces of rescue make-up. 'I can't sit next to someone who has seen my knickers in public.'

She never used to carry so much make-up, or even wear it, but then she didn't frequent such upscale restaurants, with such a stylish crowd. Leaning in towards the gilded mirror, she reapplied some foundation and finished with some Charlotte Tilbury magic powder.

'Much better,' she said, with a smile, as she snapped the gold compact shut.

Trying not to limp too obviously, she walked across the foyer in the direction of the main restaurant. Her new shoes were pinching her heels. Shouldn't have worn leather in this heat, she thought, shaking her head. Fixing her posture – chin up, shoulders back – she reminded herself to slow her pace, just as she had observed other New York women do when they walked in high heels.

'It looks like they've been in training to walk like that,' she had observed one evening to Dee.

'They are in training. Haven't you heard? There are twice as many single women as there are single men in this city. That's a tough landscape to navigate for those in pursuit of a husband.'

'No, I mean to walk that precisely, like models on a catwalk.'

'Well they are some pretty lethal heels. I think it's a case of either slow down or fall down. You can't charge across a marble floor in four-inch heels. It won't end well,' Dee had said as she sucked the end of her mojito through her straw.

Lily smiled at the memory as she paused momentarily outside the door of the restaurant, adjusting her skirt before rounding the door in the direction of the hostess stand.

'Welcome to Marea. How may I help you this evening?' the hostess asked with a wide smile that displayed perfect white teeth.

'Good evening. I'm meeting someone here. Mr Peter Allen,' Lily replied, standing up a little taller as she looked up at the elegantly dressed woman.

'Of course. Mr Allen is already here. Please follow me,' she replied, with the same automatic wide smile.

The hostess turned and made her way slowly towards the back of the restaurant. Lily caught the unmistakable flash of red from the soles of the hostess's shoes.

Louboutins! She's wearing six-hundred-dollar shoes! she thought to herself with a pang of envy. I have got to up my shoe game.

Peter was seated at the table, speaking quietly into his

phone. He winked at Lily and smiled as the hostess pulled out the chair for her to sit.

'Enjoy your evening,' she said, smiling her perfect smile and nodding to both of them before turning to return to her post.

'Sorry, this will just take a second,' Peter whispered in his soft London accent, covering his phone with his hand. 'Get yourself a drink!' he added, before returning to his phone call.

God! You look hot, Lily thought as she watched him gesture towards his phone.

He was immaculately dressed as always, this time in a lightweight, dark navy suit and a pale blue shirt. The tie had already been discarded and the top button opened. Lily had come to learn that this was his way of transitioning from the workday to dinner, unless of course the restaurant called for a jacket and tie, in which case he would loosen the tie just a smidge.

'Sorry!' he mouthed across the table.

'No, no problem!' Lily said, waving her hand in dismissal.

'Can I get you something to drink perhaps ma'am?' a waiter asked, having appeared to her right.

She recognised him but couldn't remember his name. John ... James ... something like that, she thought, running through a list of names in her head.

Peter knew everyone's name as this was one of his favourite restaurants.

'Um ... yes. Do you have a Prosecco by the glass?'

'No ma'am, but we have several champagnes by the glass. Would you like to see the drinks list?'

'Oh, sure, thanks,' she said, feeling a flush of

13

embarrassment rise up her cheeks. Of course they don't have Prosecco, Lily, she admonished herself silently. This isn't your friendly local. They don't do Prosecco. They do *real* champagne.

The waiter returned and handed her a heavy, leather-bound drinks list, which he held open at the page listing champagne by the glass.

Sweet Jesus, the price of them! she thought in quiet horror. Normally, Peter did all the ordering as he was particular about what wines he did or didn't want to drink, and as a result, Lily was blithely unaware of the prices.

The cheapest glass of champagne was twenty-seven dollars, the most expensive an alarming two hundred dollars.

'Um . . . I'll have a glass of this please,' she said, pointing to the least offensive option.

'Right away,' he replied with a smile, as he snapped the leatherbound book closed.

She sat back into her chair, admiring the soft décor of the room. It was exceedingly elegant, but welcoming, and was already filled with well-dressed people, engaged in quiet conversations. Lily shifted in her chair and flicked her long, dark brown hair back over her shoulder. She glanced down at the buttons of her dress to make sure they were still firmly in place. The second button down had threatened to pop out before she left her apartment, so she had secured it with a safety pin. She tugged self-consciously at the fabric now, as she sat casually surveying her surroundings.

'Thank God. I'm so sorry – I thought he'd never let up!' Peter said, slipping his phone into his pocket and leaning across the table to squeeze her hand. 'The guy is on the west coast so it's still middle of the day for him. Either he can't tell the time, or he doesn't care that I'm in New York. Anyway,' he said, grinning, 'you look great! Wait – where's your drink?'

'Thanks. I just ordered one,' she replied, beaming.

The barman returned at that precise moment, brandishing a bottle of Louis Roederer.

'Jamie, what the hell is that?' Peter asked, a look of mild amusement on his face.

Jamie! thought Lily. That's his name!

'The lady ordered a glass of Roederer,' the waiter replied slowly.

'Good God, man. You should know better than that. She must have been mistaken. Bring a bottle of Billy rosé please. Thank you, Jamie.'

'Right away, sir,' Jamie replied, without batting an eyelid.

'You can't drink that rubbish!' Peter said, with a large laugh. 'Either drink good champagne or none at all. Nothing worse than a cheap champagne headache, my love.'

'Cheap? That was twenty-seven dollars a glass!' Lily exclaimed.

'Exactly!' Peter laughed.

'What did you order instead?'

'Billy. The rosé. It's excellent. You'll like it.'

'Billy? That's the name of the champagne?'

'Well, no, Billecart-Salmon is the proper name, but everyone calls it Billy.'

'It sounds ridiculous, like a joke name.'

Peter shrugged. 'Yeah, I suppose, but it's no different than calling a bottle of Dom Perignon "Dom", or calling guacamole "guac".'

'Are you serious? You call guacamole "guac"?' she

giggled. 'Honestly, for someone so sophisticated, you can sound really ridiculous at times.'

'Thanks. That's the nicest thing you've said to me so far this evening,' Peter joked.

Jamie returned and poured Lily a taste of the Billecart-Salmon champagne. Peter nodded in approval.

'That's lovely, thanks,' she said, smiling across the table at Peter. 'It is good, to be fair. Definitely not your average Prosecco.'

Peter rolled his eyes in mock exasperation. 'Cheers,' he said, clinking her glass. 'You look great. Did I already say that? Well, in any case you do. How was your day?'

The conversation rolled along easily as they made their way through multiple courses, with the odd interruption of a buzz from Peter's phone. He would remove it from his pocket, glance at the message or number, frown and tuck it back into his pocket, refusing to engage in a text-message conversation. 'Never stops,' he sighed, repeatedly. 'When did people stop talking on the phone? All I get these days are these passive-aggressive text messages. Whatever happened to just picking up the phone and calling someone?'

Peter had started a headhunting firm in London eight years earlier that now employed almost sixty people globally. He relocated to New York three years later to open the US office, and the addition of an office in Tokyo last year meant that he was constantly juggling different time zones. He had an impeccable work ethic, as did most of the successful people that Lily had come across in her four years in New York, but he also seemed to thrive on being busy. Lily loved her job as senior copywriter at a hugely successful media company, but she also relished her slow, lazy weekends. Peter, on the other hand, managed his weekend as he did his weekday calendar, planning his personal training sessions, sailing, waterskiing and multiple social events that were not always entirely social, but merely another way of maintaining and enhancing his network in New York. He had bought a home in Sag Harbor in New York's very affluent Hamptons the year he made his first million, so summer weekends were all about the Hamptons.

Lily had quickly learned that America's seasonal rituals were written in stone. Her experience with New Yorkers had taught her that Thanksgiving was spent with family, spring break meant a trip to Florida, or preferably a Caribbean island, and once the first official weekend of summer (Memorial Day weekend) rolled around, there was a mass exodus to the Hamptons. Entire families decamped to their summer homes, some rambling mansions, others more modest versions of the American Dream. For the majority of these families, the man was the major breadwinner and so apart from his two-week vacation in July or August, he would commute to the Hamptons from his Manhattan home every Friday afternoon, returning late Sunday night or early Monday morning. The two-lane highway leading back to Manhattan was mostly filled with large, fancy cars and their sole male drivers on Sunday nights and Monday mornings.

Peter's phone buzzed again as the waiter handed them the dessert menu.

'Sorry, Lily, I have to take this,' he said, shaking his head as he stood up from the table. 'I swear to God if this guy had one single useful idea it would die of loneliness in his head,' he ranted, placing his napkin on the table. 'I'll be right back.'

Lily sighed and slumped back into her chair, letting her shoulders sag. Her lower back muscles ached from having had to maintain perfect posture for the past hour and a half.

'Famous last words,' she mumbled, tipping back the last sip of wine in her glass.

Lily knew well enough by now that if Peter needed to leave the table during dinner to deal with a phone call, then it was serious, and he would not be 'right back'.

The waiter reappeared to fold Peter's napkin. 'Another drink, perhaps?' he asked, with a smile.

She grinned up at him. 'God, was I that obvious?'

'Just call it a special power that I possess.'

'Do you have this by the glass?' she asked, gesturing to the empty bottle of wine in the wine cooler. 'The bottle is gone . . . sad face,' she said, mimicking the sad face emoji.

'Of course! I'll be right back,' the waiter said with a wink.

Lily couldn't help but giggle to herself. The waiters all knew Peter well by now, some of them even well enough to recognise his telltale traits and nuances. 'I'll be right back' could mean as much as twenty minutes before Peter reappeared. She pulled out her phone and scrolled aimlessly for the next fifteen minutes. She had seven WhatsApp messages from Ellen back home in Ireland, all referencing Dee's upcoming wedding in Ischia and the fact that Ellen was more than ready to run away from her husband and five children. Each of the messages was filled with multiple grin and sunshine emojis.

'Someone's excited for our trip!' Lily giggled, as she sipped her new glass of wine.

There were two Instagram messages from Kitty in London, both of which showcased outfits that she had seen advertised and deemed suitably 'island chic'. It was clear to Lily that Kitty had sent them in the hopes that Lily would actually buy them for the trip and up her wardrobe game. The glaringly obvious sentiment made Lily smile. She hadn't seen Kitty in months – in fact, not since she'd started dating Peter six months ago.

Kitty was the more glamorous of the group of five girl-friends, which also included Dee, Ellen and Morgan. They were all in their thirties, except for Morgan who, at forty-one, was the oldest of the group and considered herself to be the most sophisticated. Lily, Dee and Ellen had been schoolfriends in Dublin, while Kitty joined the group in their university years, having transferred from London to Trinity College Dublin. Several years later, following Dee's move to New York, Morgan was eventually added to the group.

'Sorry about that. Are you okay?' Peter gushed, as he leaned over and kissed her cheek. 'That guy's an idiot. He has got to go. Okay . . . how about an espresso?'

'Sure, I think I have two sips of wine left,' she agreed, as Peter signalled the waiter for two espressos.

He pulled his phone out again and frowned at the screen.

Jesus, now what? she wondered, stifling a sigh as she watched him scroll.

'So . . . ' he said, slowly drawing out the word. 'It looks like I can leave town as early as four o'clock tomorrow. Can you get out early? I can swing by and pick you up.' He grinned up at her from his phone.

'No, I can't go tomorrow. Remember? I have that baby shower Saturday morning.'

'Are you kidding me? You're blowing off a weekend in the Hamptons for a baby shower?'

'I know. I'm really allergic to the idea of it, but I have to go.'

'If you don't want to go then why are you going?' he asked, matter-of-factly.

Peter was nothing if not pragmatic, and he could never understand people who sacrificed their time, especially leisure time, for something they felt compelled to do.

'Peter, I have to go. She's my boss. Well, okay, not my actual boss, but she's definitely superior to me and I don't want to piss her off.'

'Oh, come on,' he cajoled, taking her hand across the table. 'I'm taking the boat out tomorrow, it's set up already. I was going to give you that waterskiing lesson. The weather is absolutely perfect this weekend! And it's the first time in weeks that we don't have visitors, so we'll have the whole place to ourselves.' He winked. 'I do recall you liked that faux fur rug in the den . . . ' His voice trailed off provocatively.

'You are very convincing, but I RSVP'd so I have to go. I'll follow you out in the afternoon.'

'Baby shower,' he said, as he raised his glass in a mock toast. 'What a nightmare. I'm very grateful that part of my life is behind me.' He tipped back his espresso and asked the waiter for the bill.

'What do you mean you're grateful that's behind you? It's just a baby shower, Peter, no one is asking you to adopt it,' Lily said, a slight frown forming on her face.

'Kids. Jesus. I mean, don't get me wrong, I love my kids, but I'm glad they're practically grown up. I'm so done with that period in my life. I was definitely hoodwinked into that.'

'What were you hoodwinked into? I'm not following.'

'Having kids! Raising kids! The whole experience is bloody chaos from start to finish. I don't know, maybe my ex-wife made it harder than it needed to be, but I can't say it was more pleasure than pain. I swear to God, Lily, it's like coming out of a haze or a fog when they finally start to morph into real people. The lack of sleep is brutal, perhaps bordering on torturous. Anyone who doesn't admit that to be the case, frankly, is lying to you.'

'But you said your kids had nannies growing up.'

'Yeah, and it was still like living in an aquarium and having to come up for air every so often. If it wasn't for the nanny, I don't think we'd have lasted as long as we did. My ex-wife wasn't exactly the level-headed type. She was born without a coping mechanism. Everything was unnecessarily dramatic. Without the nanny, everything would have imploded years earlier,' he said, shaking his head as he gestured with both arms up over his head.

'That's more like exploded,' Lily replied, mimicking his gesture. 'Imploded would have been much more subtle.'

'What?' he asked, squinting at her as if trying to follow this new direction in the conversation.

'Nothing,' she snapped, shaking her head in an attempt to disperse the cluster of confusing thoughts lodged in her brain.

'What the hell happened? I left the table for five minutes to take a very important call and I came back to a raging shit-storm?'

The incredulity of his accusation, along with his

sarcastic tone of voice, sent Lily from simmering to boil in seconds.

'Firstly, you were gone for more than twenty minutes, not five, and secondly, every goddamn call you ever take is always "very important",' she said, using the two-fingered fake air quotes that she despised so much. 'If I'm not mistaken, you just told me, casually over dinner, that you're done having kids. Like, that's not something you think you should have, I don't know ... *shared* at some other point? We've been together for six months, Peter. Why hasn't this come up before?'

'Lily, please keep your voice down. I'm not getting into an argument with you in this restaurant. We are finished with this conversation,' he said firmly, signing the bill with a flourish.

He stood without waiting for her to answer. He had clearly made the decision for her. They both gave the waiter a fake smile, thanked him and headed for the door.

Chapter Three

The heat outside was oppressive as they walked the four blocks to Peter's apartment in silence. Lily knew that she was prone to a short temper, and she was usually quick to apologise, but she fumed as she played back the conversation in her head. Had he actually just told her that he didn't want children? Out of the blue over dinner?

Peter pushed open the door to his apartment, the cool, air-conditioned room a welcome respite from the humidity of the city streets. His phone buzzed in his pocket, but he ignored it.

'Drink?' he asked, opening the door of the drinks cabinet. He pulled out a bottle of Japanese whisky. Lily didn't like whisky and he knew that.

He's just being a prick now out of spite, she seethed. 'Yes. A gin and tonic, please,' she said shortly. He sighed, as she knew he would. Peter loved to host parties but despised mixing drinks.

He said nothing as he pulled out a tall tumbler and poured the gin over ice.

'So, hello? Are we going to talk about this like normal humans or are you going to put me on mute like you do your employees who misbehave?' she asked, sarcastically.

'Christ, Lily. We've talked about this. We've had this conversation. What exactly do you want?' Peter asked, exasperated.

'What do I want? Are you serious? I want to know what the hell you meant when you said you were done having children. That's what I want, Peter. I want to understand what the fuck is happening here. I also want someone who wants to be in a relationship with me, and everything that comes along with that. What I *don't* want is to subscribe to a predetermined map of the future according to Peter Allen. I thought we were doing okay. Was I wrong? Did I just imagine it, Peter?'

Peter sighed and ran his hand over his mouth. 'It's my fault. I wasn't vocal enough about this, obviously.' He shook his head and reached out his hand to her. 'Lily, it's okay. Calm down, please. It will be okay.'

'What do you mean by that? How will it be okay? And do not tell me to calm down, Peter. I hate being told to calm down. You've just told me that you don't want to have kids. Just like that, out of the blue after being together for six months – and I'm supposed to calm the fuck down?'

'Are you being serious? Lily, this can't be a complete surprise to you. I've been really clear from the beginning. This is not new news. This should not be a surprise to you after all this time.'

'I shouldn't be surprised? Why, because you've got two arrogant, entitled sons who piss you off – your words, not mine – and you had a shitty parenting experience, and now you live this perfectly choreographed life, so you're done and you're not going back? Is that it? You're just done?' Her voice was loud now, and she could feel herself getting upset. Do not cry, Lily. Do not cry, she repeated silently, digging her fingernails into the palms of her hands to distract her thoughts.

Peter slammed his glass on the coffee table.

'Yes, that's exactly right. I *am* done, Lily, and I believe that I made that perfectly clear to you early on in this relationship. It's not like this is the first time we've had this conversation. Lily, we talked about this months ago at a restaurant and you're the one who got all fidgety and changed the conversation. Don't you remember?'

'Can you please stop using my name like that? You're using it in every sentence, and it sounds like you're scolding me. And what are you talking about? That is precisely the problem – it *is* the first time we've talked about it. Does this sound to you like someone hearing for the first time that her boyfriend of six months is dead set against having children? We've had a conversation about maybe moving in together in the next few months, and yet you evade the baby conversation! If you were so goddamn set against it then don't you think you should have mentioned it before now? You know, just casually drop it into a sentence: "Oh hey, Lily, pass the salt, please, oh and by the way I don't want to have any more children." Or, "Lily, do you want another glass of wine, and by the way, I'm never having any more kids."'

Peter stood and stared at her. 'Are you serious?'

'About being pissed off? Yes, I'm serious,' she replied, feeling the rage start to well within her now.

'No, Lily, are you seriously telling me that you think this is the first time we've had this conversation? You honestly think I'd keep something that significant from you and not address the issue straight up?'

'Oh my God. The issue? This is about the most personal thing we could talk about right now and you're calling it an issue? Are you out of your mind?'

Peter looked at the floor, put his hand over his eyes and pinched his nose. It was a signature move that he used when he was frustrated or angry. Up until now she had thought it was endearing, but then she hadn't been the cause of the frustration. Now even the move annoyed her.

'Lily . . . ' he said slowly.

Another signature move. He always spoke slowly and calmly as if he were in charge and was taking back control of the conversation. This bugged her now, too.

He had run his hand through his hair in frustration and part of it was now sticking up on the left side of his head. She instinctively wanted to reach out and flatten it but decided that he could look ridiculous instead. She folded her arms across her chest.

'Lily, we did talk about this. Don't you remember? The night at Bistrot Aix, a few months ago. Remember, the table alongside us with the toddler twins going abso-lutely nuclear?'

Lily stared at him incredulously. 'The twins? The ones who flung chunks of baguette at the waiter because they weren't buttered and then roared hysterically when their dad gave out to them? That scene? The one where you said something about them being a nightmare? They *were* a nightmare, Peter. They were two-year-old brats – what did you expect? What does that have to do with any of this and your big, massive declaration that you don't want to have any more children?'

Peter sighed again and shook his head. 'I definitely recall

saying something along the lines of "What a nightmare, I'm so glad I'm done with that," and you said, "Done with what?" To which I replied that I'm so glad my kids are grown up and I don't have to deal with that shit any more.'

'What?' she asked, her voice rising to a high-pitched squeal. 'That's the conversation you think covered the fact that you are done with kids for the rest of your life? What? Yeah, that was *so* clear.'

She could hear her voice rising and knew that Peter detested arguments, always claiming that he had had more than his fair share with Betty, his ex-wife, but she couldn't stop it, nor did she really want to.

'Peter, all toddlers are like that, for Christ's sake. I figured you were just losing your mind over the chaos at the next table, not making some declaration about the rest of your life.'

'And you know this how, exactly? Because your experience with children is so vast?' Peter responded sarcastically.

'Are you deliberately trying to be an asshole now?'

'I'm sorry. Look, at least you remember. I'm not playing games here, I meant it then and I mean it now.'

'But Peter ... '

'What?' Peter prompted.

'That was ... I don't know ... we were like, five weeks into the relationship. I didn't really know you like I know you now. I thought you were just being cranky about the nutty kids. How was I supposed to realise that your throwaway comment was actually a prophecy about your future?' Lily looked up at him now, biting her bottom lip in an attempt not to get teary. 'I had no idea that I was unknowingly agreeing that night to sign away or waiver or whatever the proper legal term is . . . ' She paused and shook her head.

'Waive what?' Peter asked, a confused look on his face.

'Any right or option to have children . . . with you, I mean.' She clasped her hands together and dug the fingers of her right hand into her palm, the pain temporarily distracting her from the threatening tears. 'What I'm trying to say is that I didn't think that was what you meant. I know a lot of men who aren't keen to have kids, but then they meet the right person, and something changes. I suppose I just thought that was what it was. Or hoped, or something. I don't know.' She paused and looked up into his face. Peter stared at her, shaking his head.

'Lily . . .' His voice trailed off as he sat down alongside her. 'I can't believe this is happening. I can give you everything but that one thing. I didn't think you even wanted kids.'

'I don't know whether I do or not . . . not for certain, but I didn't think I'd have to decide right now. But if I stay with you then you are making that choice for me. You're closing it off to me.'

She looked around the room as if seeing it for the first time. Clearly no woman had ever had any impact on the colour scheme or the furniture in this apartment. It was decidedly masculine. How had she not noticed this before? She had been in this room dozens of times in the past six months. The cool, dark colours had been a welcome retreat from the searing heat of summer, and she had loved nothing more than to sink into one of the oversized love seats and wait for the air conditioning unit to return her Irish skin to something resembling a more normal tone. Now she stood looking around the elegant room with its cool, dark undertones, realising it was all him. His suits were exactly the same simple, cool, dark colours. There was no doubting his power or his success when he dressed for work. Impeccable three-piece suits that he wore with a great deal of confidence.

Here, in this new penthouse apartment, he was back in full control of his life, with his ex-wife fully out of the picture and his kids off to college. He knew exactly what he wanted and where he was going, and it was becoming clear to her that he was not willing to adjust course.

'Wow, I really got this all wrong, didn't I?' she said slowly, looking back down at her hands again.

'Lily, you don't have to decide any of that now. Come on,' he implored. 'Just come out with me to the Hamptons tomorrow, blow off the stupid baby shower and we'll have a nice, quiet weekend and we can talk about everything.'

'You're not going to change your mind, are you?' she asked, her gaze steadfastly down.

'Not on this one, no,' he replied quietly. 'I'm sorry. Everything else is up for grabs but I can't do that again. That part of my life is over.'

'Well, then I believe you just decided that for us.'

Chapter Four

The United Airlines flight from New York touched down at Naples International Airport just after seven o'clock on Friday morning. The past two weeks had been a disaster on so many levels. Once Lily had made it clear that she wasn't simply being dramatic, but rather she was serious about wanting to keep her options open, Peter announced that there was no way forward for them and he immediately switched from adoring lover to silent menace.

As part of their earlier plan to build an Italian holiday around Dee's wedding in Ischia, Peter had booked business-class round-trip flights to Naples for both of them. The day after the disastrous argument, Lily received an automated email informing her that her flight had been cancelled. Later that same day, Peter's assistant emailed her a UPS tracking number for the personal belongings she had left at his apartment that were being boxed up and shipped to her. She hadn't heard a single word directly from Peter since she had stormed out of his apartment. It was clear he had cut her off.

With less than two weeks to the wedding, Lily had to rebook her flight and cash in her coveted American Express points for a middle seat in economy. It was that or pay 2,400 dollars. Now, bleary eyed from lack of sleep and one inflight gin and tonic too many, Lily stumbled off the plane and into the chaos of the international airport, joining the massive queue for passport control. Hundreds of people converged into one single, meandering line that curled around a series of rope borders, reminding Lily of images of sheep or cattle being herded through county marts on their way to be sold or slaughtered.

'Amal Clooney doesn't have to put up with this shit,' she muttered, as she rooted in her bag for her mobile phone. 'No signal. Of course, there's no signal. Good thing I printed that bloody thing,' she moaned, referring to the details of the chauffeur service Morgan had booked to take her from the airport to the ferry terminal. 'One drink in the air equals two on the ground, meaning you had six G&Ts last night you idiot. You should have known better, Lily. It's not like this is your first flight ever,' she sighed, pulling a crumpled A4 page from her carry-on bag.

The cavernous, impersonal room was stifling hot and tragically devoid of air conditioning. The stale air smelled of people who hadn't showered in hours, if not days. 'Why would a country in southern Europe not have air-conditioning? It smells like feet in here,' she moaned, checking her phone for the second time. 'Nothing ... no signal. Piece of shit,' she hissed at the phone. She was desperate to power up her phone to see if Peter had tried to reach her. In reality she knew it was unlikely, as he was stubborn to a point, but a small part of her still hoped that he would reach out. She missed him desperately, but she knew that she had to stand her ground. This hadn't been an ordinary argument that had been blown out of proportion. She had meant what she had said about wanting to be able to choose in the future, but it was becoming increasingly apparent that Peter stood by his own words just as rigidly.

'*Signora, no!*' a uniformed attendant said sternly, shaking her head as she pointed at Lily's mobile phone.

Lily shoved the phone back in her bag. 'Don't worry, it doesn't work anyway. No signal in this bloody place.'

Kicking the carry-on bag forward with her foot, she held her suit bag in one hand and a half-empty bottle of water in the other. Morgan had insisted she transport her official maid of honour outfits in a suit bag, rather than risk losing them in her checked suitcase.

'Look, you can buy another swimsuit or pair of flip-flops, I'm pretty sure they sell all that stuff there, but you are not going to find another couture dress or outfit on a small Italian island,' Morgan had admonished in her strong New York accent. 'And honey, I don't mind telling you that if those outfits go missing you will not be standing in official photographs wearing some local strappy sundress and a pair of wedge sandals. You will be pointedly M.I.A.' Morgan had said it with a smile, but there was no mistaking the tone of voice.

'Goddamn stupid awkward suit bag,' Lily moaned, yanking the hangers from the palm of one hand and into the other.

Kicking her carry-on bag another couple of steps forward, she squinted at the small print on her confirmation document, advising her that her driver would be waiting for her with a sign at Arrival Door C once she cleared passport control.

'Door C, okay,' she mumbled, shuffling slowly forward in the queue.

Her moisturiser was beginning to run down her face. She drained the bottle of water and wiped beads of sweat from under her eyes. When her turn came, the immigration officer gave a cursory glance at her passport and waved her through.

'Jesus, at least make it look like this massive queue was worth it. He didn't even look at it!' she said with a tsk sound of disapproval.

Retrieving her overloaded suitcase from the luggage carousel, she made her way to Door C, fatigued and dehydrated. She saw the sign with her name on it and made her way gratefully towards it. The holder of the sign was built like a rugby player and greeted her with a massive grin.

'Ah, Signora LeeLee!' he said, moving towards her and taking her suit bag and suitcase. '*Sono Giuseppe. Piacere,*' he said, shaking her hand. 'I take the bags.'

'*Grazie,*' she said, rubbing her fingers under her eyes for fear that layers of smudged post-flight mascara languished beneath them.

'*Andiamo, signora!*' he said, grinning again, as he took off towards the exit.

She followed him through the crowd towards a waiting Mercedes.

Thank God for Morgan! she thought, sinking into the cool interior of the car while Giuseppe loaded her luggage into the boot.

'*Ecco,* Signora LeeLee,' he said, indicating towards the bottled water and cool face cloth wrapped in plastic.

Lily smiled at the exaggerated pronunciation of her name and opened the mirror function on her phone.

Mother of God, look at the state of you, she thought, as she pulled her hair from its current knot and ran the cool cloth over her face. 'Time for some emergency repair work,' she mumbled as she whipped out her travel make-up kit.

Giuseppe took off at breakneck speed and Lily devoted the first few minutes to applying some undereye concealer and fresh mascara. Fixing her hair in a more refined knot using a clip, she finally sat back and breathed a sigh of relief as Giuseppe lurched through one-way streets and trundled across tram lines for the next twenty minutes. Lily peered out of the window, noticing that the buildings got taller and grander the closer they got to the ferry terminal.

'Your ferry, she leave at ten o'clock, no?' Giuseppe asked, turning to look over his shoulder at her.

'Um . . . yes, ten o'clock,' she replied nervously. Just watch the road, Giuseppe, she thought as she instinctively reached for the handle above the window. I don't want to be roadkill in Naples.

'*Ah, perfetto.* This is good. You will have time for a coffee. You would like a coffee, no?'

'Oh God, like a camel in the Sahara, Giuseppe.'

'Good. I take you there. No problem, Signora LeeLee.'

The car lurched around corners and shot through roundabouts for another twenty minutes.

'We have to make detour, so I go this way . . . to Il Lungomare . . . is the road of the sea. Is nice, no? *Il mare,*' he said, pointing to the sparking blue sea that opened up before them.

Lily made an involuntary and audible gasp as she took in

the spectacular scene before her. The sea was phosphorescent and glittered as though winking at her, inviting her in. The city of Naples curved around the bay before splintering off into narrow streets, each of which rippled up into the hills behind, giving the impression that the city itself was like a mini Vesuvius, the famed volcano that towered over it. As they made their way along the Lungomare, the land to her right jutted out like a pointed finger, far into the Bay of Naples beyond. The neighbourhoods along the peninsula were some of the more affluent areas in the region, with elegant villas dotting the lush, green landscape. Her eyes traced the small villages, with terracotta roofs and church steeples gathered in sporadic clusters, until the land suddenly appeared to drop precipitously into the sea. To her left, a series of grand hotels lined the wide street with elaborate balconies that must have dated back to the 1800s. As they rounded the corner, the street opened up into a vast piazza with at least a dozen pizzerias, each with signs claiming to make authentic Pizza Napoletana.

'The pizza. Is from Napoli. Is originally from Napoli. You know this?'

'No, I didn't know that. I just thought it was . . . like, from Italy, in general.'

'Ah *no, signora,* the pizza is from Napoli, from the year of 1889. The Queen of Italy, Queen Margherita, she come to Napoli and a chef . . . he make the pizza in her honour. He . . . ahh . . . *come si dice* . . . make the pizza same colour as the flag of Italy, with the colours . . . ahh . . . red, white and green. The red, is *pomodoro* . . . how you say . . . tomato. The white is mozzarella, and the green is *basilico* . . . basil! *Sì.* He . . . ahh . . . make this pizza for the Queen Margherita and he call it the Pizza Margherita,' Giuseppe announced, with a flourish of his right hand.

'Are you serious or are you making that up?'

Giuseppe frowned in the rear-view mirror. '*No capito, signora*. I don't understand.'

'I mean, is that real? Is that the truth . . . the story of the Margherita Pizza?'

'*Sì. Sì certo, signora! È vero!* This is the first "Pizza Margherita", for the Queen Margherita!' Giuseppe replied, gesturing furiously.

Based on Giuseppe's response, Lily figured that this was obviously a matter of national pride. 'Well, I'll have to have one then!'

Giuseppe laughed an uproarious laugh. Everything about him seemed larger than life and his enthusiasm was contagious. He swerved wildly around a few more corners and Lily could make out the port ahead. As they got closer to the ferry port, she noticed that the neighbourhood began to look a little seedier, and she was glad to have Giuseppe as her guide. The car bounced over some railroad tracks and he drove around the back of a large warehouse. Suddenly she could see a host of different ships, in various sizes and with different markings.

The terminal building itself was a string of individual ticket offices, each with ten to a dozen paper signs stuck haphazardly to the windows. Throngs of people milled about, lugging suitcases over the cobblestones, like ants scattering in different directions. Lily peered anxiously through the car window as Giuseppe brought the car to a stop. She had absolutely no idea which ticket office she needed, or which ferry she was booked on. The place was utterly chaotic.

'*Ecco ci*,' Giuseppe announced as he jumped from the car. 'We leave everything in car. Come. We get coffee, no?'

'Oh, yes please. Giuseppe, how do you say please in Italian? I know I should know this, but I forget. Jet lag . . . '

'*Per favore, signora!*' he replied with a grin, extending a hand to help her out of the car.

After a restorative coffee, sitting outside in the sun with the strong scent of sea breeze filling the air, Lily began to feel more human. Giuseppe stowed her luggage safely on to the ferry and enthusiastically waved goodbye as the ship pulled away from the shore. Lily ran up the steps to the top deck and nabbed a seat up front. Plumes of white smoke belched from enormous white chimneys as the ferry slowly pulled away from the shore.

She watched the city of Naples grow smaller and smaller behind her, before turning her attention ahead as the ship navigated a wide right-hand turn out into the open sea. Commercial boats, fishing boats, sailing boats and speed boats all competed for the same stretch of water that con- nected the port of Naples to the open sea and the islands of Ischia, Procida and Capri beyond.

Lily had never been to Capri, but she had heard plenty about it and had seen the glamorous images on social media and on websites promoting Italy as a holiday destination. Capri was renowned for its luxurious hotels, elegant restau- rants, electric-blue water and rugged, dramatic vistas. She had been to the usual hotspots in Italy, including Rome, Milan and Venice, but any time she had considered a trip to Capri it had always been far above her budget.

She sat on the top deck now, staring ahead into the vast blue waters of the Bay of Naples, with nothing but ocean as far as the horizon. The islands were as yet out of sight, and she knew that Procida would be the first island she would see, with Ischia tucked out of view behind it. As she leaned over the railing, waiting for her first glimpse of the islands, she wondered why, in all the years that she had heard about Capri, she had never heard a mention of Ischia. Reading Dee and Morgan's Save The Date announcement was the first time she had heard of the island, and she had had to turn to Google to learn that the correct pronunciation was 'Iss-keeya'.

Morgan, a devoted fan of luxurious, boutique hotels, had read about the San Montano Resort on the island of Ischia years earlier and had vowed to get married there one day. Dee was happy to agree, on the condition that she didn't have to get involved in the details, so as with most things in life, Morgan got her wish. Given that the three of them were travelling from New York, they decided to make a nine-day trip of it from Saturday to the following Sunday.

News of the nine-day trip to an Italian island quickly reached Kitty in London and she had her assistant block her calendar immediately, thus beginning her sartorial research into the latest season's resort wear. Ellen, the mother of five young children, had initially planned to join the girls just for the wedding weekend, until Dee intervened and put her foot down. For the first time in her life, Ellen made a choice for herself over her family, and was happy to flee and let her husband and her mother-in-law figure out how to keep all five children alive for nine days without her.

The ship ploughed easily through the sea, leaving Naples in its wake, and as they rounded the edge of the penin-sula, Lily heard someone point out the island of Procida directly ahead. Leaning over the railing, she watched Procida loom larger as it came slowly into sight. A long, narrow, rugged island of only four square kilometres, it was dotted with a tangle of tiny pastel-coloured houses. A church steeple stood proudly midway along the coast, with the land sloping down to the port and marina below. From her vantage point it looked quaint and charming, and she made a mental note to check the boat options from Ischia to explore it further.

Finally, as the ship steamed past the island of Procida, she got her first glimpse of Ischia: a volcanic outcrop ten kilometres long. Lily stared in wonder at the lush landscape of dense forests and volcanic rock, rising up to a majestic peak that loomed large over the island. As they inched closer, she could make out busy marinas, chock-full of a variety of boats and languorous cove-like beaches, the translucent sea lapping gently on to their shores. Individual villas dotted the hillsides while the clusters of small towns consisted of colourful, haphazard buildings crammed together and facing directly out to sea.

With this being the only stop on the journey before the ship made its return trip to Naples, all of the passengers surged forward to disembark simultaneously. A handful of locals sauntered ahead empty handed, with the rest of the two-hundred-strong crowd scrambling to retrieve suitcases from the luggage hold and squeeze down the narrow sets of stairs. Lily emerged from the dark hull of the ship, out into the bright sunshine, clutching her suit bag and dragging her oversized suitcase down the steep metal gangplank. She stepped on to the pier, disorientated and unsure of what direction to go in, and was grateful to see a

San Montano Resort sign a few metres ahead. She pushed her way through the throng of people, her suitcase veering from side to side as she dragged it on the uneven surface.

'I definitely packed too much,' she muttered, trying to avoid standing on the heels of the people in front of her. 'I bet I won't even wear half this stuff.'

She raised her left arm as best she could, half waving her suit bag at the man holding the sign that read SAN MONTANO RESORT. As she did so, her foot caught on the end of the bag, causing her to stumble forward and bump into the lady directly in front of her.

'I'm so sorry!' she said, attempting an apologetic smile as the woman turned and snarled at her.

'*Cavallo! Attento!*'

'It was an accident! Jesus,' she hissed.

'*Buongiorno.* Signora Ryan?'

Lily looked up to see the man holding the sign reach towards her and grab both her suitcase and suit bag.

'Yes, um ... *sì*. Thanks ... *grazie*,' she said, relieved to be rid of the bags.

The crowd milled around her as she followed him down the length of the narrow pier to the awaiting shuttle bus. The scene was one of absolute chaos. Families spilled about, eyeing the stream of disgorging passengers, shouting greetings or calling names. Drivers waited to pick up inbound hotel guests, and luggage handlers battled the crowd with trolleys' standing by to load luggage on to. The collective noise level was so great that everyone seemed to be shouting, but it struck Lily that they were all happy-sounding exclamations. The excitement was palpable in the air.

As she paused to look around at the scene around her,

she lost sight of the man who had greeted her as he was swallowed up by the churning crowd. She wondered momentarily about the chances of him being a fake and absconding with her luggage, but she decided that at this point she really didn't care. Exhausted from the overnight flight and the ensuing journey from Naples airport, she was finally here. She took a deep breath and continued in the direction of the branded shuttle bus, taking in the sights as she shuffled forward.

Chapter Five

The marina was filled with boats and yachts of varying degrees of affluence, bobbing about gently in the late-morning breeze. The narrow road that flanked the marina was lined with cafés and restaurants, each touting its daily specials on chalkboards set up outside. Lily hesitated momentarily in the crowd before spotting the driver waiting patiently ahead. As she passed the cafés, she eyed the various pastries and breads on display and realised that she hadn't had breakfast. Her stomach grumbled in obedient response as the driver held the door open and she gratefully stumbled into the air-conditioned interior. A bottle of water and a small packet of cookies awaited her, along with an ice-cold towel that she rubbed across the back of her neck and pressed to her forehead.

'*Allora*, Signora Ryan, in ten minutes we arrive at San Montano.'

'Great ... *grazie*,' she said, sinking back into the cream leather seat, as the driver inched his way through the crowd and on to the main road.

Once safely beyond the crowd, the driver whizzed along the two-lane road that ran parallel with the coastline.

After a kilometre or two, the marina gave way to a beach, furnished in true Italian style with individual beach clubs, providing access to loungers, changing facilities, showers and, of course, the requisite beach restaurant. The beach was a narrow strip of sand, leading to a calm, limpid, turquoise sea. Small children splashed about at the water's edge, closely guarded by adults wading in ankle-deep water, while sailing boats glided gracefully along the horizon.

At the beginning of the next town, the driver slowed and turned on to a narrow, cobbled road with a sign that read LACCO AMENO. To Lily's left was an endless string of colourful cafés and restaurants, their tables and chairs spilling on to the pavements outside. Interspersed among them were small, elegant boutiques, each of which had a display rail outside, showcasing soft Italian linens that fluttered in the early-morning breeze. Lily peered through the window of the shuttle bus, marvelling at how foreign and classically Italian everything looked, the unfolding scene helping her to forget temporarily that she was hungry and exhausted.

The driver followed the cobblestoned road to a fork at the foot of a hill, gearing down to make a sharp right-hand turn up a steep incline. The shuttle bus revved as it edged its way up and around a series of curves, the town below disappearing behind her, giving way to the dense, green hill. The higher they went, the thicker the foliage seemed to become, adding to Lily's sense of anticipation. At the top of the hill the trees parted to reveal an even narrower lane that disappeared under an old stone arch. A gleaming brass plaque for San Montano Resort was hung to the right of the entrance. San Montano was part of the luxurious Small Leading Hotels group worldwide, the brass plaques proudly displayed at the entrance to each member property. Now, trundling along under the arch, the road made one final sweeping curve, eventually opening on to a vast stone courtyard.

'*Eccoci, signora,*' the driver said, announcing their arrival.

As Lily gathered her sunglasses and her bag, the door of the shuttle bus slid open.

'*Buongiorno, signora. Benvenuti a San Montano.* Welcome to San Montano. I am Marco. Signora Ryan, *sì?*'

He was more than six feet tall, lean, not a rib of hair on his head and the greatest smile that Lily had ever seen. It was contagious and she felt herself instinctively smile back.

'Yes, I'm Lily,' she replied, as she stepped out into the sun.

He hesitated for a moment and glanced down at his clipboard, the slightest frown flickering on his face momentarily. 'I see that your reservation is for two persons. The other person will come later?'

Fuck, she thought, a sense of panic rising inside of her. I never changed the room reservation to one person. Idiot! She had booked the room back when they were a happy party of two and had used Peter's loyalty number to guarantee an upgrade. 'Oh. Yeah . . . right,' she sighed. 'I forgot to change that. No, it's just going to be me. He . . . umm . . . couldn't make it, so it's just me.'

She could feel her cheeks flush, but if he noticed, Marco didn't miss a beat.

'Ah okay, Signora LeeLee, no problem. *Allora* . . . now don't worry. We take care of everything. Leave everything here, *signora,*' he said, pointing to her luggage. 'Come with me. I take you to the reception to do the check-in, and then you can relax,' he said, guiding her along the path.

She had only taken a couple of steps when she stopped,

letting out an audible gasp. 'Wow,' she said quietly. She turned in a semicircle, taking in the view around her as Marco explained that the site where the courtyard stood had once been an ancient olive grove. Out of deference to the majestic trees, some of which were over four hundred years old, the pathway had been built around them. As a result, the olive trees seemed to lean to and fro as Lily made her way along the meandering path beside Marco. The façade of the hotel was series of arches, each of which was covered with purple and red bougainvillea in full bloom. A sign pointed to a lemon grove to her left, tucked away behind an old stone wall, but it was the view to her right that had caused her to stop.

A cluster of black, wrought-iron round tables and chairs sat in the grass, tucked among the olive trees. Just beyond them, a low stone wall signalled the boundary of the property and on the other side of the wall, the cliff fell spectacularly to the sea below.

'Ah, yes, this is Negombo Bay. We call it San Montano Bay. Come, Signora LeeLee, take a look,' Marco said, inviting her to step over the kerb and on to the grass.

She followed him to the edge of the property and stared down at the bay. The water was flat calm, its colour morphing from cobalt blue to aquamarine as the sun bore down intensely. Even from this height, several thousand feet above sea level, she could hear the faint sound of waves hitting the shore below. The bay was protected by a mountainous promontory that jutted far out into the sea. Marco pointed towards the horizon, explaining that the mountain protected the beach and helped to keep the waters calm and warm almost year round. Lily's eye followed the dense, jungle-like foliage that led down the mountain from San Montano to Negombo beach below. A long, narrow beach-shack restaurant hugged the edge of the forest canopy, its tables and chairs interspersed in the sand, and lines of neatly arranged sun loungers faced out towards the bay, their accompanying umbrellas flapping in the light breeze.

'From here, you cannot see it, but behind all those trees is the Negombo thermal spa,' Marco said, pointing to the cluster of trees just behind the beach. 'Is famous for the healing waters. While you are here, you must go and experience this one day. We will arrange everything for you. It is a very special place . . . and good for the relax!'

'Wow, what a view. It's really spectacular,' Lily replied, still staring towards the sea.

'Yes, is very beautiful. I am lucky to work in a place like this. But the best part is the sunset. You will see tonight. This is the best place on the whole island to see the sunset. Is like magic.'

'Unreal,' she said, shaking her head as she followed him along the path towards the hotel.

The check-in procedure was swift and efficient and included a welcome lemony drink.

'You would prefer the alcohol or the no-alcohol lemon drink, *signora?*' the lady behind the reception desk asked with a smile.

'Oh, the alcohol version, thanks,' Lily replied, without hesitation.

She realised that she had no idea what time it was, nor did she care. Her head was fuzzy from lack of sleep, and her stomach growled again. She couldn't remember what time

46

the girls were due to arrive, but she knew that hers was the first flight to land. She had made a note of it somewhere and would have to check as soon as she got on Wi-Fi.

Once registration was complete and her passport had been photocopied, Marco accompanied her to her room, explaining with a wide smile that she had been upgraded to a duplex suite.

'Holy shit!' she exclaimed, entering the suite and gazing upwards at the soaring white ceiling overhead and out through the double doors at the elegantly landscaped terrace, complete with a personal plunge pool. 'Umm, Marco . . . is this room for one or . . . ?' Her voice trailed off as she was unsure how to phrase the awkward question.

'Don't worry, Signora LeeLee. I have prepared for you an upgrade to this room. Is for one person or two, so do not worry that you are alone. You like it?' he asked, with another wide grin.

'How could I not! It's stunning. Thank you.'

Once the preliminary functionalities of the suite had been explained to her, Marco handed her the key and departed. Lily climbed the stairs to the bedroom suite – *la zona di notte*, as Marco had called it – and sank back into the white linen-covered queen-sized bed.

'Can't fall asleep, Lily. That would be a really bad idea,' she mumbled into a pillow. She pulled out her mobile phone and texted Dee.

> Forgot to change the reservation so I'm
> in some kind of massive suite.
>> I swear, even Meghan Markle
>> wouldn't turn her nose up at this!

I got lost looking for the bathroom . . .
But am terrified to check the nightly rate.
Have you landed?
When do you get here?

Forcing herself upright, she threw open her suitcase and rooted around for a bathing suit and sundress.

'Sunblock . . . sunblock . . . where are you?' she mumbled, as she felt around under the piles of clothes. She had packed two different types. One was Nivea factor fifty, the other was Banana Boat factor eight. 'Let's see how strong the sun is before we go whacking on the fifty. God knows you could do with a bit of colour,' she said, as she leaned over to peer at her face in the mirror. She unrolled two maxi dresses and shook them out. 'Not too wrinkly . . . better hang you guys up, but this is the extent of my unpacking for now. Oh, and a sarong in case of emergency . . . in case of extreme urgent need to cover body from passing strangers.'

A blue and white striped canvas beach bag hung in the wardrobe with a 'with compliments' sign attached.

Nice touch, she thought, pulling the bag down and tossing her phone, sunscreen and her new book inside.

As she did so, she noticed two pairs of navy-blue his 'n' hers flip-flops on the shelf below.

She plonked one pair on the floor and stuck her feet into them.

'Fuck you,' she hissed at the second pair, as she grabbed her bag and headed for the door.

A few minutes later, shortly before noon, Lily was stationed by the pool. She had read the same paragraph four times but retained none of it. She had checked her phone at least a dozen times. Nothing.

'*Scusi*, Signora LeeLee?' Marco said, approaching her with his trademark wide smile.

As Marco stood alongside her lounger wearing a two-piece suit, she suddenly felt very naked in her two-piece bikini.

'*Ciao*, Marco,' she replied, self-consciously reaching for her sarong.

'The driver has just informed us that he has picked up the bridal party from the ferry. They will be arriving any minute here at the resort.'

'Oh, brilliant!' she replied, reluctant to jump up and release her sarong. 'Thanks, Marco. I'll be right there!'

As he walked away, she tugged her sundress over her head. She made her way through the marble-floored lobby to see that the shuttle bus had already pulled up beyond the olive grove. A luggage trolley containing a towering stack of Gucci luggage signalled that Dee and Morgan had definitely arrived.

'There she is!' Dee exclaimed, wrapping her friend in a big hug.

'It's the bride and bride!' Lily shrieked with excitement. 'How are you guys?'

Morgan stood at the check-in desk in an enormously wide-brimmed black hat and oversized sunglasses.

'Give her a wide berth for the moment,' Dee whispered under her breath.

'Why? What's wrong?'

'Oh, nothing serious, just a raging hangover,' she exclaimed, rolling her eyes. 'She's always a bit precious with a hangover.'

'What? It's only a seven-hour flight. How can she have a raging hangover already?'

'You forget ... only the best for my betrothed, remember? We flew Emirates, business class. They pour Veuve Clicquot instead of water.'

'Uh-oh, a champagne headache?'

'Yep. She almost called the whole thing off on the ferry ride over. I think she swore off champagne, Italy and me in the forty-five-minute ride.'

'What about you?'

'Oh yeah, same. Raging headache, but nothing that a massive bowl of pasta and a nap won't sort.' Dee laughed. 'Maybe not in that order. I think I need to lie down.'

They both turned to face Morgan, who was trying to understand the strong Italian accent of the young girl checking them in, and clearly struggling to remain standing.

'No, perhaps you don't understand,' she said, sighing dramatically. 'Okay, honey, it's like this. You're telling me *a lot* right now. I need this information on an absolute need-to-know basis. Right now, I don't care what time breakfast is tomorrow. So, can you please just tell me what I need to know, *right now*, so that I can get to my room and lie down? I'll come back another time for all the other stuff, okay?'

Marco swept in behind the desk, rescuing the girl who was pinned down under Morgan's gaze.

'*Va bene*,' he said, with the same wide grin. '*Sì, signora.* Don't worry. We will escort you to your room now and then later we can talk about everything else that you might need to know, *va bene*? Is this okay?'

'Yes, marvellous. Thank you. Okay,' she replied with a nod. 'Dee, let's go. Hey, Lily, honey, I've got to lie down or I'll vomit on you.' Morgan pressed a cold towel to her face. 'Save us a spot for a late lunch, will you? And if I decide to get married on a remote Italian island ever again in the future, someone please shoot me. My next wedding is either going to be in my time zone or it's not happening.'

'Sure,' Lily replied with a grin. 'Go have a nap. Just ping me when you are up and about later.'

Dee leaned in and whispered into Lily's ear: 'Don't wait for us, go have lunch yourself. This one is about to collapse into a coma. We'll see you this evening is my bet.'

'Dee, for the love of God, let's go!' Morgan roared across the lobby.

'Coming, my love!' Dee called back. She hugged Lily again. 'How are you doing?'

'Oh, I'm grand. Don't worry. I'm fine. Just go or you'll be single again before you're even married.'

'Okay.' Dee laughed. 'We can chat later.'

Lily made her way back to the pool and had barely sunk back into her lounger when her phone buzzed. Every time her phone issued any sort of notification, her heart gave a leap. It had been two weeks and she hadn't heard a single thing from Peter. She knew how stubborn and single-minded he was – it was part of the reason he was so successful in business – but a part of her had expected, or at least hoped for, some sort of follow-up message or attempt to have a conversation. She couldn't believe he was willing to throw everything away without even engaging in another conversation.

She unlocked her phone and opened her messages. They were all from Ellen.

OMG. Landed!

I'M IN ITALY. ALONE!

WITH NO CHILDREN!

IT'S HOT AS HELL AND I LOVE IT!

Will text when on ferry.

What time is lunch?

ORDER WINE!

Don't eat without me!

WOOHOO!

The text was followed by a string of emojis: champagne, Italian flag, boats, sunshine and dancing girls.

Lily couldn't help but smile, despite the disappointment that it hadn't been from Peter.

Ellen had a hard time of it at home in Dublin. With five children under the age of eight and the youngest barely a year old, her life was utter chaos. Her husband was a decent sort but pretty useless. He had been out of work since the previous December, having been fired for saying something mildly racist at the office Christmas party. Or at least, Ellen had said that it was mildly racist. Lily had never managed to get the real story as to what he'd said, but apparently it had been enough to get him fired. The fact that he worked in human resources made matters worse as he should have known better, and now, having been fired without a reference, it was tough to land another position.

After six months of job hunting, he decided that perhaps it was a sign from God and began working on his novel. Understandably, Ellen lost her mind at the thought of him not securing a full-time job and things between them had been beyond tense since then. So, when Ellen suggested that she couldn't afford a nine-day trip and could only justify a weekend away from the kids, Dee had refused to take no for an answer and had gone ahead and booked her room and flight.

'Neither are refundable, so do not tell me that you're not getting on that plane,' Dee had admonished when she had called Ellen from New York. 'Now get that useless lump of a husband to look after his own children for a few days and don't tell me he's not capable. Isn't his mother down the road always whining that she doesn't see enough of them? I want you at my wedding, Ellen. Don't disappoint me or I'll set Morgan on you!'

No one had expected Ellen to pull off nine days away, but it turned out that her mother-in-law was only too keen to take charge of the household temporarily. Ellen suspected that the woman also intended to take charge of her son and whip him back into shape.

Lily smiled again, thinking of Ellen making her way to the island, and lay back on the lounger, her face turned up to the sun. Lying quietly, with the sun beating down on her, she did the time calculation in her head. If Ellen was already on the ferry, then she'd arrive on the island in less than an hour and get to the resort a short ten minutes later. She checked her watch. It was eleven o'clock. She signalled a passing waiter and asked if she could book a table for lunch approximately an hour later. He pointed in the direction of the bar and pizza restaurant at the other side of the pool.

'*Sì, signora*. Is open, the restaurant. Any time you want,' he informed her with a smile.

Lily was fairly sure that Ellen wasn't the kind to worry about unpacking, so it was a pretty certain bet that she would dump her bags in her room and head immediately to lunch.

'What am I waiting for? Eleven o'clock is a more than respectable time for a drink on holiday,' Lily mumbled, tugging her sundress back on over her head.

As she shuffled alongside the pool in her free blue flip-flops, her phone vibrated again. The on-screen preview of just the first few words made her smile as she unlocked the phone to read the message in its entirety.

SWEET JESUS!

The hottest Italian EVER just picked me up at airport.
    My God he's divine.
    If they are all like this will be a fab holiday!

Grinning as she typed, Lily asked:

Is it Giuseppe?

YES!

Yep, hot all right, but you do recall you have
a husband and five children, don't you?

Be still my beating ovaries! I'd go for six with this fella!

A waiter guided Lily to a table in the shade and placed three menus on the table.

'Oh, um . . . do you mind if I sit at that one?' she asked, pointing to a table in full sun.

'*Sì, ma c'è il sole, signora. È troppo caldo oggi, no?* Is too hot, no?'

'Oh no, I don't mind. I love the sun.'

The waiter laughed and scooped up the menus. '*Certo, signora.* You are English or Irish?'

'Yes. Irish. Guilty. Is it that obvious?'

'*Ah, sì, signora*, the English and the Irish, they love the sun.'

As she moved to the table in full sun, Lily's phone buzzed with another text message.

> If I die in this car, please tell my
> mother that I died happy.
>> This fella is a LUNATIC DRIVER.
>> Still divine though.
>> Keeps looking at me in the mirror.
>> Think he fancies me.
>> I'VE STILL GOT IT!

The message came with six wink emojis and three flamenco dancers.

The waiter explained the different menus, asked what kind of water she wanted and quietly disappeared. She was the only person sitting on the terrace. She tipped her head back and turned her face up to the sun, sighing an audible sigh of pleasure. The restaurant was tucked away behind the pool, with spectacular 180-degree views of the island. On one side she could see the marina, where she had arrived a few hours earlier, and beyond it the sea stretched all the way towards Naples, with Mount Vesuvius clearly visible in the distance.

In the other direction, directly opposite her table, she could see the small town of Lacco Ameno hugging the coast, the radiant blue of the sea interrupted only by various sizes and shapes of boats, most of which were uniformly white. From her vantage point, the boats moved as if in slow motion, and she found the entire scene utterly transfixing. Directly behind the town, the land swept dramatically upwards, culminating in the majestic peak of Mount Epomeo. It reminded her of a weekend trip to St Lucia and the Pitons, the lush, green, mountainous volcanic spires covered in tropical forest.

The top half of Mount Epomeo was covered in dense green forest, thinning out halfway down to reveal vineyards clinging to the precipitous sides. From the midway point individual villas and houses dotted the green backdrop, becoming more voluminous in number as the mountain continued its descent to the sea below. The top half was entirely uninhabited, such was the density of the forests, and strict local planning laws ensured that it remained in its natural state.

Lily hadn't expected anything like this level of lush, verdant foliage on a Mediterranean island. Sighing happily at the incredible beauty all around her, she flipped open the wine list. She ran her finger down the list of white wines offered by the glass, realising that she recognised none of them. Tapping her fingers to her lips, she read the list for a second time, hoping to glean some snippet of information from the Italian descriptions.

'*Buongiorno, signora,* may I help you choose some wine?'

She looked up to see a friendly smile, a handsome face and a checked navy, tailored three-piece suit. Lily couldn't remember the last time she had seen any man wear a three-piece suit, apart from Peter.

Peter, she thought. Not a word . . .

'*Signora?*'

'Oh God, sorry. Jet lag. Sorry, my mind just wandered off there,' she replied, mortified.

'Ah, no problem, *signora*. A nice glass of wine perhaps and relax in the sun. You will feel better, no? You arrive from America today? For the wedding?'

'Yes, just a few hours ago.'

'I am Rafaele. I am the restaurant manager, *signora*,' he said, extending a hand to shake hers. 'We are all very excited for this wedding.'

'I'm Lily. Nice to meet you. Yes, me too. The rest of my friends get here soon, or today some time. I'm not really sure.'

'The bridal party has arrived, you know this?'

'Yes, I know this. I mean, I do,' she corrected herself. 'Sorry, I'm sleepier than I thought. Umm . . . my other friend will be here in about half an hour and we'll have lunch here. Is that okay?'

'*Sì! Sì!* Signora LeeLee, of course. This will be your table for as long as you want it. Now, can I help you to choose some wine?' he asked, peering at the list through his tortoiseshell-rimmed glasses.

'Yes, but I actually don't recognise any of them. Can you recommend something?'

'*Certo.* White wine?' he asked, leaning down over the menu.

'Yes, please.'

'*Va bene. Allora* . . . ' He pointed to three different wines by the glass. 'All of these are from Ischia and are very good.'

'Oh great. Ischian wine. Perfect. Okay, whichever you think is best.'

He closed the menu and stood up straight. '*Subito.*'

'Okay, *subito,*' she repeated.

Rafaele laughed. 'Ah no, *signora. Subito* is . . . right away . . . It means, I will bring you the wine right away. The wine you will try is Forastera. Is nice and light . . . perfect for lunch.'

'Oh, right. I thought *subito* was the name of the wine. Sorry . . . I'm blaming it on the jet lag.'

'Don't worry, *signora.* No problem,' he said with a kind smile.

Lily's phone buzzed again as Rafaele walked away.

On ferry. See you in an hour.
    OMG! SO excited!
    There's a bar on the ferry!
    Best boat ever!

Rafaele returned a moment later and poured her a taste of the Forastera wine.

'That's lovely,' she said, nodding her approval, as he poured her a generous glass.

She sat back in her chair, taking another sip of the wine. The only sounds she could hear were birds chirping and the familiar clattering of dishes from the kitchen. In less than an hour Ellen would arrive in a cloud of noise and drama, like a small animal that had been set free after years in captivity. Dee and Morgan would wake from their slumber, and Kitty would arrive ... she couldn't remember when Kitty was due to arrive, but certainly no later than tomorrow.

Rafaele stuck his head out of the restaurant door and gave her a nod. 'Is good?' he asked, both of his eyebrows rising with the question.

'Yes. *Sì*. Very good, thank you. I mean, *grazie*.'

'Good. Now, you are here in San Montano. From now on, everything will be good. *Buon appetito!*'

She couldn't help but smile back at him, wanting to believe more than anything that 'everything will be good'.

'It certainly doesn't suck at the moment, Lily,' she said, under her breath, savouring the wine, the sunshine, the view and the soon-to-evaporate peace and quiet. San Montano was about to get a lot louder, and she couldn't wait to drown out the voices in her head.

Chapter Six

Lily made her way down the sweeping, grand stone stair-
case from the main building towards the outdoor terrace
where breakfast was served. Her flip-flops echoed loudly on
each step, the sound reverberating off the old walls. It was
already warm, even though it was not yet seven a.m. She
paused momentarily, stifling a yawn, one hand to her eyes
to shield the glare from the sun. White tablecloths graced
tables, each of which had its own oversized white umbrella
standing ready to host guests for breakfast. Four-foot-tall
ceramic urns, each containing an exquisitely gnarled olive
tree, sat on either side of the entrance.

As she made her way across the terrace she recognised
Franco standing at the door, his hands clasped together, a
warm smile at the ready. He had served the three of them
last night at dinner, which surprisingly had been a rather
subdued affair. Morgan had stayed in bed with a migraine
and Lily, Dee and Ellen had had dinner together at the
resort restaurant. Both Lily and Dee had struggled with
the effects of jet lag, but were resolutely determined not to
let the first night be a concession to exhaustion. Franco had
regaled them with stories of the history of San Montano

and the island over multiple bottles of crisp, white Ischian wine, and they had chatted happily around the table until after midnight.

As he greeted her again this morning, Franco gave her a warm smile. '*Buongiorno, signora.* You have slept well last night?'

'*Buongiorno*, Franco. Yes, thanks,' she replied, wondering if it was considered rude to keep her sunglasses on. She dared not take them off, as last night's late dinner with the girls, followed by a fitful sleep, had resulted in red-rimmed, puffy eyes. Glancing around the room she realised that there was no sign of the girls. In fact, she seemed to be the first person down for breakfast.

That's a first, Lily. You're normally legging it in at the last minute before they take the last few slices of ham off the buffet table, she thought.

'*Fuori, signora?*' Franco asked, indicating a table just outside.

'Yes. *Sì, grazie.*' She nodded. Definitely outside so I can hide behind these sunglasses, she thought as she shuffled after him in her flip-flops.

The sun was already high and the breeze warm, hinting at the promise of another hot day to come. Birds chattered in the trees behind her and the thunderous sound of the thermal pool waterfalls mimicked the waves far below her.

'*Un cappuccino*, Signora LeeLee?'

'*Sì, grazie.*'

'*Subito, signora,*' he replied, with another wide smile.

She looked around the empty terrace and sighed.

'Loser,' she mumbled, as she adjusted her chair to face away from the buffet station and out towards Mount Epomeo and the sea below. 'You can't even lie in bed like normal people on holiday.'

She checked her phone for the fourth time that morning.

Nothing. Shocker. What exactly were you expecting, Lily? she thought, blinking away the first threatening tear of the day. For a moment she considered leaving the table, but the thought of a perfectly creamy cappuccino was too much of a temptation. Her head hurt behind her eyes from lack of sleep. The coffee would help.

Four waiters hovered out of view behind her. She sat quietly and alone, staring ahead at the spectacular view, but not actually seeing it. Her mind was far away in New York.

In the reflection of the glass doors to her right, she saw Franco gesture to the waiter heading in her direction, as if he wasn't moving fast enough. Perhaps he could tell that she needed the coffee urgently.

The waiter placed the cup gently on the table, the cream of the cappuccino forming a perfect meniscus on top. She realised, as he left the table, that she didn't even know if he had said hello. He must have done. They all did, all of the time.

Get it together, Lily, for Christ's sake.

She shook her head, agitated that her thoughts were once again back in New York with Peter. She felt like resting her face on the tabletop, but decided against it, given the number of waiters she knew were hovering somewhere behind her. She sipped the cappuccino, savouring the creaminess of the foam and the tang of hot coffee just beneath.

How does it always taste so much better in Italy? she wondered.

As she cradled the cup in her hands, her phone lit up with a WhatsApp message. It was Kitty.

Are you at the resort?

Yes. Where are you? Have you landed?

Yes. Feels like I've landed in fucking Calcutta.

WHAT??

Tell me the resort is FAB or I'm on
next plane out of this shithole.

What? Where are you?

Naples. Zero air-conditioning! Plus, had
to get a bus from plane. A BUS. Do you
know when I was last on a bus?

Lily stifled a laugh as she typed back.

Resort is divine. Ignore the airport. And the taxi ride to
the ferry too. Just get here. Hurry! It's fab. I promise.

Okay. They better have a stellar wine list.

They do.

How long from here? To resort?

Two hours from airport.

FML

There's a bar on the ferry.

Thank God

OK. LMK when you're on the ferry.

Will, if I don't throw myself off it.

LOL.

Lily smiled to herself, secretly hoping that Giuseppe was about to make another trip to the airport, as he would most definitely brighten Kitty's morning.

The sound of church bells from the village below echoed across the mountain, signalling seven thirty a.m. and shattering her reverie.

Have I been here for half an hour already? she wondered, looking around the terrace and the restaurant behind her hosting a vast array of breakfast food. It was still empty except for the waiters, but other guests would start arriving for breakfast soon. The northern Europeans would be first, Germans and Dutch taking the lead, followed by the French. Apart from Morgan's loud encounter at check-in, she hadn't heard an American accent yet on the island, but no doubt if they were here, they'd arrive soon in workout gear. The Brits and the Irish usually showed up at the last minute, hustling through the door, desperate to secure a place to sit and a coffee before the buffet was disassembled.

Relieved to note that she still had the place to herself, Lily made her way to the elaborate buffet station. Tiny red tomatoes were stacked high in bowls, glistening and calling out to be drowned in tangy, local olive oil. The cheese and charcuterie platters sat safely tucked inside glass domes, surrounded by multiple baskets of bread in various shapes and forms, along with artistic displays of fruit, berries, yoghurt and muesli. A circular table took pride of place in the centre, displaying a dozen types of pastries, still warm from the oven, the unmistakable smell of sweet pastry lingering in the air.

Eggs, Lily thought. Eggs would be good. If you keep consoling yourself and your sad life with bread at the rate you've been doing for the past two weeks, it's going to get really ugly and none of those new swimsuits will fit.

A small wicker basket filled with fresh eggs sat alongside an egg-boiling contraption. It was obvious what it was, even though she had never seen one before. The long pan of water simmered on a low boil, with small metal baskets dangling from the sides, each one the perfect size to hold one egg. It didn't look too dissimilar to her mini deep fat fryer at home, just with water in place of the wildly unhealthy frying oil. Lily figured that just as she would dunk in the basket with the chips and haul it out when the light went off, it most likely was the same procedure for the eggs.

It wasn't clear how long she should boil them for, but she figured that three minutes or so should be sufficient for soft-boiled.

'How hard can it be?' she mumbled, gently placing an egg in the wire basket and lowering it down over the edge of the water contraption. The basket tilted and the egg hopped out, rolling its way to the far corner, deep below the water.

'Dammit,' she muttered, tucking a strand of hair behind her ear. She tried to fish out the errant egg, but the spoon wasn't long enough, and in the process she splashed boiling water on her fingers.

'Goddammit!'

Picking up a second egg, she repeated the procedure, this time slowly lowering the metal basket down over the side. She turned the handle to hook it over the edge, but it rolled to one side, tipping the egg into the boiling water once again.

'Seriously? Goddamn caveman contraption!' she growled at the machine.

'*Menaggia*,' came a voice from directly behind her.

She turned and looked up at the man grinning at her. He was at least a foot taller than her, with tousled brown hair, deeply tanned skin and a perfectly ironed white linen shirt over a pair of swim shorts emblazoned with pink pelicans.

'Pardon?' she asked, confused and frustrated at the same time, rubbing her singed fingers. She had no idea what he had just said to her and she definitely wasn't in the mood for conversation.

'*Menaggia*,' he repeated, this time with a hand gesture to match. 'It's Italian for Goddammit. I thought it might be useful.' He had a soft American accent.

'Oh, sorry. I didn't mean to say it out loud, but I just lost two eggs to that bloody thing,' she said, pointing at the stainless-steel apparatus.

'Ah yes, well those two are well on their way to being overcooked at this point. What's your preference?' he asked, stepping forward towards the table.

'Sorry?' she said, with a little frown.

'Your eggs. Hard boiled or soft boiled?' he asked, dropping an egg into a mesh basket.

'Oh, um, soft boiled, please.'

'Sure. Did you actually want two or was the second just

a repeat of the first failed attempt?' he asked, grinning at her again.

She smiled despite herself. 'No, I actually wanted two. I just didn't know what I was doing.'

'There's a trick to it. Like this, see?' He turned the basket deftly and hooked it over the side.

'Okay, now I just feel stupid. I could have stood here for an hour and not thought to do that.'

He shrugged his shoulders. 'I learned the hard way too.'

Lily peeked down again at the bright pink pelicans under the perfectly ironed shirt and now that he was closer, she noticed that his hair had that salt-and-pepper colour. It made him look distinguished, even while wearing ridiculously colourful swimming shorts. She was suddenly acutely aware that she looked as if she had just rolled out of bed while this handsome creature looked like he'd just stepped off a boat.

'Are you Irish?'

'Yep, guilty. What gave it away?'

He laughed as he dropped two more egg baskets into the water. 'I have a couple of Irish friends back in New York. Your accent is similar.'

'Oh, you're from New York? I live in the city.'

'No kidding. Where?'

'Upper West Side. Eightieth between Columbus and Amsterdam.'

'I'm right across the park from you. Seventy-seventh between Lex and Park. I'm Matt, by the way'

'Lily,' she said with a small smile. 'I love that neighbourhood. I go there most weekends, actually. Coffee first at Sant Ambroeus then a tour around the Metropolitan Museum of Art and lunch at Serafina.'

Matt laughed. 'You just described my average Sunday. I love Serafina. Great pizza! It's a wonder we haven't bumped into each other there.' His smile revealed perfect white teeth. 'First time in Ischia?'

'Yes, we have a wedding here next weekend so we decided to come in early and make a proper vacation of it. It's always so hard to get time off work, so we all decided to take advantage of the wedding.'

'Right. Americans really suck at taking vacations. Are you staying here for the week? At the resort, I mean?'

'Yes, I am. I love it already and it's only my first morning. It's fabulous.'

'It is. It's a big island though and there is so much to explore. I can give you some local tips if you like?'

'Okay, that would be great. We were thinking of renting a boat today, but it looks a bit rough out there,' Lily said, nodding towards the horizon. 'We're not exactly hardcore boat people. I'm more of an aspirational boat person, if you know what I mean.'

Matt gave a glance at the timer and leaned back against the counter. 'It's usually flat calm here. That's the tail end of some storm that passed by down south, but it should be totally fine again by this afternoon. Where were you going to go on the boat?'

'I'm not sure. We don't really have a plan. We were just going to ask at reception. I know Procida is close, I passed that on the ferry on the way here. What about Capri? Is that close to us?'

'Not really ... I mean, you could do it, but you'd have to rent a private boat. The ferry doesn't run from Ischia to Capri. But honestly, there is so much to explore on Ischia,

I don't think you'll even want to leave. I've been to Capri a few times. It's not for me.'

'How come?' Lily asked, curious as to why he preferred Ischia over Capri. 'Everyone in the world has heard of Capri, but I'd never even heard of Ischia until this trip.'

'And that is precisely the answer,' he replied with a grin. 'Capri is beautiful, for sure, with dramatic scenery and all that, and it has super expensive, glamorous hotels, which attracts a certain crowd, but it's not my scene. Ischia, on the other hand, feels a lot more real, a lot more Italian. For some reason it has been under the radar of the international set for years, and as a result it's a lot less developed and less touristy, which I like.'

'I didn't have much time to do much research before leaving, so apologies if I sound like the most geographically vapid individual you've ever met.'

Matt laughed and shook his head. 'Not at all, but to be honest you'll find more than enough to do here on Ischia.'

The egg timer pinged loudly, and Matt scooped out the four eggs.

'There you go,' he said, placing two eggcups on the counter in front of her. 'You're all set. Franco!' he called out with a wave, then rattled off a stream of Italian. 'You need to put a sign up here to show people how to work this thing,' he translated to English for her benefit.

'*Sì, sì* . . . ' Franco said with a shrug of his shoulders, as if this were a regular occurrence.

'Franco is a master at this,' he said, smiling as he dangled the empty baskets back on the side of the machine.

'*Allora*, Signora LeeLee, *siedeti*. Sit down,' Franco said, indicating back towards her table outside. 'I bring this to you. No problem.'

Lily turned to thank the American, but he had disappeared. In his place stood two Germans in hiking boots and shorts. She smiled to herself, realising that she had correctly identified the breakfast buffet's early-morning guests. She filled her plate with some fresh balls of mozzarella cheese and some ruby-red tomatoes, stopping momentarily to drizzle dark green olive oil over the top. She made her way slowly back to the table and, sinking back into the chair, reached for her sunglasses.

The air was warm and still and she closed her eyes and turned her face to the sun. Franco quietly placed her eggs on the table in front of her and smiled, giving her a small nod before he shuffled back in the direction of the buffet. The terrace was still empty, apart from Matt who was sitting at the table on the other side of the double doors, deeply engrossed in his iPad. Lily checked her phone again. Nothing.

You've got to stop checking that thing, she muttered, as she hacked at the sides of her egg.

'Cranky person. Ten letters,' Matt said, loud enough for her to hear.

Lily turned to look in his direction. 'Um, are you talking to me?'

'Sorry, I didn't mean to say that out loud. I was talking to myself. I'm two clues away from finishing the *New York Times* crossword and it's driving me nuts. What's a cranky person . . . ten letters?'

'Curmudgeon.'

'Is that a real word? How do you even know that?'

'It's my job to know words,' she replied matter-of-factly.

'You're a writer?'

'No, but I write for a living.'

Matt picked up his cappuccino and frowned. 'Okay, is that supposed to be cryptic? How can you write for a living but not be a writer?'

Lily smiled. 'I'm a copywriter. I write for a living, but it's just blurb for adverts and products – like marketing copy and promotional jargon, that kind of stuff – so I honestly can't call myself a writer, not in the true sense of the word. Does it fit? Curmudgeon, I mean.'

'Spell it for me,' Matt said, leaning back over his iPad.

As she did so, he typed it out. 'Yes! Okay, last one. Don't abandon me now!'

Lily tried to smother a laugh. He was funny in an unassuming kind of way. 'Okay, let's hear it.'

'Fickle weather. Another ten letters, beginning with C.'

'Capricious.'

Matt looked up from his screen. 'You're like some sort of crossword Olympic champion!'

This time she laughed. 'I never usually do crosswords, I don't have the patience for them. I just need to know a lot of words in my line of work because you can't keep saying the same thing over and over.'

Matt typed the last remaining word into the open spaces. 'Awesome!' he said, punching the air with a small fist bump. 'That was a Friday one, too. Thanks for bailing me out.'

'What's the difference with a Friday one?'

'The *New York Times* crossword runs Monday to Sunday. Monday is the easiest day, and they get progressively harder every day. Saturday is the toughest. I don't even bother trying on a Saturday. That's for Harvard English students, or the likes of you.'

'What about Sunday?' she asked, ignoring the compliment.

'Good question. Sunday is the biggest, but not the toughest. It takes longer but it's kind of like mid-week difficulty level.'

He glanced down at his watch and tipped back the last sip of cappuccino foam. 'I've got to run, but before you go sailing off to Capri, there are a few things you should do on this island.'

'Okay,' Lily said, pulling out her iPhone to take notes.

'Okay, off the top of my head . . . the thermal springs and thermal waters here on Ischia. A lot of people believe that there is a feeling or a sensation you get just by being here – it's very quiet, very calming, almost a feeling of wellbeing. It's not spiritual exactly but it's definitely a unique feeling of some sort. I'm not sure how to explain it – it's just a combination of calm and contentment. The waters are considered therapeutic, so the thermal spas are definitely a draw for a lot of people. Second, there are all these different beach towns, and casual beach restaurants tucked away, some of them can only be reached by boat, but they all have a pretty unique vibe, which is fun to explore. Oh, and third is the mountain.'

His enthusiasm was contagious, and she typed a series of words frantically.

'The mountain?' she asked, pausing to look up at him.

'Yes. Mount Epomeo.' He pointed at the towering, verdant mountain that dominated the view ahead and to the right of them. 'It dominates the whole island, creating a microclimate that maintains this lush rainforest vegetation and tropical weather system. Look at those clouds sitting right at the top there,' he said, pointing up towards the peak. 'You don't often associate that type of cloud with an Italian summer, do you?'

'No, they look moody.'

'Moody clouds – right. Anyway, you can take a car up so far and then hike to the top. You'll be rewarded by an epic lunch at a great local restaurant. Rabbit is their speciality,' he said, smiling at her as he stood up to leave. 'They're wild and the island is overrun with them, so cooking them is the locals' way of keeping the numbers under control, without having to do a mass cull.'

'Okay, zero sympathy for the bunnies. I have this image in my head of local chefs out foraging for them in the mountains.'

Matt laughed. 'You're probably not far off, and the mountain restaurants are the best places to try it. There are a few that are renowned. Ask the guys at reception to make a reservation for you because they're always packed.'

'Okay, I will. How do you know so much about the island?'

'I've been coming here for years. Trust me, once this place gets under your skin you will never be able to forget about it. It will keep pulling you back time after time. It's like the island that time forgot, and you feel like one of the privileged few to know about it. One last tip: *aperitivo* hour outside on the terrace is not to be missed. It's the best spot on the island to watch the sunset,' he said with a grin as he tucked his iPad under his arm and strode off.

'Thanks for the tips,' Lily shouted after him. And for

taking my mind off of Peter for the first time in weeks, she thought. She crossed her legs and sank back into the chair, happy to not feel the overwhelming weight of sorry-for-yourself sadness, if only for a little while.

Chapter Seven

'You're up early!' Ellen said, stifling a yawn as she joined Lily at the table. 'How long have you been here?'

'Dunno, half an hour . . . maybe more. How'd you sleep?'

'Are you joking? With no children swinging off me? Like the dead. My God, those croissants in there look amazing. Did you see the bread display? Breakfast is included in the room rate, isn't it?'

'Yep, knock yourself out,' Lily laughed.

Ellen returned with a loaded plate. One plain and one chocolate croissant, a chunk of crusty bread, two slices of ham, a piece of ricotta cheese and two mini pastries.

'You know you can make multiple trips, don't you?' Lily mocked.

'Yep. I fully intend to. Just getting my bearings. Did you seriously just have eggs?' she asked, looking at the discarded eggshells on Lily's plate.

'Yeah, they were good.'

'What's wrong with you? You can have eggs at home. You're in Italy, Lily. *Italy.* The home – no the *birthplace* – of bread and carbs.'

Ellen broke off a corner of a croissant and stuffed it in

her mouth, rolling her eyes with pleasure. 'Jesus ... amazing. You don't know what you're missing. God, this view is stunning,' she said, turning to take in the view. 'Anything from Peter?'

'Nope. Not a word.'

'Unbelievable. What a knob. It's like he never existed.'

'What are we talking about?'

Both girls turned to see Dee approaching the table, with Franco in hot pursuit.

'*Buongiorno ... Buongiorno*,' he said, with a smile for all three of them. '*Cappuccino, signora?*' he asked Dee.

'Yes, urgently. Thanks, Franco. *Grazie.*'

'*Un altro cappuccino*, Signora LeeLee?'

'*Sì, grazie.*'

'Me too, please,' added Ellen. 'Peter. We were talking about Peter and the fact that she hasn't heard a single word from him since that night.'

'Unreal. Prick,' Dee said, shaking her head.

'I don't want to talk about it. Can we change the subject? It's too early,' Lily said, putting her head into her hands. 'Where's Morgan?'

'She's moving slowly this morning, but she's on her way. Okay, fair enough, we'll embargo the Peter conversation for now. So ... on to more important things. How are the croissants?'

'Divine. I'm going for round two,' Ellen said, disappearing from the table.

'*Allora ...*' said Franco, placing the cappuccinos on the table.

Both girls sat in companionable silence for a moment, taking in the view, each lost in her own thoughts. The terrace began to fill up with couples and families, all dressed in colourful pool attire. The outdoor tables were clearly a premium choice as they were first to fill up. Lily noticed several displeased faces, mostly women, as they were informed that the terrace was full and they would have to sit inside.

'Couldn't we just move a table outside?' asked one woman in a loud American accent. 'There's plenty of room right here. If we just moved this one over a little, we could easily fit another table right here.'

She was gesturing furiously at the space alongside Dee's chair, indicating where she felt a table could be slotted in.

'*No, signora*. Is not possible. Inside only,' Franco said firmly.

Morgan appeared silently at the table, dressed from head to toe in Missoni.

'What's going on? What is all the racket about?' she asked, placing both of her hands over her ears.

'It's this one over here,' Dee responded, nodding at the offending American. 'She's trying to rearrange the furniture,' she said loudly. 'She'd like to sit on my lap, actually, I think.'

Morgan turned and glared at the woman, a deadpan expression on her face. 'Well, honey, try getting up earlier tomorrow morning. Then you can sit where you like.'

The American woman glared at Morgan but seemed to think better of engaging further in conversation.

Franco moved around the table to take Morgan's coffee order.

'Oh, yes, I'd love a cappuccino please, double shot. And do you have wholegrain bread?'

'*Sì, signora*, of course.'

'Great, I'll do two slices of wholegrain toast, well done, and two soft-boiled eggs, please. Oh, and do you have avocado? I'd love a side of avocado, if you have it.'

Ellen leaned forward and put a hand on Morgan's arm. 'Morgan, it's a buffet!' she whispered.

'No point, Ellen,' Dee said, shaking her head.

'Buffet? That's just a suggestion for people who don't know what they want,' Morgan said with a wave of her hand. 'I know exactly what I want.'

'*Certo, signora. Subito.*' Franco replied, winking across the table at Ellen.

He had clearly seen it all before. The girls spent the next hour languishing over breakfast and multiple rounds of coffee. The conversation focused mainly on the wedding the following weekend, interspersed with different suggestions for activities and trips that had been recommended for the next few days.

'I'm not leaving this resort,' Morgan announced, patting Dee's thigh with one hand.

'Don't be daft ... there's a whole island to explore!' Ellen laughed.

'If there's a sailboat involved, by all means count me in, but I'm not going on any of those crazy hikes you guys were talking about.'

'What about the vineyard trip?' Lily asked. 'That sounds amazing!'

'Does it involve a hike?' Morgan asked, spearing a strawberry with her fork. 'You're not going to trick me into any physical exertion just by dangling a vineyard at the end of it. I've seen the wine list here. They have all the wine I could ever drink, and I don't have to leave this terrace.'

Dee shrugged her shoulders while Lily and Ellen laughed in unison. There was no denying that Morgan knew exactly what she did and did not want, and she wasn't afraid to share her opinions with anyone.

'Are you guys ready to go?' Morgan asked, eventually, folding her napkin on to the table.

The sound of high heels on the stone floor was unmistakable.

'I just got here, darlings, so hold your horses. What are we drinking?'

Kitty strode towards their table in a long, flowing red linen dress that fell to her ankles, oversized black sun hat and oversized dark sunglasses. Lily glanced down at her shoes. They were either Jimmy Choo or Manolo Blahnik. She knew she had seen them advertised but could never tell the two designers apart.

'You just got off a flight. How the hell do you look like that?' Lily asked, in admiration.

'Business class,' she said in her posh London accent. 'And I don't drink on planes ... wreaks havoc with the skin.'

Morgan visibly shivered as she recalled her overindulgence in Veuve Clicquot the previous day. 'It's all too raw ... I can't even think about that flight over here.'

'Looked like you were living your best life at the time,' Dee teased.

'Coffee? Cappuccino? Is that really the best you lot can do on your first morning? We're on day one of an Italian extravaganza.' Without waiting for an answer, and still standing, Kitty turned around and caught Franco's eye. 'Darling, may we please have a bottle of your best Italian bubbly ... something good, but nothing too sweet. Would that be all right?'

Lily could have sworn that Franco's eyes lit up, possibly at the promise of all kinds of escapades to come. He appeared by Kitty's side brandishing the wine list.

'*Certo, signora.* I can suggest this one.'

'Perfect!' she gushed. 'This is going to be fun. Five glasses please.'

A waiter appeared with a fifth chair. '*Buongiorno, signora,*' he said, not taking his eyes off Kitty.

'He's hot,' Kitty said, smiling widely as the waiter departed.

'Kitty, please don't turn your charms on the waiter,' Dee said, feigning a sigh. 'We haven't even been here twenty-four hours and there's a very expensive wedding happening here next weekend. We don't want to get barred or banished for your behaviour.'

'Seriously, he's divine,' Kitty replied, ignoring Dee's quip as she turned to stare after the young waiter.

As Franco poured the drinks, Morgan held her hand out over her glass. 'I'm going to stick to coffee for now, Franco. I'm still too fragile.'

'Well, you know your own body and what's best for you,' Kitty said with a smile as she carefully removed her hat.

All four of the girls stopped and stared at her.

'Who are you?' Dee asked, with both her eyebrows lifted high.

'Pardon?'

'Who are you and what have you done with my cynical friend?' Lily chimed in.

'What do you mean?' Kitty asked, feigning innocence. 'I'm merely being supportive of Morgan's choices ... Oh, all right,' she sighed. 'I'm trying to improve upon my future self. If I don't do something drastic, I think I will remain single for the rest of my life. These are desperate times, darling.'

'Okay, again ... what? Your future self?' Lily asked, leaning across the table towards Kitty.

'My coach told me to be more positive and express more interest in other people and their lives.'

'Your *who* told you to *what*, exactly?'

'Oh, stop it, lots of people have life coaches now,' Kitty said dismissively as she raised a glass to make a toast. 'Cheers, darlings, to an unforgettable week!'

'I've had a life coach for months now,' Dee said with a grin, as she clinked her glass against the others. 'Morgan set me up with one as a gift and now I can't live without her.'

Ellen's eyes opened wide as she imagined the possibility of having a coach in her life. 'Oh my God, am I the only one who doesn't have a coach?' she asked. 'I don't even know what they do exactly, but I can guarantee they'd make a better hand at my life then I'm doing right now.' She sighed. 'Imagine if I could pay someone to help me get to the next level of myself.' She sighed again, her eyes gazing into the distance. 'I could be so fabulous!'

'It's a good thing you live in Ireland, Ellen. You'd be in full-time therapy if you lived in the US. It's addictive,' Morgan said, topping up her glass.

'Seriously, I love the idea of being able to pay people to listen to me. Imagine. For one whole hour they'd *have* to let me talk.'

'It's actually more like forty-five minutes by the time you get seated and started,' Morgan corrected.

'I don't think I've ever had anyone's full attention for forty-five minutes. I'd definitely be addicted. You know I think I have ADHD,' Ellen said calmly, as she tipped back her glass of champagne.

'You don't have ADHD, darling. You *are* ADHD,' Kitty said, trying to explain the difference between the two expressions.

'Yes, I know, that's exactly what I was thinking. I mean, I really need to get my life together, so I did that self-assessment thing that's been going around the internet, you know the one to see if you are actually ADHD?'

'Um, no, I don't know what thing on the internet. And please don't tell me that you are self-diagnosing from some random internet quiz,' Lily said, shaking her head and waiting for Ellen's latest catastrophe to unveil itself.

'No! It's real, I swear. I did the test and it turns out I am totally ADHD. Not even just on the spectrum but like WAY the other side,' she gushed, continuing undeterred. 'I've figured out that I just need to do three things: first, get an official doctor's assessment so I can get a prescription and fix my life. Do you know that it takes me a month on average to even post a letter? I carry the goddamn thing around in my bag for two weeks before I even think of getting a stamp. Then I'm at the post office without the letter, and it takes me another two weeks to get around to sticking the stamp on the letter. Honestly, getting a real diagnosis is going to change my life!'

'Okay, so what's number two and three?' Dee asked, all four of them now insanely curious as to where this might be heading.

'Oh right. See ... I had even forgotten that I was telling you my three things. Okay, so number two is actually get the pills and start taking them so I'll be able to do thing number three.'

'Which is . . . ?'

'Oh . . . I don't remember. I took too long telling you that story. Don't worry. It will come back to me eventually,' she said, triumphantly pouring herself another splash of champagne.

It was the first time that all five of them had been together in over a year and there was much catching up to be done. Lily put an embargo on discussing Peter and the breakup until drinks that evening, insisting that such a topic was not really suitable for breakfast. Morgan decided it was futile to fight the urge when the second bottle of champagne arrived, and the next hour descended into a cacophony of stories and laughter. When the waiting staff started to set the tables around them for lunch it was the signal to take the marathon catch-up session to the sun loungers and continue the chatter under the searing Ischian sun.

Chapter Eight

The layout and geography of the island of Ischia is such that sunset is only visible from one stretch of coastline, and San Montano was in prime viewing position. Mount Epomeo, the mountain that loomed tall behind the town of Lacco Ameno, obscured the view of the setting sun from the rest of the island. This was a huge selling point for the resort, and to further celebrate the fact, they had adopted the charming custom of ringing a bell each evening at precisely fifteen minutes before sunset. No matter where you happened to be on the property, you had time to make your way to the expansive outdoor olive garden and claim a seat for the greatest nightly show in town.

The bar at San Montano was off to the right of the vast, marble-tiled lobby, but it had its own entrance from the olive garden just outside. It had been cleverly laid out to maximise the view of the setting sun, with a cluster of small tables and chairs nestled among the ancient olive trees. Every evening at six o'clock, Enzo took his place at the grand piano in the corner of the bar and commenced his nightly renditions of the classics. The double doors to the olive garden were opened fully, and the easy tunes carried across the light summer breeze. Ambrogio, dressed to perfection each evening in a three-piece suit, took up his position as bar manager behind the long marble-topped bar counter. An expert mixologist, he liked to create speciality cocktails, but the definitive, go-to drink of choice at sunset was the Aperol Spritz.

'*Allora, signore, buona sera!*' Ambrogio said, greeting them with a warm smile. '*Benvenuti.*' He held his hands wide to welcome them to the bar. 'Welcome to San Montano. You arrive yesterday, no?'

'Yes,' Lily said, returning his smile. 'We got here yesterday, but we had travelled all night so we were wiped out.'

'Wiped out?' Ambrogio repeated, with a slight frown.

'Oh, sorry, I mean, we were exhausted, so we just had a quiet night.'

'But not tonight, Ambrogio,' Ellen said, with a huge grin.

'*Eccellente!*' Ambrogio laughed. 'Yesterday, it was my day off. This is why I do not see you last night. But tonight . . . *Eccomi!* Here I am. *Allora*, you are just in time for the sunset. I have reserved a table outside for you. But first . . . what would you like to drink?' he asked, clasping his hands together.

'Aperol Spritz!' Lily said, without hesitation.

'I second that!' Ellen said, excitedly. 'Probably four of them, right?' she asked turning to face the other three.

A unanimous positive response settled the drinks question.

'*Allora* . . . come. I will show you your table,' Ambrogio said, gesturing to the double doors. 'From here you will enjoy the sunset. I have reserved this table here for the bridal party.'

He guided them down the narrow path that wound its

way through the olive grove. The building and development had been extremely sympathetic to the ancient gardens, and so the olive trees remained in place, the path conceding to their age and winding its way carefully around them. The fact that there were no straight lines or new plantings only added to the sense of raw, uninhibited beauty, the sense that this place had been here for ever, and that its visitors were merely passing through to enjoy it in this moment.

Ambrogio came to a stop at one of the prime tables and glanced quickly around. 'Ah, but you are not all here. We wait for one more. *Mi dispiace.* I am sorry. You would like to wait, to order the drinks?'

'No,' Lily said, shaking her head, as she realised that Kitty had yet to appear. 'We're definitely not waiting. Aperol Spritz ASAP, please.'

'There is only one more to join us this evening, but you can definitely go ahead with those drinks,' Dee offered, by way of explanation.

'*Sì, sì,* yes, okay. Four Aperol Spritz,' he said, gesturing to a nearby waiter. 'We don't wait for the groom, no?'

'Ah,' Dee said, a small smile spreading across her face. 'You were off yesterday, so you probably missed the arrivals information. Don't hold your breath, Ambrogio. There won't be any groom.'

It was clear that Ambrogio was trying hard to follow Dee's strong Irish accent, but the sentiment was not lost on him. His face registered a look of confusion for a moment. He looked from Dee back to Lily and back to Dee again.

'But . . .'

Dee laughed and, not wanting to embarrass him, put one hand on his arm. 'Ambrogio, my love, there is no groom.

There are only two brides. This is a gay wedding: me, and my beloved here,' she said, putting one arm around Morgan's shoulder.

'Going to be all kinds of fun!' Ellen said with another grin.

Ambrogio put one hand to his face. '*Sì, mi dispiace, signora.* Yes, I have heard this, but I did not know that it was this wedding. *Eccellente!*' he said, laughing. 'Two brides. *Meglio così* ... better like this, no?'

'I dunno, honey. I'll let you know in a year,' Morgan said with a grimace.

'*Allora, signore,* here are your Aperol Spritz,' Ambrogio said, as a waiter arrived with a tray of orange-coloured cocktails, and a selection of nuts, breadsticks and small bites.

'I will come back when the other ... person, they arrive. *Buon aperitivo!*' he said with a little bow, before leaving them to enjoy the drinks and the view.

The girls gathered around their table, each picking up a cocktail and staring at the horizon.

'What a view,' Dee said, in quiet admiration. 'That beach looks nice, I might check it out tomorrow.' She pointed down towards Negombo beach.

'You look great tonight, Ellen,' Lily said, admiring her friend's pale-yellow maxi dress.

'Thanks! I feel like I'm dressed like a real girl again, not my usual ratty leggings and jumper. And no one has vomited on me so that's definitely a plus. I packed for my best self for this trip.'

Lily snapped a photo on her iPhone. 'You look great. That's a great colour for you. Look ... ' She turned her phone around to show Ellen the photo.

'Hmm ... it's okay. In real life I think I look a bit skinnier, don't I? Maybe it's the light. Or just the phone. They say the camera adds ten pounds, maybe it's the same with iPhones. Don't post it anywhere,' Ellen said assertively, as she gathered up the long skirt of her dress and sat back into one of the cushioned chairs. 'What a view,' she added, appreciatively.

'We're not in Kansas any more, that's for sure,' Morgan said, raising her glass to the other three girls. 'Cheers, ladies.'

'Cheers,' they replied in unison, with happy smiles on each of their faces.

Lily had never seen a sunset like it. She stared silently at the enormous round orange ball in the sky, thinking it was probably the largest sun she had ever seen. She had read that *tramonto* was the Italian for sunset.

'*Tramonto*,' she said out loud, the round vowels rolling over her tongue. It sounded far more dramatic than 'sunset', she decided. 'Sunset' was just plainly descriptive. The sun was about to set, period. No drama. What was that American saying she had heard so often from Morgan? 'It fell short.' Well, the word 'sunset' certainly fell short of describing what she was seeing here this evening. There was nothing pretty or delicate about it; rather, it was a large, blazing, fiery display. This sun was not going down without making its presence felt, and it worked.

Silence fell on the crowd of people who had gathered to watch it, layering a hush across the resort as the sun sank heavily below the horizon. Those merely walking by were compelled to stop and stare as it left their view dramatically. No trickling yellows or pinks, it was there one second, large and bold, and gone the next, blazing big reds across the smattering of wispy clouds.

'How does it just disappear like that?' Lily asked in awe, taking her seat alongside Dee, Morgan and Ellen.

Dee stuck her straw deep into the bottom of her glass. 'That's just what it does. Happens every day.'

'No, I know it does, but like . . . *how*, you know? It's there one second and gone the next. Poof! Heading off down to Australia for their tomorrow morning,' Lily said, still gazing at the horizon.

'Why are you being weird?'

'I'm not being weird; I've just never seen a sunset like that before. That one was fiery and bold. It had balls, you know?'

'That's the first time I've ever heard of a ballsy sunset, but I guess it kind of was. What's going on with you, anyway? You still haven't heard a word?'

'Not a thing.'

'Are we talking about Peter? Finally! You've shut me down every single time I tried to ask you. Now, spill. I want all the details of what happened. I can't believe I always vouched for him, the little turd.' Kitty announced her late arrival loudly and sat down, swinging the skirt of her emerald-green dress around with a swoosh.

'Since when were you his biggest fan?' Dee asked.

'I never said I was his fan, just that I vouched for him. I thought he was good for you, actually. You seemed to respond to him in a way that I hadn't seen happen before. Sartorially, the man worked wonders for you. I mean look at you—'

'Respond to him? Changed everything about herself for him, you mean!' Dee shrieked.

'Eh, hello? I'm sitting right here,' Lily retorted.

'Okay, changed, didn't change, who cares. What matters is that you look fabulous. Don't you feel fabulous? That's got to count for something. But enough of he said, she said,' Kitty said, nodding her head in Dee's direction. 'What the hell actually happened?'

Lily's shoulders slouched. She took a deep breath and repeated the conversation and the events of her last evening with Peter as accurately as she possibly could. The four girls sat in respectful silence around her, as she recounted the throwaway comments about the baby shower, followed by Peter's incendiary announcement about having already decided that children were not in his future, and the ensuing argument back at his apartment until such time as Lily decided it was best that she leave. The onslaught of questions was fast and furious.

'And you've heard nothing since?'

'No.'

'Have you reached out to him?'

'No.'

'Are you going to reach out?'

'No, why should I? He made his position perfectly clear.'

'What about your stuff? The bits and pieces you had at his place?'

'He had his assistant courier them to my office.'

'What a jerk.'

'Asshole.'

'Do you miss him?' Ellen was the only one to ask the burning question.

'Yes,' Lily said, not making eye contact with any of them.

Silence fell on the group momentarily as each of them weighed up Lily's answer.

'I'm not sure this question is allowed, but I'm going to ask it anyway,' Morgan said, sitting up straighter in her chair. 'You aren't sure you want to have kids, right?'

'Well, no. I mean, yes, that's right. I don't know for sure.'

'And you love this guy, right? You were crazy about him?'

'Well, yes, I was, until—'

'So, why are you giving up a man for a baby you don't know you actually want?' Morgan asked, verbalising the very question each of them had been wondering.

'But why should I give up the chance to have a baby for a man who already has that, just because he is done with that part of his life? What if I change my mind? What if I wake up one day soon and decide I do want one? Then what?'

Dee gestured in the direction of the hovering waiter that he should bring another round of Aperol Spritz. 'Then you spend the rest of your life resenting him for taking the choice away from you, or you trick him and get pregnant by fake accident. Are you really either of those kinds of women? Because I sure as hell don't think so.'

'If you're not even sure about wanting a baby in the first place, then why are you giving all this up? Everything else was perfect, right?' Morgan asked, determined to get to the bottom of Lily's rationale. 'I mean, it's not like you desperately want kids or anything, and frankly if you haven't wanted them by now, chances are that's how it will stay.'

'But why should that matter? Shouldn't I be allowed to make that decision? What if I do decide that I want them? I mean, I'm thirty-four years old, what if in a couple of years, I decide that I do want kids? Then what? I've blown my chances with someone who made it perfectly clear that, if I choose him, I lose the baby option.'

'I don't know, Lily,' Ellen said, slowly. 'It's bloody hard work. Granted I have five of them, which is complete over-kill by any idea of normal, but still, any number of them are hard work. I mean there are honestly days I'd like to sell them, followed by days I'd happily give them away for free. Then they do something adorable and cute, and I feel like the world's worst mother.'

'Don't be so hard on yourself, everyone has a bad day now and again.' Kitty shrugged, tipping back her Aperol Spritz to drain the last drop.

'No, no,' Ellen replied, shaking her head. 'Maybe I wasn't clear . . . I alternate between the days I want to sell them, and the days I would happily give them away for free . . . like, every other day!'

'Well, I can't say that I can see the attraction,' Kitty said, dryly. 'Never have done. I don't know how you cope with five of them, Ellen. I mean, what happens if you have them and then you realise that you're not really cut out for it? Or worse, you realise that you don't even like them? You can't just give them back.'

'Yes, that is the official take on the subject,' Dee said, grinning over at Kitty.

It was hard to tell if she was joking or actually being serious.

'But isn't it a pity that you can't give them to someone who really wants to have kids?' Kitty said, sighing loudly.

Dee gestured with both hands. 'I believe that's frowned upon, Kitty.'

'No, I know that, of course, but still, it's a pity, isn't it? I mean, look at all the people who really want kids and can't háve them. Think of all the people who'd benefit from a solution like that.'

'Kitty, I really hope you're not considering having kids . . . ever,' Lily said, laughing for the first time that evening.

'No, darling, my womb is officially closed for business. I mean, there are elements of my life that I might change, like not be so bloody single all of the time, but still, it's my life and I like it. I simply cannot imagine having to put all those small people and their needs ahead of my own. Lily Ryan, you had a fabulous life with Peter. You were living the high life in New York with the best of everything! I think you need to be really, really sure before you throw it all away.'

'She had a great life *before* Peter, too,' Dee interjected. 'You were perfectly fine pre-Peter. Don't go thinking that you need him back in your life to make everything better.'

'No, I know. I don't think I will change my mind – about the baby thing, that is. But it's just that I know lots of women who decide that they want to have kids when they're older, like in their early forties. If I go back to Peter, then I'm doing so with my eyes wide open, and closing the baby door for ever.'

The other four sat in silence, mulling over her closing statement. It was hard to argue with the logic. Peter had been perfectly clear, so the decision, and the next move if there were to be one, was definitely Lily's.

Morgan stood up, brushing crumbs from her lap. 'Okay, on that note, I think it's time to end this little chat and move on to dinner. And for the love of God, can someone please be on point and keep me away from all these little bowls of nuts and breadsticks? I have a dress to fit into in six days and this is not the way to achieve that goal.'

Morgan had spent her entire life battling her weight. Over the years she had subscribed to every fad diet invented by mankind, the most recent being the ketogenic, which had proven to be hugely successful. The golden rule was no carbs, and she had stuck to it religiously. She had bought several recipe books and followed ketogenic influencers on social media, and with a wedding looming she had followed the advice and directives to a tee. Five months and twenty-five pounds later, she was thrilled to be hovering at her goal weight.

But her greatest weakness in life was carbohydrates.

Now, with less than a week to the wedding, she was presented with a seemingly unending selection of carbs at every single meal. The choice ran the gamut of croissants, pastries, cake, breadsticks, bread (white, wheat, ciabatta, focaccia, and the most dangerous of all, the *pane di campagna* – country bread, dark brown and exceedingly crusty on the outside and soft, light and spongy on the inside). Then, of course, there was the wide variety of pastas offered at lunch and dinner, and every woman's diet killer: pizza.

'I'm in the home of pizza. The actual birthplace of pizza, right where it was invented ... right here in Campania. And, as if that's not bad enough, I'm in a country that serves cake for breakfast. I mean, who doesn't love cake for breakfast? How the hell does anyone stay skinny here?' Morgan ranted, as the girls gathered their things and made their way down the path to the restaurant.

'Six days, ladies. Just six days until I fit into that dress, and after that all bets are off. All the photos are to be taken from now until Sunday morning. Then, I'm going dark. Under cover, off the radar, missing ... presumed wallowing in one form of carbohydrate or another. Now, let's go have fish and green vegetables,' she said, rolling her eyes in mock despair.

The girls were accompanied to a table for five overlooking Negombo Bay. The restaurant was situated in such a way that most tables enjoyed a view of the sea. The exterior wall curved around in a semicircle and was made entirely of sliding glass doors. This evening they had been slid back fully and a light breeze provided relief from the heat of the early evening.

The beach below was now empty. The loungers had been tidied into neat rows and the sand combed in preparation for another sunny day. The moonlight reflected on the still water of the bay below, casting shadows across the soft rippling waves. The scene was totally transfixing, with the water moving mellifluously with the rolling waves. Franco greeted the girls with his usual warm smile and proffered the wine list for their consideration.

'*Buona sera, signore.* You have the best table in the house. Especially for you. This is the best view on the island. You like it, no?' he asked, proudly gesturing to the sweeping view of the bay.

'It's quite amazing, Franco,' Kitty said, tearing her eyes from the view to make eye contact with him. 'I've never seen anything like it. It's almost hypnotic.'

'*Grazie, signora. Sì, è bellissima,*' Franco replied, the pride evident in his voice. '*Allora,* tonight, what wine would you like to drink?'

'Franco, sweetheart, I don't recognise a single bottle on this menu,' Morgan said, as she flipped the wine list closed and handed it back to him. 'As long as it's white, dry and fabulous, I really don't care what you bring.'

'*Bene*. I bring a bottle from Ischia called Frassitelli. It is excellent, *signora*. If you don't like it, I drink it myself!' he said, grinning.

He proudly explained that the wine was produced locally by Casa D'Ambra, a vineyard high up on Mount Epomeo, and was owned and run by two sisters. The sisters had grown up on the property, their grandfather having bought the land and planted the vines about seventy years ago. The locals had initially told him he was crazy to invest in a property up so high, and that the altitude would impact the quality of the vines, but he continued undeterred. He had been convinced that the high altitude, responsible for a dramatic drop in temperatures by night, would be beneficial to the vines, and so he prevailed despite all advice to the contrary. He struggled for the first few years, but eventually produced a decent wine. Learning from his earlier mistakes, he changed the position of the vines to access more direct sunlight, and the result two years later was a stunning white wine. He passed the vineyard down to his son, who in turn passed it on to his two daughters. The two sisters boldly invested in additional land, and with several years of dedicated attention and recent advances in technology, they were able to augment the quality of the wines to win their first award.

'*Allora*, the wine is coming, but first here is a welcome drink on the house,' Franco said, reappearing at the table. A second waiter approached the table and handed Franco a bottle of something sparkling.

'This sparkling wine is Franciacorta. Is from Northern Italy. I think that you will like it,' he said, carefully pouring the sparkling wine into the five glasses. 'Then, I bring you the white wine, and if you like it you can visit the vineyard,' Franco said, topping up their glasses once the initial fizz had settled. 'It is up there.' He pointed through the window towards the peak of Mount Epomeo.

'That's pretty cool, that it's run by two women. We should definitely check it out!' Lily said, enthusiastically. 'This is delicious, Franco. *Grazie.*'

'As long as I don't have to hike there, I'm game. Vines, yes, climbs, no,' Morgan said, raising her glass to make a toast. 'To women-run vineyards. May we see a lot more of that in the future.'

'Well, I'm loving this bubbly, for starters. I think I'll be shipping a few boxes back to London. This is actually very good. Franco, can I see that bottle please?' Kitty said, turning to ask Franco over her shoulder.

'I actually can't tell you when I last had a glass of bubbles,' Ellen said, taking a photo of the bottle with her phone. 'Do you think this costs a fortune? I could bring a few bottles home and close my eyes next week and pretend that I'm still here.'

'Ellen, darling, you look really good tonight. What have you done to yourself?' Kitty asked. 'Have you had work done?'

'I said exactly the same thing!' Lily said, nodding in agreement.

'No, sad that you all think I've done something as dramatic as cosmetic surgery. I just made an effort, to be honest. I lost my mind shopping for this wedding. I packed for a version of myself that doesn't exist in real life, or not in *my* life, at least. I have accounts on several online shopping sites now. Did you know that they all deliver for free? So dangerous. I think I have a bit of an addictive personality because I couldn't stop ordering stuff online. I bought a hat for forty euros on ASOS. I'm not even a hat person.'

'Well, that dress is divine on you, darling. You look marvellous.'

'Thanks, Kitty,' Ellen said, blushing. 'I packed way too much stuff, though. I got a bit carried away. I was on the ASOS app one night and had a bunch of things saved to my favourites that were out of stock. Then I realised that you could set a notification when they come back into stock. Honest to God, I might as well have been in Vegas. The app kept telling me that something was back in stock and they say something like "Go! Go!" to get you to jump on to the app and buy it. Then it would flash up "Last one left" and I'd lose my mind trying to add it to my cart. My God, the stress of it all. Actually . . . the night I bought this dress I was sitting on the edge of the bathtub. Little Jim was in the bath whining, but I kept shushing him because I fell in love with the dress, and it was flashing up "Last one left". I couldn't type fast enough to get it in my cart and hit "purchase". I was completely distracted. Turns out he had got his toe stuck in the tap because Mommy was shopping for a new dress. I'm such a bad mother,' she finished, rolling her eyes. 'Is there any more in that bottle?'

'Yeah, same . . .' Lily said, shaking her head. 'I bought two hundred and twenty euros' worth of new underwear. What a waste. It's not like anyone is going to see that here. I think I was still programmed from buying new underwear for every date with Peter. Stupid. My credit card is maxed out. I had to bring my emergency card for this trip, and I already put about eighty euros on that buying

Tom Ford cosmetics that I can't afford in duty free. I'm a financial tragedy.'

'Oh, don't be so hard on yourself. We all lose the run of ourselves in new relationships,' Dee said, kindly.

'New? I was with him for six months and was spending the same amount on underwear and new outfits as I was on rent! Honest to God, my credit is maxed out. I need to get my act together after this trip and start paying it down or American Express will have me in debtor's court.'

'Darling, that's what emergency credit cards were made for,' Kitty said supportively.

'Yeah, so what ... you spent like a baller for a few months,' Dee said with a shrug. 'Big deal. You work hard and you'll get back on track again after this trip.'

Lily pursed her lips and stared across the table at her best friend. Dee had always been practical and level-headed, and Lily was grateful for her words of encouragement. Despite her self-imposed woeful financial situation, she felt herself relax a little as she took solace in what Dee had just said.

'You're right,' she replied with a sigh. 'I'll start over and save like a maniac as soon as we get back to New York.'

As the girls were ordering dinner, an elegantly dressed couple passed by their table. The woman wore a long, white, broderie-anglaise dress that had a hint of a train at the bottom. Her brunette hair was piled up in a chic chignon and she walked confidently in perilously tall nude sandals. The man wore a soft, pale blue linen suit, with an even paler blue shirt underneath it. He caught Lily's eye as he passed by and smiled.

'*Buona sera,*' he said, hesitating slightly before his brunette companion tugged on his arm. She never even turned her head towards them.

'Who the hell is he?' Kitty whispered loudly.

Lily blushed and gave a small, self-conscious wave back. 'Oh, no one. I don't know him. I just met him at breakfast.'

'Well ... I'm going to have to start getting up earlier, aren't I. Good Lord, they don't make specimens like that any more, darling,' Kitty replied, her head turning to follow him across the room.

'Kitty!' Lily hissed. 'Stop staring!'

'Lily, darling, when the good Lord made men like that, he intended them to be stared at. What time exactly did you have breakfast at?' she joked.

'Well ... a) I was down for breakfast at six thirty, and if that's not enough of a deterrent for you, then b) the glamazon hanging off his arm should do the trick.'

'Jesus, I'd feel like a smurf standing next to her,' Ellen said, her eyes following the woman in admiration.

'Zero per cent body fat,' Morgan added. 'I bet she hasn't had a sandwich in a decade. Pass over those breadsticks, please, Dee, and don't try to talk me out of it.'

Dee pushed the basket of breadsticks across the table towards Morgan. 'Just before we drop this topic entirely, can I ask what exactly you mean when you say you "met" him at breakfast? I didn't think people *met* at breakfast. Aren't most folks just stumbling about in search of their first coffee? Expand please, my dear.'

Lily put her head into both hands. 'It was kind of embarrassing actually. I—'

'Ooh, even better!' Kitty interjected, rubbing her hands with glee. 'Do continue!'

'I was trying to be healthy, you know ... ignoring all the lovely bread and pastries, so I thought eggs would be a good idea. I didn't realise that there was a basket of hard-boiled eggs over by the cheese, I just saw the fresh eggs and the egg-boiling thing.'

'The what?'

'I don't know what it's called. It's a big metal thing with boiling water for boiling your own eggs.'

'This is why I don't do buffets,' Morgan said, slathering some unsalted butter on a slice of ciabatta bread. 'Who the hell has the patience for all that? Boiling your own eggs? Doesn't sound like much of a holiday to me. Dee, this bread is really delicious. You should try some ... Sorry Lily, go on. But you guys, this is the only piece of bread I'm allowed, okay?'

'Jesus, Morgan, it's like trying to watch a two-year-old with you. Give me that basket of bread,' Dee said, grabbing the basket from the centre of the table. 'Sorry, Lily. Go on ...'

'It was nothing. I was trying to cook my eggs, I dropped them into the water by mistake and he appeared and showed me how to do it properly, that's all.'

'Wait. I thought that the whole point *was* to drop the eggs into the water? Am I missing something here?' Ellen asked, a confused look on her face.

'Search me. You lost me at "cook your own eggs",' Morgan replied, shaking her head.

'No, you're supposed to put the eggs into these little wire baskets and lower them into the water, then lift them back out when they're done. But mine fell into the water, so I couldn't get at them.'

'Honey, this is sounding more like being a line cook at a two-bit diner than breakfast at a five-star resort,' Morgan continued. 'Here's an idea ... how about tomorrow you let the nice Italian people make the eggs for you?'

'But if she'd done that she never would have met that hunk over there, so there is something to be said for it,' Ellen said, turning to look in his direction again.

'Do people still say hunk?' Kitty asked. 'I thought that went out with the eighties.'

'I dunno – could have. I don't get out much,' Ellen replied, a sideways grimace on her face. 'Did you talk to him, Lily? Or was it just "let me fix those eggs for you"?'

'No, he pretty much just fixed the eggs and showed me how to do it for next time. Then he called Franco over to finish it for me. When I got back to my seat he was sitting at a table across from me and he gave me some tips about where we should go on the island. That was it.'

'Well, that's disappointing. Zero drama, then ... Oh, here's our food,' Dee said as Franco approached the table with two waiters in hot pursuit.

All five of them had ordered fish, and Franco introduced each dish as it was placed in front of them.

'Allora ... pesce di spada ... this is the swordfish. Branzino is the sea bass,' he said, as two plates were placed on the table.

'Orata nel sale per due, this is the sea bream cooked in salt for two persons. Who has this fish tonight?'

Lily and Ellen raised their hands in unison, staring at the huge mound of solid, white salt.

'Is our fish actually under all that salt?' Ellen asked.

'Yeah, they cover it in salt and bake it in the oven,' Lily replied, peering at the hard mound of salt. 'Apparently, it keeps the fish super moist. I read about it before the trip. It's kind of a speciality here. That and rabbit.'

'There's rabbit in there too?' Ellen asked, a look of horror on her face as she stared at the large mound of salt.

'No, rabbit is another speciality here in Ischia,' said Lily, laughing. 'This is just the fish ... the *orata* ... or whatever he called it. Is it *orata*, Franco?'

'*Sì*, Signora LeeLee, is the *orata*.'

'*Allora*,' he continued. '*Finalmente, abbiamo il pezzogna all' acqua pazza. Pezzogna* is the fish ... is a local fish and is cooked whole in *acqua pazza* ... in crazy water,' he said, giggling at the translation. '*Signora*, we will do for you, no? We will take it off of the bone, no?' he asked, turning to Kitty.

'Oh, yes please, darling. Wonderful. I'm absolutely rubbish at doing it myself. That's precisely why I refuse to cook fish at home.'

'*Va bene*. We do it here,' he said, setting the dish on a side table.

Using two spoons, he removed the head and tail, discarding them on to a side plate. Then he carefully removed the chunky white flesh, placing it on a plate, and scooped up the tomatoes, vegetables and broth that the fish had been cooked in. The aromas were heady and intoxicating, smelling of briny sea and sweet tomatoes.

Morgan tasted her fish and then reached down for her purse, pulling out a small, flat, rectangular box. It was white, with green letters printed on it. From where Lily sat it looked like a travel-size box of mints. She watched as Morgan slid back the lid of the box and took out a pinch of something white. From her vantage point, it was impossible for Lily to see what might be in the box. By now, Ellen and Kitty were also watching what was happening across the table.

Dee looked up from her fish and saw the three heads staring across at them.

'Umm ... Morgan ... ?'

'This whole scene is rather fascinating from this side of the table. I really do hope it's something highly illegal that we might all be invited to try!' Kitty said, leaning sideways to get a better view. 'Is it some kind of ecstasy? I must say I've never tried it, but I would certainly be game, especially if someone of your standards had purchased it. I wouldn't be the type to try street-corner drugs, but the high-end stuff from the best of dealers ... well, that's rather tempting, I must say!'

'I can't tell if you are joking or half-serious,' Lily said, looking sideways at Kitty. 'Morgan, what the hell is that?'

'It's salt,' she said, looking from one to the other of them.

'Salt?' Lily repeated.

'Sure. Salt,' Morgan nodded, as she sprinkled a minute quantity on her fish.

'Morgan, why do you have salt in your purse?' Lily asked. 'Is this a joke or something?' She looked at Dee. 'I don't get it.'

'I always travel with salt,' Morgan replied, matter-of-factly. 'The shit you get in restaurants is mostly chemical. This is real, pure salt. You can't imagine the difference until you've tried it.

'Are you for real?' Ellen asked, looking at Dee for confirmation. 'Does she really travel with salt?'

'Yep,' Dee replied, stifling a giggle.

'Wait, I'm confused. What's wrong with sea salt? These

are sea salt crystals,' Lily said, pointing to the salt grinder on the table.

'Sea salt is fine,' Morgan replied. ' But you never know if you'll actually get sea salt or some cheap, processed crap.'

'So, what's that? In your little box there?' Lily asked, now more intrigued than ever.

'It's one of the best in the world. It's from Japan and it's called Hana Flake. It's super fragile, so I carry it in this tin box to protect it.'

'Is it expensive?' Ellen asked.

'Yes. It comes in tiny jars, kind of like the way they sell saffron in tiny packets, for the same reason.'

'Why? Is saffron expensive? I'm beginning to feel very culinarily uneducated at this point,' Ellen said, spearing a piece of fish with her fork.

'Honey ... saffron is the most expensive spice on the planet! How do you not know this? It comes from these little purple crocus flowers, and it takes about four hundred of them to make just one ounce of saffron. Based on weight alone, it's more expensive than gold.'

'That's mental. I need to start reading more,' Ellen said, shaking her head.

'This conversation is unnecessarily painful,' Kitty said, waving at Franco. 'Franco, darling, can we please have another bottle of that lovely wine?'

'*Subito, signora,*' he said, a big grin lighting up his face.

'Good call, Catherine. Get him to put a third on ice when he comes back,' Dee said, with a wink.

'Not if you call me Catherine, I won't,' Kitty replied, in a mock-threatening voice.

'Why? What's wrong with Catherine? Did you used to

be called Catherine at one point?' Lily asked, turning to face Kitty. 'I'm learning all kinds of things about you all tonight. Do go on . . . Catherine.'

'Marvellous. Now look at the can of worms you've opened up.' Kitty rolled her eyes as Franco reappeared with a second bottle of Frassitelli wine.

'Ah, Catherina, this is your name? This is my favourite name,' Franco said, twisting the corkscrew into the bottle. 'It was the name of my grandmother. *Allora* . . . you will try, Catherina, no?'

Kitty glared across the table at Dee. 'Sure, Franco. I'll try, but I'm not called Catherine any more. I'm called Kitty now.'

Franco shrugged, 'Ah, this is nice too. I like this name, too. Is good, the wine?'

'Yes, delicious, *grazie*.'

'*Prego, signora*,' he said, grinning at them all as he poured the second bottle into the five glasses.

'You can get another one of those ready there, Franco, please. Won't take too long to work our way through this one,' Dee said, reaching for the fresh glass of wine.

Franco laughed and nodded, shuffling off to put another bottle of Frassitelli on standby.

All four of them stared at Kitty, waiting for the backstory to her name change.

'It's not much of a story, really,' she said, sipping her wine. 'I was born Catherine to very affluent, successful upper-class British parents. I rebelled when I was younger and changed my name to Kate. My mother was furious, of course, as she didn't believe the name was very becoming, but she agreed to put it aside. A year later, I was dating this artist from Cambridge and she claimed that I was only doing it to upset her, so she threatened to disinherit me. Idle threats often have a habit of backfiring, as did this one. I took it one step further, got engaged to the artist – temporarily, of course – changed my name legally to Kitty, and haven't seen or heard from her since.'

'And you think that's not dramatic?' Lily asked, her jaw dropped.

'Darling, it's just family nonsense. All families are twisted in some way, but those with means, those with serious wealth, are the most screwed up of all. They think that money is something they can use as leverage for most of life's challenges, and they don't hesitate to use it against their own families if it's to their advantage. I'd had enough so I left.'

'Wow. So did your mother really disinherit you?' Ellen asked, her fork paused in mid-air.

'I have no idea. I'll tell you when she's dead.'

'Excuse me, I'm sorry ... am I interrupting something?'

They all turned to face the voice coming from behind them. His reflection was cast in the window, so those facing directly forward first saw him cast in the glow of candlelight. He was standing behind Kitty's chair and moved slightly to her right so that he came into view.

'Excuse me, ladies. I came over to introduce myself, but it sounds like I might be interrupting an important conversation,' he said with a polite smile.

He towered over the table, wearing a textured dark blue blazer, a white shirt open at the collar and a pair of dark jeans with a dark brown belt. From the other side of the table, Lily couldn't see beyond the belt, but she was willing to bet a hundred dollars that his shoes were the same shade of brown. His jet-black hair was slicked back, his skin gently tanned, and his eyes crinkled at the corners when he smiled.

'Please, don't apologise. We were done with that conversation anyway. I'm Kitty,' Kitty said, extending her hand to shake his, her eyes not leaving his face.

'It's a pleasure to meet you. My name is Antonio. I am the manager of the resort. I apologise that I was not here to welcome you all when you arrived, but I was in the US on business. Now, which of you five lovely ladies are the brides-to-be?' he asked, a genuinely warm smile spreading across his face.

Dee and Morgan raised their hands and introduced themselves. He shook each of their hands, introducing himself as he did so. 'Everything is prepared for your wedding next weekend and you will have a formal meeting with our planning and events team at your convenience. You are also on holiday, so you must feel free to schedule the meeting when it suits you. We are here for whatever you might need. Ah, I see that you are almost out of wine, but you still have a little food left. Allow me.'

He turned to signal Franco, who nodded and returned immediately with another bottle.

'This is on the house, ladies. Welcome to San Montano,' he said, handing each of them his business card. 'If there is anything you need, please don't hesitate to contact me. My mobile number is here too. Now, I will leave you to enjoy the rest of your dinner. *Buona serata*,' he said, with a small nod of his head, before he turned and walked swiftly away.

'Did that just happen, or did I dream it?' Kitty asked the table.

'I didn't think people that good-looking existed in real life,' Ellen said, staring after him. 'I mean, not with real jobs, you know. Models and actors maybe, but the manager of a resort on an Italian island? Are you joking?'

Lily's phone pinged loudly in her bag. 'It's like we've landed in the middle of an Audrey Hepburn movie, or something,' she said, ignoring her phone. 'He was ridiculous, but they are all gorgeous and *so* nice! It's as if they don't even realise they are so good looking.'

'Antonio ...' Kitty repeated his name quietly. 'Did anyone notice if he was wearing a wedding ring?' she asked, a sly smile crossing her face.

'Kitty Thomas, if you do anything to jeopardise my wedding next weekend, your mother won't be the only one to disown you! And if I disown you, I warn you that I'm taking custody of this entire group so you will die lonely!' Morgan said, waggling a fork in her direction.

Lily's phone pinged again.

'For the love of God, will you silence that thing?' Dee growled.

'Sorry! I forgot to before dinner.'

Pulling her phone from her bag, she frowned at the screen. 'That's weird,' she mumbled.

The messages were from three different work colleagues.

Have you seen the email? Call me!

WTF? Did you know about this?

Call me when you get this. Shit!!!

'What's up?' Dee asked, seeing the increasing frown on Lily's face.

'I don't know. These are work messages. Something's wrong. I have to check my email,' she said, opening her Gmail app.

The first three emails were from the same colleagues forwarding the offending email, along with their choice of obscene comments. Lily scrolled until she got to the original email. It was from the HR director, John Slate, known internally as Teflon John because nothing ever stuck to him. He was a smarmy sycophant who hid behind forms and best practices but refused to engage with the employees as a human being.

The subject line read: 'Company Update: Layoffs'.

'Oh my God,' Lily said, as she scrolled slowly down the lines of text.

The four girls stopped and stared at her.

'Oh my God ... ' her voice trailed off.

'*What?* What is it?' Ellen asked, leaning in to read the email over her shoulder.

'Oh my God,' she repeated. 'Does that mean you, Lily?'

Lily looked up from her phone, the colour draining from her face. 'I think I've just been fired.'

Chapter Nine

Ellen leaned across towards Lily and yanked the phone from her limp hand. 'You haven't been fired, Lily,' she said as her eyes scanned the lines of email. 'It says layoffs, it doesn't say anything about being fired. Hang on, let me read it properly.'

'Shit,' Dee said. 'When did this happen?'

'I don't know. It looks like the email was sent out before my phone started going nuts. Oh my God, this is a disaster,' she said slowly, putting both hands to her face.

'It says it's a cost-cutting measure to be implicated company-wide ... blah blah blah ... due to the recent loss of the Disney contract ... blah blah blah ... effective imme-diately ... Jesus, they are laying off forty people,' Ellen said, scrolling through the email.

'And I'm one of them ...' Lily said, her voice barely a whisper. She put her forehead to the table and banged it three times. 'This is a disaster. My life is a financial car crash and I have just been fired—'

'Laid off, Lily, not fired,' Ellen corrected.

'Financially it means the exact same thing,' Lily said, banging her forehead on the table again and groaning.

'I think she's in shock,' Kitty said, in a low voice. 'She's not swearing. She's just doing a kind of Rain Man move on the table there. Perhaps we should get her a whisky.'

'Sorry . . . is this a bad time? It looks like this might be a bad time. I'm sorry, I don't want to interrupt.'

Lily lifted her forehead from the table as the other four girls turned to follow the voice.

Matt stood two feet away, as if reluctant to come any closer.

'No, it's fine. Lily just got some bad news, that's all, so . . .'

'I'm sorry to hear that. I hope it's nothing too terrible,' he said, a look of genuine concern on his face.

Lily stared at him in silence. She wasn't sure how to form the words to communicate what she had just learned.

'Her company is laying off a bunch of people and she's one of them,' Morgan explained. 'No one has died or anything. It's just a shock, obviously. She just found out.'

'Oh gosh, I'm so sorry. That's awful, and to hear about it here while you guys are on vacation. I'm sorry to interrupt, I just wanted to say hello, but I'll leave you guys alone. If there is anything I can do to help, please give me a call.'

Lily nodded, attempting a smile that didn't quite work. 'Thanks,' she replied quietly, as Matt placed a business card on the table and walked away.

Ellen handed the phone to Dee, who then passed it on to Morgan and Kitty. All five of them were silent as they read the email. Moments later, Franco arrived at the table carrying a small silver tray and five small shot glasses.

'*Allora, signore.* Matt asked me to bring this to you. Is our local grappa. He said to me that you have had a shock. This is good for the shock.'

'Who? Dee asked, a confused look on her face. 'Oh, the eggs guy?'

Lily shook her head. 'I don't believe this. First Peter and now this ... I mean, what god did I piss off? Could this year get any worse? You know how you hear about people having a bird shit on their head? Like a seagull or something. Well, I feel like there is a cow hovering overhead, shitting down on me.' Her voice trailed off as she dabbed away a tear from the corner of one eye. 'Sorry ... I'll pull myself together in a second.' She blinked furiously.

'*Salute*,' Franco said, placing the bottle of grappa on the table. He patted Lily's shoulder lightly and shuffled quietly off.

'Oh, please ... what are you apologising for?' Kitty asked. 'Is this your first time getting fired?'

'She wasn't fired, Kitty. She was laid off,' Ellen corrected again.

'Who are you, her agent? It doesn't matter. Fired ... laid off ... it all feels the same and it all represents the same implications – financial and emotional. I've been fired twice. The second time was the impetus to start my own company.'

'I was fired once. I was working at a McDonald's one summer and they caught me eating the fries. Can't even look at a McDonald's now without feeling bitter,' Dee said, tossing back the grappa.

'Yeah, but you guys all own your own apartments and are sensible with money. I've spent the past six months blowing my entire savings at Victoria's Secret buying sexy underwear and ordering new outfits online like I was one of the Kardashians. God forbid I'd show up in the same outfit twice. I bought two pairs of Jimmy Choos so I'd "fit in" to all the fancy restaurants I was going to. Who the hell did I think I was? I probably have two month's rent in the bank and I'm currently sitting on an Italian island and charging it to an American Express card that I won't be able to pay back. I'll have the Amex cops chasing me around New York. Oh my God.' She groaned, putting her face into her hands.

'Here, get this into you,' Dee said, pushing a glass of grappa across the table. 'It can't hurt. Look, you're here now, so let's just focus, okay? Don't freak out. You're in Italy for this lovely week and we'll figure it out. This happens to everyone, Lily. It sucks right now, but you are very talented, and you'll get another job. We'll help you. You're just having a really crappy run right now, but no one is dead. This too shall pass. Now, drink!'

Dee's tone was a combination of motherly care and admonishment and it was loud enough to jolt Lily back to the present. The Irish had a tendency to revert to death at any signs of bad news, and if no one had died then the present situation surely couldn't be considered all that tragic. As the girls rallied in support of her and swapped stories about being fired or laid off, Lily tried her utmost to engage with the conversation, but for the most part she remained lost in her own thoughts. She felt the warm liquor slip down her throat and sank back into her chair. Her shoulders sagged as she tipped up the glass, releasing the last drop on to her tongue.

'I think the universe is trying to tell me something,' she said to no one in particular.

Dee poured another shot of grappa into their glasses. 'Maybe this is its way of telling you to draw a line under everything and start over.'

Lily leaned forward and rested her chin in her hands. 'Well, the universe has crap timing. It could have waited until after my Italian holiday to start telling me to change my life. I don't think I can even afford to be here right now! My life is a mess. I thought your twenties was supposed to be the rough part and we'd have it all figured out in our thirties? I'm going backwards.'

'Okay, I'm not going to allow you to wallow here,' said Dee. 'Look, getting laid off is crap. Breaking up with Peter sucked, but you have worked really hard to build a new life for yourself in New York and you love it, right? I've known you for fifteen years, Lily Ryan. You'll figure this out. You'll brush yourself off and you'll find another job. As for Peter, you were fine before him and you'll be fine again. Cut yourself some slack. I know you don't want to hear this because it all looks shit right now, but your life is not a mess. Don't be so hard on yourself. If you have to draw a line under everything then what better place to be, what better place to do that?'

Lily nodded her head. 'Starting over is scary.'

Kitty leaned forward and placed a hand on her arm. 'Darling, what's scarier still is ending up where you never intended to be. We've all had to course correct. It's just your turn, that's all.'

'God, you all sound so together. I have to course correct once a week, and at *least* once a month I wonder what possessed me to get married in the first place. There should be an AA equivalent for married people to help us stick with the programme,' Ellen said, leaning her chin in one hand. 'Do you know what? I just realised that I'm the only one of us married! I never thought of that before.'

'That's really helpful. Inspiring even. You're really selling the dream,' Morgan said, pouring another grappa.

'Oh yeah ... sorry about that,' Ellen giggled, a sheepish look on her face as she took the bottle of grappa from Morgan.

As they raised their glasses noisily with one final round of grappa, Lily smiled despite herself. Everything else in her life might be absolute chaos right now, but she definitely wasn't alone.

Chapter Ten

Lily stood at the edge of the saltwater pool facing the bay, her hands on her hips, breathing deeply and dripping wet. The swim had felt good. She had pushed herself to complete thirty lengths, hoping that the physical exertion would help dislodge the thoughts of Peter swirling around in her brain, and the email from the night before.

If he were here with her, he would make everything better. He'd give her a pep talk about finding a better job and would take her mind off the whole nasty situation. Instead, she had lost Peter, too, and had to figure her own way out of this mess.

He would love it here, she thought, gazing at the wide expanse of Negombo Bay, rippling in front of her. She sighed quietly, shaking her head at all that had transpired over the past few weeks. 'You've made a complete bollocks of everything, Lily,' she mumbled. She tried to slow her breathing as she wrung out her hair and tied it into a knot at the nape of her neck.

The voice came from directly behind her.

'Great view.'

She turned to see Matt standing about six feet behind

her. He was staring over her right shoulder, directly towards the bay. She frowned instinctively and stared at him, wondering if he was being facetious, or if he had really been referring to the view of the bay, but he continued to stare at the horizon, not meeting her eyes.

Lily was suddenly very conscious that she was in a bathing suit, dripping wet, and self-consciously wrapped her hands around herself. The swimsuit wasn't even one of her favourites. It was a sensible Adidas racer-back, perfect for swimming lengths, but Lily thought it flattened out her boobs too much. She had planned to have a quick swim before breakfast and hadn't expected to have to deal with other humans at that hour of the morning. The clinking sounds of cups and glasses inside indicated that the waiters were setting up for breakfast, but apart from that, there was no one else around.

Lily, you're such a bloody narcissist to even think he might have been referring to you, she admonished herself in her head. 'Yes, it's beautiful,' she replied, her eyes darting around to locate her kaftan.

'Here, allow me,' he said, picking up a rolled pool towel and tossing it in her direction.

'Thanks,' she said, catching it in mid-air. It was not quite seven o'clock and the air was already warm, but she shivered involuntarily as she wrapped the towel around herself.

'I'm not following you, I promise. I wanted to get a swim in myself before breakfast and I prefer this saltwater pool to any of the others,' he said, slipping off his flip-flops. 'You're an early riser. This is two mornings in a row.'

'Not usually. I'm normally the last one running down to

grab a croissant, but I didn't sleep very well last night so I just gave up.' She shrugged.

'You were swimming pretty hard. Looks like it was a good workout.'

'Well, I plan on spending the rest of the day inhaling carbohydrates so I figured I may as well earn it.'

He laughed. 'Hey, I'm sorry about your news last night. That sucks. Are you okay?'

'Yeah, I'm fine. It does suck, though,' she said, sitting down heavily on the lounger. 'I definitely didn't see it coming.'

'Crap timing to find out on your vacation, too.'

'Yeah, my one week off,' she replied, pushing her sunglasses up on her nose. 'The idea of trying to find another job in New York ... God, it's exhausting just to think about it.'

'Look, I know this is probably easier said than done, but try not to sweat it this week. I know it's easy for me to say but look ... you said it yourself, this is your one week off, so you owe it to yourself and your friends to make the most of it. I know you won't be able to just wipe it all out of your mind, but try ... I don't know ... try smashing it with a rock in your head whenever those negative thoughts creep back in.'

Lily looked up at him as he sat on the lounger opposite her, his forearms leaning forward on his knees. His hair was dark and dishevelled with a strand in front falling down to his eyelashes. She stared from behind the safety of her sunglasses and noticed that every time he blinked the strand of hair moved. She felt an overwhelming urge to reach out and sweep it back, wondering if he had just rolled out of bed

119

and not bothered to brush it. He wore an earnest look on his face and raised his eyebrows in question as if prompting a response. She smiled despite her mood.

'Are you a shrink or something? It's awfully early to be having a conversation about "negative thoughts" if you're not.'

'Hell, no!' he laughed. 'Have you ever had a shrink give you advice like that? I'm not sure shrinks are allowed to recommend things like smashing your thoughts with a rock. That would probably get me disbarred or whatever the shrink equivalent is.'

'You forget that I'm Irish. We don't do shrinks. We just gather up a friend and go to the nearest pub and talk it to death.'

'Hey, it's cheaper than therapy,' he replied with a grin.

'That depends on the number of rounds you order.'

His grin was infectious, and she found herself smiling for the second time that morning. 'Actually, I think even Freud said something about the Irish and therapy. Something along the lines of the Irish being the "one race of people for whom psychoanalysis is of no use whatsoever".'

Matt laughed loudly. 'Is that right? That's too funny. Yeah, I like your pub idea. I might have to try that one on next time I need to be talked off a ledge. So, what do you and the girls have planned for today?'

'We might take a stroll down to Negombo beach; have lunch at one of the restaurants,' she replied.

'Negombo is great. The water is warm and salty so it's amazing to swim in, but don't have lunch at the beach, go in behind the first thermal pool instead. There's a small outdoor restaurant in there that's straight out of *Alice in*

Wonderland. The owner is a bit odd, don't take any notice of him. He's French,' he said with a shrug. '*But* the food is absolutely insane. The guy's grandmother is about eighty-seven years old and she's in there six days a week cooking up a storm. The place only opens for lunch, and they close when they run out of food, which usually happens before about one thirty, so go early.'

'Oh, that sounds great, thanks. I normally have a whole plan for what to see and where to eat when I travel any-where, but everything was a bit chaotic before I left, and I just didn't have time . . . ' She hesitated, not sure what to say next, but resolutely not wanting to get into the messy details of her breakup with a perfect stranger. 'Anyway, that place sounds great.'

'Sure. Honestly, there are so many good options. I've never had a bad meal on this island, but you know how it is . . . some places are just really special and not to be missed. Make sure you get out on a boat, too. It's the best way to see the island.'

'Yeah, a boat trip is definitely on the list. We've got a wedding at the weekend, so we'll be jamming in all the sight-seeing between now and Friday, but to be honest it's pretty tempting to just stay here.' She put her hand to her eyes, shielding the glare of the sun. 'This view . . . it's magical.'

Matt laughed. 'Yes, I can see how it would be tempting to just hang out here, it's a great resort. I've been coming to Ischia for years. The manager is a good friend of mine, he'd be happy to hear that you like it so much,' he said, tugging his T-shirt over his head as he walked to the edge of the pool.

Lily tried not to stare, but caught a glance as he walked

past her. Her eyes ran from his broad chest down along his arms. They were strong, but not overtly muscular. Her eyes languished momentarily on his abs – the man was clearly in great shape – but she couldn't supress a smile as her gaze continued down to his navy swim shorts resplendent with a pattern of yellow ducks. Matt turned around and caught her smile and glanced down at his shorts, his face breaking into a wide grin.

'I have a thing for colourful shorts,' he said, raising both hands in the air in fake surrender.

'I can see that. Yesterday it was pink pelicans and today it's yellow ducks. Is it a bird thing or just colourful wildlife in general?' she joked.

'No, only things that live on the water because, that way, they make sense. You see, if these ducks were elephants or lions that would be completely ridiculous.'

'Yes, they might be the most sensible, logical shorts I've ever seen,' she replied, unable to stifle a giggle. She turned to look in the direction of the restaurant. 'I can hear the sounds of breakfast, so I better go get a table before it gets busy.'

'The sounds of breakfast?'

Lily turned her head to one side, wondering how to best put words to what she meant. 'Yeah, breakfast has its own particular sound. I think it's because breakfast is kind of . . . I dunno . . . *dainty*. Like . . . tiny spoons clinking against small bowls. I'm not sure how to describe it, but I think everything about breakfast is unique. No one is drinking, people are just waking up, so they are quieter than normal, and the food is kind of pretty . . . especially in a place like this.'

'Huh, that's true,' he said, turning his head to listen to

the sounds she was referring to. 'I never thought about breakfast having a different sound, but I guess it does. You're good at this.'

'At what?'

'This ... describing things. You have a good way with words.'

Lily shrugged. 'I'm used to it, I suppose. I do it for a living ... used to, at least.'

'You obviously have a talent for it. Maybe you should do something with that. Look, I run an ad agency and I can tell you that trying to find good writers is a constant struggle. You could make a killing if you put yourself out there, especially in a place like New York.'

'I don't know. It's all so superficial, so fake, isn't it? All those cheery slogans and captions, and most of them are total lies, by the way. No one ever magically drops two dress sizes in a week, it's all bogus.'

'So do something real, something authentic. What do you love to do more than anything?'

Lily squinted up at him. 'Are you sure you're not a shrink?'

'I was in the same spot as you a couple of years ago. It was really complicated, and I had to reinvent myself. A friend had exactly this same conversation with me and it forced me to think about what I really wanted to do; what I'd actually enjoy doing for a living.'

Lily hesitated. You are sitting in a towel, damp through to your skin and some handsome stranger with cheese-grater abs is telling you to dig deep and figure out what you want to do with your life, she thought. This is bizarre, and I haven't even had coffee yet.

Matt was staring at her expectantly.

'Well,' she began reluctantly. 'If I'm to be totally honest, then travel is what I love to do more than anything.'

'Great. So do that,' he said matter-of-factly.

'Do what?'

'Do something in the travel industry, with your writing skills. Just think about it. Look, there isn't a week that goes by that our agency isn't contacted by someone in the hospitality industry looking for representation to promote their brand – some resort or hotel chain. They are all looking for ways to stand out from the competition, but we don't do hospitality.'

'Hmm . . . ' Lily said uncertainly.

'You know that old saying that when one door closes another one opens? Well, I've been there, I've had the door slammed in my face and it sucks. The only solitary advantage to that shitty situation is you get to start over, and if you get to start over, wouldn't it be cool to do the thing you love instead of just some other rote job that pays the bills?'

Matt's phone vibrated on the lounger and he strode towards it. 'Sorry, I'm not usually this philosophical in the morning, I just happen to have had experience with this particularly charming setback. Excuse me just a second.' He glanced at the screen. '*Ciao amore . . . sì . . . sì. Va bene. Non preoccuparti. Vengo subito.*'

I have no idea what he just said, but *amore* translates in any language, Lily thought, as she stared down at her blue flip-flops. Everything is blue here, she thought idly. I wonder if that's on purpose.

'Sorry about that. So much for my swim. I've got to run,' he said, turning back to face her. 'Oh, by the way . . . try the fig jam at breakfast. Wild figs from the island. The pastry chef is shortlisted for some sort of culinary award for it.'

'I don't like jam. Or sweet things,' she said, a little more petulantly than she had intended.

'This isn't really jam—'

'You just said, "try the fig jam".'

'Right . . . I did,' he said with a smile. 'Sorry, I should learn to keep my opinions to myself. Anyway, I better go. *Arrivederci!*'

She waited for him to disappear out of sight, pulled her kaftan on over her head and made her way up to the terrace. 'Serves you right, thinking you can have some cute conversation with an American stranger before you've even had coffee. Idiot. What were you thinking?' she muttered as she pulled back a chair and sat facing the bay.

'Who is the opposite of Einstein?'

Lily turned to see Ellen shuffling towards her, mobile phone in one hand and a champagne glass in the other.

'Where'd you get that?' Lily asked, eyeing the champagne glass.

'Franco gave it to me. He said you were out here, and as I was passing the buffet he handed this to me. Did you know they have Prosecco at breakfast? And it's the good stuff, too. Best breakfast ever!'

'No, I didn't, but it sounds like a great idea right now.'

'What's wrong? You seem pissed off. Oh my God, did you hear from Peter?'

'No, nothing's wrong, and no, I still haven't heard from Peter. Anyway, what were you saying when you came out?'

'About what?' Ellen asked, a confused look on her face.

'Jesus, Ellen, it was only two minutes ago. You said something about Einstein.'

'Oh yes, I was wondering who might be considered the opposite of Einstein. Because that is who I married.'

'You're making less sense than usual.'

'I just got a text message from Mike telling me that he fixed the dishwasher.'

'Wait, what does this have to do with Einstein?' Lily asked with a frown as a waiter approached their table.

'*Buongiorno, signora. Cappuccino?*'

'Yes, um ... *sì*, two please.'

'*Due. Subito, signora.*'

'Oh, and can I have one of those too, please?' she asked, pointing to Ellen's champagne glass.

'*Certo, signora,*' he replied, with a smile.

'He thinks he's a genius now because he fixed the dishwasher, but there actually wasn't anything wrong with it. He was pissing me off the day before I left for Italy. He was sulking because he wasn't going, and I was trying to pack, so I poured a glass of water on the floor in front of the dishwasher and told him it was leaking.'

Lily threw her head back and roared laughing. 'You did NOT.'

Ellen giggled. 'I did. I had to do something to distract him. He was getting on my nerves.'

'What did he do?'

'He went all Bob the Builder, getting his toolbox out and he had to change his clothes, because he was wearing his good jeans.' Ellen giggled again at the memory of it. 'Anyway, that's all I know, because I left him at it and went back to my packing.'

'And he was texting you just now to tell you that he'd fixed it.'

'Yeah, he thinks it was a blocked filter. I have lines of details that I don't understand or care about, but basically, he took apart any bits that were removable and put it back together and he's delighted with himself.'

'Oh my God, that's the funniest thing I've heard in a while,' Lily laughed, as she pushed her chair back from the table. 'C'mon, let's check out the buffet.'

The two girls loaded up their plates with a selection of charcuterie, cheese and sliced country bread. They took a plate of fruit to share and two small bowls of home-made Greek yoghurt and granola. Alongside the cheese display, Lily noticed two blue and white ceramic bowls, each with a handwritten sign. One was labelled SPICED APPLE and the other ISCHIA FIG. Hesitating for just a moment, she took a spoonful from the Ischia fig bowl and placed it next to her cheese.

'God, I wish I could have breakfast like this every morning,' Ellen mumbled through a mouthful of bread. 'I don't even eat breakfast at home. I don't have time to eat myself by the time I've fed all five of them. Breakfast in my house takes an hour and a half.'

'That sounds torturous.'

'It is. I'm not kidding,' Ellen said, slathering another lump of butter on to her bread.

'I don't eat breakfast in New York, either. I get a cappuccino on the way to work and that's it. I don't know who I think I'm fooling here, eating all this food, but I can't not, if you know what I mean.'

'Well, it's all good food, Lily. All fresh and local.'

'Who's fresh and local?' Kitty asked, as she pulled back one of the chairs. 'You two were down early.'

'How do you possibly look so good first thing in the morning?' Lily asked, admiring Kitty's floor-length cover-up. 'Are you wearing make-up?'

'No. Just some mascara and lip gloss.'

'Mascara is make-up,' Ellen retorted, rolling her eyes.

'It's just mascara. I don't understand why any woman would leave the house without mascara. It's like a secret weapon. And, one never knows what – or who – the day will bring. Ooh, champagne! Now that's a damn sight better than yesterday's excuse for a breakfast. Well done, ladies.'

'Blame Ellen,' Lily said, as she tentatively trailed some fig jam over her slice of locally made soft Toma cheese.

'What's that?' Ellen asked. 'Looks fancy.'

'Fig jam.'

'I thought you didn't like sweet things?'

'I don't, but it's figs, so it's not like regular jam. The figs grow wild here in Ischia and apparently the chef is up for some sort of award for it. Thought I'd try it,' Ellen shrugged.

'Darling, you are a little font of knowledge this morning. How do you know all this?'

'Oh, um . . . I read it in the magazine in the room I think.'

'I might have to try some myself,' Kitty said, calling Franco over to the table. 'Franco, darling, is this fig jam really as good as Lily says it is?'

Franco's eyes widened in delight. '*Ah sì, signora*, the chef, he . . . *come si dice* . . . he is to win an award . . . *come si dice* . . . *Kilometro zero*. It means zero kilometre from where the food is grown, to your table. These figs are grown here in Ischia. You must try. I take you some. You would like some cheese too, *signora*?'

128

'That would be wonderful, Franco. *Grazie* ... I only understood half of what he said, but he certainly looked excited about this award.'

The soft flavour of the fig melded perfectly with the smooth nuttiness of the local Toma cheese. Lily closed her eyes and sat back in her chair. She ran her tongue over her bottom lip, tasting the combination of flavours.

'Wow, that *is* amazing. He was right.'

'Pardon?' said Kitty, scooping out her second passion fruit. 'Who was right? Franco?'

'Nothing, sorry. So, what's the plan for the day?' Lily said, changing the subject. 'I think the other two are doing some wedding stuff this morning, so we won't see them.'

'Well, that sounds like Morgan's code for "I'm having a lie in so you can all bugger off", if you ask me,' Kitty said, grinning as she bit into a grape.

'Are you really not going to have any bread or croissants? Just fruit and cheese?' Ellen asked, a look of desperation on her face.

'Darling, every woman has an allowance of carbs on a daily basis. It's entirely up to each of us how we choose to ingest them; bread, crackers, pasta, pizza, potatoes, rice, wine – or any sort of booze, actually. I would prefer to eat fruit and cheese now and save my allotment for pasta and wine at lunch and dinner. I'm thirty-six, Ellen. Once you hit your mid-thirties every carbohydrate is like a freight train heading your way. It's merciless and relentless.'

Ellen stared at the half croissant in her hand and replaced it on the plate. 'That's so sad.'

'Hard choices, Ellen. Hard choices.'

'I don't care. We're only here for nine days so don't you

dare depress me about food and calories. I'll worry about all that again when I get home,' she replied, as she stuffed the remainder of the croissant into her mouth.

'What do you think of going down to Negombo beach?' Lily asked, folding her napkin and picking up her phone and sun hat. 'I heard that there is a great restaurant hidden away down there. Some quirky kind of place with great food, but you have to get there early because they close as soon as they run out of the daily specials.'

Ellen pushed her chair back from the table and stood up, grinning. 'Sounds good to me. Personally, I feel right at home in quirky places. I'm going back to get my book and put on some mascara. I didn't realise that was Kitty's secret to leading the perfect life. Meet you all out front in ten minutes.'

Chapter Eleven

The pedestrian descent to Negombo beach was via a series of almost four hundred steps that curved their way down the hill, descending slowly into a lush, dense rainforest. At the bottom, the girls followed a path that took them through enormous, overgrown palm trees and gigantic wisteria bushes, bursting with violet flowers. The foliage was so dense that it created a canopy overhead, providing welcome shade from the searing sun. The forest was alive with the sound of birdsong and chatter, and even though the girls craned their necks to follow the sounds, the instigators remained perfectly camouflaged and invisible. It sounded to Lily like a tropical forest soundtrack as they made their way through the shaded path, one behind the other, each lost in her own thoughts.

Suddenly, the forest opened to a clearing and the bay revealed itself directly in front of them. The girls kicked off their flip-flops and walked barefoot on to the hot, soft, golden sand. To their right were dense gardens that housed the famous thermal pools and spas, and to their left were two beach-shack restaurants, each with small, rickety wooden tables and chairs lined up in the sand. Beyond the restaurants were several lines of navy-blue loungers, reserved for residents of the resort.

The girls were greeted with cold, jasmine-scented face towels and a glass of home-made jasmine iced tea. Soft, thick, blue-and-white-striped towels were laid out on their loungers, which directly faced the bay. Lily lay back and pressed the cold towel to her face, inhaling the heady scent of jasmine. She groaned as her phone buzzed from deep in her canvas beach bag.

'That's probably Dee and Morgan wondering where we are,' she said, from underneath the cool facecloth.

'I'll bet Dee is looking for an escape from all that wedding talk, and Morgan's worried that she's missing a fabulous lunch somewhere. I knew she wouldn't last long,' Ellen replied, pulling down the straps of her swimsuit.

'I'll answer it in a minute,' Lily mumbled. 'Or one of you get it and tell them where we are. It's in the inside pocket of my bag.'

Kitty leaned forward and poked around in Lily's bag. Pulling out the phone, she stopped and stared at the screen. 'Lily.'

Her voice was enough to pull Lily from her reverie underneath the cold towel. Sitting up, she stared first at Kitty and then down at her phone.

'It's Peter,' Kitty said, handing the phone to her friend. 'You have a missed call and a voicemail. Your phone must have been on silent.'

Lily stared at the transcribed voicemail: 'Call me.' Her stomach flipped upside down seeing his name on her phone for the first time in weeks.

'Call me?' she repeated, aloud. She could feel a

surge of rage rise up inside her, followed by a swell of disappointment.

'Is that all it says?' Ellen asked, sitting up and tugging her swimsuit up across her chest. 'Is there more?'

'Nope. Just that. "Call me." Period.'

'Not that it's any of my business, but does he actually expect you to respond to that? Is that how he normally communicates with people?' Kitty asked, leaning over Lily's shoulder to read the message again.

'Is this some kind of joke?' Lily asked. 'I hear nothing – not a single word – since the night we broke up, and now out of the blue I get summonsed to call him? Is he out of his mind? Well, I'll be damned if I'm going to respond to that, and if he thinks that's going to work then he really doesn't know me at all.'

'But don't you want to know what he has to—'

Lily cut Ellen off mid-sentence. 'Are you joking? Absolutely not. Not if that is the way he reaches out. He's clearly too used to firing off instructions to his little minions and he thinks of me no differently. Well, he can stick his two-word instruction up his arse, along with his manners,' she fumed, ramming the phone back in her bag. 'What a nerve! I can't believe I wasted six months of my life with this git.'

Kitty stood up and pulled her beach dress over her head in one swift movement. 'I know we basically just got here, but I'd say this is as good a reason as any to break for lunch. Forget Peter and his commands. Come on, ladies, let's go find this oddball in the forest with the insane food.'

The three of them made their way across the hot sand, with Kitty taking the lead and Ellen behind her, followed by a fuming Lily, who stomped in a quiet rage. They bypassed the two beach-shack restaurants in search of Matt's recommendation, turning right at the first thermal pool and making their way deeper through the dense green foliage. The thermal pool was shielded by tall bamboo trees, but loud voices rose up from the steaming waters and followed them as they trekked along the narrow path under the thick green canopy.

Kitty stopped and peered through a gap in the bamboo trees towards the hot, steaming waters of the thermal pool. 'It's like human soup,' she giggled, referring to the two dozen people bobbing up and down in the simmering water.

The three continued along the path for another few minutes in silence, until Kitty came to a stop in front of a pair of three-foot-tall painted mushrooms, one red and one yellow. She turned slowly to face Ellen and Lily. 'I think we may have found the quirky place.' Flicking the latch on a narrow bamboo gate, Kitty stepped gingerly inside. The entire place had been constructed out of bamboo, including the walls and tables. Even the dangling lampshades were 100 per cent bamboo, with naked bulbs hanging beneath.

A dirt path wound between various plants and trees, with tables and chairs interspersed seemingly randomly among them. The mushroom theme continued inside, with painted mushroom structures scattered here and there, adding to the sense of haphazardness. The leaves of the bamboo trees created a canopy many feet overhead, casting natural shade across the seating area. The tables were set with mismatched, colourful crockery and the drinking glasses were irregularly shaped coloured glass.

'I see where Matt got the *Alice in Wonderland* reference,' Lily said, running her hand over the rough edges of a bamboo table.

They heard a crash of metal or steel from behind one of the bamboo walls, followed by the hissing of steam.

'*Ah, merde!*' a male voice roared, followed by a second crashing sound. A young man pushed his way out through the bamboo door, letting it slam behind him. Spying them, he stopped dead in his tracks. '*Oui?*' he asked, gruffly, flicking back his blond hair.

'Hello, are you open for lunch?' Kitty asked politely.

'We are closed.'

'Oh, I see. Are you closed all day, or are we just early?'

'Do you 'ave a reservation?' he asked, in a thick French accent. He was tall and lean and wore a dark red Bruce Springsteen T-shirt that stretched across his chest. He was deeply tanned, and his face showed day-old stubble.

'Sweet baby Jesus, he's delicious,' Ellen whispered, unable to stop staring at him.

'Ah, no, I'm afraid we do not. Do you have room for three?' Kitty replied in her fake polite voice.

He sighed loudly. 'Do you 'ave allergies?'

'Allergies?' Kitty asked, a slight frown on her face.

'*Oui.* Allergies. Do you 'ave any allergies? If you 'ave allergies then we are fully booked,' he replied, folding his arms across his chest.

'And if we don't have allergies?'

'Then there is no problem,' he said, showing the hint of a smile and gesturing with both hands.

Kitty looked at the two girls. Lily shook her head.

'I'll do whatever he wants me to do. I'm allergic to coriander, but I'll deal with any possible side effects as long as he lets me stay,' Ellen whispered, quietly.

'No ... no allergies,' Kitty confirmed.

'*Ah bon!*' he said, his face breaking into a wide grin. 'Sit where you want. We open in ten minutes. You want something to drink?'

'Who would ever say no to anything he ever asked? Ever?' Ellen asked, staring at the tall Frenchman.

'Yes, definitely. Whatever you recommend,' Lily said, remembering Matt's suggestion to go with the flow.

He laughed. '*Ah bon*, I bring you something good.' He disappeared back behind the bamboo door.

The three girls just looked at each other.

Ellen shook her head as she watched him leave. 'Seriously, are all the men on this island good looking or have I just not left Ireland in a very long time?'

'He's like a French James Dean, and you just know he's a bad boy,' Kitty said, drumming her fingers on the table. 'I could imagine getting into all sorts of trouble with this one.' She reached across the table and squeezed Lily's hand. 'We'll get you something to drink and then we can bitch about Peter some more.'

'Wow ... I had momentarily forgotten about his psycho voicemail. Do you think he meant it? About the allergies, I mean ... or was he just messing with us?'

'I have no idea, but I wasn't about to find out. Like Ellen said, if he was giving us a table, I'd dance on it for him if I needed to. What a divine creature. Far too young for me, I realise that, but still.'

The Frenchman reappeared holding an ice bucket in one

hand and a bottle of wine in the other. The corkscrew was sticking out of his jeans pocket.

'Oh, to be that corkscrew ...' Ellen muttered, as he approached the table. 'Gorgeous creature.'

'Pardon?' he asked in this thick French accent, turning to face Ellen.

'Oh, gorgeous ... *place*. This place is gorgeous,' she said blushing.

'*Ah bon, merci. Allors* ... here we go. This is perfect for the hot, sunny day. You don't want something too high in alcohol or you will be asleep before your lunch. This rosé is perfect. You will see.' He poured Ellen a taste.

'Delicious,' she said, nodding her head in approval. 'Oh, it's French rosé!' she said, eyeing the label.

'Of course. The Italians they make great wine, but only the red and the white, not the rosé. French rosé is the best in the world and Provençal rosé is the best. Why drink anything else?'

'Delicious,' she repeated, subconsciously licking her lips.

'Only the best, madame,' he said, with a wink. He stuck the corkscrew back into his jeans pocket and flicked his hair back with his right hand. '*Allors* ... this is today's menu.' He propped a piece of black chalkboard on a chair alongside them. It had five dishes scrawled in chalk on it. 'My grandmother is the cook. She decides every morning what to cook, after she has been to the market.'

The bamboo gate creaked open behind them and a young couple in swimsuits and shorts rounded the corner.

'*Ah bonjour,*' he said, with a grin, pointing to a table in the corner. 'Welcome back. I will be right with you.'

137

The young couple smiled back and followed the path to their table.

'Anything that you recommend?' Lily asked.

'*Oui*, all five of them. Perhaps you can share, no? Up here is the window to the kitchen. Each dish is made fresh. You choose the dish you want, and you return when you want another. The best way is to try all of them. If you like something, and you want more, you take some more. Is the same cost. It is like the Spanish . . . how they do the tapas . . . I think you will like this way of eating. Is all about tasting and sharing,' he said, with a shrug of his shoulders.

'I love that it's all written on a blackboard,' Ellen said, idly fingering the chalky lettering.

'*Oui*, we are one hundred per cent plastic free, madame. We do not use plastic here at this restaurant. Everything is recyclable or compostable.'

'As if she needed any more encouragement,' Kitty said, across the table to Lily.

'You might as well have told her that she looks like Heidi Klum. You just made her day,' Lily said, nodding towards Ellen.

'*Ah, oui?*' he said, giving Ellen the benefit of his grin. 'I like this. For me, is important, and is easy to choose. It is up to each of us, *non?*'

'Yes, I totally agree,' Ellen replied enthusiastically. 'We're all responsible for the mess we've made of the planet and it's up to us all to fix it. I love that you are plastic free. That is so cool.'

'*Bon*, I like to hear this. More people need to take responsibility.'

'Trust me, she means it. I showed up at her house in

Ireland once with a plastic straw . . . it was like I was bring-ing cocaine into the house,' Kitty said, rolling her eyes.

He bent down and pulled a small wicker basket from under the table. 'And now, your phones, please.'

'Sorry?' Lily asked, looking from him to the basket.

The bamboo gate creaked open again and a group of four rounded the corner.

The Frenchman turned and stared at them. '*Oui?*'

'Oh, umm . . . do you have a table for four?'

'Do you 'ave a reservation?'

'Oh . . . no, they didn't say we'd need a reservation. The guy at our hotel just told us to turn up early.'

'How many you are?'

'Four.'

'Do you 'ave any allergies?'

'Um . . . you mean to food?'

'No, I mean to humans.'

The spokesperson for the group frowned and glanced sideways towards the others. 'Sorry?'

'Yes, to food. Of course to food,' he replied, gesturing with impatience.

'Oh . . . um . . . ' He turned to the others and there was a ten-second conference.

'Yeah, um . . . yes, my friend is allergic to tree nuts.'

'No. We are fully booked. *Au revoir.*'

The foursome hesitated, not sure if he was being seri-ous or not.

'Out!' he shouted, pointing in the direction of the bamboo gate.

'What a nutjob,' one of them muttered as they turned and walked away.

'*Pardon,*' he continued, turning back to the table. 'Your phones, please. You are here to eat. Be present. Talk to each other.' He nodded his head towards the basket.

Lily looked down at the text message languishing on her phone, daring her to respond.

The Frenchman waggled the wicker basket in front of them.

'No phones and no plastic. I think I just walked through the jungle into the year two thousand and thirty,' Lily sighed, looking down at her phone.

'Just give him your phones,' Ellen hissed, as she dropped her phone into the basket and smiled up at him. 'I'm not leaving.'

He nodded in approval as the other two followed suit and dropped them in. He placed a small wooden circle on the table with the number eight. 'This is your table number and your basket number. *Bon appetit!*'

'Okay, I have a mad idea I need to run by you two,' Lily said, as the Frenchman hoisted up the chalkboard and strode towards the kitchen to place their orders.

'Ooh, I love mad ideas. I have them all the time,' Ellen said excitedly.

Kitty topped up their glasses. 'I'm all ears.'

'I was tossing and turning again last night, thinking about what I'm going to do next. You know, about work. I've been drifting along in a job for the past few years that paid well, but which I didn't really love. I mean, the money was good, and it allowed me to build a life for myself in New York, but the work itself was so boring.' She sighed, taking a sip of her rosé wine. 'You two both love what you do, and I know Dee does too – I'm not sure about Morgan but she tends to whine a lot anyway, so it's hard to know what she's really thinking. So, anyway, I just don't want to settle for something average or boring again, I want to figure out what it is that I will actually *enjoy* doing.'

Ellen went to speak but Kitty placed a hand on her arm. 'Go on,' she said.

'Okay, so I love the part of my job that's actually about writing. The biggest problem was that I didn't love what I was writing *about*. Then I got to thinking about what it is I love to do more than anything, and that's travel. So, if I could pull this off, I'd find or create a job where I could merge the two of them and live happily ever after!' she said with a laugh. 'See? Easy, right?'

The Frenchman placed a basket of bread and the first of the dishes on the table.

'You mean be a travel writer?' Ellen asked, dipping a piece of bread into a small bowl of dark green olive oil.

'Not exactly. I don't think travel writing pays that well and I think a lot of it is freelance, so I couldn't guarantee making rent in any given month. I've spent the past couple of years building out websites for all these companies and brands, you know, with copy, slogans, blog posts – I had to learn all that stuff the hard way – so what about building a simple website with a travel-based theme, but instead of talking about brands, I talk about places. Like Ischia, for example.'

'So, this website would focus on Ischia as a destination?' Kitty asked, leaning forward on the table.

'Yes, exactly. I mean, no one knows anything about this place. We hadn't even heard of it before Morgan started planning the wedding, and I think I could create a simple website to tell the story of Ischia, get hotels and restaurants to pay to be featured on it. If you fast forward to the future, maybe you could book stuff via the site, restaurants or tours or whatever, but initially, just to get it up and running, it could be a "pay-to-play" proposition, whereby different businesses in Ischia pay to have a presence on the site.'

She looked from one to the other of them, waiting for a response.

'I think it's brilliant, frankly,' Kitty said. 'It's like a platform for destinations. There are all sorts of ways to generate revenue with a platform like this. The local properties pay you to be featured and you could court other travel companies – airlines, travel publications and the likes – to advertise on the site and get their own brands in front of the people they know are going to be travelling. Very clever, Lily. I like it.'

'I love it,' Ellen said, clapping her hands in support. 'You'd be brilliant at it!'

'You absolutely have to test out your theory while you're here,' Kitty continued.

'Yeah, I was thinking the same thing. God, the thought of it makes me want to throw up a little. I don't even know how to pitch it and sound marginally intellectual. Plus, I have nothing to show people right now. It's just a mad idea.'

'The best ideas often are, darling. Don't worry about the logistics of it all. I've been in your shoes, selling my own mad idea before I even had a business card. Tell the story from your heart. Get it right in your own head first and then test it out on humans. But yes, if you are seriously considering doing this, then you absolutely must test-drive the theory while you are here.'

'God, the thought of it is almost enough to put me off my lunch.'

'Welcome to the joys of working for yourself, darling. Why do you think I'm so skinny? Once you start your own business you're always selling. It's nerve-wracking on a day-to-day basis, but when it goes right, it really is the most exhilarating high! Apart from great sex that is,' Kitty added, as the Frenchman placed a steaming platter of sautéed clams and mussels in front of them.

Lily speared a steaming clam with her fork. 'Well, having so rudely been made single recently, it's safe to say that any exhilarating highs I'll be getting will only be coming from mental exertions for the foreseeable future,' she said, as the three of them started on the first of many dishes and fell into a happy, amicable silence.

Chapter Twelve

Lily stepped out on to the terrace at San Montano and turned her face up to the evening sun. The breeze was stronger this evening and she pulled her light grey wrap around her shoulders. Tonight's restaurant was supposedly fancy, so she had chosen one of her favourite new dresses – a long, pale lemon maxi dress with a billowing chiffon skirt. She had bought it for the trip as Peter had said earlier that summer how fabulous she had looked in a similar-colour sundress. She had imagined that she would be wearing it here with him on the island, but that was no longer the case.

It had cost her an absolute fortune, and in the chaos that had followed the breakup she hadn't thought to exchange it before leaving New York. Ambrogio waved from behind the bar inside, indicating that he would be right out. Adjusting her sunglasses on her nose, she turned to make her way towards one of the clusters of chairs facing the bay, awaiting sunset.

'Where the hell were you lot all afternoon?' Dee's voice came from directly ahead, but Lily's view was blinded by the glaring sun.

Squinting from behind her sunglasses, and holding one hand over her eyes, she could make out the outlines of Dee and Morgan at the furthest table. 'Oh, hi! We went to that place in Negombo for lunch.'

'Negombo? It might as well have been fucking Mars. We tried calling all three of you for three solid hours.'

'Yeah, sorry, waste of time. You're not allowed to have phones there. They take them off you and put them in a basket until you leave. Like, they actually *physically* make you put your phones in a basket or else you can't stay for lunch,' Lily explained, taking a seat alongside the two of them.

'Are you kidding me?' Morgan asked, leaning towards Lily. 'No phones? Not going. Anyone who tries to tell me that I can't keep my phone on is dead to me.'

'But you texted me in capital letters saying that Peter had called you, and you had all sorts of freak-out emojis asking me what I thought you should do!' Dee said, gesturing wildly with both arms. 'When I couldn't reach you, I thought you'd gone and thrown yourself off Mount Epomeo or something. What the hell?'

'Yeah, sorry. I sent it and then the owner made me drop the phone into the basket,' Lily replied sheepishly. 'I did call you on the way back up here, but it went straight to your voicemail.'

'I was taking a nap. So . . . what did he say?'

'"Call me."'

'That's it?'

'Word for word.'

'What a first-class knob. Honestly, you're better off without him if that's his attitude.'

'Yeah . . . I know,' Lily said, slowly. 'I was raging when I first saw it, but to be honest now I just think he has a bit of a nerve. I'm not even going to dignify it with a response.'

'That's the spirit. Good riddance. So, with all the drama, how was lunch? Was the food at least good?'

'Oh, lunch was fab. Amazing, actually. We thought we'd be there for an hour or so, but we were there for almost four hours. Apparently, that's what happens to people. You show up, hand over your phone and lose all sense of time and space. The place is wacky, too, all these painted mushrooms around the garden. Oh, and there's no menu.'

'No menu and no phones. Sounds like an absolute treat,' Morgan said, rolling her eyes. 'Come on, let's have a quick drink before our taxi gets here. Love the dress, by the way, Lily. The colour suits you.'

'Yeah, thanks. It was the knob's favourite. Figured I'd wear it to spite him.'

Ambrogio magically appeared at their side to take their order.

'*Buona sera*, Ambrogio. I think I'll have a Negroni for a change.'

'Ah, may I suggest a "My-groni", Signora LeeLee?' he asked, with a smile.

'What's a "My-groni"?'

'Is a special recipe that I make. Is like my version of the Negroni.'

'Ooh, definitely, I'd love to try it,' Lily said.

'Make that three, Ambrogio. I can't handle missing out on anything else today. I think I'm suffering from FOMO,' Dee said, rattling the ice in her heavy crystal glass and tipping it back to drain the last sip of her drink.

'*Certo!*'

The next twenty minutes was consumed by wedding talk and the last-minute decisions that needed to be made. A formal meeting had been scheduled with the resort's events team in two days.

'Lily, you need to go to that meeting and keep an eye on Dee,' Morgan said, shaking her glass to release any drop of alcohol that might be trapped underneath the large square ice cube. 'Make sure she doesn't make any rash decisions. I've done my part, so I'll be at the spa that morning. Now, here's our taxi. Tip the rest of that Negroni back.'

'Where are the other two?' Lily asked, as they made their way to the awaiting taxi.

'They've gone ahead. We're meeting them in the piazza,' Morgan replied as the three of them approached the taxi.

'*Buona sera! Buona sera!*' the taxi driver greeted them.

He was tall and burly, and his face lit up with a grin as he held open the door of the car. '*Mi chiamo Giovangiuseppe.* I am Giovangiuseppe, but everyone calls me GG.'

'Nice to meet you, GG,' Dee said, sliding into the back seat. 'We're going to Sant'Angelo please.'

'*Sì, sì, signora.* Don't worry. I know everything. It is all arranged. I will take you there and tonight I bring you back,' he said, grinning in through the car door at them. '*Andiamo!* Is your first time to Sant'Angelo?'

'Yes, first time,' Lily replied as the car turned to leave the resort.

'Ah, *è bellissimo!*' he said, turning to look over his shoulder at them. 'You want to know some things about Ischia? I can be your tour guide on the way! For free!'

'Christ ... I detest tours,' Morgan mumbled under her breath.

'Yes, we'd love a free tour guide!' Dee replied enthusiastically, nudging Morgan.

Sant'Angelo was on the other side of the island, sitting high above the coast. After a circuitous thirty-minute taxi ride across the island and a non-stop commentary, GG made a right turn down a steep, winding incline. The bay glistened on their right as they slowed to navigate the steep descent towards the town of Sant'Angelo. GG came to a stop at a point where the road widened and a cluster of taxis were gathered, their drivers in a huddle smoking cigarettes and exchanging gossip. He pointed out a stone arch carved out of the mountain ahead. The arch was clearly too narrow for vehicles to pass through, so cars had to offload their passengers at this point. From here on, the entire town was pedestrianised except for the dozen or so golf carts that functioned as shuttles up and down the hill.

'We'll be taking one of those things back up here later, that's for sure,' Morgan said, staring at the steep downward trajectory of the hill. 'Come on, let's go find the other two.'

The three of them ambled slowly down the cobbled hill. On their right was a low stone wall, and beyond it the bay was filled with sailing boats and motorboats. The sea was flat calm and sparkled under the low evening sun. The left-hand side was lined with shops; individual small boutiques, most of which were decidedly more elegant than those they had seen elsewhere on the island. Sant'Angelo was a huge draw for wealthy tourists as the scenery was dramatic, the shopping was exclusive and there was a large choice of restaurants all conveniently located in the pedestrian zone.

At the recommendation of the concierge, the girls had booked a table at Il Celestino, which they passed as they made their way down the winding, cobbled street. Waiters in white shirts were setting up tables and polishing glasses. The main room held twelve tables and a huge terrace extended out to the left, with canopied tables in the open air. Everything was white, from the tablecloths to the flowers to the billowing linens that framed the windows, and it had an air of serene calm and elegance all at the same time. Its location was so desirable that almost everyone passing by on the way to the centre of Sant'Angelo below stopped to see if they might reserve a table for dinner. The answer was always the same: they were fully booked for weeks in advance and only the best concierges had the contacts to snag a last-minute table.

The road continued its descent beyond Il Celestino and brought them around a sweeping curve that opened up into the vast piazza, the heart of Sant'Angelo. The piazza was surrounded by even more boutiques, including some of the high-end Italian brands with couture-decked mannequins sporting light-coloured, lightweight Italian fabrics. Elegant Italian women dressed almost exclusively in linen drifted in and out of the shops carrying oversized shopping bags. There was nothing casual about Sant'Angelo, and even the visiting tourists seemed to have got the message to maintain the sartorial standards.

The piazza was already heaving with people as a variety of boats made their way in towards the marina and people gathered for *aperitivo* hour. Groups of young children ran among the tables and chairs, shrieking as they played, their parents, *aperitivo* in hand, oblivious to the noise and chaos they were creating.

'Over here!' Kitty called, waving an arm in the air.

Lily waved back but grabbed Dee's arm. 'I'll be right back. Order me a drink,' she said.

She ducked behind a group of children to follow the path beyond the marina. The reward for having continued further was a spectacular 360-degree view. Just beyond the marina a narrow path led down to the cove-like beach, flanked by three competing beach clubs. Lily felt an almost physical tug forward, down the narrow path towards the beach. The three beach clubs were colour coded: Aqua Beach was blue, Banana Beach was yellow and Sole Beach was orange. The sun loungers were flanked by individual umbrellas, each with a delightful frill at the bottom, flapping incessantly in the breeze, the continuous fluttering of colours making it look as if the beach had an energy of its own. At the foot of the walkway, just beyond the beach, clusters of houses and apartments in various shades of whites and blues were stacked haphazardly on top of each other, with no building taller than five or six storeys. It gave a friendly, higgledy-piggledy air to the hamlet, at once inviting and welcoming.

Even though the piazza was already filled with people enjoying *aperitivo* hour, the beach was still at least half full. Lily gazed in amazement as young children played in the water while their adult supervisors stood, knee deep in the bay, directly facing the sun, the reflection of the sun on the water expediting the sought-after mahogany-coloured tan. Italians were always looking for the maximum tanning opportunity and exposure. At least a dozen Speedo-clad men stood ankle or knee deep, eyes glued to their mobile phones, oblivious to their charges as elegant sailing boats drifted slowly by on the horizon.

Lily arrived back at the table just as the round of Aperol Spritz was being served, along with bowls of crisps and nuts and a variety of mini bites including chunks of Parmigiano-Reggiano, rolled slices of prosciutto and cocktail sticks of tomato and mozzarella, the classic Italian *caprese*.

'I love all this free food you get with drinks here. They should start doing this at home,' Ellen said, biting into a chunk of Parmesan.

'I could eat like this all day long,' Kitty said, reaching for another *caprese* spear. 'Simple and delicious. I must say, the Italians really do have life nailed, don't they? Summer especially . . . they really know how to summer. Lily, where did you disappear to? You're not all depressed over that text message and just trying to put on a brave face, are you?'

'No, I just wanted to see the beach, that's all.'

'How many times did you pull your phone out in the six minutes you were down there?' Dee asked, tilting her chin down and staring hard at Lily over the top of her sunglasses.

'Four,' Lily replied with a grimace.

'Darling, breakups are hard by definition. You really must try to not take the whole thing personally. I know that's not easy, but honestly, it's the only way forward. Trust me. I've had more than my fair share of experience,' Kitty said, putting a hand on Lily's arm.

'Whatever happened with you and that guy you were dating from Cambridge?' Morgan asked.

'He shagged the horticulturist,' Kitty said, spearing a

chunk of Parmesan with her toothpick. 'A lovely, lithe, organic-looking creature with long auburn hair, just his type.'

'You had a horticulturist?' Ellen gushed, shaking her head at the realisation of how vastly different their lives were. 'Wow, even your problems are sophisticated. A crisis in my house is if the Coco Pops at the bottom of the bowl are in any way visible under the layer of Cheerios on top.'

'No, I didn't personally have a horticulturist. The horticulturist was his – in more ways than one. She works the land at his estate. In true cliché fashion, I arrived early one Friday evening to surprise him. Turns out I was the one who got the surprise. Dirty, cheating bastard,' Kitty hissed. 'Now, Morgan, how many more days do we have at this place before all the crazy relatives start to show up?' she asked, desperate for a change of subject.

'Oh God, don't remind me. I should have listened to Dee and just gotten married with you three as witnesses. I think the first of them start arriving the day after tomorrow.'

'Any crazy uncles?' Ellen asked, with a grin.

'Doesn't everyone have crazy uncles?' Dee asked, draining her drink and standing up from the table. 'Come on you lot, our reservation awaits.'

Il Celestino was already more than half full by the time they arrived.

Ellen's phone buzzed in her pocket. 'You go ahead, I'll follow you in ... some crisis at home,' she said, rolling her eyes in anticipation of this evening's parenting challenge.

Lily, Kitty, Morgan and Dee stepped through the front door and were greeted by a tall, tanned man with slicked-back, jet-black hair. He was dressed head to toe in black, in stark contrast with the waiting staff, who were dressed entirely in white.

'*Buona sera*,' he said with a smile, gesturing for them to come inside.

'It is now,' Kitty mumbled under her breath as she looked him up and down. 'A very *buona sera* . . . '

Dee elbowed her and moved to step in front. '*Buona sera*. We have a reservation for eight o'clock under the name Ryan.'

'Ah, from San Montano. *Bene. Benvenuti* . . . welcome . . . I am Paolo. Please, follow me,' he said, gesturing to the corner table on the terrace.

'Brilliant!' Lily gushed. 'Look at this table!'

'Ah, but you are only four? The reservation . . . it said for five people, no?'

'No. I mean, yes, there are five of us. There is one more just outside the door,' Lily explained.

'*Bene. Bene. Allora* . . . *ecco* . . . ' he said, handing them menus and placing a heavy wine list on the table.

Ellen rushed back to the table. 'Sorry, sorry. Jesus, who's the Adonis at the front door?'

'Dunno, must be the manager or something. Good-looking lad all right,' said Dee, nodding in agreement. 'Everything all right back home?'

'Oh, for fuck's sake,' Ellen said, shaking her head in frustration. 'My father-in-law's teeth are missing.'

'I beg your pardon?' Kitty said, half coughing and half laughing. 'His what now . . . ?'

'His teeth are missing. His false teeth. He stayed over last night with my mother-in-law to help Mike with the kids and when he woke up this morning his false teeth were missing. Last night they were in a glass in the bath-room and now they are gone. And my husband decides to call me in Italy to see where they might be and what he should do about it. This is my life.' Ellen sighed, shak-ing her head.

The four girls were in peals of laughter around the table.

'It's not funny!' Ellen protested. 'Well, I suppose it is, but honestly, this is my life on a daily basis. It's ridiculous. I swear, I might not go back.'

Paolo returned to the table brandishing a bottle of spar-kling wine. 'Ladies, this is a welcome drink. It's one of my favourites,' he said as he popped open the bottle and poured a glass for each of them.

'It would be rude to say no,' Dee said, with a grin. 'Thank you, Paolo. Is this your restaurant?'

'Yes, I have had this restaurant for ten years now.'

'And the concierge told us that you're always full,' Lily said, watching as he slowly poured each glass. Like most Italian men, he was deeply tanned. He was tall and lean, and his black pants and shirt were so perfectly fitted that Lily thought they must definitely be tailored. He wore the top button open, adding a slightly casual air to an otherwise very elegant outfit. He looked like he had just stepped off the pages of a magazine.

'*Sì, signora*. Ischia is a small island, so the good restaurants are always full. We only serve the freshest food from Ischia. We import nothing,' he said with a smile. 'When people find something that they like, they talk, so we are always full. *Allora . . . salute!*'

'What a great country,' Ellen said, with a sigh. 'Cheers, ladies.'

Lily, Dee and Morgan raised their glasses, but Kitty was still staring after Paolo.

'Um ... hello? Kitty?' Lily said, prodding her with a finger.

'Yes? Oh, sorry ... I was distracted. What a divine creature ... I was just having sex with him in my head.'

'Oh my God,' Morgan mumbled, shaking her head. 'You mortify me at the most random of moments. Honestly, Kitty, do you not possess any filter?'

'How was it?' Ellen whispered conspiratorially, leaning in across the table towards her friend.

'How was what?' Kitty asked, looking genuinely confused.

'The sex! Was it good?'

'Of course it was good! It was in my head. When else do you have great, intense sex? Not in real life, not me at any rate. In real life I'd be fumbling about the place, but just now I was a sexual goddess with perfect, glowing skin and perfectly toned abs and the Adonis there was raking his fingers across them in admiration.'

'I'm even envious of your fantasy. How sad am I?' Ellen said, pulling the bread basket towards her.

'Funny, but I find it hard to imagine you fumbling about the place,' Lily said, tasting her champagne. 'You always seem so ... I don't know ... together and sophisticated.'

'I work hard to make it appear that way, darling. I have to if I want to survive in my industry, but in reality, I'm like the proverbial duck: calm and serene on top and scrambling about furiously underneath it all!'

Dee picked up her menu and waggled it in the air. 'Kitty, I say this with love – interesting and all as this is, can we please order? I'm starving!'

'Hangry, much?' Morgan asked, as she peered at Dee.

Lily sat silently hunched over the table, her finger running down the length of the menu, salivating at the descriptions of the seafood dishes. 'Everything sounds delicious.'

'Who wants to share the whole fish cooked in salt with me?' Ellen asked. 'I definitely won't be getting it when I go home, so I'm making the most of it.'

'Yes, I will,' Lily replied as her phone pinged for a second time.

Kitty waved an arm in the air at Paolo. 'How about we just ask him to bring some appetisers to share and then we can order our fish?'

'You are finally making some sense,' Dee said, snapping her menu closed.

'Just no octopus, please,' Ellen said, quietly. 'I can't eat octopus any more. It's too sad.'

'Why do I sense a tragic or environmentally disastrous story coming?' Morgan said, as she put a hand on Paolo's arm. 'Paolo, honey, we are ready to order, but can you first bring us another bottle of bubbles?'

'*Certo. Subito!*'

She turned to face Ellen. 'Now, Ellen ... what's the problem with octopus exactly? Or do I even want to know?'

'I read that book, *The Soul of an Octopus*, and it changed everything. Do you know that they actually possess consciousness? They have a brain in every one of their legs and they are *extremely* clever. They can taste with those little suckers that they have. That's how they recognise people – they recognise their taste. And ... ' she continued, pausing for dramatic tension. 'They are masters at escape. One time, a baby octopus manipulated the lock on its tank, crawled out and made its way down the stairs. The people in the aquarium were looking for it for hours and eventually found it hiding in a teapot! Honestly, they are like little puppies . . . they are that clever.'

'Got it. No octopus because they possess consciousness,' Morgan said, as Paolo returned to the table. 'Paolo, we're going to order fish, but can you please bring us some appetisers to share? Whatever you recommend . . . just no octopus, or we won't be able to sleep tonight.'

'Ah, you have an allergy? To octopus?'

'No, honey, but it would be too much like eating puppies for some of us, so let's not.

'I don't understand.'

'Neither do I, to be honest, but don't worry about it. Just don't bring any octopus.'

'*Va bene,*' he said, with a shrug.

He took the rest of the orders around the table and then recommended a bottle of local white wine to go with the appetisers.

'Paolo, we might as well be realistic and get two bottles right from the start. One is going to disappear into the five glasses immediately and the other can be standing by on ice. I promise you it won't last all that long,' Kitty said as she turned and smiled up at him.

He laughed and nodded. '*Subito!*'

'Did he just wink at you?' Ellen asked. 'How do you do that? I mean, you're gorgeous and tall and skinny and you have perfectly arched eyebrows . . . but how do you get men to react to you like that all the time? I feel invisible next to you.'

'Darling, I'm single. You're the one who is married.'

'Don't remind me,' Ellen sighed. 'I better call home again

before it gets too late – and before our food arrives. Don't talk about important stuff until I get back.'

She shoved her chair back from the table and weaved her way out through the adjacent tables to the cobbled street.

'I'm not following or stalking you guys, I swear!'

The girls turned to see Matt standing behind them with the manager from the resort. 'Have you met Antonio?' he asked, gesturing towards Antonio alongside him.

'*Buona sera*, yes, we have met earlier in the week,' Antonio said, with a smile. 'I hope you are all enjoying your stay?'

'Yes, marvellous. We've got to stop meeting like this, people might talk,' Kitty said, a coy smile on her face.

'This is true,' Antonio replied with a laugh. 'Ischia is a small island and the best restaurants are always full. So, *signora*, I'm afraid it is inevitable that we will continue to bump into each other.'

'The small Italian island you've never heard of,' Lily said with a smile.

'She's a writer,' Matt said, turning to Antonio.

'Yes, and she has this very interesting idea to create a website to promote the island of Ischia,' Kitty interjected.

'You do?' Dee asked, unable to hide the surprise in her voice.

'Um ... yes, it's a new idea and I haven't really thought out all the aspects of it yet, but the idea is to create a website to promote Ischia as a destination.'

'Really? Tell me more about this idea,' Antonio said inquisitively. 'Perhaps you can solve my problem,' he enthused, folding both arms across his chest.

'What problem is that, Antonio?' Kitty asked, leaning across the table towards him.

'*Allora* . . . I have a five-star hotel on an island that no one knows about. The Americans, they don't come . . . except for this one, but even he has a long history with the island, so this does not really count,' he said gesturing to Matt. 'We have a few American tourists, but not many. In fact, Americans are . . . how do you say . . . the exception more than the rule? We have mostly the northern European countries and most of them, they found us by mistake when they were looking for Capri.'

'I thought exactly the same thing earlier in the week,' Lily replied. 'Ischia really is still off the beaten track. It's still an undiscovered gem.'

'See? That's the writer talking,' Matt said, nudging Antonio.

'*Esatto!* This is my biggest problem. *Allora*, how would this idea work?'

'Well, the idea is that the website would function as a platform, not just for advertising but to actually tell the story of Ischia as a destination,' Lily began, not yet sure what she might say next. 'Well, not the story exactly, but um . . . the website would feature different businesses, like hotels and restaurants, and *they* would tell their story, to promote Ischia.' She could feel herself beginning to blush. 'I'm not doing a very good job of describing it because it's all kind of new, but the idea is to have a place, a website . . . online that would promote Ischia in general as a destination.'

'Hmm, I'm not sure I understand exactly, but I would like to know more. In the middle of summer Ischia is full of Italian tourists, but we would like to have more international tourists, especially in the quieter months. This is true, Paolo, no? For your restaurant too?'

Paolo nodded his head and shrugged his shoulders. 'Yes, everyone who comes here falls in love with Ischia and comes back again and again, but all of them say that they had never even heard of Ischia before they planned their first trip. We're always full in the middle of the summer, but I would love to have more business for the other months too, but it is hard to convince people to try a place that they have never heard of. They prefer to go to Amalfi or Capri ... places they already know.'

'Capri!' Antonio scoffed. 'It is full of more Americans than Texas. Fancy hotels and expensive restaurants. It is no longer the real Italian experience. It is an Italian experience for wealthy people with no imaginations! Now, I don't want to interrupt your dinner any longer, but perhaps we could discuss this more, later in the week? In the meantime, it is easy to stay at San Montano, but you must see and explore everything that our island has to offer.' He gestured widely with both hands.

'Actually, I'm taking a boat out in the morning if you guys fancy a boat ride,' Matt said. 'It's the best way to see the island, right, Antonio?'

'*Certo!* To see Ischia from the water is magnificent!'

'Nothing fancy ... a friend of mine has a great beach restaurant on the other side of the island that is only accessible by boat. It's super casual but a really fun place right on the sand and they do amazing shellfish. No pressure if you have plans, but—'

'No plans!' Dee said loudly. 'Absolutely no plans tomorrow. Count me in. I love boats!'

'What boat? What's happening? What have I missed?' Ellen asked, breathlessly rejoining the table.

160

'Matt just invited us to go on a boat with him tomorrow.'

'You have a boat?' Ellen asked, still out of breath.

Matt laughed. 'No, a friend of mine – Angelo – has a boat service. He takes people out to those restaurants that can only be accessed by boat and he has a few that are available for rent too. When they're not all booked, he lets me take one out.'

'Brilliant! I'm in!' Ellen said, raising one hand in the air. 'Are we going? I mean, are you guys going? What the hell, I never get to go anywhere, so I'll go, Matt!'

Matt laughed and turning to Lily raised his eyebrows.

'Yes, definitely, sounds like fun!' she replied.

'All right then, meet me at the pier in Ischia Ponte at ten a.m. Here's my number in case you need to reach me, but don't be late. We're going to take a ride before lunch,' he said with a wink. As he placed a business card on the table in front of Lily, his phone rang.

'*Ciao, amore. Sì, arrivo ora.* Sorry, excuse me,' he said placing his hand across the phone. 'See you guys in the morning.'

'What kind of boat is it? Did he say what kind of boat?' Morgan asked, a nervous look on her face.

'Don't worry, my love. I'm sure it will be perfectly seaworthy,' Dee joked.

'How kind of him to invite a bunch of perfect strangers on his boat. He doesn't even really know us,' Kitty said as she reached for her glass.

'I don't care. I'd go off with a total stranger in a balaclava if he invited me on a boat ride,' Ellen said enthusiastically. 'Let's face it, this week could be my one chance at true happiness!'

'Well, I'd say he's very keen to get to know us . . . some of us, at least,' Dee said, a wide grin on her face as she nodded across the table towards Lily.

'Dee, stop exaggerating everything, he asked all of us, and don't forget about the "*amore*" on the other end of those phone calls . . . but yes, Kitty, it was sweet of him to invite us.'

'Yep, very sweet,' Dee said, a quiet smirk settling on her face. 'Now, what's this new idea? This is the first I've heard of it.'

'We discussed it at length at lunch, darling,' Kitty said with a smirk. 'That's what happens when you choose not to participate!'

'God, I made a complete bollocks of describing it, didn't I?' Lily said with a groan.

'Not your most eloquent moment, darling, no. You did a much finer job at lunch. What happened?'

'God, I hope I didn't blow it and he thinks I'm an idiot,' Lily said, putting her hands to her face. 'I just got nervous and then I couldn't get a decent sentence out. Was it really that bad?'

'Honey, I don't know what this idea is about,' said Morgan, 'and I don't know what you were trying to say, but I'd have paid you to stop talking.'

Lily groaned.

'Morgan, for fuck's sake, couldn't you be a bit more supportive?' Dee shrieked.

'I *am* being supportive. No point sugar-coating a bunch of lies. If she's serious about this thing then she'll have to get better at talking about it.'

'No, she's right,' Lily said slowly. '*Brutal* . . . but right. Can we change the subject? I need time to figure out what it is that I am actually trying to say – what I want to *do* for this island – and practise my pitch.'

'That's the spirit, honey,' Morgan said, nodding approvingly. 'I'm happy to sit and listen to you anytime if it will help, but for the love of God don't go talking to any more potential clients until you know exactly what you're going to say to them.'

'Deal. Now can we please talk about something else for a change? I'm tired of listening to myself talk.'

Tuning out of the conversation, Lily sank back into the chair, hoping she hadn't blown her chances with Antonio. She had wanted desperately to make a good first impression, but her nerves had got the better of her.

Nerves and a lack of preparation, Lily, she chastised herself silently, vowing to spend some time perfecting her pitch. You've got one week here, so if you want to make this work then it's entirely up to you. Get your shit together and figure it out.

Chapter Thirteen

'I was born for this kind of life,' Kitty said later, sipping her wine, her voice trailing off as she sat back in complete contentment and stared out to sea. 'I need to figure out a way to free myself from the office so that I could work remotely a bit more. I would love to rent a villa for a month somewhere and work remotely for a few hours a day to keep things ticking over.'

Dee leaned over, pulling the bottle from the ice bucket. 'So why don't you just do it? You own your own company, you're your own boss.'

'Just the small matter of half a dozen employees awaiting direction on a daily basis, darling. Once I have a plan figured out for them then it's entirely possible.'

'Don't you wish you could live here all year long?' Ellen asked, sinking back into her chair with a happy sigh.

'No,' Morgan replied, matter-of-factly.

'What? Are you serious? What's wrong with you?'

'I'd get bored,' she said with a shrug.

'You actually love your job, don't you?' Kitty said, shaking her head in disbelief.

'I do.'

'What's that like?' Kitty asked, learning across the table towards her friend.

Morgan laughed and shrugged again. 'I just enjoy work. I know if I were here for more than a few weeks I'd get restless. I like being busy. I like diversion. Too much of the same thing becomes monotonous, even island life, believe it or not.'

'I honestly don't know how I'm going to go back to regular life after this,' Ellen sighed. 'It's just all so dull when you see how other people live, isn't it? I mean, they really know how to live here, in fairness to them. Don't get me wrong ... I love my children, but no one tells you that somewhere along the way you lose yourself, or part of yourself. I don't know how to describe it, but most days I feel like I exist to keep these small people alive and the best I can hope for is when they are all reared and gone that I can start digging in the dirt to see if I can resurrect the parts of me that got buried along the way. God ... that's really deep, isn't it? See, I'd be great at therapy,' she concluded with a self-satisfied smile.

'I need to do something with my life. Something else. Corporate finance is just so goddamn uninteresting,' Dee said, signalling a passing waiter.

'What do you want to do?' Ellen asked, relieved that she wasn't the only one disenchanted with her current life.

'If I knew that I'd have done something about it already,' Dee sighed. 'I'm stuck. Once you go down the corporate route, your options become limited.'

'But I thought you liked your job, and don't they pay you ridiculous amounts of money?'

'I used to love it. It was fun at the start, you know, it used to be challenging. Now it's easy and there's no option to do anything else or learn anything else. And yes, they pay me a shedload of money which is exactly *why* I'm stuck ... I mean, what kind of lunatic walks away from a three hundred thousand-dollar package?'

'Oh, to have your problems,' Lily teased.

Paolo arrived at the table with a tray carrying five tall glasses filled with a white foamy drink.

'*Allora, signore*, before you leave, you must try the best dessert in Ischia. It is called Il Celestino.'

'How come we haven't had it anywhere else?' Dee asked, as he placed a tall glass in front of her.

'You can only find it here at Ristorante Il Celestino,' he said, placing a glass in front of Kitty with a wink. 'We invented it.'

'Ooh, you have paper straws! Well done, Paolo,' Ellen said, clapping her hands excitedly.

'*Sì, signora.* We are a small island so we must respect the environment and the nature that we have around us.'

'I love this little island more and more every day,' Ellen said, sucking her white drink through the paper straw.

'Me too ... I find myself drawn to the people,' Kitty said, grinning up at Paolo as she stirred her drink with the environmentally friendly non-plastic straw. 'What's in it?'

'Home-made sorbet, fresh lemon juice, vodka and Prosecco. *Salute!*'

'My kind of dessert,' Dee said, holding up her glass. '*Salute!*'

Kitty ran her finger around the rim of the glass. 'I'm not sure I even want to stay in London long term. I think I'd move back to Ireland and buy a farm, if all things were equal and money weren't an issue.'

'What's that now?' Dee said, staring at her in disbelief.

'Not be an actual farmer or anything ... at least, not a real one with cows and milking parlours. No, I'd open an *agriturismo*, like they have here. Like a modern-day guesthouse for foodies, but an elegant version. I'd buy an old rambling farmhouse and renovate it. I'd have exposed old stone walls and Irish linens in white, beige and sand and a seasonal restaurant using only local organic ingredients. And I'd rescue donkeys and sad farm animals from around the country, so the place would actually be self-sustainable.'

'So, kind of like Ballymaloe House?' Lily asked.

'Yes, but smaller. And with rescue chickens.'

'I'd love to open my own yoga studio,' Ellen said, gazing at a sailing boat passing by the restaurant.

'Why don't you?'

'Because I don't have a magic pit of money. In case you've forgotten, I have five children, an unemployed lump of a husband and a massive mortgage. I can't just chuck in my job. I have to keep my well-paid, boring day job and labour on.'

Dee leaned forward and put her hands flat on the table. 'You know, Lily ... I know that this sucks right now, but you're actually the only one of us that has the option of clearing the decks and starting over. I know the reason you're in this situation is miserable, but now you are free to do whatever you want.'

'I'll trade you the starting over thing for some peace of mind and a not-fucked-up relationship,' Lily retorted, tipping her head back to drain the last drop of creamy white deliciousness from the glass.

'Well, I don't think it qualifies as a fucked-up relationship if it's over, so you're not entitled to feel bad about that. You dumped his sorry ass,' Dee corrected.

'You're right. Now I don't have any relationship.'

'Beats being in a fucked-up one!'

'Yeah, I suppose,' Lily agreed reluctantly.

Paolo brought the bill along with five tiny, thin glasses of home-made limoncello, which he explained was a classic Italian after-dinner drink. This one was made from their own lemon trees, from their farm on the other side of Sant'Angelo. Lemons, sugar, water and alcohol were the only ingredients, the alcohol varying depending on what part of Italy you found yourself in. The texture was almost viscous. Lily could feel it warm her throat as she sipped it, but contradictorily, her lips were left stained with an intense sweetness. All five of them sipped their drinks quietly until Ellen's phone pinged loudly.

'He found his teeth,' Ellen said, shattering the reverie.

'I beg your pardon?' Kitty asked, her eyebrows raised quizzically.

'My father-in-law. He found his teeth.'

'The way your mind works is honestly quite astounding to me sometimes,' Morgan said, shaking her head. 'Dinner is on me tonight, ladies,' she added, waving her American Express card to get Paolo's attention. 'We'll have another round of these limoncellos for the road, Paolo, please.'

'*Certo, signora!*' he replied, with a smile.

'Yep, turns out Woody had taken them.'

'Woody?' Kitty asked, both eyebrows raised again.

'Yes, my six-year-old, Woody. His front tooth fell out recently and he got a euro from the tooth fairy, so he saw grandpa's teeth and figured he'd make a killing. He took the dentures out of the glass and stuck them under his pillow.'

The absurdity of Ellen's story of the hijacked teeth combined with too much wine and limoncello gave the girls the emotional release they needed. All five of them laughed until they had tears running down their faces. Paolo returned to the table with Morgan's card and receipt.

'*Ora, fate bene!*' he said with a grin, before starting to laugh in tandem with them. 'This is the kind of moment I hope to see from these beautiful girls on *vacanza*! *Meglio così*. This is better. *Buona notte, signore*. Come and see me again. I have ordered your cars for the hill. They wait outside.' He winked at Kitty as he left the table.

'A girl doesn't have to be asked twice,' Kitty said, her eyes following him.

'Right, you lot, I'm not about to risk missing that golf cart. Bottoms up!' Morgan said, slamming back her second limoncello. 'Oh, I'm going to regret that in the morning,' she muttered, placing a hand on the back of her chair for balance. 'Our chariots await!' she shouted, charging towards the door.

'She doesn't get out much,' Dee said, shaking her head. Leaning over she hauled Lily up from her chair. 'Come on, you. Hey, Paolo! How do you say, "Let's go" in Italian?'

'*Andiamo!*' came the reply from the other side of the restaurant.

'Thanks. *Grazie!* Right. *Andiamo*, Lily! We have a boat to catch in the morning.'

'*Sì* ... *andiamo*,' Lily replied as they stumbled ever so slightly to the door.

Chapter Fourteen

Lily sat with her head in her hands on the top step outside the door of the resort. She was massaging her temples when a pair of Prada espadrilles came to a stop directly in front of her.

'You too?'

Lily looked up and squinted in the glare of the sun. 'Don't talk about it. Jesus, Dee, how much wine did we have? I have a shocking headache but I didn't think we had gone nuts.'

'Well, I'll put it to you like this,' Dee said, sitting down on the step alongside her. 'Morgan found the dinner receipt crumpled up at the bottom of her purse this morning and almost got whiplash when she flattened it out and read it. She had no idea what she was signing last night.'

'Oh God, poor Morgan,' Lily groaned.

'I think it was the limoncello at the end that did the damage.'

'Oh,' Lily groaned again. 'I had forgotten about that. God, I can taste the sweet stickiness of it now that you mention it. Did we book a taxi to get to the pier? I don't even remember getting back to the resort.'

'Yes, we asked GG to come and get us. He should be here any minute. Any sign of the others?'

'Not yet. I'll text them to tell them haul ass,' Lily said, poking in her bag for her phone.

'Hang on, I can see Morgan and Kitty inside,' Dee said, craning her neck to look back into the foyer. 'Here's the taxi. Text Ellen to hurry up.'

'What the ... oh, holy fuck ... ' Lily exclaimed, staring open-mouthed at her phone. 'What the ... oh my God.'

'Oh no, what did you do?'

Lily groaned and put her face into her hands. 'No ... do not tell me ... I should never be let out.'

Dee took the phone from her hands. The call log showed five attempted calls to Peter, followed by a seven-minute conversation. 'Oh, you tool. What did you do?'

'I have no idea. I don't even remember talking to him.'

'Uh oh ... well, this might help jog your memory. You sent a string of text messages to him too. The general theme appears to be that you miss him.'

'Oh my God, I did not,' Lily said, grabbing the phone out of Dee's hand. As she tentatively scrolled back to the top of the messages, her phone rang. It was Ellen.

'Where are you guys? I'm the only one here.'

'Where is *here*, Ellen?' Lily asked, her head in her hand.

'At breakfast. On the terrace. Where is everyone?'

'Ellen, there is a taxi waiting out front to take us to the pier. Remember? The boat ride with Matt? We have to leave right now.'

'Shit. Sorry. I totally forgot. I'll be right there.'

Two minutes later all five of them were clambering into GG's minibus, with Lily still doing damage control on her phone. Morgan, white as a sheet, requested that no one speak to her for the duration of the journey as breathing was about all she could do right now. Ellen had a croissant hidden in a hotel napkin and spent the twenty-minute ride breaking off minuscule pieces and chewing them slowly. Kitty popped three different pills and downed an entire half-litre bottle of sparkling water.

'What are those pills for?' Dee asked, her head stuck out the window of the minibus.

'One is a vitamin C tablet – I swear by them when I'm hungover – and the others are paracetamol for my head-ache and ibuprofen for my legs.'

'What's wrong with your legs?'

'When I drink too much the muscles above my knees ache,' Kitty explained, matter-of-factly.

'Can I have a paracetamol, please? I've a shocking wine headache,' Dee moaned, pulling her head back inside the minibus. 'Are they the big dose?'

'Yes, five hundred milligrams.'

'Perfect. Horse one over here so. How do you look so human this morning, anyway? What's your secret? I'd scare small children, the state of me this morning.'

'It's the vitamin C. I took one last night and another when I woke up. They're magic. Do you want one of those, too?'

'Can't hurt. Go on.'

'Does anyone else need medical intervention?'

'Nobody talk to me,' Morgan groaned, her forehead against the taxi window.

Lily stuck out her hand and Kitty obliged with a par-acetamol and a vitamin C tablet.

'I'm just trying to keep this croissant down,' Ellen said,

taking deep breaths in between bites. 'How long is this going to take? I might die before we get there.'

The twenty-minute journey to Ischia Ponte felt like an eternity. The series of winding roads didn't help matters and all five of them got out of the taxi feeling – and looking – worse for wear.

Matt spotted them and waved, striding towards them in a fresh white linen shirt, navy shorts and a beat-up pair of espadrilles. 'Morning, ladies . . . glad you made it. I wasn't sure you'd show up, to be honest. It looked like you guys were on course for a big night out!'

'It's all very hazy to be honest, Matt,' Lily replied, standing alongside him. 'It's lucky we even remembered that we had an invitation this morning.'

'Oh dear,' he said with a grin. 'So, you girls did it up right last night then?'

'Is it that obvious?' Dee asked.

'Well, I'm impressed that you all showed up under the circumstances. *Bravi!* Come on, let's get a coffee before we head out. It will help. This place over here is good,' he said, pointing in the direction of a cluster of tables and chairs at the head of the pier.

'Nice hat,' he said to Lily, as they reached the café. 'Are you a hat person?'

'Oh, thanks. Not really, but I figured I might need one if we're going to be on the boat for a while.'

'Looks great . . . you should be a hat person. Okay, cappuccinos all round?' he said, turning to the others.

Lily blushed at the compliment before berating herself for having such a conspicuous reaction. *He was just being kind, Lily. A good-looking man can't pay you a compliment, but* you turn bright pink? So, it's a cute hat, that's all. He said *it* looks great, not *you* look great, and don't forget about the *amore* tucked away in the background. She's probably a hat person. She shook her head to dispel the mental image of Matt's Italian *amore* and turned her attention back to the table.

The cappuccinos and sweet croissants seemed to have magical, medicinal powers and one by one the girls slowly started to come back to life. Lily closed her eyes with the first sip of her cappuccino. For a moment she savoured the delicious creaminess of it, until her mind flashed back to the drunken calls to Peter. She felt a surge of embarrassment rage through her, resulting in a flush of red rising up her neck.

'I can never understand how something so simple tastes so good here. Why is it so difficult to get a good cappuccino elsewhere?' she asked no one in particular, desperate to think about anything but Peter.

'Works like a charm every time,' Matt said, grinning, unaware that his top lip had a light dusting of sugar. Lily involuntarily licked her lips as she watched him speak. 'I think it's the combination of the hardcore coffee and the sugar kick from these croissants. Plus, they will line your stomach before getting on a boat. Never a good idea to get on a boat when you are feeling shaky.'

'Thank God for you,' Dee said. 'I'm starting to feel human again.'

'It's beautiful here,' Lily said, looking around. 'I feel like I've stepped back in time with all these ancient stone walls. I fell asleep for a while on the way here, so I've got no clue as to where I am, like on a map. All I know is that there is

a pier, a boat and a beach with lunch and I saw two different towns on the map called Ischia, which makes no sense
whatsoever.'

'This is Ischia Ponte,' Matt said, topping up her glass
with sparkling water. 'We're on the south-west side of the
island. And yeah, I can see how the Ischia names thing
could be confusing. There's Ischia Porto, the main town on
the island and also the largest port, and Ischia Ponte. *Porto*
means port, like a marina, and *ponte* means bridge. This
neighbourhood gets its name from the long stone bridge
that leads out to the castle.'

'We haven't seen the castle yet, have we? Or have I just
missed it?' Ellen asked, scooping out the froth from the
bottom of her cup.

'Would you like another one of those?' Matt
asked, grinning.

'Oh God, yes, could I? Would you mind? I mean, I
don't want to hold everyone up if we're on a schedule or
something.'

'No worries. The boat is moored two minutes from here,
so we'll leave when we're ready. Anyone else for a second?'

A unanimous yes was uttered by all as Matt continued
to explain the history of the castle.

'No, you haven't missed the castle. Trust me, you'll
know when you see it. It's the most spectacular sight on
the island. Okay, so real quick,' he said in his soft New
York accent. 'Here's the history bit. The castle is actually
a medieval citadel with a bunch of churches, convents and
houses all enclosed behind this massive wall. Once upon
a time it was an island but at some point they built a long
bridge to connect it to the mainland ... hence the name

175

Ischia Ponte. First it was a settlement, then a fortress and I think it was even used as a prison at one point. Anyway, it was abandoned for the longest time until an Italian family bought it at an auction in 1912 and restored it, so today it's open to the public. You'll see it as soon as we get to the top of this street and we'll go right by it on the boat. It's pretty spectacular.'

'Imagine rocking up to an auction one day and buying a castle,' Ellen said, shaking her head. 'Some people just have the most interesting lives, don't they?'

'Right ... so how big a part of today is the actual boat ride?' Morgan asked, speaking for the first time that morning. 'I'm not a huge boat person, so I'm wondering how long we're going to be on the vessel itself.'

'Well, that's really up to you guys. We can stay out on the water as long as you want. We've got a lunch reservation at one o'clock and the restaurant is only fifteen minutes away, so what we do beforehand and how long we mess about on the boat is up to you. I would recommend doing a spin around the base of the castle at the very least. I mean, you can cross the bridge and see it on foot, but it's pretty awesome to see it from the water.'

'If you insist,' Morgan said, reluctantly.

By ten thirty a.m., the six of them were appropriately caffeinated and made their way through the labyrinthine, narrow, cobblestoned streets towards the pier.

The streets were buzzing with life. Lily pulled out her mobile phone to snap the myriad images she was accosted with. Everywhere she looked seemed to be a photo waiting to be taken. Matt pointed out ancient churches tucked away down narrow alleyways as they walked, promising that at the top of the hour they would be treated to the most magnificent chorus of church bells they had ever heard. As they ambled slowly along the cobbled paths, taking in the sights and the sounds, Lily trailed further and further behind.

By the time Lily had caught up with the group, Matt had stopped outside a bakery and delicatessen named Boccia. It was an unassuming-looking spot on the ground floor of an apartment building, but Matt explained that it was the most famous bakery on the island, its fame evident by the line of about a dozen people queuing to get in. Smells of freshly baked bread wafted through the air, proving to be an invitation almost impossible to ignore.

Small delivery vans unloaded fresh fruit and vegetables, and large sacks of flour for the local pizzerias and restaurants. Lily stood and stared at the heaped crates of fresh, local produce and marvelled at how enticing they all looked. The tiny vine tomatoes all had stems still attached, the carrots had earthy roots dangling and long, green fronds on top. Most of them seemed to have a layer of dried earth, indicating that they had only recently been tugged from the ground of a nearby farm, and not lying idly wrapped in clingfilm in some gigantic supermarket. Dark red cherries and round grapes were piled in high heaps, and bulbous figs sat plump under the morning sun. She wanted to taste everything at once, including the things she couldn't even name.

All the buildings had wrought-iron or wooden doors that opened from the street into internal narrow staircases, weaving their way up to apartments upstairs. Pushchairs remained parked outside front doors to allow more room inside. But the size of the apartments didn't matter because everyone lived outside for eight or nine months of the year.

'Okay, we just have to cross the piazza here,' Matt said, indicating to turn left where the narrow street gave way to the main square. Lily walked along behind him, noting that from where they stood they could smell the sea. The sounds of scooters, cars, children playing and waves slapping up against the sea wall created a cacophony of warm, happy sounds that wrapped her in a delicious feeling of being somewhere warm and foreign. With a quick glance in the direction of the rest of the group, Lily ducked down a narrow, shaded alley, sheltered from the sun by the tall buildings flanking it on either side. The street was entirely residential apart from one small café. She paused by one of the circular wrought-iron tables, framing the bright yellow door of the café on her phone camera.

Jogging back up the street, Lily could see Kitty in the distance. It was always easy to spot Kitty in a crowd as she was usually head and shoulders above most other people. The piazza was thronged with families making their way to the pier to take one of Angelo's boats to one of the nearby beaches, and young children darted about excitedly, chattering and shrieking loudly in Italian. Dodging groups of small children, she peered over the wall at the blue sea just below. In contrast to the chaos of the piazza, the sea sparkled quietly, glinting under the morning sun as if winking at her. She could see Matt, already bent over and untying a series of ropes as the others waited patiently, Kitty and Morgan in the shade and Dee and Ellen sitting determinedly under the sun.

Lily was breathless as she reached the group. She stopped

dead in her tracks as her eyes followed the girls' gaze out towards the sea and rested on the castle. She gasped at the sight of it, rising up from the sea like a fortress, towering over everything around it. It was at once gracious and formidable and it commanded everyone's attention, silencing those who saw it for the first time.

'Wow,' she said, quietly.

'It's something, isn't it?' Matt said, turning around to face her. 'Wait until you see it from the water. I think awesome is the best way to describe it.'

His phone rang in his pocket. He answered it in the manner that all Italians answer their phones. '*Pronto?*'

Lily heard a string of '*Sì ... sì ... certo,*' before he hung up again.

'Wow, that's stunning,' she replied, her hands on her hips, trying to catch her breath. 'Really stunning. It's like a fortress out there in the middle of the sea ... ' Her voice trailed off as she stared at the castle. The sea was almost iridescent in the morning light, sparkling furiously under the intense glare of the sun. 'You know, I think this island has its own shade of blue ... Ischia blue.'

Morgan glanced at her. 'I'm fairly certain there is a definitive set of Pantone colours and Ischia blue is not one of them.'

'Well, it should be. It's different, striking. It's *so* blue.'

'I think you might be right,' Matt said. 'I don't think I've ever seen a blue like it either. I like that ... Ischia blue ... ' He turned and smiled at Lily. 'I might have to borrow that. It should be on that website you were talking about.'

She blushed involuntarily at the veiled compliment. 'Yeah, well I used to get paid to come up with stuff like that.

179

At least I know I'm good at it. God, I made a real hash of talking to Antonio about it.'

'I wouldn't worry about it – he'll just blame it on his English. He did say he wanted to hear more, right?' Matt said.

Lily looked sideways at him. 'Are you always this positive?'

'Glass half full!' he said with a grin.

Lily laughed, but secretly she was terrified. She had behaved recklessly over the past six months, blowing her salary on new designer outfits and expensive restaurants, determined to pay her way with Peter at least some of the time. Now, she was *literally* paying the price as she had less than two months' rent in the bank, twelve thousand dollars in credit card debt and, given the current state of the economy, it would take some time to find a new job. Though the thought of a potential new career venture was exciting, she knew she appeared lot braver than she actually felt.

Chapter Fifteen

'Okay, I'll be right back,' Matt said, stepping over a rope that tethered the boat to the pier. 'My friend Giovanni whose restaurant we're going to just asked me to pick up something for him. Can I get a volunteer to give me a hand?'

'Sure, I'll help,' Lily said, handing her beach bag to Ellen. She'd do anything to get her mind off her current financial situation.

'Won't be a minute,' Matt said over his shoulder to the others.

'Where are we going?' Lily asked, trying to keep up with Matt as he strode along.

'Back to that bakery I pointed out earlier. Boccia. They supply the bread to all the good restaurants around here and for some reason Da Maria didn't get their supply this morning.'

'What's Da Maria?'

'Oh, sorry, that's the name of the restaurant we're going to for lunch – Ristorante Da Maria. The little place on the beach. I probably didn't mention that last night – I didn't want to say too much. I get really enthusiastic about this kind of stuff – boats, local restaurants, basically anything about Ischia, and I didn't want to come across as a stalker or anything. I was trying to sound really casual.' He gave a shy smile. It was the first time she had seen anything but a grin on his face.

'Stalkers don't usually invite five people to join them on a boat. If you'd invited one person it might have seemed a bit psycho-murdery, but not when you invited all five of us. We're pretty loud and aggressive. If we were ever kidnapped, we'd probably be given back in a hurry.'

Matt laughed loudly and turned to look down at her. 'You're pretty funny, you know that?'

'I dunno . . . my life is a total cluster right now, so I don't know what I'm doing being funny. I should be back in the hotel sitting in the dark, facing into a corner trying to manifest what I need to do next to fix my life, not lollygagging around here about to spend the day on a boat.' She stopped short. 'God, sorry, that sounded very ungrateful. I didn't mean that I shouldn't be here . . . I just meant . . . I mean—'

'Lily, has anyone ever told you that you worry too much?' Matt turned around and stood directly in front of her, a kind smile on his face. 'Look at where you are,' he said, as he spread his arms wide and gestured around the piazza. 'You are in the most spectacular part of Italy for one week. *One week!* People have all kinds of stuff to deal with all the time and it will all be waiting for you to figure out when you get home. Just don't go wasting these next few days stressing over something that you can't control. I think your idea is great. Just give it the time it needs, figure it out and talk to people about it while you're here . . . and stop overthinking it!'

Lily bit her bottom lip and stared down at her sandals.

'I know, you're right. I'm sorry, I didn't mean to sound ungrateful ... I am happy to be here. It's just that the girls have everything figured out with their lives and I kind of thought I did too, and now everything is shit again and I feel like I'm walking on quicksand and everything is shifting beneath me. You know what this feels like? It's like, if this were a game of Scrabble, they'd all be winning with ten-letter words and I'd have ... like ... six or seven of the letter z and not a vowel in sight.' She finished with a loud sigh.

'Lily, have you ever actually played a game of Scrabble?' Matt asked, his eyebrows raised in a combination of amusement and confusion. 'You know there's only one letter z in the entire game, right?'

Lily sighed and looked up at him. 'Look, I just broke up with someone a couple of weeks ago and it's complicated, and then I get here and find out that I'm being laid off at the end of the month and ... ' Her voice trailed off as she bit down hard on her bottom lip. 'Oh God, now I'm going to sound all weepy and you're going to regret even asking me to help you with the bread, never mind inviting me on your boat. I'm really not this emotional and unhinged under normal circumstances, I swear.'

Reluctant to look directly at him, she blinked furiously in an attempt to send the threatening tears back where they came from.

'I'm sorry, I had no idea. The job stuff is bad enough but having to deal with a breakup at the same time ... well, that sucks, especially the complicated ones. Trust me, I've had first-hand experience of just how painful that can be. I know how awful it feels, especially in the early days of trying to process it all. Sorry if I sounded like a jerk, I was just trying to pull you out of a hole, but I didn't realise just how deep it was . . . ' He put his hand underneath her chin and gently tipped her face up. 'Hey . . . how about we forget about all this, go get the bread and get back to the boat? I can't promise that it will all go away, but I *can* promise that you'll feel a little better. If nothing else, it will take your mind off all this for a couple of hours. What do you say?' he asked with a kind smile.

'Yes, that sounds good,' Lily replied, returning his smile. 'And sorry again for—'

'Ah!' he said, stopping her short. 'We're forgetting about all this, remember?'

She smiled again. 'Yes, you're right. Sorry.'

'And stop saying sorry!'

'Okay, sorry.'

She slapped her hand across her mouth and stifled a laugh as Matt rolled his eyes in mock frustration.

Two enormous stacks of bread stood wrapped in brown paper outside the door of the bakery. Matt scooped one up and placed it across Lily's outstretched arms, exchanging a few words with the owner before scooping up the second.

Minutes later they were back at the pier. Dee and Ellen were sitting on the boat ramp, their feet dangling in the cool, turquoise water, while Morgan and Kitty sat in the shade of the pier wall. Matt handed his bread package to Dee before stepping lightly aboard the simple wooden outboard motorboat.

'Come aboard, ladies. Take your shoes off and toss them underneath the seats.'

'*Seats* is a bit of a stretch, wouldn't you say?' Morgan

hissed at Dee. 'I thought we were going sailing, not bobbing about like fucking Moby Dick on a fishing expedition.'

'Oh relax, it will be great. Come on, my love ... think of it as an adventure. When else would you ever be in a boat like this with someone who knows his way around the island?'

'Well, never at all, frankly, if I had my way.' Morgan grabbed on to Dee's hand and reluctantly stepped down on to the boat, letting out a small screech as it wobbled under her.

'Oh, this feels very safe,' she hissed sarcastically, holding on with both hands.

Matt held out a hand to help Kitty and Ellen on to the boat, then stood up to take the bread from Lily. He tucked it carefully to one side before reaching out to take her hand as she stepped on to the boat, holding on to it until she took a seat alongside him.

'*Andiamo*,' he said as he powered the engine and steered the boat slowly from the marina out into the bay.

'Oh my God, this smells amazing,' Dee said, inhaling the scent of freshly baked bread.

'No life jackets I guess, right?' Morgan asked, gripping on to the side of the boat with both hands.

'Don't worry, you'll be fine.' Matt grinned at her as he revved the engine. 'We're not going far. You can swim, right?'

'Yes, I can swim, it's just that I prefer to step gradually into the water, if that's okay with you.'

'Yeah, she's not really the leaping sort,' Dee grinned mischievously, nudging her soon-to-be wife.

'Got it! Okay, off we go.'

Much to Morgan's relief, Matt made his way slowly and carefully out from the pier, skirting left and right around the myriad boats moored in the bay.

'Look at the colour of this water. It's incredible! A sort of greenish blue,' Kitty said, her hand trailing in the water.

'Well, if you came out from behind those massive, polarised, titanium-grade, tortoiseshell sunglasses that take up half your face, for just half a second, you might actually see real colours and what the world actually looks like. I swear to God, you're going home with the weirdest suntan lines on your face, Kitty,' Ellen teased.

'Darling, I have zero intention of coming out from behind these things. Do you have any idea of the sun's radiation levels? Wreaks havoc with the skin.'

Matt navigated his way expertly out of the bay. As he pushed the throttle forward and increased the speed, the girls sat back quietly, taking in the scene around them. The morning sun was high in the sky now, the boats coming to life one by one. All around them engines were revving, and greetings were being thrown from one boat to another. Seagulls swirled overhead and squawked, following the boat on its path to the open bay.

Once they got beyond the pier wall, Matt charged the engine, and the boat took off at speed towards the castle. Morgan hung on for dear life, her knuckles turning white as she gripped the sides of the boat. Ellen dangled over the edge with one arm trailing in the water, Kitty pulled a sun visor down over her eyes, and Lily and Dee sat side by side in silence, the rush and intensity of the wind deeming it both unnecessary and challenging to speak.

As they reached the base of the castle, Matt slowed the boat down to barely a purr, explaining that the waters around the castle were protected, and had strictly imposed speed limits to protect the native bird colonies that nested throughout the year. As they chugged around the rugged, blackish rock, Matt pointed out nests large and small, tucked into crevices, their occupants safely hidden away out of view. High above the waterline, natural rock gave way to layers of stone and concrete and the girls could make out windows that had been carved out thousands of years ago.

They slowly followed the baseline of the castle, and when Matt rounded the curve of the rock, with the island of Ischia hidden from their view and only the vast bay ahead of them, he cut the engine. The boat bobbed up and down until it settled in the aftermath of the engine's wake. Lily leaned over the edge of the boat and stared down into the abyss of water beneath it. She had never seen water so crystal clear.

'Ischia blue,' she whispered.

Fish darted about and nibbled at underwater foliage on the rock's edge, hinting at a world of life out of sight beneath them.

A sailing boat coasted by them serenely, with two women sunbathing at the front.

'That's how I envisioned my day,' Morgan said, her eyes following the sailing boat as it glided silently by.

'Sorry about that, Morgan,' Matt said, with a laugh. 'I prefer these little runabouts. You can get into small spaces that those bigger boats just won't allow.'

'That may be, but they sure are pretty,' Morgan sighed.

Matt stood and tugged off his T-shirt. 'This is a great spot for a swim if you guys are up for it. The water is divine.'

Lily turned to answer him, but her breath caught in her throat. God, he's hot, she thought, trying not to stare.

He was lean and tanned a deep, golden brown. Dee wasn't quite as diplomatic. 'Jeez, Matt, work out much?'

He laughed, bending to hook the ladder over the side of the boat. 'Religiously. It's my thing. I think I probably have an addictive personality and I'm addicted to working out. It's also my stress buster, to be honest. Keeps me sane.'

'How can I take my clothes off now?' Ellen whined, as she began to unbutton her sundress. 'Christ's sake, Matt.'

'Last one in pays for the drinks,' he quipped, before diving in head-first.

'I'm not taking my clothes off and I'm certainly not leaving this boat,' Morgan said, shifting to one side, away from the ladder. 'Knock yourselves out, ladies.'

'I'm in!' Dee shouted with a loud whoop as she stripped down to her swimsuit and jumped in, followed by Lily and Ellen.

The water was exquisitely clear and refreshingly cool. Lily lay flat on her back, staring up at the deep blue sky. With the sound obscured by the water in her ears it felt like she was in a far, distant, silent land. She closed her eyes and floated, breathing slowly and deeply, her thoughts dissipating and her mind slowing down. She was unsure how long she floated there for, but it felt like a release, as her mind and body relaxed in the cool, crisp water.

The squawk of a seagull overhead pulled her from her reverie, and she turned and swam slowly towards the base of the castle. The crystal-clear, turquoise water alternated between patches of warm and cool as it lapped softly at the craggy rocks where Lily paused for breath. She couldn't determine where the sky stopped and the sea began as she was surrounded by a hazy vibrant blue.

'Ischia blue,' she whispered as she trod water.

She realised she hadn't felt this free in months as she floated on her back, the tension easing slowly from her as the water provided a restorative release. She felt worlds away from her life of the past six months with Peter, as a rapid stream of memories flashed through her mind: expensive French wines, craft cocktails, fancy restaurants, high heels and designer dresses. The images were jarring against the intense simplicity and natural beauty of her surroundings in Ischia, and she dived below the water to dispel the visual slideshow. Bursting to the surface moments later, she heard Matt whistle, calling her back to the boat.

Matt turned the engine over and slowly navigated the boat away from the rock face, continuing around the base of the castle in the direction of Cartaromana Bay.

'I didn't think you were ever coming back,' Matt said as he adjusted the throttle.

'Why? How long was I out there?' Lily asked, tying her wet hair into a knot at the nape of her neck.

'About half an hour. I'm starving!' Dee said as she towel-dried her hair.

'Okay, ladies. Time for lunch! Next stop: Cartaromana Bay. This place is awesome, and Giovanni is an old friend,' Matt said, cranking the engine into high gear. 'Hold on to your hat!' he shouted to Lily over the sound of the engine, as the boat took off at speed.

The fast, ten-minute journey from the castle to Cartaromana Bay took them west along the coast. The bay was full of pleasure boats, their occupants sunbathing or swimming before lunch beckoned. Lily turned her face up to the sun and closed her eyes, relishing the feeling of the sea breeze whipping against her skin. Matt made a wide right turn, slowing the engine as he did so, and easily navigated the boat in towards the curve of Cartaromana beach. Da Maria restaurant was built on stilts, into the grey-black cliff that hugged the beach. Squinting to see it better, Lily realised for the first time how hungry she was. Matt dropped anchor, as dozens of other boats had done, and cut the engine.

'Now what?' Morgan asked, a look of horror on her face, looking from him to the white outline of Da Maria restaurant.

'Now we wait.'

No more than four minutes later an even smaller motorboat pulled up alongside their boat. A heavyset, jovial-looking man in a white polo T-shirt stood as he navigated the boat towards them, a huge grin on his face.

'*Buongiorno!*' he shouted, in greeting. '*Matteo, tutto bene? Buongiorno a tutti! Buongiorno!*'

'The Italians like to find an Italian version for everyone's name if at all possible. For the duration of lunch, I'll be Matteo,' Matt explained, as he reached out and shook hands with his friend. 'This is my dear friend Giovanni. *Buongiorno!*'

Still grinning, Giovanni hovered his boat alongside Matt's and held out a hand to help the girls on board.

'Oh my God. This is not going to end well,' Morgan

muttered, letting out a low squeal as she stepped from one boat to the other.

Giovanni laughed and helped the other three on board, followed by Matt.

There was a loud, rapid conversation in Italian between the two men, complete with good-natured back slapping and hand gestures, before Giovanni returned his attention to the engine.

'*Andiamo!*'

The small boat zipped in towards the pier and Giovanni threw a rope around a large peg to secure them to it. Morgan tried not to squeal again as she stepped up on to the pier, realising as she did so that it wasn't fixed permanently, but rather it was a floating pier made from recycled barrels. As it moved beneath her, there wasn't a single person on the beach who didn't stop to stare at the American woman howling, as she dropped to all fours and crawled along the floating rubber pier.

'I'm mortified,' Dee said, her hand to her face, as she followed along behind her. 'Absolutely mortified. What am I marrying? Do you think it's too late to call off this wedding?'

Giovanni didn't seem to be the type to be bothered by much and he merely shrugged as he scooped up the packages of bread and followed them to the shore. Giving Matt a big clap on the back, he disappeared up the stairs with the parcel of bread. 'Your table is ready whenever you want ... *A dopo!*' he shouted over his shoulder.

Morgan collapsed on to a lounger clutching a hand to her chest. 'My heart is racing. Literally racing. I can't believe that I have to get back on that thing to get back to the resort. I hope to God there's another way off this beach,' she gasped, as she lay back and covered her face with her hands.

Kitty sat under an umbrella as Dee and Ellen raced for the water. Lily stood ankle deep in the bay, taking in the scene. Two neat rows of sun loungers sat facing the sea, with the beach curving around in a semicircle to the left and right. Behind them was a high, sheer rock wall protecting the beach and providing shelter to the bay. The water was warm, benefiting from thermal pools on the far left beyond the restaurant. There was nothing else on the beach except for two changing cabins tucked away next to the restaurant, and two outdoor showers. It was delightfully deserted and understated, which was in some way explanation for the lack of crowds. Lily walked the length of the beach in ten minutes and after a dip in the bay, lay back on a lounger under the gloriously hot midday sun.

Couples and families started to gather their belongings and make their way to Da Maria for lunch. Kitty sat up and adjusted her sunglasses as she watched Matt wade slowly out of the waves.

'Honestly, he's like something out of a movie. He's fit!' she said, her eyes following him as he strode up the beach.

He sat down heavily on a lounger on the other side of Lily, catching her eye as he reached down for his towel. 'Nice beach, huh?'

'It's gorgeous ... you look chiselled!'

'Ha!' he laughed. 'Chiselled? I've certainly never been told that before. You're funny.'

'I'm not sure I meant to say that out loud ... but I

couldn't help it. You look like a magazine ad. You know, *Men's Health* or one of those.'

Matt laughed again. 'You read *Men's Health*?'

Lily blushed. 'No . . . I . . . I've just seen it . . . you know . . . back in New York.'

She had seen multiple copies in Peter's apartment. He subscribed to several men's magazines and that was one of them. He kept the issues that he liked and would frequently refer back to saved articles. He was another gym fanatic, showing up religiously at Equinox on the Upper East Side at six o'clock every morning. On the nights that Lily stayed over, she'd barely be out of bed by the time he was back at the apartment at eight o'clock.

'Chiselled . . . ' Matt said again, laughing quietly to himself. 'Let's see if we can get these two fish out of the water and go to lunch.' Putting two fingers to his mouth he let out a shrill whistle. Dee and Ellen waved in acknowledgement and swam towards the shore.

'That's cool. I always wanted to be able to do that,' Lily said, pulling her feet up on the lounger. 'This beach is gorgeous, Matt. I'm surprised it's not more crowded.'

'Well, you can only get here by boat, so it keeps the masses away, which is a plus in my mind. Giovanni's place is a real draw. Most of the boats plan their day around lunch here. It's pretty ideal. I don't like crowds.'

'You don't like crowds, yet you live in Manhattan?'

'Yep, you've got me there. I run an ad agency and that's where my client base is. Not much demand for my line of work in a place like this,' he said, rubbing his hair roughly with a towel.

Lily wrapped her arms around her knees and gazed out

at the sparkling bay. 'God, this place is magical. You read about places being a hidden gem, but this really feels like it's under the radar. And we haven't seen the half of it.'

'I told you, this place will get under your skin and cast a spell on you. You won't be able to forget it.'

'Part of me is terrified about doing something myself for the first time, and the other part of me is excited. I just don't know where to start. I mean, I don't know the first thing about building a website.'

Matt ran his hand through his hair and laughed. 'And you think anyone who has ever built a website was born knowing how to do it? Lily, stop looking for obstacles!' he said, standing up and extending a hand to her. 'There are all kinds of DIY website-building tools now, it's just click and drag and there you go! Your very simple, basic website is built. I could help you do it in an hour, swear to God. It's that easy.'

She took his hand and he pulled her up.

'It might just be the maddest thing I've ever considered, but I can't think of a single reason why not. I have literally got nothing to lose.'

'That's the spirit. Right, what day is the wedding?'

'Saturday, why?'

'I'll give you a few tips if you like ... stuff you can do over the next couple of days, and I can introduce you to some folks you could talk to about this idea of yours – unless you're going to be busy with wedding stuff?'

'God, no. Morgan has this thing organised to within an inch of its life! Right, Morgan?'

Morgan sat up and draped her Missoni wrap around her shoulders. 'Dee only agreed to marry me on one condition – that she had absolutely nothing to do with the planning of it. I like the sound of this scheme of yours, Matt. I knew nothing about this island before I picked it as a wedding destination. Now that I'm here and getting to experience it, I can't believe I've never even heard of it.' She nodded in the direction of the motorboat moored out in the bay. 'That little boat ride aside, it has been unadulterated magic ever since we got here.'

'Right, I think Morgan just seconded the idea. Let's see what Giovanni has to say about it all. I can't think of a better judge – he'll tell you exactly what he thinks,' Matt said with a definitive nod. 'Let's gather up the others and get some lunch.'

Chapter Sixteen

The top floor of Da Maria's had a surrounding wall that came up about four feet, and from there to the ceiling was completely open to the roof, offering a full 180-degree view of Cartaromana Bay. Giovanni greeted them at the top of the wooden steps with a wide smile before they were shown to their reserved table at the front of the restaurant. They had a sweeping view of the bay and a welcome sea breeze wafted through the open space, each of them happy to have some temporary respite from the blazing sun.

'Amazing view, Matt!' Morgan said as she leaned on the low wall and stared out at the bay.

'See, this is exactly the kind of place that I would feature on the website. I mean, just seeing this online would make you want to book a trip!' Lily said, standing alongside Morgan.

'Yeah, it's my favourite spot for lunch on the island. So, are you guys taking a honeymoon after this?' Matt asked as he pulled back a chair.

'No ... you're on it, honey! I have a big court case next week, so we fly home on Monday. This was the only weekend that the resort had free in months, so we decided to do it in reverse and take the time before the wedding.'

'So, you guys are gatecrashing the honeymoon?' Matt asked, turning to Lily.

'Well, I suppose so . . . yes. I never thought of it that way.'

'Thought of what?' Kitty asked, flipping the pages of the menu.

'That we're gatecrashing their honeymoon.'

'Oh that. Trust me, it would be far less interesting without us here, and Morgan is simply not very good at downtime . . . are you, darling?'

'No, I'm not. Vacations give me anxiety.'

'What?' Matt asked, incredulous.

'I go to the bathroom for two minutes and I come back to a conversation about Morgan's anxiety triggers. How far down the list have you got, my love?' Dee asked, patting Morgan's thigh.

'Just started – with vacations.'

'There's a list?' Matt laughed, gesturing towards the waiter.

'Pharmacies, elevators, flies . . . You don't know what you've started, Matt.'

'What's wrong with pharmacies?' he asked, quizzically.

'Sick people go to pharmacies,' Morgan replied.

'So? It's not as if they're breathing on you.'

'No, but they have to pay, right? And key in their pin code. So, they're touching those buttons with the same fingers that have been up their nose or applying cream to their hideous rashes.'

'Jesus.'

'Exactly!'

197

'You've just ruined pharmacies for me for ever. Okay . . . elevators?'

Morgan looked at him blankly. 'Are you joking? You don't see the problem with several hundred people touching the same little button every hour? I mean, when you're a kid you're taught to not put money in your mouth 'cause it's dirty. And why is it dirty? Because so many weirdos have been handling it and those same weirdos have been calling elevators by touching that one button! One button . . . all day long!'

'Seriously, I'm going to look like a nutjob from now on trying to press the elevator button with my elbow. I guess people long ago had one less thing to worry about because elevators used to have attendants in the old days,' Matt said, as he poured water into their glasses.

'They still do at Tiffany's,' Kitty offered helpfully.

'Great, so Tiffany's is safe.'

'Yes, darling, only good things happen at Tiffany's.'

'So, I'm guessing that the fly phobia goes down a similar path? That they carry disease or something?'

'Yeah, we should probably get this out of the way before we order food,' Dee said, already glued to the menu.

'Well, yes. Flies eat shit. That's a fact,' Morgan said bluntly. 'I'm sorry, but there's no polite way to put it.'

'She wanted to buy one of those dreadful electrocuting lights for the apartment. I drew the line at that, so instead she whacks them with magazines.'

'And that works?' Matt asked, both eyebrows raised at the strangeness of the conversation.

'It does. A fly's brain can only work in one direction, so if you come at it from the left, he'll fly to the right, and vice versa. If you come at it in both directions at the same time, its brain can't process it and it is momentarily confused and freezes. That's when you whack it.'

Just at that moment, Giovanni arrived at their table with his notepad and pen.

'Oh, thank God,' Dee said. 'Morgan, I'm officially cutting you off now. This conversation is vile, as is your obsession with wiping out the planet's housefly colony. And, before we move off topic entirely, can you please stop using my copies of *Food & Wine* magazine to whack them? I like to hold on to the recipes, and fly-gut smudges on the cover are just not appealing. Now, moving right along . . . Matt, if there is anything that we absolutely must try here, then I'm all for it. I love being told what to do when it comes to food.'

For the next two and a half hours, Matt willingly played the role of gracious host. It was clear that he had been coming here for years and Giovanni and he were old friends. To Lily's ear, Matt's Italian was perfect, and he laughed and joked easily with Giovanni. There was no rigid plan as to how the food arrived at the table, but plate after plate showed up, delighting the girls one dish after another, ranging from Italian classics to innovative takes on well-worn traditions.

The food parade began with a plate of classic bruschetta and *bruschetta di mare*, the toasted bread topped with warm, lightly cooked clams and mussels. Lily whipped out her phone to capture the images as each dish was placed on the table. A platter of prosciutto, melon, buffalo mozzarella and an assortment of charcuterie arrived next, along with a large calamari salad. It was warm and light and quite unlike anything the girls had tasted before. The squid had been marinated overnight in garlic, olive oil, parsley and fresh lemon juice, rendering it juicy and tender. Dishes of fresh anchovies marinated in oil and lemon, sautéed mussels, sautéed clams and a mixed tempura seafood special of octopus, squid, shrimp and anchovies. Baskets of freshly baked crusty bread were used to mop up the juices, and bottles of crisp, local white wine accompanied the seafood extravaganza perfectly. Ellen avoided the pieces of battered octopus and one glare from Dee was evidence enough that they didn't need a repeat of the octopus story. Instead, the conversation around the table had ceased entirely unless it was related to the dishes being served.

'That was amazing,' Ellen said, appreciatively. 'I don't think I've ever had a meal like that before. Seriously. I didn't think seafood could taste like this, and what a view.'

'Well, that's good to hear,' Matt said, patting her shoulder. 'That was just the appetisers.'

'What?' Ellen asked. 'There's more? Oh my God, that's the best thing I've heard in a long time.' She clapped her hands in pure joy.

'Oh my God, I need a section just for food on the website!' Lily said, flicking through the photos she had just taken.

From their table out front the girls had a perfect view of Giovanni running the shuttle to and from the boats moored in the bay. They watched him pull up alongside elegant fifty-foot sailing boats and casual ten-foot motorboats. Everyone was at once welcome and everyone, regardless of their affluence or status, was treated the same.

After a short break, the next batch of dishes was served

family style. Big, steaming bowls of pasta were placed in the centre of the table, along with a stack of napkins, in anticipation of the gastronomic mess that was about to be made. Spicy spaghetti with garlic, mussels and red pepper, the classic *spaghetti alle vongole*, with plump, fresh clams, linguine with shrimp and tomatoes, and the local favourite *paccheri alla maria*, a short, tube-shaped pasta with a light tomato-based mixed seafood recipe. All of this was leading up to the house specialty: *risotto alla pescatora*, fisherman's risotto. Da Maria's risotto sells out every day in summer, so those in the know order it in advance, sometimes at the previous day's lunch. Matt had had the foresight to do that earlier that morning.

Traditional risotto calls for *carnaroli* rice, which slowly absorbs the seafood broth made fresh every morning, along with some white wine, onion and tomato, while the chosen seafood is added towards the end of the cooking process to ensure it retains its firmness and doesn't overcook. Seafood risotto recipes differ around the country, depending on local traditions and availability of different types of fish. Da Maria's recipe hasn't changed in over twenty years and is a fiercely guarded secret, beloved by returning guests year after year, featuring the day's freshest clams, mussels, calamari and shrimp.

'Wait! Do you mind if I just move this for a second?' Lily asked no one in particular. She pulled the steaming dish of risotto towards her and snapped a photo with the bay in the background. 'There! Look at that!' she said, replacing the bowl carefully in the centre of the table. 'These photos are going to tell a story all by themselves. I think I need an image gallery of some sort for the food.'

The table fell silent again as they devoured the steaming dish, the only sounds being murmurs of appreciation. Bottles of ice-cold, local Ischian white wine were the perfect accompaniment and as arms reached across the table to scoop up the last scraps of seafood risotto one by one, the girls sank back into their chairs, beginning their descent into a food coma.

Morgan was the first to break the silence. 'I may have been traumatised coming down that pier, but I've gotta say, this alone was totally worth it. I would happily crawl back down the pier to have this dish again. And if neither of us has said it already, Matt, we'd love to have you join us at the wedding this weekend.'

'Wow, that's high praise, given how much of a spectacle you made of yourself,' Dee teased. 'But yes, I've got to agree. This risotto was insane. Matt, thank you for inviting us here today, and yes, please do come to the wedding. It should be a lot of fun.'

'I'd be honoured! I'm pretty sure this is going to be the event of the year!'

A round of espressos and complimentary limoncellos rounded off the meal as Matt gallantly insisted that lunch was his treat.

'Where's Giovanni?' Lily asked, stopping abruptly as they made their way down the stairs and on to the sand. 'I wanted to say goodbye.'

Directly behind her, Matt stopped short, placing a hand on her shoulder so he wouldn't bump into her and scraping his elbow against the wall. 'Ouch! Sorry! I wasn't expecting you to stop just then. Um ... he's probably already at the boat to take us back out.'

'Shit, sorry,' she replied, turning to face him. 'I shouldn't have just stopped like that. Are you okay?'

'Yeah, just a graze.'

Lily reached out and turned his arm so she could see. 'Oh no, I'm so sorry. I'm so clumsy,' she said apologetically, although the feeling of being so close to him was not something she could pretend to regret.

Giovanni appeared from around the side of the building and in one fluid movement bent down to scoop Morgan up in his arms. After an initial screech, she fell completely silent and held her breath as he carefully and confidently made his way down the wobbly rubber pier, depositing her safely in his boat at the end of it.

'What the hell was that back there?' Dee whispered into Lily's ear.

'I stopped short and to avoid me he scraped his arm against the wall. The man takes us to an epic lunch, and I send him home injured. I'm so clumsy,' Lily whispered back.

'Yeah, well ... I dunno ... I just turned around and saw you right up against him, and him staring down at you. Anything else you'd care to share?' Dee said, a wicked grin on her face.

'Cut it out!' Lily hissed, as they reached Giovanni's boat and clambered aboard.

'Hey, Giovanni, Lily has an idea she wanted to run by you,' Matt shouted as Giovanni revved the outboard engine and took off in the direction of Matt's boat.

Giovanni turned to Lily and raised his eyebrows.

'Oh, yeah, I have this idea ... to build a website to promote Ischia to tourists in America and Europe, to tell the story of Ischia and these great restaurants, these amazing views . . . '

'*Bene.* Good. Yes, good. We need this. Tell me what I need to do, and I do it. This island is like a big secret. It is time for the world to know Ischia,' Giovanni concluded with a nod.

'Great, okay, thanks, Giovanni . . . *grazie.* I'll let you know when it's ready.'

'*Sì, bene, bene.* Matt has my number. When you are ready, we will talk.' He raised his cap an inch off his head as they each climbed aboard Matt's boat. '*Arrivederci!*' he shouted, with a big wave and an even bigger grin, as he turned his boat back in the direction of Ristorante Da Maria. 'Until next time! *A la prossima! Ciao!*'

Chapter Seventeen

Lily sat in the foyer waiting for Dee, tossing her mobile phone from one hand to the other. She checked the volume for the fourth time that morning.

Yes, Lily, it's still on ... loser, she admonished herself quietly. Not a single message or notification.

She opened her Gmail and swiped down her screen to refresh the app. Three emails from Patty in HR about next steps and best practices, one from a friend in sales who was also one of the lay-off casualties, an automated message from her gym reminding her that she hadn't checked in for four weeks and an Instagram message telling her that they had updated their terms of use. Nothing from Peter.

Wow, about as uninspiring as an inbox could be, she thought. Fuck you, Patty, with your safe HR job.

She checked her messages app. There was one message from her mother that read, 'hope u having lovely time', and one from her landlord informing her that her rent cheque had bounced.

'What the hell ... Oh, for Christ's sake,' she groaned, putting her head in her hand. 'How did that bounce? I transferred four thousand dollars before I left!'

She opened her banking app and attempted to sign in. 'What's the goddamn password?' she mumbled, stabbing at the screen. After three failed attempts her account was locked. 'Shit! Now I'll have to call them and turn on roaming. Will cost a goddamn fortune from here. Shit, shit, shit ...' her voice trailed off as a quintessentially happy-looking couple in gym outfits strode by her.

'Good morning,' the spandex-wearing blonde said in a light, breezy tone.

'Morning,' Lily replied with her best fake smile. 'Fit, smug bastards,' she muttered, once they were safely out of earshot. She put her head in her hands and sighed loudly. 'Another problem ... bounced rent cheque and a locked banking app.'

'What's the matter with *you*?'

She looked up to see Dee towering over her. 'What are you doing in a bathing suit and a kaftan? This is a meeting about your wedding!' Lily shrieked. 'I even put a bra on for this!'

'God, this is all so unnecessary.' Dee sighed. 'Honestly, it's just a bunch of us gathering in a garden to exchange vows and guzzle champagne afterwards.'

'Well, it's a good thing that Morgan is more romantic than you are and planned this whole thing or we'd all have been gathered around a manhole cover on a street in New York to see you get married.'

'She warned me that I had to handle everything once we got here, that the advance planning of it was her responsibility but that making it happen on site was mine. But I didn't think there was much else to organise. We just gather in the olive grove, right? Anyway, what's up with you? What's with all the sighing a minute ago?'

'Oh, nothing. I just locked myself out of my banking app so now I'm going to have to call them from here, which will cost me an arm and a leg. My rent cheque bounced, and I can't log in to see what happened. I'm totally locked out.'

'Probably for the best. I wish I could lock myself out of my credit cards.'

A formidable-looking team of three young women, dressed in the same navy and white skirt suit uniform as the receptionists, hustled towards them.

'See, I told you that you should have worn proper clothes!' hissed Lily. 'They are wearing uniforms, Dee!'

'They are at work, Lily. I'm on vacation for the first time in two years. I'm not getting out of my bathing suit for anyone.'

Laura introduced herself as the events manager, the other two girls were part of the support team to make sure that everything was planned appropriately and the wedding went smoothly on the day. One girl took furious notes the entire time, while Laura did most of the talking. She ran through a list of what she wanted to cover in the meeting, causing Dee to glance at Lily, a look of desperation on her face.

'Okay, so maybe we can get through this kind of quickly. I think everything is pretty much planned already, isn't it?' Lily asked.

'Allora... so you have planned the wedding for five o'clock on Saturday ... but I just want to tell you that you should maybe think to have it, maybe at six o'clock. At five o'clock it will still be very hot, and your guests will be in the sun.'

'That's fine, most of them are Irish and don't see the sun from one end of the year to another. They'll be delighted.

What else is there?' Dee asked, leaning forward to look at the woman's folder.

'What about the priest?' Lily asked. 'Do we need to meet him or a rehearsal or anything?'

'The priest ... I don't know ... ' Laura said, a look of confusion on her face. 'I don't know who is the priest?'

Dee and Lily looked sideways at each other, and back to Laura.

'What do you mean you don't know who the priest is?' Lily asked, watching shock register across Dee's face. 'You're supposed to have booked the priest.'

Dee interjected. 'Hang on a minute. First of all, this is a gay wedding, so you won't find a priest within screeching distance of this thing. Second, I wasn't involved in much of the advance planning, but I know that someone on your team emailed Morgan and said that they had an official that they used for weddings.'

'*Sì, signora*, yes, we have this person here in Ischia that we use for the weddings ... *come si dice* ... an official person, but we have not booked him for this wedding,' Laura said, shrugging both shoulders and gesturing with both hands. 'No one has asked us to do this.'

'So, who exactly did you think was going to marry us?' Dee asked, her voice rising.

'*Allora, signora*, many people, they bring this person ... sometimes it is a friend who will do this, so for us ... this is not so strange. *Allora*, you do not have this person?'

'No, I don't happen to have a random officiant. I didn't think I needed to pack one for this trip,' Dee replied sarcastically. She took a deep breath and exhaled slowly.

'Okay,' Lily said, placing a hand on Dee's arm. 'Laura,

can you call the officiant that you use to see if he's available? That should be the first thing we do, before we panic unnecessarily.'

'*Ah, mi dispiace*,' Laura replied. 'I am sorry, but this is not possible. I know that already he is busy with another wedding on Saturday ... in my town.'

Dee folded her arms on the table in front of her and put her head down with a moan. 'I don't believe this is happening. I *cannot* go up to the room and tell Morgan that we don't have someone to marry us. She will go into a spiral and lose her mind entirely.'

'And I suppose there is only one official on the island of Ischia?' Lily asked, already knowing what the answer was likely to be.

'*Sì, signora.* Just one,' Laura replied, looking nervous for the first time.

'Okay, stop freaking out, Dee. I'm sure this is not the first time that this has happened. There has to be a solution in this day and age, and we have a couple of days to figure it out. For God's sake, just don't say a word to Morgan. She doesn't need to worry about this. Laura, can you see if you can find some kind of officiant nearby from Procida or Capri, or even the mainland? We can pay for them to travel here, you know, cover their expenses and all that.'

'*Sì ... sì ... certo.* Of course, Signora LeeLee. I will check today and let you know,' she said, as her colleague scribbled frantically in her notebook.

Dee sank back into the oversized armchair in dismay as the conversation continued. Laura confirmed that Friday night's cocktail party would take place on the terrace overlooking the bay. A well-known local trio would play all the Italian classics, and hors d'oeuvres would be hosted outdoors. The pizza restaurant facing Mount Epomeo had been reserved from eight o'clock for a casual dinner, with music and dancing to continue until midnight. Set-up for the wedding would begin late Saturday morning, with seating for forty people. The string quartet would perform pre-chosen pieces during the ceremony and would continue afterwards for the champagne reception in the olive grove.

'So, we will do a rehearsal on Friday morning, yes?' Laura asked, as she closed the folder on her lap. 'We can go now and have a look at the space.'

'Is that really necessary? I mean, it's just a bunch of people in the olive garden ... not really all that much to rehearse,' Dee said, standing up as Laura and her colleagues took off in the direction of the olive garden.

'Jesus, Dee, it's your wedding!' Lily reprimanded. 'We have to at least go out there and see where everything is going to be set up to make sure it looks okay. And, you know, walk through the ceremony and where to put the musicians and how you'll arrive, all that kind of stuff.'

'The ceremony is going to last four minutes. "Do you take? Yes, I do ..." That kind of idea. Morgan has a few people doing readings, and the string quartet are playing two tunes. That's about it. Four minutes.'

'Dee, people are travelling a very long way for this wedding. They expect a proper ceremony. It can't be over in four minutes, otherwise they could have just dialled in on a Zoom call, for Christ's sake. Like ... how are you going to arrive?'

'Arrive where? I'm already here!'

'No! To the olive garden, Dee!'

'I'm planning to walk there, Lily – unless you have notions of me arriving on horseback or something?'

'You can't just rock up. You're one of the brides! I mean, Morgan will walk down the aisle in her dress, but how will you arrive? Do you want to walk down the aisle too?'

'Are you joking? Two brides walking down the aisle? No, that's not happening. Anyway, it's an olive grove for God's sake, there *is* no aisle. It's grass!'

'You're definitely missing the bride gene. I'll say it again – it's a good thing the planning of this thing wasn't up to you or we'd be having dinner in a soup kitchen.'

Dee sighed. 'I just don't want the traditional, fussy wedding, that's why I agreed to come here in the first place, to escape all that nonsense.'

'But it *is* a wedding, Dee. You have to do some of it!'

'I'm not arriving in any special way to the olive garden, okay? I'm just going to rock up and talk to people, like a normal human being, before Morgan makes her big entrance. End of conversation.'

'Fine . . . jeez!' Lily joked. 'I don't see this side of you that often, thank God!'

'It's my go-to work demeanour. I'm a total bitch at the office.' Dee grinned. 'Okay, let's go stake out this olive garden and get it over with.'

The next thirty minutes were spent following the three women in suits up and down the length of the olive garden, as they explained the layout of the space, the placement of the altar and the chairs, the set-up for the string quartet and the champagne station that would be staffed at the end of the ceremony.

'Okay, three things,' Dee said, turning to Laura. 'One, this is not a Catholic wedding, so there is no altar or anything religious, right? Morgan will lose it if she sees a crucifix or a holy picture, so just don't use or refer to any religious stuff and we'll be fine. Two, the champagne station is going to be slammed immediately following the ceremony. You're going to need more than one person pouring champagne. Trust me on this, these people will start reaching for the bottles themselves, so please have three people on hand to pour drinks. Three, can we get a bottle of that wedding champagne out here now, please, and two margherita pizzas? We don't need tables and chairs, we're just going to sit over here on the grass and have a little lunch picnic. Can we do that?'

Laura seemed relieved to be able to solve one problem easily and said she would arrange it immediately.

'Do you want to call Morgan and have her join us?'

'No, she's at the spa and I don't see her really getting the idea of sitting on the grass with pizza when she could do the same in the very comfortable restaurant up behind the pool.'

'Fair enough. I think the other two have gone off shopping. They were afraid they'd get pulled into wedding stuff if they didn't disappear.'

'I'd disappear if I could. I hate all this fuss.'

Ambrogio, the bar manager, appeared around the corner carrying a bottle of champagne. He stopped, spread both his arms wide and with a big laugh said, *'Bravi! Bravi! Che bella idea!'*

He was flanked by two waiters armed with an ice bucket, champagne glasses, plates and cutlery. They spread out a tablecloth under the shade of an olive tree as Ambrogio opened the champagne.

'*Buona idea!* No one uses this olive garden, only for weddings. This is a great idea ... to have pizza and champagne! *Bravi!*'

He poured their champagne, stashed the bottle on ice and disappeared as quickly as he had appeared.

'Cheers!' Dee said, raising her glass to Lily's. 'Sorry if I was painful to deal with back there. Thanks for helping.'

'Cheers! Don't worry about the minister thing. We'll figure something out. Can you believe you're going to get married here in four days' time?'

'I know, it's crazy,' Dee replied, turning to look around the olive garden. 'I can't believe that they don't use this garden more. It's gorgeous. I can't believe we're only here for another week ... actually, less ... that's depressing.'

'I know. Sitting here in what feels like our own private olive garden, drinking champagne. This must be how Bridget Bardot felt, all those years ago, living the life,' Lily said, sighing as she leaned back on one elbow and sipped her champagne.'

'She was French.'

'Oh right. Okay, Sophia Loren then.' Lily laughed.

'So, what's going on with Peter? Any word since?'

'No, I was too embarrassed to call him again after that late-night drunken conversation that I can't even remember and he hasn't called back, so I don't know what to think.'

'But you've no idea what was said on the phone?'

'No, I don't remember a word of the conversation and the texts were all just from me to him stating how much I missed him. Jesus, I'm such a lost cause.'

'Well, that's not very helpful. So, what are you going to do? Are you ever going to call him? You can't just leave things hanging like this.'

'I think I'll just deal with it when I'm back. There's enough going on here and I kind of don't want to let him back into my head, if you know what I mean.'

'But what if he's changed his mind and wants to get back together? You could have already agreed to that, for all you know.'

'Dee ... this is Peter we're talking about. Have you ever known him to change his mind about anything, or admit he had been wrong?'

'Fair enough. Look ... in the grand scheme of things you're probably right to put him out of your head as best you can and just enjoy being here. You can always call him next week when you're home and deal with it all then,' Dee replied, as she stood up and stretched. 'Right, I'm off to the pool and I'm not budging until dinner time. God, champagne in the middle of the day is such a great idea. I feel so chilled right now.' She grinned. 'What's the plan for tonight?'

'We're having dinner at eight o'clock at that place down in Lacco Ameno. I don't remember the name of it ... it begins with a P. Hang on, I have it in my phone ... Pignattello. It's the sister restaurant to this place down in the town square. I asked Marco at reception about it and he told me that it's as good as a Michelin star restaurant, but they don't have a star yet. Apparently it's one of the best restaurants on the island and we should definitely have the tasting menu. He said it was already booked for us, so someone else must have made the reservation.'

'Morgan must have planned that one, then. She's all about her tasting menus. Right, drinks here at seven, then?'

'Sounds good! I'm going to rehearse my pitch by the pool,' Lily said, brushing pieces of grass off of her sundress. 'I'll see what they think about my idea tonight; see if I can line up another restaurant!'

'You know you're actually on vacation, right? I mean, you do remember how to be on vacation, don't you? It's supposed to be a lot of lolling about, reading a trashy book, drinking in the afternoon ... that sort of thing.'

'I know, but this restaurant is supposed to be fabulous so maybe they'd be keen to support my website idea. I might pick up a client while at dinner, so what have I got to lose? Anyway, I have to get better at the pitch. I think it sounds a bit wooden ... or maybe I sound a bit wooden, I'm not sure which, but either way I think I can make it better.'

'I don't think I've ever seen you this excited about work,' Dee said, squinting at Lily.

'This? This doesn't feel like work! I'm telling these people that I'm going to promote their fabulous island and hopefully they are going to pay me to do so! What's not to love?' The excitement was unmistakable in Lily's voice.

'I remember this version of you. It's been a long time since she showed her face. In fact, I think she became a missing person case about, oh I don't know ... six months ago, give or take.'

'Yeah, yeah, you never approved of Peter, I know.'

'Lily it wasn't that I disapproved of Peter, it was just that it was hard to recognise the person you became after you met him. I'm just glad to see this version of my friend show up again.'

Lily rolled her eyes and raised a hand in protest but couldn't think of a single sarcastic thing to say.

'Now, off you go. Get to work. I'm going to drag my soon-to-be wife from the spa. See you for drinks at seven – if you can tear yourself away from your new obsession that is.'

'Okay, seven o'clock!' Lily said with a wave as she disappeared around the corner of the ancient stone walls.

Chapter Eighteen

The shuttle dropped the girls off at two minutes past eight in the centre of Lacco Ameno, a short stroll from Il Pignattello. The restaurant had vast bay windows that overlooked the cobbled piazza in the centre of town and the eighteenth-century church in its rear corner. A group of ten old men played boules to one side, with still more standing by watching. Couples strolled arm in arm in the Italian tradition of taking a *passeggiata* – a stroll before dinner – while young children darted in and out of the grand fountain.

As they made their way across the piazza, Lily stumbled and grabbed on to Morgan's arm.

'Why are you wearing those heels? This whole place is cobblestones. Those heels are ridiculous in a place like this.'

'I have gammy legs. I can't help it. They look better in heels. I look like a munchkin in flats,' Lily said, straightening her high-heeled sandal back on her foot.

'What the hell is gammy? What does that even mean?'

'Morgan, how can you be about to marry an Irishwoman and not know what gammy means?'

'I don't know, I must have missed that delightful lexicon tutorial. You people have your own entire language of ridiculous words – craic, donkey's years, banjaxed, eejit, jammy. So, what precisely does gammy mean?'

'Oh, like ... wonky ... you know, not working properly, or looks funny ... funny odd or weird, not funny haha.'

'*You* people are weird,' Morgan said, laughing her big laugh. 'Gammy indeed. Come on, get your gammy legs moving because I'm starving.' She dragged Lily to catch up with the rest of the group.

The restaurant was lit entirely by candlelight, and as the evening wore on, wrought-iron streetlights cast a soft orange glow over the exterior of the building, colouring the tables just inside the window a warm gold. The girls were accompanied to a corner table just inside the window. The place settings were simple, white, handmade crockery and elegant Riedel glassware. Michele, the restaurant manager, greeted them and handed out several menus.

'*Buona sera* ... welcome to Il Pignattello. My name is Michele, the restaurant manager, and here are the menus for this evening. There is a tasting menu, the à la carte menu, and a wine list. All of them are printed on eco-friendly rice paper, so they feel a little different.'

'Rice paper! That's fantastic,' Ellen gushed, running her hand over the paper.

'*Sì, signora,* our restaurant is one hundred per cent plastic free and we are the first restaurant in Ischia to achieve the green star for environmental awareness.'

'I love that! Who picked this restaurant? I'm so glad we came here tonight.'

Morgan rolled her eyes. 'I did, but I normally reserve judgement until after I've tasted the food ... no disrespect to your eco-friendly initiatives, Michele.'

'No, *signora*, you are right. Tonight it is all about the food. *Allora*, I will leave you to look at the menus and the sommelier will be right over.'

Moments later, a tall, slender brunette wearing slim-fitting dark grey trousers and a fitted white shirt appeared at their table. Her hair was tied up in a meticulous chignon and her deep brown eyes were accented by perfectly executed cat-eye eyeliner.

'*Buona sera!* My name is Lucia, I am the sommelier, and I will be delighted to assist you this evening. But first, perhaps a drop of something sparkling to start the evening?' she said in pitch-perfect English. 'This is from one of my favourite producers in Campania. It is made using the traditional method of the Champagne region.' She slowly poured five generous glasses. 'I hope that you will like it. *Salute!*'

The girls pored over the menus, which had been thoughtfully translated into English alongside the original Italian.

'I want everything. This all sounds amazing,' Lily said as Michele arrived back at their table.

'So, the tasting menu is five courses, and we have a wine-pairing menu also, if you would like to do this,' Michele said, pointing to both menus. 'All of our seafood is sustainably caught, and our vegetables are organic from our own gardens.'

'Oh wow, that's impressive!' Ellen gushed enthusiastically.

'Tasting menu. No question,' Dee said, closing the menu. 'I don't even need to read it. That's the way to go.'

'I'll do the tasting menu as long as there's no octopus,' Ellen said, handing her menu to Michele.

'Ah, okay, you have an allergy, *signora*?'

'No, I just feel sorry for them.'

'Here we go,' Morgan said loudly, putting a hand across

her eyes. 'Michele, trust me, you don't want to hear the whole long, sorry story. Let's just call it an allergy and eliminate the octopus, for the love of God.'

'*Sì, signora.* No problem.'

'And we'll take a bottle of this champagne that we're drinking, please,' Morgan added.

'You would like to speak to the sommelier?'

'Sure, in a little while, but let's get a bottle of this to get us started. And I'll do the tasting menu too, thanks, Michele.'

Lily and Kitty nodded in agreement.

'*Grazie ... grazie,*' Michele said, gathering up the menus. 'I bring you the champagne.'

Morgan leaned across the table towards Ellen. 'Honey, you do know that he's got a bucket full of dead octopus back there, don't you? I mean, you not ordering octopus won't actually save any lives ... they're already dead. It's not like lobster, all hanging out happily in a tank of water until someone comes along and orders one. Those poor creatures are plucked from the tank and scalded alive. That I could understand.'

'Lobsters aren't smart. Octopuses are smart, and if fewer people ordered octopus then they'd fish less of it, so I still feel like I'm doing my part to protect them.'

'Oh, thank God,' Dee sighed, as Lucia arrived at the table. 'It was beginning to feel like I was having dinner with David Attenborough and he was judging my choices.'

'Right – as maid of honour I want to check in on all things wedding really quickly before we get stuck into dinner,' Lily interjected.

'Ah, you are the wedding party from San Montano for this weekend?' Lucia asked. 'I did not realise. Which one of you is the bride?'

Morgan raised one hand and nudged Dee, who reluctantly did so too.

'It's a gay wedding, darling,' Kitty said, matter-of-factly. 'Just in case you didn't catch that one.'

'Oh, marvellous! I lived in New York for a few years and many of my friends were gay. Gay weddings are my favourite!' Lucia said, laughing. '*Salute*, ladies!'

Kitty turned to watch her sashay between the tables as she left. 'Isn't she a divine creature? The figure on her!'

'Yeah, and she's a sommelier, so she gets to drink wine for a living,' Ellen said, staring after Lucia.

'Yes, but I don't think she drinks it by the jug, quite like we do, darling,' Kitty said, draining her glass.

'Okay, so . . . wedding update,' Lily said, clinking her glass with her fork. 'Everything is set for Friday night's cocktail party. We kick off at six o'clock with cocktails on the terrace and a fun pizza dinner after. Then we have spa appointments on Saturday morning, hair appointments Saturday afternoon and the ceremony is at five o'clock.'

An older couple entered the restaurant and were seated at the table alongside the girls.

'I can't see a damn thing in here, Ruby,' the gentleman said, in a loud American accent. 'What are all these for?' he asked, leafing through the menus. 'Can't I just have one menu?'

Michele patiently explained the various menu options and left, to allow them time to read the menus.

'Earl, can you just sit quietly and give me a minute to read these? I need a flashlight.'

'Can't see a damn thing . . .'

The lady pulled out a tiny yellow torch from her purse. She flicked it on, lighting up the entire corner of the restaurant.

'I'm sorry,' she said, in a strong southern drawl, turning to the girls' table. 'I won't be a minute. I just can't see with these candles.'

Morgan nudged Dee.

'Sure, no problem,' Dee said, politely, realising that Morgan didn't want to engage in the classic 'where are you from' conversation with fellow Americans.

Lucia arrived to pour a glass of champagne for the couple, only to have Earl put a hand on her arm. 'Honey, bring me a mint julip, instead of that frog water.'

'Make that two,' Ruby responded, not lifting her eyes from the menu.

'What the hell is all this? Ruby, all I want is a bowl of spaghetti or that rice dish that I saw a photo of . . . what the hell do they call that thing?'

'Risotto, Earl,' she replied loudly as Michele returned to the table.

'We're not gonna do the tasting menu. We're gonna order from the à la carte menu.'

'Certainly,' Michele said, his pen poised above his note-pad. 'What would you like?'

'Can I get the mushroom risotto, but without the mush-rooms actually in it.'

'*Non ho capito* . . . I don't understand,' Michele replied, frowning deeply. 'This is a mushroom risotto.'

'Yes, I get that. That's what I want – the mushroom risotto, but could you just have them take out the mush-rooms when it's cooked.'

'*Allora*, this is not possible, *signore*. Maybe you would like instead another risotto?'

'No, the mushroom risotto is fine, but can you just take out the mushrooms at the end? You know, like when it's made, just have the guy remove the mushrooms.'

'Ah, *il signore ha un allergia?* An allergy?'

'No,' his wife interjected, with a loud sigh. 'He just has a problem with mushrooms.'

'*Ma, signora* ... madam ... is not possible to remove the mushroom from the risotto. Is made with mushroom. Many, many, small pieces of mushroom. Is impossible to remove them.'

'Earl, they can't take out the mushrooms, so just pick something else if you can't deal with that, okay?' she said, with another loud sigh. 'He won't actually die if there are mushrooms in there. He doesn't have an allergy.'

'Yeah, it's more psychological.' He shrugged. 'Should be fine if they are small pieces and they don't look like actual mushrooms,' he said, handing the menu back to the waiter.

Michele paused momentarily, looking from one to the other of them. 'So, is okay ... the mushroom risotto?' he asked, warily.

'I guess so,' she replied, snapping the menu shut before glaring at her husband. 'I'll do the spaghetti with clams, and you can leave the clams in, honey.'

'Of course. Shall I send over the sommelier?'

'No, there's no need,' the lady said, handing Michele their menus. 'Do you have Chianti? Just bring us a bottle of Chianti.'

Michele hesitated and Lily watched as he mentally

223

considered talking the woman out of ordering Chianti with dishes as delicate as *spaghetti vongole* and mushroom risotto, but he decided against it, nodded and left the table.

Morgan dipped her head and shook it slowly. 'We're such an embarrassment to ourselves when we're abroad,' she said mournfully, as the first course started to arrive.

After the girls had devoured the first platter of seafood, Antonio stopped by their table.

'*Buona sera, signore,* I am happy that you have chosen our sister restaurant for dinner tonight.'

'Oh, *buona sera*, Antonio,' Lily said with a warm smile. Marco told us about it earlier in the week. Said we had to come.'

'Good, good, yes ... tonight you will have a feast fit for a king,' Antonio said, gesturing with both hands. '*Allora*, I don't want to interrupt your dinner, but I did want to invite you to a party. It is tomorrow night, at the Casa D'Ambra vineyard. The owners, they are good friends of mine.'

'Oh, the two sisters? We've heard of them,' Ellen said, her eyes lighting up at the idea of any kind of party.

'Yes, they are the two sisters. *Allora*, they have won many awards for their wines ... incredible wine. Tomorrow night they will hold their annual party for all of their customers and friends. You should come. I will call them to add your names to the guest list.'

'Sounds wonderful. Will you be there, Antonio?' Kitty asked casually.

'Yes, of course, *signora*—'

'Kitty, please,' she insisted with a smile.

'*Va bene* ... Kitty.' He smiled back at her. 'Yes, I would

not miss this party. It is definitely one of the highlights of summer. Ah, but you will see for yourself ... as my guests, no?'

'How very kind of you. I can honestly say that I cannot wait,' Kitty said, her eyes not leaving his.

'Very good. Now I must go,' Antonio said. 'Tomorrow evening at six o'clock. Just one thing ... the party is a white party, so you must wear only white. Ask Marco at reception for the details in the morning. He will tell you everything that you need to know. Now I will leave you to enjoy the rest of your meal. Ah, Lily, perhaps tomorrow evening you can tell me more about this idea that you have to promote Ischia. I am very interested to hear it. *Buona sera.*' He gave a wide smile, and a small nod in Kitty's direction.

'Good Lord, the man moves like a panther. I can just imagine—'

'Kitty, for the love of God, give it a rest,' Morgan said, rolling her eyes and shaking her head at the same time.

'I make no apologies, darling,' Kitty asked, as unperturbed as ever. 'He's a divine specimen of a man and based solely on how those trousers look on him he has thighs made of steel. My imagination is running wildly rampant right now and I doubt that a man like that would disappoint.'

Ellen sighed loudly. 'Are you having great sex again in your head? God, I'm so jealous.'

'Well not any more, more's the pity ... and it was all looking so promising, too. What a shame. Now, can anyone tell me if we are finished here? I've lost count entirely of how many dishes we've had.'

'I can't believe I have to pitch to Antonio tomorrow night. Jesus, he's like the linchpin to this whole thing.

Imagine having San Montano sign up. They'd totally be an anchor client,' Lily said, putting both hands to her face.

'Anchor client. *See*, you already sound like you know what you're talking about to me,' Ellen said, nodding supportively.

'I think you could be on to something with this,' Kitty said, her fingers drumming on the table. 'I mean, look, I hadn't even heard of Ischia before we started talking about this wedding and everyone you've spoken to seems really keen to explore the idea. Antonio is no fool and he is determined to hear you out. That says to me that there is a real demand for what you are planning to offer. Look, I run a PR firm and I can tell you that first impressions are more important now than ever before. People's attention span has dropped to nothing. You have seconds, or you'll be scrolled over. People no longer want to be sold to – those days are over. Today, people want to buy into something, feel like they're part of something.'

'God, it's very sexy when you all start talking work-talk. I honestly have the smartest friends,' Ellen said, as she pulled the white wine bottle from the ice bucket. 'I sound so dull by comparison. Oh, sad face, it's almost empty. Do you think—'

'Yes,' Morgan and Dee replied in unison.

'You've got nothing to lose, Lily,' Kitty continued. 'You're a very talented writer. Don't just take my word for it, Matt has been pushing you to do this too. Literally every time we see the man he has some comment about your idea, so I'm not the only one who believes in it. I think you can actually pull this off, and if you don't I'll hire you. I could do with someone like you on my staff.'

'Not a chance,' Lily laughed. 'We wouldn't last a week together.'

'Yes, you're probably right. I really am a witch to work for. I couldn't do that to you, darling.'

Michele arrived with a selection of desserts for the girls to share. Lily sat back in her chair, rerunning what Kitty had just said through her head, completely lost in her thoughts.

'Lily!'

'Sorry, what?' She looked up to see all four girls and Michele staring at her.

'Coffee! Do you want a coffee or what?'

'Sorry, yes, an espresso please,' Lily answered, smiling and making an effort to rejoin the conversation as her thoughts drifted away again, this time to Matt. Why did Kitty have to mention him? Now he was stuck in her head again. She couldn't help but picture his *amore* in her head. Classically Italian of course, tall and slim, tanned, brown eyed with long, lustrous dark brown hair and that innate sense of style that all Italian women seem to be born with.

As the coffees were placed on the table and a round of after-dinner Ischian *digestivo* was offered on the house, Lily shook her head rapidly to disperse the mental images of the elegant Italian woman.

'*Allora*,' Lucia said with a smile, arriving back to the table and holding aloft a tall bottle. 'This *digestivo* is made here in Ischia. Rucolino. It is made from rocket leaves. It helps you to digest the meal and it is delicious. Michele and I will join you to toast your wedding,' she said, as Michele placed seven square, crystal glasses on the table. She poured an inch of the viscous, chocolate-brown liquor into each of them. 'Um ... Antonio told us about the idea that you have to do something – a website, to promote Ischia,' Lucia continued, slowly. 'We too would be very interested to hear about your proposal. All of our clients are people who come here and stay locally or at the resort, but no one knows of us before they get here. We would love to be able to tell the story of our restaurant and perhaps be part of the reason people come to a place such as this . . . '

'Yes, I know what you mean,' Lily said, her mind racing wildly. 'You would prefer to be part of the decision for people to choose Ischia, instead of just a happy coincidence.'

'Yes, exactly! When you are ready to share some information with us, please do. I think that we would really love to be a part of this. *Salute!*' With a smile, she raised her glass to toast them.

'*Salute!*' the girls replied in unison, clinking all seven glasses together over the centre of the table and toasting yet another great Italian meal.

Chapter Nineteen

The shuttle pulled up in front of the resort at five thirty p.m., allowing just enough time for the thirty-minute journey to the vineyard. As the five girls made their way towards the shuttle, Lily nudged Dee.

'Look who it is!' she whispered loudly. 'It's the American from last night . . . the mushroom guy!'

'The who?' Dee asked, turning to look in the same direction as Lily. 'Oh Christ, not the two from the last night. Are they staying here?'

'I guess so, and it looks like they are taking the shuttle with us, too.'

Morgan followed their line of sight and rolled her eyes. 'No one speak to me on this bus. I refuse to get dragged into a conversation about America while I'm running away from my life for a week on this Italian island,' she said, climbing up into the bus.

'Morgan . . . no offence or anything, but what exactly are you wearing?' Lily asked, trying not to smile behind her sunglasses.

'I'm calling it my midlife-crisis jacket,' Morgan replied

confidently, referring to the three-quarter-length white faux-leather jacket with silver shoulder studs.

'Are they shoulder pads?' Ellen asked, with a giggle. 'I haven't seen those since my Madonna-worshipping days.'

'They are and I love them. They make me feel more powerful.'

'Good for you, darling. I wish I were a little bolder. I'm always so bloody conservative,' Kitty sighed. 'I could be mistaken for a Laura Ashley advert in this dress,' she added, referring to her broderie anglaise Reiss midi dress.

'I don't know who that is, but at least you are tall and skinny. I'm short and I feel like the shoulder pads might catch people's eyes and keep them from wandering down the rest of my body,' Morgan replied with a grimace.

'Well, they catch your eye all right, my love, but I'm not sure that it's for all the right reasons,' Dee said, grinning. 'Now come on, sit down!'

The small crowd was silent for the first few minutes of the drive, until the American couple began whispering loudly in the seat in front of them.

'Ruby, what are you doing?'

'I'm checking my Facebook,' the woman whispered in her slow southern drawl. 'I want to see if Delilah has put on any weight since she got married. She's been on a diet for the past two years since her husband ran off, determined to bag herself another rich husband.'

'What does that have to do with her putting on weight?' he asked, in a conspiratorially loud whisper.

'Well, I reckon now that she's remarried, she won't have to try as hard any more, and she always did have a fondness for pie ... hmm ... how do you zoom in to these things?'

she asked, moving her fingers around the screen. 'There you go,' she drawled, holding her phone up for her husband to see. 'I mean, at the most basic level she needs a bigger size in that dress.' She sounded quite pleased with her discovery.

'Ellen, what on earth is *wrong* with you?' Kitty hissed. 'It's like sitting next to a jack rabbit.'

'I'm wired.'

'What do you mean you're wired?'

'I drank all the little fun-size cans of Coke in the minibar in my room.'

'You did *what*? Why on earth would you do that?'

'I got back from the pool and I was melting from the heat, so I thought one little can would be nice, but it was tiny, and I never get to drink Coke at home. The kids are nuts enough as it is, so I can't bring that stuff into the house. Then I had a second and then it was like I was possessed ... I couldn't get enough of it, so I drank all six.'

'Good Lord, you need a chunk of bread or something to soak up all that wanton sugar. Now sit still, for crying out loud.'

The shuttle bus made its way up the hill towards Forio, with striking views of the sea on the right. They continued in the direction of Sant'Angelo before suddenly making a sharp left turn up a steep country road. The rough stone road wound its way up and around a series of tight bends, the sea falling further and further below them with every turn. As the bus continued uphill, they could see the town of Forio receding from sight far below. The bus continued on to a narrow country lane and they were suddenly surrounded by long lines of lush green vines, stepped into the hill in perfect symmetry.

The bus eventually came to a stop in front of tall wrought-iron double gates. Beyond the gates lay an enormous circular stone terrace surrounded by rows of vines as far as the eye could see. The land continued up behind the vineyard to precipitous heights while below them the bay of Citara sparkled, reflecting the sun high overhead. Sailing boats passed by on the horizon as if in slow motion and, with the height of their vantage point, they had a 360-degree view of the island. Even the birds were below them as they watched hawks swoop and hover over the vines in search of their prey.

The house of Casa D'Ambra was an imposing two-storey building with a flat roof, characteristic of most of the buildings in Ischia. Lily stood on the edge of a vast lawn, adjacent to the terrace, transfixed by the scene in front of her. Two hundred or so elegantly dressed guests, all of whom were dressed in white, mingled and chatted amicably, the sounds of laughter and the clinking of glasses filling the hot summer air. Three outdoor wine bars had been set up alongside long tables covered with crisp white linen tablecloths. Black-tie waiters walked the grounds, some offering platters of tiny *aperitivi* and others trays of chilled Frassitelli, the vineyard's award-winning white wine.

Lily turned and plucked a glass of cold, white wine from a passing tray, before realising that the girls had wandered off and she was now alone. She scanned the crowd but could see no sign of Antonio and immediately felt an involuntary nervous swell in her belly at the thought of initiating a conversation about marketing the resort. She still hadn't figured out how she might do it, or what exactly she would say, but she had been able to think of nothing else all night, so she had to find out if the notion even had any merit.

It was easy to lose someone in the crowd when everyone dressed alike, but Lily figured that the girls were certain to be at one of the outdoor bars. She spotted Morgan's shoulder pads in the distance and made her way gingerly across the lawn towards them, her heels sinking into the grass.

'Should have worn wedges, dammit,' she muttered, trying to walk on her tippy toes.

'Certainly not like any party I've been to before,' Ellen sighed, as Lily stood alongside her. 'Definitely no bouncy castle, and I doubt there'll be chocolate Rice Krispie cakes. Look at these women. Do you think they've ever had a sandwich or a couple of potatoes?'

'Probably not,' Dee said, with a grimace.

'I still don't understand how Italian women are so thin, you know . . . with all the great food that they have here – the bread, the pasta, the pizza . . . God, I'd give anything to look like that,' said Ellen, eyeing up two tall, slender Italian women in front of her.

'Kate Moss famously said, "Nothing tastes as good as skinny feels,"' Kitty said, holding her wine glass to her lips. 'I tend to agree with her.'

'Well, that's because you're as skinny as Kate Moss, Kitty. The rest of us normal humans will never look like that, no matter how hard we try,' Ellen retorted. 'And to be honest, if looking like that means never having a sandwich or a potato again, then I'm not sure it's worth it.'

'Wow! Who is the siren in the red dress?' Morgan asked, pointing to the far side of the lawn. 'And what is she doing wearing red?'

Lily turned to see who Morgan was referring to. It was impossible to miss her. She wore a high-collared dress that fell to her ankles, belted at the waist with a wide, flowing skirt. A daring slit cut to her upper thigh, which flashed into view as she moved through the crowd. Her dark hair was piled loosely on top of her head, and spectacular teardrop diamond earrings flashed in the sunlight.

'Oscar de la Renta earrings,' Kitty whispered. 'I'd know them anywhere.'

'Wait! There are two of them!' Ellen shrieked, pointing at another brunette in a long, strappy red satin dress. 'My God, she's divine, too.'

'They must be the two sisters ... the ones who own this vineyard,' Lily said, gaping at the second woman dressed in red. 'How cool to host a white party and show up wearing red. That's deadly! I'd love to be that brave.'

'I'd love to be that interesting. Imagine owning your own vineyard,' Ellen said, her eyes following the two women as they made their way through the crowd.

'I assumed that people who worked in vineyards would be earthy sorts, in dungarees and wellies, with scratched-up hands from the vines and dirt under their nails,' Lily said. 'I can't see these two getting stuck in the bushes.'

'Well, they probably hire people for that part of it, to be fair,' Dee said. 'Either that or they do dungarees by day and satin dresses by night. Maybe they're dying to get out of the bushes and the dungarees. Jesus, those earrings could start a fire, the way they're flashing.'

'I'm telling you – Oscar de la Renta. She has good taste, I'll give her that,' Kitty said admiringly. 'You see, travel really does broaden the mind. Here we are in a vineyard owned and run by two women, surrounded by all this elegance at the top of a hill, on an island we didn't know existed six months ago. Speaking of which, is anyone up for a trip later this year?' Kitty sipped her glass of wine.

'You do realise that we are currently *on* a trip, don't you?' Morgan asked, sarcastically.

Kitty rolled her eyes. 'Don't be silly. This is a wedding week, it's different. I'm talking about a week in Morocco later this year, maybe around November when it starts to get cold and miserable in London.'

'I don't think you understand just how crap American holidays *are* exactly. I have ten days for the year. This is it for me,' Dee said.

'I run my own business. I don't get any. This is it for me for the year, too,' Morgan chipped in. 'Where is that waiter? That wine is divine and I'm dry.'

'In another life, before I got laid off and realised that I'm on the express train to financial ruin, I'd have gone in a heartbeat,' said Lily. 'Essaouira is on my list.'

'Ess ... what? Are you just making up random sounds or is that an actual place?' Ellen asked, sucking down the end of her glass.

'Are you joking?'

'No, I never heard of ... whatever you said the place was called.'

'Essaouira. It's in Morocco, on the coast. It's meant to be a real fisherman type of village, less touristy than Marrakech, so more ... real. I've seen photos and read about it in a few magazines. It looks fabulous and it's all the rage right now as an under-the-radar sort of destination.'

'Oh right. Glendalough is on my list. It's the next village

over. Supposed to be less touristy, more real . . . very under the radar, too,' Ellen replied, rolling her eyes as she did so.

'Sorry, Ellen,' Kitty said, putting her arm around her friend. 'I keep forgetting that you are financially responsible for five other people.'

'Six,' Ellen corrected her. 'Don't forget about the husband who decided to move to the country to write his novel. My God, is this how you all live while I'm back in Ireland with five kids? I mean, am I imagining it, or is this just unreal?'

'Certainly not how I spend my nights, that's for sure,' Morgan said, waving at the passing waiter. 'I'm usually at home with a stack of casework. This is the first European vacation I've taken in years, not counting a couple of trips to Ireland to see Dee's family. I had forgotten just how amazing Italy was.'

'Okay, I'm going to see if I can talk to the sisters about this Ischia website idea before I have too much to drink and lose my nerve.'

'I'll go with you,' Ellen volunteered.

The two girls wandered through the crowd, arm in arm, picking up another glass of wine from a passing waiter as they strolled. The crowd appeared to be mostly Italian, but they could hear the odd German or Dutch accent; neither of them could tell the two apart, but they decided it had to be one or the other.

'Hang on, let's go up here to the vines for a minute. I've never seen one up close,' said Ellen, turning in the direction of the vineyard that ran alongside the main house. 'I just drink their offspring. Sounds kind of sadistic, doesn't it?'

Lily stopped and grabbed her arm. 'Look! Is that her, do you think?' she hissed.

'Is who who? Who are you talking about?' Ellen followed Lily's stare towards a small cluster of people. One of them, a tall brunette in a simple, white satin maxi dress, stood with her arm draped casually over the shoulder of a man in a white linen suit. He laughed at something she said and, turning to face her, Ellen could see his face in profile. 'Is that Matt?'

'Yes,' Lily said quietly. 'Is that his *amore*, do you think? You know, the one he's always on the phone to? The one who was with him at the restaurant the other night? It looks like it could be her, doesn't it?'

Ellen stood silently, squinting at the group in the distance. 'Dunno . . . it's hard to tell from over here.'

Though she didn't like to admit it, Lily was more disappointed than she'd thought she'd be. 'Well, just as well I didn't throw myself at him. Imagine how mortified I'd be right now if I had.'

'You don't know the circumstances,' Ellen said, turning to look at Lily. 'Anyway, it's probably for the best. The last thing you need right now is another man in the picture.'

'Yes, no . . . you're absolutely right. It's nothing . . . just a turn of phrase. Well, anyway, I doubt that she's his sister, judging by the way she's dangling off him.'

'Yeah, she's like a Christmas-tree decoration, hanging off him like that,' Ellen said, staring at her over the top of her wine glass. 'I dunno, I did think he was into you, especially that day on the boat, and I'm usually good at reading people. The way he looked at you was kind of intense, but what do I know?'

'Well, that looks intense enough to me,' Lily replied, nodding in their direction.

'What looks intense?' Morgan asked, as she stood alongside them.

'Matt and the brunette bombshell over there,' Lily said quietly.

'That? Oh, Lily, you're better off, honey. Holiday romances might sell books and movies, but they rarely end well in real life and you don't need the complication right now. You've got other shit to figure out, including what to do with this idea of yours and your life in general. Just be glad you didn't jump into anything messy,' Morgan said sternly. 'Honestly, go find those women and pitch them your idea. Focus on that. Everything else will eventually sort itself out . . . things usually do. You'll see.'

'Look! There's Antonio. Come on, Lily Ryan. No time like the present.'

'Okay,' Lily replied, a flush of nervous energy surging through her again.

'Come on,' Kitty said firmly, as she linked her arm through Lily's. 'I don't need any excuse to get up close to that man. I can be your motivation or your crutch to lean on, or whatever.' She tugged Lily in Antonio's direction.

'*Buona sera*,' Antonio said, as he kissed them both on each cheek. 'You are enjoying the party, no?'

'It's divine!' Kitty replied, with a smile. 'It's so kind of you to have invited us.'

'You both look wonderful. I am glad that you had packed something white in your suitcase.'

'No, actually. I'll have you know that this cost me a small fortune at the boutique in your hotel this morning!'

'Well then, I am glad that we could be of service,' he replied with a wink.

'And Lily, I would like to hear more about your idea to promote Ischia. We didn't have time to talk properly the last evening.'

'Yes, of course. Well, I was thinking that what you needed was a social media campaign to tell your story, the story of Ischia.' She took a deep breath and continued. 'Because today people respond more than ever to stories. You know – more than just ads. They no longer want to be sold to, they want to be included in the conversation, they want to feel like they are part of something, part of the story of a place.'

She stood up taller. Antonio was staring at her and listening intently. He stood silently with his arms folded at the chest, his right hand to his mouth.

'People value experiences over products today,' she continued, 'which is why ads that are selling something tend to fall short of expectations. When I'm writing to sell a product, I don't talk about the "what", I talk about the "why" and I talk about the benefits. Like ... why should you care about this product, why does this product even exist, why will it make your life better? So, if you just stick a photo of a swimming pool on social media it will most likely be scrolled past. If you stick a photo of a model lying by the pool, it will definitely be scrolled past, especially by all the women scrolling, because she's just going to piss them off. They can't see themselves in her, which means that they can't see themselves here.' She paused momentarily, and cleared her throat. 'Your story, or your message, has to resonate. You have to connect with your audience and pull them a little closer. If they like what they read then they'll like or follow your brand, or they'll subscribe to your newsletter, and that gives you even more ways to connect with your audience. Today, you have to build a relationship with the customer before they will part with their cash, so it's your job to give them the reasons why.'

Antonio was drumming his fingers on his bottom lip. 'Yes, I like this. I like what you are saying . . . I don't know much about social media or marketing. I'm a developer, an investor. Okay, I tell you what. When do you leave Ischia?'

'Sunday,' Lily replied.

'Okay, you must go to Procida to meet with my business partner,' he said, gesturing with both hands. 'He leaves tomorrow afternoon on a business trip. He owns a luxury hotel there and several restaurants and together we are developing a new property in Campania. He is one of my closest friends, and he is one of the smartest businessmen that I know, but he is a cynic. His grandfather was in the Mafia and they built their business the old-fashioned way. Now, of course, his business is legitimate, but he does not spend money easily. If you can convince him that this is a good idea, then I will agree to it. I am tired of hearing people say that they have never heard of us or never heard of Ischia. I think it is time for the world to know Ischia, to know that we are here for them. That they can come and enjoy the beauty, the romance, the adventure . . . I apologise, I am talking too much! This happens every time I speak of Ischia.'

'No need to apologise. It's clear that you are very passionate – about Ischia, that is,' Kitty said, in a poor attempt to be coy.

'Yes, I am. But I am Italian, after all,' he replied, shrugging both shoulders as he grinned at her.

Lily looked from one to the other of them and shook her head slowly, almost imperceptibly, wondering at what point in the conversation she had become invisible. She marvelled at how Kitty did it. She was blatantly flirting with Antonio and she could feel the tension between them and dared not say a word for fear she would disperse it. Kitty was so comfortable in herself, she thought, as she watched the two of them quietly. It was clear that Kitty was attracted to him and wasn't afraid to show it, and Lily was once again in awe of her confidence and easy manner, in direct contrast with her own clumsy, awkward way.

Lily tuned back into the conversation as Antonio pulled his mobile phone from his pocket and made a call, firing off a rapid stream of Italian. He paused, taking the phone down from his face.

'*Allora* ... tomorrow morning at eleven o'clock you can be in Procida, yes?'

'Yes,' Lily said, nodding rapidly, even though she had no idea how she would get there.

Antonio hung up the call and nodded to Lily. 'Good. He will meet you at La Lampara tomorrow morning. The ferry at ten o'clock will get you there in plenty of time. It is only twenty minutes to Procida. Now, if you will excuse me, I see some other guests here. *Buona sera, signore*,' he said with a smile.

'Honestly, I feel like I have a fever or some sort of vortex raging inside me,' said Kitty. 'What *is* it about Italy? It gets under your skin and through your pores and everything is heightened and extreme. I don't think I've ever had such an erotic conversation with my clothes on—'

'Kitty! What am I going to do?'

241

Kitty rolled her eyes. 'About what?'

'His partner! He's ex-Mafia and cynical but if he thinks it's a good idea then Antonio will sign up. Oh my God!'

'Darling, his grandfather was Mafia, that's all in the past.'

'I won't sleep the night. I'm so excited! What will I say to him?'

'Exactly what you said to Antonio. You were fabulous!'

'What's happening? What have I missed?'

'Ellen! You won't believe what just happened! I'm going to Procida in the morning to pitch Antonio's business partner. If he approves the idea, then Antonio said he'll do it. He'll be a client. My first client!'

'Oh my God. This is very exciting and mildly terrifying at the same time! God, my life is so boring by comparison,' Ellen said, shaking her head.

The unmistakable clinking of metal on glass caught their attention and they all turned to face in the direction of the Casa D'Ambra villa. The crowd slowly hushed and gathered in front of the imposing building. The two sisters stood together, politely waiting for silence.

'They're fabulous, aren't they?' Ellen whispered loudly to Dee as she stood alongside her.

'Yep, and imagine they make wine for a living,' Dee replied, nodding in agreement.

The sisters made a short speech in Italian, generating much laughter and applause from the audience. Lily stood, rapt, as she watched them speak to the crowd with such ease, wondering if she could ever display such poise and exude such confidence. She had no idea what they were saying but envied them the graceful way they delivered their speech.

There was a momentary pause and the sisters pointed towards the back of the crowd. Suddenly, Lily heard one of them say Matt's name loudly, followed by more Italian and even more applause. Matt made his way to the front of the crowd, where he was hugged warmly by each of the sisters. Smiling widely, he took the microphone and gave a short speech in Italian.

Lily scanned the crowd for the brunette. She stood, beaming widely, her palms flat together at her chin, and her eyes fixed on Matt.

'The Christmas decoration looks very proud,' Lily said, nudging Dee.

'Do you have any idea what's going on?' Dee whispered.

'No. A lot of *grazie* though, so he's being thanked for something.'

Ellen leaned around Morgan's shoulder, whispering loudly: 'I feel really dim right now. What's Matt doing up there?'

'No idea,' Dee muttered.

'It's like we're at the Italian Oscars, only we can't understand anything they're saying. I'm feeling really excluded right now, like I should be happy for him or something, but I can't because I don't know what's happening.'

'Don't worry, the Christmas decoration looks happy enough for both of you,' Lily said, grudgingly.

'The what? Oh, the *amore*?' Ellen turned to look back in her direction. 'I have four children at home, so I know what a fake smile looks like. She looks bored to me ... still hot, though, in fairness to her.'

'You have *five* children,' Lily said, trying to suppress a giggle.

'Oh shit! I keep forgetting about the new one. God, that's so bad, isn't it?'

As the speeches came to an end, the audience applauded politely before dispersing towards the three outdoor wine bars.

'Yep. No fucking idea what all that was about,' Dee announced, turning to face the girls. 'But whatever it was it looked like it deserves a toast. Cheers.'

'It's quite a party, right?'

They heard Matt's voice come from behind them. He reached out and put his right arm around Lily's shoulder. She froze instantly and held her breath involuntarily. He extended his left arm and did the same with Ellen.

Lily felt herself deflate a little. What was that exactly? she wondered. One second it feels like he's putting an arm around my shoulder and the next it looks like it was just a slow-motion group hug. You're such an idiot, Lily, she thought, feeling her face burn.

She stared at the ground, willing herself to stop blushing and hoping that he hadn't noticed. One-one-thousand, two-one-thousand, three-one-thousand, she repeated over and over in her head until she could feel the heat in her face start to retreat.

'Your date is like a Victoria's Secret model, Matt,' Dee said. 'I'm guessing that she's Italian?'

'My what? Oh right,' he said, 'Yeah, she's Italian all right but "Victoria's Secret model" might make her laugh. She's a barrister.'

'Give me a break. Of course, she is,' Ellen said, rolling her eyes.

Matt laughed and squeezed Ellen's shoulder. 'And she's definitely not my date.'

Dee laughed out loud. 'Matt, she's been glued to you all evening.'

'She's my sister-in-law,' Matt replied, his expression serious.

'Your sister-in-law?' Dee and Morgan repeated simultaneously.

Lily turned around to face him.

'Yes, well, I suppose ex-sister-in-law, really, but anyway, she recently went through a very nasty divorce and even though she looks like a million dollars, she has the confidence of a dollar bill. The guy really did a job on her. Miserable insect.'

Dee looked from Lily to Morgan, unsure what to say next. 'How could you look like that and not be overflowing with confidence?'

Matt shrugged. 'Everyone's got something, Dee.'

Matt didn't offer any more information following the sister-in-law revelation and Lily grew quiet, her mind racing with thoughts.

Kitty, ever observant, didn't take long to notice just how suddenly reticent she had become and subtly pulled Lily to one side. 'What is it? What's going on in that head of yours?'

'Nothing ... I don't know ...' Lily hesitated. 'It's just that ... all this, you know?'

'All what, exactly? The fact that Matt has a past? Big deal. Or is this more uncertainty about your future?'

'Well, both in a way. I mean, look at us here tonight, at this party. It's fabulous! And maybe now this business idea ... I mean, how cool is that? I know it will be a lot of hard work, but I could totally reinvent myself and actually do something that I love, something that means something beyond just a pay cheque for a change! I mean, if I had . . . or if I hadn't . . . I don't know, Kitty . . . I'm not making any sense.'

'You're wondering if you've made a mistake letting Peter go.'

Lily didn't reply, she just stared at her friend and shrugged. 'Do you think I made a mistake? Isn't a bird in the hand worth two in the bush? Was I stupid to throw Peter away just over the baby conversation? I mean, look at all of this! I don't want a baby here! I could have had all of this and had him too. It would have been perfect,' she said, gesturing widely.

Kitty raised both eyebrows. 'I've always said that he could give you a fabulous life. Not that you can't create your own, but let's face it, the man is fabulously wealthy so it would be a hell of a kickstart to a glorious life together. Look, you were perfectly happy until you tried to figure out all the angles and peer into the future. No one can predict the future, Lily. You've got to start living life your way, and for today, not for what you think you might want some day in the future.'

'I know. I got carried away when I got here with notions of a gorgeous American showing up and being everything that Peter wasn't and living the dream. But that was just a stupid holiday fantasy thing and I know it's probably just the rebound talking, having broken up with Peter and . . . shit . . . have I made a huge mistake, Kitty?'

'There's nothing wrong with a fantasy, or a fling, but you can't fix everything at the same time. You need to focus on your work and getting the financial stuff back on track.

Then, when you're back in New York, see what happens with Peter.'

'Kitty, he cancelled my flights and basically cut me out of his life once I'd made my dramatic exit. I think I need to accept that it's over. For better or for worse, that ship has sailed and we're done.'

'Oh, stop wallowing. Peter adored you. Anyway, you can deal with that when you're back in your real life in New York – for better or for worse. This isn't real life. This is a super-sexed, highly stylised version of life. It's impossible not to get carried away.'

Kitty was right. This wasn't real life, it was a fantasy, it was a week away that had given her some perspective, and she vowed to enjoy the wedding and her last two days on this glorious Italian island before returning to New York to pick up the pieces.

They made their way back to the girls, where Matt and Morgan were exchanging stories about New York.

'Are you all set for your big meeting tomorrow?' Matt asked.

'I'm not sure. I mean, I think so, but he sounds a bit intimidating and there's a lot riding on the meeting. I really need Antonio to get on board with the idea. He'd totally be an anchor client, but I guess it's up to this guy in Procida to decide that.'

'Hmm,' Matt replied, running his right hand over his chin. 'I know Lorenzo. He's a character but he's a good guy. He spent twenty years in London. I think he was in banking. Apparently he's a very shrewd businessman.'

'Great, now I'm even more nervous,' Lily said, rolling her eyes.

'I think he's a bit of a poet or a writer or something. I have this half-baked recollection of him talking about something literary . . . anyway, I can't remember, but I think if you talk to him like you talked to me that time – you know, about the sounds of breakfast – then he'll get it.'

'You remember that?' Lily asked, surprised.

'How could I not? I was barely awake and able to speak English and there you were talking about the sounds of breakfast like it was the most normal thing in the world. You actually made me stop and think *literally* about the sounds of breakfast. Normally I'd have had a coffee and been on my way for the day, but you were able to describe this really simple, ordinary moment as something remarkable. That, my dear, is a talent.'

Lily gave a small, involuntary smile, trying not to blush with the compliment.

'Okay, I've gotta run,' said Matt. 'My Victoria's Secret model is glaring at me. I think she needs to be rescued from the mayor. The man sure does like to talk about himself. *Arrivederci*, ladies!'

He turned to leave, then hesitated and turned back to Lily. 'Oh, and good luck tomorrow. Not that you'll need it – I know he'll be as entranced as I was that day.'

A passing waiter with a tray of white wine paused in front of the girls. As they each plucked a glass from the tray, Dee stood squarely in front of Lily.

'You cannot seriously tell me that you still think he's not into you. Even *I* felt that!'

Ellen turned to look after him. 'My God, he's hot in a quiet, brooding kind of way, isn't he? And we know that the Christmas decoration isn't the girlfriend . . .'

'Yeah, but that still doesn't solve the problem. Just because it isn't her, there's still an *amore* that he fawns over.'

'But she wasn't here tonight, now, was she?' Dee said slowly. 'So, one still has hope. Out of sight is out of mind . . . isn't that what they say?'

'Okay, you guys, this crowd is starting to disperse, and I hate to be the last one to leave a party. It's shows a real lack of class,' Morgan said, tipping back her glass of wine.

'Yeah, I have to get back to the hotel to rehearse for tomorrow. I'm going to run to the bathroom. I'll see you guys at the bus,' Lily said, distractedly.

Lily replayed the conversation with Matt in her head as she made her way across the lawn. The sun had set and a series of antique, rust-covered lanterns spilled silver light across the property, leading them from the lawn back to the main house and the piazza beyond. Just as she reached the edge of the lawn, a little girl dressed in a white linen sundress and white leather sandals raced passed her through the crowd.

'Papà! Papà!' she shrieked excitedly as she ran through the crowd, her chestnut-coloured hair bouncing down over her shoulders.

Lily smiled and turned her head to watch the little girl, who couldn't have been more than four years old. She was scooped up by a man in a white linen blazer, his back turned to Lily.

Adorable, she thought with a smile. He smothered her with a bear hug before spinning her around in a circle.

Lily froze to the spot, her jaw dropping ever so slightly as the girl's father came into view.

It was Matt.

Momentarily unable to move, her mind went blank, and her heart hammered rapidly in her chest. She could feel a wave of heat move up through her body, culminating in a flush over her neck and cheeks.

'*Andiamo*,' Lily heard him say, as he settled the little girl on his hip.

'*Andiamo, Papà*,' the little girl chanted, her arms clasped tightly around his neck.

He turned and caught Lily's eye. Hesitating just for a moment, he made his way towards her, a sheepish smile on his face.

'Hi.'

'Hi,' Lily replied, her face registering something between surprise and confusion.

The little girl tilted her head to one side as she looked at her. 'What's your name? My name is Elena,' she said in a soft American accent.

'Oh,' Lily said, turning to face her. 'My name is Lily.'

'I have a friend called Lily.'

'You do?'

'Yes, she's in my class. She has a puppy. Do you have a puppy?'

'Um ... no, I don't.'

'Why not?' the little girl asked, staring intently at Lily.

'Well ... um ... I live in a very small apartment, so I really don't have room for a puppy.'

'Oh. *Papà* says I can have one when I'm bigger. Right, *Papà*?'

'Right, when you're bigger.'

'So, this is your *papà*?' Lily asked, raising both eyebrows as she looked at Matt.

'Yep, I'm *Papà*.'

'Wow, well, that's news. Funny how that hasn't come up at all,' Lily said, her expression blank. 'That's a very pretty dress, Elena.'

'Thanks,' Elena said, running her hand across the piece of ribbon around her waist. 'It has a bow, see?'

'I see that. You're lucky. I wish I had a bow.'

Elena beamed up at her. Then her head tilted up to look at Matt. '*Papà*, can I have an ice cream? Please!'

'No, it's way too late for ice cream. Didn't you just have dinner at Mia's house?'

'Yeah. Can we go now?'

'Yes, we're leaving in just a minute. Listen ...' Matt said, standing Elena down on the grass. 'This is complicated. I—'

'I'm sure it is,' Lily said, nodding. 'Hey, you don't owe me any explanations. Anyway, I've got to run. The girls are waiting.'

She bent down to Elena's height. 'It was nice to meet you, Elena.'

Elena's face lit up with a smile. 'Bye,' she said, with a wave that waggled her entire arm.

Matt opened his mouth to speak but Lily just smiled and waved. 'See you later, bye.'

Forgetting entirely about her need to find a bathroom, Lily strode quickly across the pebbled driveway. Her mind was flooded with questions as she made her way to the periphery of the vineyard.

How could he be a daddy?

How come this hadn't come up before? Why would he not have mentioned having a daughter?

What about Mommy? Is there a mommy?

Is Matt married? Divorced? Does Elena live with her? With him? Where has she been all this time?

What about all the time we've spent together? Does this mean that I really know nothing about him?

Isn't an omission as bad as a lie? Then again, does he really owe me any explanation?

God, did I totally overreact and act hysterically? I just cut him off rudely and left. Shit, I didn't even give him a chance to explain . . .

The girls were staring up at the dark, cloudless sky. One sole, blazing star looked like a splash of silver paint on a dark indigo canvas.

'That's bright,' Dee said. 'You don't see stars like that in New York.'

'Okay, you each get a wish, okay?' Ellen said, her head tilted up.

Lily glanced at Ellen, wondering what she should wish for.

You can't even decide what to wish for, Lily. Maybe that's what you should wish for – some clarity. In fact, clarity would be a definite improvement on where you're at right now. What if the baby conversation hadn't blown up your relationship? Would you want to go back and wish for 'happy ever after' with Peter? What about Matt? Was that all just in your head? What about his little girl, Elena, and what just happened? Would you wish that you weren't so attracted to him in the first place?

'Here goes. Ready?' Ellen asked, her voice shattering Lily's ruminations. 'Star light, star bright, you're the first star I see tonight. I wish I may, I wish I might. Get this wish I wish tonight.'

'That's sweet. Do you do that with your kids?' Lily asked, grateful for the distraction as the shuttle rolled slowly up the hill and came to a stop in front of them.

'Yep, all five of them,' Ellen grinned, as she clambered up the two steps and slid the door closed.

Chapter Twenty

Although it was only nine a.m. it was already blazing hot on the terrace. The morning air was still and thick, without even the whisper of a breeze. Humidity seemed to hang, as if suspended in mid-air, cloaking everything in a thin veil of moisture. Franco stood staring up at the charcoal-grey, ominous clouds that swirled slowly overhead, as if reading the sky.

'Ah, *buongiorno*, Signora LeeLee!' he said, as Lily dragged a chair back from the table to join Dee and Morgan.

'Just a cappuccino for me please, Franco,' Lily said.

'*Va bene*, Signora LeeLee.'

'Honey, can you please not drag that?' Morgan asked, her chin resting on one hand. 'It feels like it's scraping the inside of my brain.'

'What's up with you this morning?'

'Don't ask,' Dee said, trying to suppress a grin. 'She made the tragic error of hitting the minibar after we got back from dinner last night.'

'Jesus, Morgan. That's like Drinking 101. What were you thinking? You never touch the minibar at that hour.'

'Save it, oh wise one. I don't need the lecture this morning,' Morgan replied glumly.

Franco returned with a cappuccino for Lily. 'Last night we had a storm,' he announced. 'But better that we have this weather today and not tomorrow, no? Tomorrow everything will be okay. Perfect for a wedding party.'

'Damn right,' Morgan replied, hiding behind her oversized sunglasses.

'The party at the vineyard – how was it? *Elegante, no?*'

'It was fabulous, Franco, but I'm not feeling too *elegante* myself today. This storm has come at a good time because I can see a post-breakfast nap in my future.'

'Ah, *signora*, you have had too much wine at the party?'

'Yeah, I'm my own worst enemy, Franco. I forget that I'm not a young woman any more.'

'*Non è vero!* This is not true. You are young, but when you have too much wine, you don't sleep so good. *Ma, non preoccuparti.* Don't worry, Signora Morgan. I know what you need!'

Franco disappeared from the table, returning a minute later with a colourful bottle.

'*Allora.* Fernet-Branca. Is umm ... *come si dice* ... how do you say ... *un amaro* ... a bitter! *Sì!* And it has twenty-seven herbs and spices. You put it in your espresso and *ecco* ... like magic! You will feel like dancing again.'

'Whatever you say, Franco. Magic sounds good right now, so I'm game.'

'What's the story with this storm?' Dee asked, glaring at the dark grey horizon. Not a single boat had ventured out yet this morning, leaving the bay empty, like a blank canvas. High winds had raged across the south of Italy in the wee hours of the morning and huge quantities of rain had been dumped on the island, rendering everything damp and steamy in the morning heat.

'No, don't worry. This storm it will be finished soon. The worst of it was last night while you sleep. Now, the sky, she is still angry, but the storm has passed. By ten o'clock the sun will come back again. Will be perfect weather for your party tomorrow night. *Non preoccuparti!*'

'God, I had such a crap sleep last night. Tossed and turned for hours and then crazy dreams all night. I feel withered,' Lily said, stifling a yawn. 'I'm going to be so unimpressive today.'

'That's the spirit,' Dee said, scooping out the last of her cappuccino foam. 'Can't beat a positive mental attitude before a big meeting.'

'God,' Lily moaned, resting her forehead on the table. 'What am I even doing? This guy is going to see right through me.'

Lily drank her cappuccino in three sips and made her way through the lobby to drop her key at reception. She stood waiting for Marco to finish with the call that he was on, double checking to make sure she had her wallet in her bag.

'*Buongiorno*, Signora LeeLee, how can I help you?' Marco said, beaming from ear to ear with a smile.

'Oh, umm . . . I just wanted to drop off my key. I'm going to Procida this morning and I need to get the shuttle to the marina, please.'

'Ah, but you cannot go to Procida this morning, Signora LeeLee. The ferry, she is cancelled this morning, because of the storm,' Marco said, gesturing to the still grey clouds hovering ominously outside.

'What? What do you mean the ferry is cancelled? I have to be in Procida at eleven o'clock.'

Marco clasped his hands together and adopted a genuinely sorrowful look on his face. 'Sì . . . but it is not possible this morning. If you wait just two hours, the ferry will start again at noon.'

'But I have a meeting. Antonio set it up,' Lily said, trying to keep hysteria from her voice.

'Ah, Antonio, he set up a meeting for you? Ah, yes, with his partner, no?'

'Yes!'

'Yes . . . but unfortunately the ferry will not run this morning. Do you want me to call his office to say that you will be there later in the afternoon?'

'No, that won't work. He is leaving later this morning on a business trip. This was my last chance to see him.'

'Let me call his office. I will check,' Marco said kindly.

'Shit!' she muttered quietly, putting her head down on her hands. She was exhausted, hadn't slept enough, had skipped breakfast and now was going to miss her meeting.

'Sorry, I didn't mean to eavesdrop, but we were just leaving . . . '

Lily turned to see Matt standing alongside her. Surprised as she was to see him, she couldn't help but think how good he looked in his navy shorts, white linen shirt and navy New York Yankees baseball cap. He was holding Elena by the hand, also dressed in navy and white.

'He's right. The ferry is cancelled this morning. They always do that when there's a storm. They cancel in advance and then it's never as bad as they thought but they can't get back up and running for hours.'

257

Elena waved up at her. 'Hi, this is Peppa,' she said, holding a scraggly-looking pink pig.

'Hi, Elena.' Lily couldn't help but smile at the little girl. 'Hi, Peppa.'

'I can take you if you want. I know this is a big meeting. I can borrow a friend's boat.'

'Can I come too, *Papà*?'

'Maybe, let's see if Lily needs a ride.'

'But if the ferry is cancelled then how can you take a boat out?'

'Lily, look at the sea. Does it look rough to you? They cancel these services ahead of time and then sit drinking coffee for a few hours. It's a bit of time off for them. They don't care. You said you're more of a bathtub boat person, right? So, this is pretty much bathtub boat water. Kind of like the calm after the storm.'

'Oh. But . . . '

'But what?'

'Is there any other way to get there?'

'You mean any other way apart from getting in a boat with me? Probably not at this short notice.'

'Are we going in the boat, *Papà*?' Elena asked, bouncing up and down.

'Let's ask Lily. Are we going in the boat, Lily?'

Marco stood behind the desk at reception and shrugged both shoulders. 'Signora LeeLee, I think you must go,' he said, pointing to his watch.

'Shit,' Lily muttered.

'You said a bad word!'

'Oh sorry,' Lily said, automatically slapping her hand across her mouth. 'Sorry, Elena.' She looked up at Matt.

'Didn't you have plans? You just said you were getting ready to leave.'

'Yes, so we did, and now our plans are to take a boat out for a ride to Procida, right, Elena?'

'Yeah! Boat! Boat!'

'Well, if you think it's safe . . . '

'It's perfectly safe. Do you think I'd be taking my daughter out to sea if there was any danger?'

'No, probably not. Well, I . . . '

'What else can you possibly say to delay this decision?' he asked, a smile forming across his face.

'Boat! Boat!' Elena chanted, twirling round and round.

'Well, as long as it's not too much trouble.'

'This is important, right? Your whole, entire future career and wellbeing might well be hinging on this meeting, right?'

Lily groaned. 'When you put it like that . . . '

'Okay, Elena, *andiamo*! My car is right outside.'

Fifteen minutes later the car pulled up alongside the marina. The boats, moored closely together along the pier, jostled from side to side in the wind that remained, trailing in the aftermath of the storm. By the time they reached the boat, Matt had kicked off his flip-flops. He placed Elena's hand in Lily's before stepping on board.

As Matt pulled the cover off the cockpit, Lily stood admiring the sleek white yacht. The deck was polished teak, and the cushions were navy with a white trim. Matt disappeared down the three steps that led to the interior of the yacht. Lily held tightly to Elena's hand as she peered over the side of the boat. She could make out a small kitchen and a table and chairs below deck and what appeared to be additional rooms beyond it.

'This is stunning,' she said, as Matt reappeared on deck.

'Welcome aboard, ladies! Lily, take off your shoes and toss them into that basket right there,' Matt said, pointing to a neat wicker basket on the deck.

'Do you actually know how to drive something like this?' Lily asked, looking down the length of the boat.

'Sail, Lily,' Matt said, grinning at her. 'Sail, not drive, and yes, I am a qualified sailor. I've taken this beauty out a few times before, so no need to worry. Anyway, we're going with the wind so it will be a smooth ride once we get out around the tip of the island. You guys ready?'

'*Sì, Papà*,' Elena said, lifting the lid of one of the seats and pulling out a life jacket.

'Okay, help me pull up those dock fenders over there.' Matt pointed out the six navy protective cushions extended on ropes over the sides of the boat. 'Just grab the lines and tug them up and tuck them under the lip . . . like so,' he said, as he hauled the first one up and tucked it neatly under the smooth, teak edge. 'I'll get the dock line and we'll be off. He leapt on to the pier, unlooping the dock line from the cleat, and stepped quickly back on to the boat, tossing the line back loosely on to the dock.

'What's the difference between a rope and a line?' Lily asked, hauling the last one on to the boat.

'Nothing, actually, they are the same thing, but as soon as a rope gets on to a boat it becomes a line.'

'What? So, why don't they just call it a rope?' Lily asked, shaking the seawater from her hands.

'Dunno.' Matt shrugged. 'Sailing has its own language. I don't know why, but you have to know the basics.' He made his way towards the helm, instructing the girls to take a seat. 'The wind is still pretty strong. It might be a bit choppy as we make the turn to get around the coast, but once we get to the other side of the island, we'll be completely sheltered from it.'

The marina was quiet except for one other sailing boat that was pulling out from the pier ahead of them. Matt deftly backed the yacht out from the pier and turned to face the open bay. The boat listed from left to right in the swell as they made their way out towards the tip of the island. Small waves slapped against the sides of the boat and the flags whipped furiously in the strong breeze. Lily twisted her long hair into a knot and fastened it at the nape of her neck. Elena sat by her side, pressed up against her, with both hands holding on to her hat. As the boat picked up speed the wind got even stronger and sent misty sprays of salty seawater over the edge towards the girls. Elena squealed in delight and laughed with absolute abandon.

Matt stood barefoot at the hull, his eyes fixed dead ahead towards the bow of the boat, his legs wide apart for balance. Lily watched him capably steer into the wind, his shoulder blades flexing beneath his shirt. He reached up and tugged his baseball cap down tighter over his eyes. He was deeply tanned and she could make out the muscles in his calves and thighs as he flexed with every turn. She could see the side of his face, his expression calm but serious. He appeared to be quite at home as he guided the yacht out to the open sea ahead. They continued out of the bay, hugging the massive rock along the coastline until they reached the westernmost tip of the island. Slowly, Matt made a sweeping turn towards Procida and within seconds the wind had dropped almost entirely. He turned around and smiled at the girls, giving them the thumbs-up sign.

'We're good now! You okay, Elenita?'

They both smiled back at him.

'*Sì, papà*,' Elena said, grinning at him.

'What does Elenita mean?' Lily asked, bending down closer to Elena.

'It's Italian. Elenita is what *Papà* calls me sometimes because I'm still small. It means little Elena.'

'Oh, that's so cute! So, what would my name be?'

Elena frowned slightly and thought about the question. 'Do you mean if you were still small?'

'Yes, I suppose so,' Lily said, laughing. She felt herself relax, not having realised that she had tensed up in the short battle against the wind and the current

'Lilyita,' Elena said, nodding. 'It doesn't sound so good, but that would be your name ... but only if you were still small.'

'Okay, maybe I'm too old for that name.'

'Oh, I know! You could be *amore*! *Papà* calls me *amore* too sometimes.

Lily gasped involuntarily. 'Wait ... *You're* his *amore*?'

'*Sì*.'

'Yes, I've heard him call you that many times. He uses it on the phone, right?'

'Yep,' Elena nodded. 'Do you think Peppa needs a bath?'

'Well, he's pretty grubby looking.'

'Peppa is a *she*.'

'Oh, sorry. I've never met a real pig before.'

'What does "grubby" mean?'

262

'Um, kind of a little bit dirty, but not terribly dirty.'

'She likes to play in mud. So do I.'

'Yeah, me too.'

'You do?' Elena asked, eyeing her sceptically.

'Sure. I used to make mud pies when I was little. Have you ever made mud pies?'

'No. Will you show me?'

'Sure. The next time we find some mud.'

Elena seemed content with that suggestion and turned her attention back to Peppa Pig. Shortly after ten o'clock, just as Franco had predicted, the sun broke through the clouds, casting a warm glow down on them. Lily ran her tongue over her lips, salty from the sea spray.

'It's pretty straightforward from here,' Matt said, turning to face them. 'We'll be in Procida in twenty minutes. Lily, do you want to steer?'

'Yes! I've never driven a boat.'

'Steer, Lily ... you steer a boat, you don't drive it,' Matt said grinning at her. 'Elena, come on up here and sit next to me.'

Lily took up position alongside Matt. He placed Lily's hands at the ten and two position and with one foot pushed her right leg further to the side, widening her stance.

'Balance is important,' he explained, sitting and putting his left arm around Elena. 'You never know when you might run into some unexpected current. Swell from other boats is something you have to watch out for, too, and with your feet further apart you'll be more grounded.'

Tucking Elena back against the cushion, Matt stood up alongside Lily again, his right elbow resting casually against the dashboard. He leaned forward and pointed out a marker on the horizon, instructing Lily to keep the boat pointed towards that spot at all times.

'Okay, Lily. You've got the wheel.'

Once they had made the turn from the bay out into the open sea, they could see the island of Procida in the distance. On the map that Lily had consulted, Procida had been a mere speck, but now it loomed large in front of her, its jagged coastline stretching out for miles in the distance. As she stood, hands firmly gripping the wheel and eyes peeled on the horizon, Matt explained that most visitors to Procida were day trippers. There were no grand hotels on the island and not much by way of tourist attractions. Procida had somewhat of a shabby-chic, lived-in vibe to it and that was part of its charm. It was even more laid back than Ischia and more authentic than elegant but touristy Capri, which was visible in the distance as a meandering lump of rock falling sharply and aggressively down to the sea on one side.

Matt broke the silence first. 'Can we talk for a minute?' he asked, glancing in Elena's direction.

'Matt, honestly there's nothing—'

'Lily, please. Just hear me out.'

She shrugged. 'Okay.'

He shifted closer along the bench towards Lily's post and took a deep breath. 'Elena is four. I haven't lived with her mother in two years. She left . . . ' he hesitated, clearing his throat. 'She left both of us.'

Lily's jaw dropped instinctively as she turned to face him. His expression was emotionless, his eyes not meeting hers.

'Elena's mother is Italian – Roberta. She's from Ischia.

We were together for two years before we had Elena. I always wanted kids, more so than she did. Elena was barely two when ... Roberta came home from work one day and told me that she had met someone else. No explanations, no attempt at reconciliation, nothing. She wasn't even remorseful, to be honest. I was devastated, of course, I never saw it coming, but my heart broke open into tiny pieces for Elena, this beautiful, happy little baby girl who wanted nothing more than to be loved back by the two people she loved most in the world. And then all of a sudden one of them was gone, of her own free will. Just one week after she came home and confessed everything, she walked out the door and never came back to that house.'

Lily glanced from her point of navigation ahead to Matt and back again.

'To make things worse, I had quit my big job on Madison Avenue and started my own agency just two years before that. The hours were long, and I worked my ass off, but Roberta grew disenchanted and started seeing someone else. They say that there are always signs – you know, when you look back – that you should have known, should have guessed, but honestly to this day I can't see a single one of them. I was completely blindsided. I had no family in New York, and I knew that I couldn't work and take care of Elena at the same time. She had just lost her mother, so the last thing I wanted to do was dump her into full-time childcare, so I rented out the apartment, packed up our stuff and came here, to Ischia, to Roberta's family.'

He looked up at Lily and gave a small smile. 'It was a

fucking nightmare. Most of her family, her mother in particular, blamed me for her leaving. They weren't all bad, a few of them were actually really kind, but most of them blamed me. They said it must have been my fault.'

'They blamed you for her going off with another man? That's ridiculous.'

Matt's smile drew into a thin line. 'No ... she left me for another woman, actually. That's what they blamed me for. They said I mustn't have been enough of a man. Her mother in particular, she still blames me to this day. I think it was just that she couldn't understand it all and so she had to blame someone.'

'Jesus,' Lily said under her breath. 'What about now ... what's it like now? Oh wait ... that woman you were with last night, the beautiful one, the Victoria's Secret model. Is she something to do with Elena's family?'

'Yes, she's Roberta's sister, Mia, and the only one who really stood by me during the shitstorm. She adores Elena and she's the one who keeps everything on an even keel here with the family. I'd be lost without her.'

'So, is there anything—'

'God no! She's sweet, but no ... definitely not. She's gorgeous, obviously, but a bit too self-obsessed for me, and way too complicated.' Matt laughed. 'But she'd admit that herself.'

'So, where is she now? Roberta, I mean,' Lily asked, turning the wheel slightly to the right to maintain her line with the marker.

'She's still in the States. Still with the woman she left me for. So, I suppose that means something ... I'm just not sure what that is. So, yeah –' he took a deep breath '– I

266

came here with Elena and tried to figure out what to do next. It wasn't that straightforward because I couldn't just move here and live happily ever after on an Italian island. I have to work, and I couldn't run my business from here, at least not at the same level as I had been doing back in New York, so I had to cut some of my clients loose and keep the ones I knew I could manage. I did that for a year, and we settled into a kind of rhythm. Just last year we moved back to New York and put Elena in school and we came back here again for summer. She gets to spend time with her family and it's good for her to grow up with her Italian heritage, that's important.'

'Isn't her mother here with her during summer?'

'No, her mother is too busy working. She sees her for two weeks in summer and the usual holidays. Work was always her thing,' he said, glancing up at her. He hesitated before continuing. 'I didn't take her seriously when she said she wasn't sure she wanted to have her – when she got pregnant, I mean. I was the one who said it will all be fine. I guess she really meant it.'

'But ... how come you didn't mention it any of the times over the past few days ... like that day on the boat?'

Matt took another deep breath and put the palms of his hands together, staring at them intently. 'We've been through a lot, Elena in particular, and she's still the happiest, sunniest, sweetest little girl you could ever meet. I'm fiercely protective of her ... I'd fight tigers for her, as you can imagine, and I guess I've been reluctant to let anyone in.' He paused for a moment, glancing up at Lily. 'I saw a shrink for a while, after Roberta left, and she said that I couldn't keep holding on to our little bubble of two, that

I couldn't close us off from the rest of the world for fear of what might happen ... that I had to open up to other people.' He looked up at Lily. 'I guess that was a waste of money,' he said with a hesitant smile.

After a few moments of silence, Matt directed Lily to turn the boat in towards the marina. 'That's Marina Corricella dead ahead. It's the prettiest part of the island. Okay, Elenita! We're coming in to Corricella. Are you ready?'

'*Sì, Papà*, me and Peppa are ready. 'Cept ... '

'Except what, *amore*?' Matt asked, glancing over his shoulder in her direction.

'Peppa doesn't have a life jacket, *Papà*.'

'Peppa will be fine. You just hold on to her, okay?'

'NO! *PAPÀ!*' she screeched. 'Peppa can't swim! Peppa is a pig and pigs can't swim!'

'Sure they can. Pigs are great swimmers, but if it will make you feel better, we'll go look for one when we get back to Ischia. In the meantime, you just hold on tight to her, okay?'

Elena glared at Matt with a scowl and squeezed her stuffed toy pig to her chest.

'See the big church dome right up on top there?' Matt asked, leaning in towards Lily to turn the wheel slightly to the right. 'That's the highest part of the island and the marina is right below it. Just keep her pointed towards that and you won't go wrong.'

Lily nodded in response. The view directly ahead of her was breathtaking. Marina Corricella curved around in an arc, hugging the Bay of Naples, and was divided into three main parts. To her right, on the top of the hill, stood a fortress, its tens of dozens of windows all facing towards the sea and hundred-foot walls protecting it from long-ago invaders. A vertiginous cliff fell dangerously below it, making an uninvited entrance all but impossible. The middle section of the marina backing up from the waterfront contained stacks of ice-cream-coloured houses and apartments, all huddled higgledy-piggledy together in charmingly crooked lines. The third section, stretching far to her left, was a lush promontory, dotted with elegant, flat-roofed villas. Access to Corricella was limited: either directly from the sea, or via one of a series of steep stone stairs, each with more than a hundred steps leading down from the town above, tucked away from view behind the cliffs. The fact that access was exclusively by foot or by boat only added to the sense of tranquillity and respite.

Matt showed Lily how to slow the boat and adjusted her position as they approached the marina. Seagulls squawked and chattered loudly, jostling for the best views and vantage points of inbound fishing boats. Piles of fishing nets were stacked high and overflowed from large wooden crates along the pier, creating a natural barrier to the water. The windows of the surrounding houses were flung open, desperate for any hint of a breeze, but more often than not, there was none. Awnings stretched out, casting shade on wrought-iron balconies. The air was thick with heat and impossibly still now. Families sat under umbrellas at outdoor café tables, languishing over coffee and taking refuge from the heat of the sun directly overhead.

Lily could hear shouts from the various boats to an old man on the pier and she couldn't remember a time when she felt more alive. The old man ahead was the colour of dark mahogany furniture, barefoot and bare chested. He was the marina caretaker, Matt explained, and anyone who hoped to score a berth had better contact him far in advance or be well connected, as space was limited and highly desirable.

Matt nudged her left shoulder and took over the wheel as they slowed to a crawl a few metres from the marina.

'Okay, Elena, we're coming in towards the pier. You ready?'

Elena nodded, her feet tucked underneath her on the navy cushions and her chest puffed out, having stuffed Peppa head first down into her own life jacket.

A line of massive rocks, implanted decades before along the edge of the marina, acted as a breaker from the greater sea beyond. Small wooden boats jostled for position with sleek white outboard motorboats and elegant sailing boats, most helmed by bare-chested, barefoot Italians. They were all exclusively nut-brown and fit. The Italians tanned with ease, turning deeper shades of brown, not suffering from the onslaught of sunburn or the shockingly pink skin endured by those from more northern climates.

As Matt pulled the boat into position, the old man on the marina caught the line he threw.

'Lily, throw those fenders over the sides, please!' Matt shouted.

'I could totally be a boat person,' Lily said, crawling from one side to the other and tossing the navy fenders over the edge into position. 'Even the language is cool, all the special code words. It's like something out of a James Bond movie.'

The boat was secured at the marina and Matt waved

at Lily to disembark. 'Let's grab a coffee before you go to your meeting.'

'Some place with a mirror, preferably,' Lily said, trying to tease her fingers through her windblown hair.

'My friend owns a place just a little further up the marina. The Vinería di Arturo. It's a wine bar and bookstore, but they do coffee during the day. We've got a half hour before your meeting with the Godfather, and we're only ten minutes away.'

'He's not really known as the Godfather, is he?' Lily asked, stopping to look up at him, a horrified look on her face.

'No, just kidding,' Matt said, reaching out to brush back a piece of her hair that was whipping across her cheek. As his hand grazed her cheek, she could smell the salt from his skin. He stood a foot taller than her, and she realised that in her flat sandals she just about reached his shoulders. She could make out tiny lines at the sides of his eyes as he squinted in the harsh sunlight. He was dishevelled looking, his hair tousled from the strong sea breeze, but she hoped he wouldn't fix it. He looked good. He reached down and took Elena's hand, who skipped happily along by his side.

'Sorry, people tell me that I've a weird sense of humour. I've met the guy and he's actually really nice. Stop worrying, Lily! You'll do great,' he smiled, as he tucked another piece of hair behind her ear. 'There . . . now, you're perfect.'

'*Perfect*,' she thought as she touched her cheek where his hand had been.

He hesitated for just a moment, as his gaze met hers. 'C'mon,' he said with a smile. 'Coffee.'

Chapter Twenty-One

The stone-slabbed terrace of the Vinería was packed with small, round wrought-iron tables and chairs, each filled with groups of families and friends, giddy at the prospect of a day on the water or at one of the nearby beaches. They ordered two cappuccinos and sat at the only remaining free table. Lily ducked into the bathroom, desperate to do a rescue job on her wind-blown hair. By the time she had emerged the crowd had begun to dwindle, each party making their way to an awaiting boat.

She turned her chair to face the water, a cacophony of sounds filling the air. Small children, Elena among them, darted in and out among the chairs, their parents oblivious to their shrieks. Outboard engines hummed and purred, ready to depart for a day of unbridled adventure on and in the translucent turquoise sea. The two of them sat in silence watching motorboats leave white wakes behind as they pulled away from shore. Lily couldn't hear a single language other than Italian. Desperate to appear nonchalant, she tossed out the first question that came to mind.

'Matt, do you think we're the only non-Italians on this island?'

'Right now? Probably, yes. I do know one American family that has been coming here for years. They've actually got a house way over on that promontory, to the right,' he said, pointing to the far side of the bay. 'He's the only Black guy on the entire island and he's built like a rugby player, so to say that he stands out is an understatement. He's from Atlanta, I think. He's the only foreigner I know here.' Matt scooped the remaining cappuccino foam from the bottom of his cup. 'It's mostly Italian families who have been coming here for generations and have houses, or Italians coming in for a few days and renting one of the Airbnb apartments here in the marina. The foreign tourists prefer Capri, and are largely unaware of the natural beauty of Ischia and Procida. Ischia is one of Italy's best-kept secrets.'

'I'm beginning to see why. How far is La Lampara?' she asked, scouring the marina for signs of the restaurant where she'd agreed to meet Lorenzo.

'See the stone fortress all the way at the end there? It's the yellow and white building just before that, about a five-minute walk from here. La Lampara is one of the best restaurants on the island. It's his place. So ... you all set for this meeting?' Matt asked, running a hand back and forth through his hair. 'Jeez, I can feel the salt,' he laughed, sitting back into his chair and stifling a yawn.

'Sorry, I hope it wasn't too much trouble taking me here this morning,' Lily said, leaning forward on to the table and placing her chin in one hand.

'No, not at all. I was planning to go for a ride in the afternoon with Elena, so it was just a slight change of plan. I love any excuse to take the boat out.' Matt's eyes followed

273

Elena as she darted around the tables with two other children her own age.

'Yeah, I'm a bit nervous to be honest. He's either going to like the idea or not, but if he doesn't buy into it, then it's a no from Antonio, too, at which point I'll have to just accept that it was probably a mad idea.'

'Lily, seriously ... you have *got* to stop worrying! At some point you've got to get past all the self-doubt and have faith in yourself *and* your idea. Just be confident. Everyone you've talked to so far loves the idea, right?'

Lily smiled despite her nervous state. 'I suppose so.'

'Just go have the conversation and we'll meet back here in an hour. We can get lunch here before we head back to Ischia if you like. I know a great place on the other side of the bay.'

'Sounds great!'

'Okay, I'll call and get a reservation. It's a small place called La Conchiglia and it's only accessible by boat. It's one of those super-casual toes-in-the-sand types of places with the best seafood you've ever had in your life.'

'Better than Ischia?'

'Maybe. In fact I think it's possibly the best seafood you can get anywhere ... maybe even the best meal of your life,' he said jokingly. 'You've got to book way in advance in the height of summer because it draws the boating crowd, but we should be good today. It's still early.'

'So, all that stands between me and possibly the best meal of my life is this one little meeting?'

'Yep,' Matt said, smiling as he leaned back into his chair again.

'Okay, I better get going,' Lily said, scraping back her chair.

'See you on the other side. Knock him dead!' Matt said with a wave.

Elena waved goodbye as Lily made her way down the marina towards La Lampara. The church sat authoritatively on top of the cluster of mismatched buildings, hovering above the marina and its residents below. Lily noticed that most of the churches she had seen in Italy were stone or white in colour, but this was a muted pale yellow, not dissimilar to the buildings surrounding it, and had a regal grey dome as its crown.

Lines of washing hung limply outside every window, the stillness and the heat of the late-morning sun creating a haze that shrouded everything, adding to the already sleepy, soporific feeling of an Italian midsummer's day. Massive basil plants, their leaves the size of cabbage leaves, sat in terracotta pots outside front doors, at once functional and decorative. The entire marina appeared to be devoid of straight lines. Lily walked carefully along the uneven pavements that weaved in and out, worn over thousands of years by the relentless sea.

Each restaurant had its menu posted outside, vying for the attention of passing day trippers. Speciality dishes focused heavily on the sea, with the local tiny, silvery fresh anchovies featuring on every menu as *alici marinate*. *Spaghetti al limone*, another local favourite, was to be found at every ristorante and trattoria, as well as fish of more shapes and sizes with exotic-sounding names than Lily had ever seen. She stopped to read a chalkboard menu that stood behind a refrigerated display of that morning's catch.

'*Orata, spigola, pezzogna* …' she said under her breath, rolling the sounds around on her tongue.

She arrived at La Lampara a few minutes early and was shown upstairs to a corner table in the shade overlooking the bay. Lorenzo arrived moments later, dressed meticulously in a sharp grey linen suit, black open-collared shirt and grey fedora. He introduced himself as he placed the fedora on the table in front of him and shook Lily's hand. He was accompanied by two young men dressed entirely in black. One carried a tray of espressos, the other had a tablet poised in his hand. At seventy-two years of age, Lorenzo spoke perfect English, having spent twenty years working in London's financial centre. He had a full head of steel-grey hair, combed back to perfection, and his manners were impeccable. Everything about him suggested that he paid attention to detail and Lily surmised instantly that he didn't suffer fools.

Lorenzo explained that the two young men were his assistants, one of whom placed steaming espressos on the table, while the second documented every nuance of the conversation on his tablet. Lorenzo explained that his father had been a diplomat so from a young age he had lived in different cities around the world. His father had insisted, however, that Lorenzo spend every summer in Procida with his extended family, and as a result had developed a deep love of the island.

As they sat there, perched high above the chaos and the noise of the marina, church bells rang out every fifteen minutes, the only other sounds being the gentle rumble of an outboard motor and shrieks of happy children. Lorenzo motioned in the direction of Capri and explained how it saddened him that so many people were familiar with it, while so few had ever experienced the magic of Procida.

'Most people want what they know ... what they can be sure of, but choosing that path means you are forced to travel it along with everyone else.' He shrugged. 'They believe that if ninety-five people have been to Capri but only five have been to Procida then Capri must be the better choice, because surely ninety-five people cannot be wrong. They don't realise that travelling in a crowd like this limits the ability to really see a place for what it is because the crowds will obscure your vision. Can you believe that Procida is actually closer to Napoli than Capri is? And yet it remains a hidden gem and I think it is time that the world knew of its existence. So ... tell me what you have in mind?'

He leaned back in his chair and pulled out a pipe as Lily told him of her idea to create a digital platform for Ischia and, on Antonio's suggestion, Procida. She explained her theory of people seeking more from travel today, and travellers valuing experiences over physical things and of people opening up more to the idea of unexplored, less touristy destinations. She proposed that the way to reach people today was through stories and that messages of and from Ischia and Procida should be more aspirational.

Lorenzo puffed twice on his pipe. 'Very well. Antonio was right. This is a big idea, but a necessary plan for our islands, and I will support it on one condition.'

Lily stared at him, unsure of what to say.

'If this is to be authentic, then it must showcase the entirety of both islands as a real destination. It should tell the true stories of the islands, and it should promote the region and its experiences organically. It will not be successful if only the big hotels or restaurants can afford to pay money to be featured and promote their business.

Of course, they must pay, but this must also tell the story of the small, individual businesses, the family businesses – the people who for generations have been the fabric of Ischia and Procida.' Lorenzo paused and puffed on his pipe.

'To do this, I believe that you must experience Procida properly, as you would want your readers to experience it, so you must live it. Procida is a way of life, it is the sea, the sounds, the food, the people, and these are the stories that you must tell. You must come back here and get to know its people. I have many properties here on Procida so we can make a small apartment available to you, that is not a problem. Signora Lily, I don't think you can accomplish what is necessary in one week. I think you will need to return to Ischia and to Procida and see all of it for yourself. If you can commit to that, then it will be easy to work out the details.'

He turned to his assistant. '*Hai capito? Hai scritto tutto?*' he said, making sure that his assistant had documented the pertinent details.

The young man nodded, not taking his eyes off his screen. '*Sì, certo, signore.*'

'Yes, definitely. Trust me, that would be a pleasure,' Lily said with a wide smile.

'Very well then, I must go. Now, I believe that your captain awaits to take you to La Conchiglia. If it is not the best lunch that you have ever had then let me know and I will have the chef shot.'

Lily's eyes widened momentarily until she noticed the glint in his eyes.

'*Arrivederci,*' he said with the smallest hint of a smile. He placed the fedora back on his head and winked at Lily.

'*A la prossima* . . . until next time,' he said, before disappearing as quickly as he had arrived.

Lily made her way back to the marina in silence, lost in her own thoughts. Matt stood waiting next to a small motorboat which acted as a free shuttle from the marina in Corricella to La Conchiglia at the other side of the bay.

In the short five-minute journey, Lily filled Matt in on the conversation as the shuttle boat whizzed across the bay, depositing them on the rickety, wooden pier that stood ten feet up from the sea. The restaurant was as unassuming as a barn, with crumbling pink paint on the ground floor and an open-air top floor with a simple, curved roof.

'Oh my God, I love it!' Lily shrieked, stepping gingerly on to the wooden pier. She turned to extend a hand down to Elena.

'*Grazie*,' Elena said, beaming up at Lily as she took her hand. Elena held on tight as they made their way down the rickety wooden pier.

'Where did you go? Did you have to go to work?' Elena asked as she jumped down on to the sand.

'I did, but I'm finished now. It was just one meeting.'

'But I thought you were on vacation?'

'I am, but I have this idea for a new job, and I had to have one meeting to see if this one guy thought it was a good idea.'

'What's your new job?'

'Well, it's to build a website so that people from all around the world can find out about Ischia and Procida and then maybe they could come here on vacation.'

Elena bent over and kicked off her sandals. 'Everyone likes Ischia.'

'Yes, that's true.'

'Lily, can you hold these, please?' she asked, dangling her sandals up in the air, completely losing interest in the conversation.

'Sure,' Lily replied, as Elena darted across the sand.

Matt was greeted by hugs from various staff members, and they were immediately shown to a table where a carafe of house wine, bread and platters of food started to appear.

'You can order off the menu, but I prefer to do the chef's specials,' Matt said, pouring two glasses of wine. 'Is that okay with you?'

'God, yes!' Lily said, salivating. 'I don't know what half those fish are anyway. Are you hungry, Elena?'

Elena nodded as she dipped a chunk of bread in olive oil and stuffed it in her mouth.

The three of them chatted easily for the next two hours, with each platter of food outdoing the previous. There were fresh anchovies that tasted of the sea, marinated in peppery olive oil, seafood salad, chargrilled octopus, tuna, fresh spicy calamari, and *bruschetta* piled high with luscious deep red garlicky cherry tomatoes. Lily hesitated for just a moment before she speared a piece of octopus with her fork. She smiled to herself as she imagined Ellen's heartfelt objections. Sorry, Ellen, but these look too good to pass up.

She closed her eyes, savouring the delicate briny taste of the sea, and made a mental note to take a photograph of the menu before leaving. These dishes needed to be featured on her website as this was definitely food worth travelling for.

Two steaming bowls of linguine and spaghetti were

placed on the table, the waitress explaining that they were 'rich man's linguine' with five types of shellfish and 'poor man's spaghetti' with anchovies, green pepper and cheese. A round of espressos and a bowl of gelato for Elena rounded out the meal and Lily happily decided that there was no need to shoot the chef.

'Incredible,' Lily said, happily satiated. 'Delicious. Everything was just delicious.' Tipping back her espresso cup she drained the last drop of the sharp coffee 'So, how come you're staying at the resort if you have a house here?'

'The house is being renovated. It was old when I bought it, but I had no choice other than to move into it right away, so it desperately needed some modernisation. I finally got around to doing it this summer and I'm at the resort just for the really messy part, which is almost finished. Once the dust settles, I'll be able to stay there again. Elena's staying at her grandmother's place, so it's been nice for her, but given that I'm the devil incarnate, I figured the resort was a much better option.'

'I'm going to have a new bedroom and a new bed, right, *Papà*?' Elena asked, as she coloured on the paper tablecloth.

'That's right. A really fancy new bed.'

'Do you want to have a sleepover one night?' she asked, turning to stare up at Lily.

'Oh, that sounds lovely, but I have to go home to New York in a few days and my friends are getting married this weekend, so I need to stay at the resort.'

'Is your friend going to be the bride?'

'Yes, she is,' Lily said, bending down to pick up an orange crayon from the floor.

'Does she have a white dress?'

'Of course! I haven't seen it yet, but I bet she'll look like a princess.'

'*Papà*, can I see the bride?' Elena asked, not looking at anyone in particular.

'They're getting married in the olive garden, so we'll be able to see her then.'

'Hey, tomorrow night is the rehearsal dinner, but it's at the pizza restaurant at San Montano. You two should come! It will be fun.'

'I love pizza,' Elena said. 'Can we go for pizza, *Papà*?'

'You don't think Dee and Morgan would mind?'

'Of course not. There'll be live music and a bunch of crazy relatives, so you'll fit right in.'

'Gee, thanks,' Matt said, joking. 'Okay, if you think it would be okay, that would be fun. Tomorrow is our last night at the resort. What do you say, Elenita? Pizza party on our last night?'

Elena clapped her hands in glee. 'Yeah, I'm going to see the bride!'

'Now, gather up those crayons because we need to get back to the boat. Look, there are two under the table down there.' He turned to Lily and rolled his eyes. 'What is it with girls and weddings? She's only four and she's all about the white dress.'

'Happy ever after is an easy sell, I guess,' Lily said. 'It's a simple recipe. Find the right person, put on a white dress, say "I do" and live happily ever after.'

'If only it were that easy in real life, right?' he said, bundling Elena's bits and pieces back into her pink backpack.

By the time they were dropped back at their own boat, the marina was packed. The old man acting as the marina superintendent was barking orders at the constant stream of boats coming or going. Their drivers, exclusively male, bare-chested, barefoot and nut-brown, stood guiding their motor craft, one hand lightly on the steer. Babies with remnants of an afternoon gelato ringing their mouths shrieked up and down the pier as adults took shelter under umbrellas from the afternoon sun.

As the afternoon progressed, families and friends gathered along the pier for *aperitivo*. Old men in shorts and flip-flops smoked rolled-up cigarettes as they traded the day's gossip, not waiting for each other to finish a sentence. Matt slowly backed the boat out from the marina, as Lily and Elena sat behind him on the navy cushions.

'*Pronto*,' Matt said, as his phone rang. He stalled the engine while he took the call.

Lily turned and stared, transfixed by the colourful scene taking place on the marina as returning yachts spilled out their salty-skinned, suntanned people, each seeking out a late lunch or an early *aperitivo*. It seemed to her in that moment that Procida was possibly the most colourful place she had ever witnessed, as all around her people indulged in the simple, yet hedonistic pleasures of a summer day on a tiny Italian island. But she couldn't help feeling envious of all the couples and lovers enjoying the best that summer has to offer, content in the knowledge that they had someone to share the evening and the night with, too.

She shook her head, chastising herself for allowing her gloomy tendencies to creep in, having had the most perfect day so far. But when life was being played out all around her in such gloriously rich colour, it was hard not to think about it. She had said no to a life with someone because she had been afraid that she might want it all. Yet here she was off the south coast of Italy, relishing this simpler version of life. She certainly wouldn't be able to do any of this with a baby in tow, she thought, as Matt revved the engine again. In fact, how could she consider starting a new business if she had a baby to take care of? She had no idea if the business would work, but she was determined to try, and surely to do that justice she'd have to dedicate herself entirely to it. A baby would just screw everything up right now.

She could tell that Matt was winding down the conversation, his hand idling on the throttle. She stared at the back of his head as he reached down and revved the engine again. There was no doubt that she was attracted to him and he had been nothing but kind to her, but this was one of those impossible situations with no happy ending: he with a messy past and she with a messy present. Her thoughts rolled round and round in her head until Matt turned around to face them. 'Ready?' he asked with a smile.

She felt her stomach do a little flip. Get a grip, Lily, she thought. The man hasn't said or done anything to indicate that he is even remotely interested in you beyond just being kind.'

'Yep,' she said, nodding.

'Me too, *Papà*,' Elena said with a yawn. 'Lily, can I sit next to you?'

'Oh, sure. Come on up here. Are you sleepy?'

Elena nodded as she clambered up alongside Lily. She curled up into a little ball and rested her head on Lily's lap. Matt reversed slowly out from the pier and turned the boat around to face out into the bay. Lily placed her hand on Elena's head to stop her silky-soft hair from blowing on to her face, her thoughts racing as the boat sped along.

She looked down at Elena and smiled. She was already fast asleep, her eyelids twitching as she dreamed. She had turned around to face Lily and, one hand curled into a tight fist, had at some point clutched on to her dress. Lily gently moved the strap of the life jacket to keep it from pressing into the side of Elena's face and placed her hand back on the side of her head. How can they have such absolute trust as to fall asleep like that in the lap of an almost perfect stranger, in the middle of all the engine noise and the rush of wind, she wondered. She thought perhaps children's ability to trust implicitly was due to the fact that they had no reason to suspect otherwise. Undoubtedly some human would come barging into Elena's life at some point in the future and break that trust, casting a shadow of doubt on to her world. Perhaps that was the point at which everything changed, pure innocence shattered by human intervention.

But Elena had already known disappointment and had experienced the fragility of human relationships in her four short years. She had been disappointed by the very person who was supposed to love her the most. Lily felt a surge of emotion and hoped that at only two years of age she had been too young to understand what was happening and feel the pain of separation, of being left behind. Based on what Matt had told her, she didn't have a mother, at least not one who was really present. What would it be like to grow up without a mother, without a female figure in your life, Lily wondered, holding the little girl tighter in to her. It was an instinctive feeling to want to protect the small person asleep on her lap, one she hadn't felt previously, and she wondered how her own mother had been able to walk out of her life.

Matt looked over his shoulder at them, smiling to see Elena curled up asleep on Lily's lap. 'Are you okay?' he mouthed silently over the roar of the engine.

Lily nodded and smiled. She could feel the warmth of Elena's small body through the material of her dress. Feeling strangely protective of her, she held on tightly to her for the duration of the boat ride back to Ischia, determined that at least for the next fifteen minutes, Elena would sleep soundly, and without worry, in the safety of her arms.

Chapter Twenty-Two

The previous day's storm had passed over Ischia without incident, and in its wake the entire island looked even more vibrant than before. The sea sparkled an iridescent turquoise, twinkling under the harsh glare of the morning sun. The torrential downpour appeared to have contributed overnight to an explosion of colour from every angle. Bougainvillea blossoms had burst open in vibrant pinks, magentas and purples, spilling down from the eaves of the resort. Dense foliage surrounding the property appeared to have turned a deeper shade of green, the dust of summer having been rinsed away in rivulets, and the earth below steamed, the heat of the sun causing the rain-soaked soil to release some of its moisture.

Lily had had a fitful sleep the night before, tossing and turning, thinking about what she should do only to immediately second-guess that decision. She ruminated once again about Peter and the decision she had made. It had felt like the right decision at the time, but had it been? Had she been too dramatic about the whole baby thing? She couldn't imagine actually having a baby right now, and she never had done, so had she been wrong to strike him out just in case she might change her mind in the future? She was thirty-four years old, and she hadn't changed her mind yet, so why was she making a case for doing so in the future?

None of it made any sense and when the sun came up, she decided that hoping to get any more sleep was a waste of time. She had texted Dee to tell her that she was skipping that morning's massage and would see them all at breakfast. Her stomach growled with hunger now as she made her way towards the terrace in the warmth of the early-morning sun. She pulled out a chair and sat down, not noticing that Matt was already seated at the table alongside her.

'Good morning,' he said, removing his sunglasses.

'Oh, hi, good morning. I didn't see you there,' she said, startled.

'It looked as if you were miles away. Where are the girls this morning?'

'Oh, they're at the spa. I couldn't handle another massage in silence. It gives the voices in my head the chance to take over.'

'Isn't that the whole point of going to the spa? I'm not really a spa kind of guy, but I thought massages were supposed to quieten those voices and make you more relaxed?' he asked, turning to face her.

'Yes, but there's way too much going on in my head right now. A few zen vibes from a massage don't stand a chance of beating out the noise in there.'

'Why, what's all the noise about? I'd have thought you'd be feeling pretty good after yesterday. You had a great meeting, right?'

'Oh, I'm just overthinking it all. I just don't know where to start or what to do first.'

'Lily Ryan, you really do worry too much, do you know that?'

She liked hearing him say her full name. 'I know, but I've made such a mess of things at home and now that my salary has basically dried up, I'm going to have to figure out how to make this new idea work fast. My anxiety has kicked in, it's on overdrive.'

'You've just been given the go-ahead by two of the biggest businessmen on Ischia and Procida. Once word gets out that you're doing this, I guarantee you others will want to follow suit. People here have been desperate to raise awareness of these islands for so long and have tried to do just that on their own. This will work because everyone wants it to work. It might be hard at the start, but isn't everything?' He smiled at her. 'Don't worry, just get stuck into the details. Talk to Kitty and get her to help you structure it. She runs her own PR firm, right? So, she had to do the same thing at the start.'

Lily said nothing, but continued to look at him, not wanting to turn away.

God, you're gorgeous, she thought. Why do I always meet the wrong guys ... or the right guys at the wrong time? Jesus, what is *wrong* with you, Lily? she ranted in her head. So, he's hot and you're attracted to him. So what? That happens all the time to people on holiday. Cop on!

She directed her eyes back towards her table. He was being sweet and kind and she was overthinking it again, exaggerating feelings that just didn't exist. Just appreciate this for what it is, she admonished herself. He's trying to help and offer advice and you're unbuttoning his shirt in your head. She swirled her cappuccino round and round in her cup.

'I know, you're right,' she said, sitting up straight. 'It's just one more thing to layer on right now. I feel like I'm standing on quicksand.' She hesitated. Before she knew what she was doing, she had opened the floodgates and started pouring out her thoughts in all their disorderly glory. 'I made a bit of a hash of things back in New York. The breakup . . . well, it was all my fault. I wanted the fairy tale . . . I wanted it all, and even though he was offering me everything I thought I ever wanted, it still wasn't enough. So, in a huge dramatic gesture, I broke up with him and walked out. Then he cancelled my flight to Italy, so I had to rebook and the whole thing was a nightmare, and I haven't heard from him since, so I'm pretty sure he hates me or thinks I'm a total psycho, or maybe both.'

Matt stared down at his coffee cup silently. 'Sorry,' he said slowly. 'I hadn't realised that it was all so recent. I mean, you had mentioned something, but I didn't know it was all still so raw. That must be tough, especially being here for a wedding, surrounded by happy people. Mind if I join you?' He pushed back his chair and moved to her table.

'No, not at all.' She sighed quietly. 'It's been lovely here, I've loved every minute of it. God, I sound so ungrateful, don't I? It's just that everything I knew for sure three weeks ago is now kind of upside down, and I'm so excited about this new business idea, but also a little bit terrified, to be honest.'

'Hey, terrified is a good thing. It keeps you sharp. Look, I had to do something very similar after my ex-wife walked out. I had to figure out how not to destroy the business I had built, and I had Elena to consider, so I know what you mean about walking on quicksand. It's as if you can't rely on anything or anyone and that's a very lonely feeling.'

'Sorry if I sound like a moan. I'm so lucky to be here and everyone has been so sweet and so supportive.' She turned to face him directly. '*You've* been so sweet and supportive, and thank you again for yesterday. Where's Elena, by the way?'

'Mia picked her up earlier this morning but she's coming back for the party tonight. She has already decided what dress she's going to wear.'

Lily couldn't help but notice that his face lit up whenever he spoke of Elena.

'Aw, that's so cute. Well, I promise I'll have hauled my arse out of this current pit of misery by the time tonight comes.'

Matt stood up to leave. 'I hope so. You have the greatest smile and I'm hoping I might see it again some time. You know . . . just once. Let's not get carried away.'

Lily couldn't help but laugh. 'Okay, deal. But tonight is the last time you'll ever see it.'

'Well then, I'm going to have to live with that,' Matt replied with a grin. 'See you tonight.'

As Matt left, Lily folded her arms on the table and placed her head down on to them. 'Why did you have to go spilling your messy inner thoughts out to this poor man at breakfast? What is wrong with you? A cute guy is nice to you and you reward him by spewing all this shit about Peter that you're not sure you even believe to be true,' she groaned quietly. 'Get a grip, Lily, get a grip.'

Minutes later she could hear them coming. Looking up,

she saw the four girls making their way noisily towards her, four pairs of blue flip-flops slapping against the stone floor. 'I don't want to hear about how perfectly zen you all are and how in tune with the universe.'

'Who bit you on the arse this morning?' Dee asked as she sat down.

'I didn't sleep very well last night,' Lily mumbled.

'*Scusi* ... Franco! Emergency coffee needed over here,' Dee roared, pointing to Lily.

'*Certo, signora! Subito*,' Franco replied with a grin.

'So, what were you muttering to yourself about when we got here? You do know you look a little nuts when you do that, don't you?'

'Oh, just that I was having a bit of an emotional moment and Matt came along and I kind of dumped it on him,' Lily groaned.

'Lily, you have got to get it together!' Morgan said sharply. 'Seriously, just get over it already and be present!'

'Morgan! Cut it out!' Dee admonished. 'What's with everyone this morning? You'd better all adjust your attitudes before five o'clock, that's all I'm saying. Christ almighty, you'd swear it was a public flogging we were going to tonight. Liven up people, it's a party!'

'Sorry,' Morgan replied, her cheeks flushing red.

'Why are your cheeks red? That usually happens when you tell lies.'

'Sorry, Lily ... I think my anxiety is kicking in. That was mean. Forgive me?''

'It all sounds like fun to me, even if you were a bit of an emotional basket case,' Ellen sighed, tapping on her phone. 'I miss all that flirting shite. Once you're married it all changes and once you have children it's about as rare as flying monkeys.'

'There is *actually* such a thing as flying monkeys,' Dee said, staring at Ellen.

'Is there really?' Ellen gasped. 'Oh my God, I'd love to see that!'

'Who are you texting? Your cappuccino is getting cold,' Lily said, keen to change the subject.

'My husband. He just texted me.'

'See! You're always complaining that he doesn't text you or call you. Cut him some slack, Ellen.'

'Yeah. Okay ... sure ... he just texted me this: "Hi. Watching farming programme here. They're giving a ram a vasectomy. They showed it being cut and clamped, then they twisted the clamp till his bit fell off. Ellen ... no fucking way I'm doing that. Don't care how many more kids we have. I'll take care of them. Miss you." And they say romance is dead,' Ellen said, as she typed a response.

'That is both vile and sweet at the same time,' Morgan said. 'Is that what they actually do to them? You know what, I don't want to know. I don't need another sorrowful version of the octopus story. What are you typing? How do you even respond to something like that?'

'"Turn off TV and put kids to bed. Miss you too." That's it verbatim.' Ellen stuck her phone back in her pocket. 'I'm going to have to get my tubes tied. I can't cope with any more children. I draw the line at five. Molly was the last thing to be launched out of my vagina.'

'I still can't believe that you've got five children. How do you manage to keep them all alive? I think I've probably come close to death just trying to take care of myself on many a night out in London,' Kitty said, staring aimlessly into her cappuccino cup.

'It's a daily struggle. Anyway, I have to do something. My sister got hers tied a couple of years ago. She said it was brutal. I had to stop sending her baby pictures when Molly was little because she texted me back one day to say that her ovaries had twinged, and she actually emailed the consultant and asked him about a reversal.'

'I never saw the attraction, personally,' Kitty said, applying zinc stick to her lips. 'I like my life the way it is, not having to answer to anyone. What is it with all these women who start having babies the moment they get married? Honestly, you'd think it was some reproductive indoctrination: follow or be damned.'

'Yeah, or at the very least "follow or be judged",' said Ellen. 'I didn't have my first until two years after I was married. The amount of times I was asked when we were going to have a baby . . . it drove me nuts. I was buying fish one day and this old woman, a friend of my mother's, asked me if we were having trouble getting pregnant. She told me that I should sit with my legs up the wall every evening before bed.'

Kitty spat out her coffee and descended into a fit of coughing.

'Yeah, but you always knew you wanted them, didn't you?' Lily asked earnestly.

'Yes . . . I did. I would have had them on my own if I hadn't met Mike. I always thought that Sandra Bullock was cool – she was getting ready to adopt that kid when she found out her slime-bag husband was having an affair and she went ahead and adopted him anyway.'

'See!' Lily wailed. 'That's the kind of conviction that I'm missing. You knew you always wanted to have them, Kitty always knew that she'd never have them, and even Sandra Bullock was determined to get one in the middle of her divorce drama. Conviction! Everyone seems to be convinced one way or the other and I can't make my mind up. I don't know if I do, and I don't know if I don't. I think I don't, but what if I really do and I just don't know it yet?'

'I don't know whether I want them or not,' Dee interjected.

'Let me help you with that one, my love. We don't,' Morgan said, drawing her hand across her throat.

Dee shrugged. 'Fair enough. I'll get a snickerdoodle.'

'What's a snickerdoodle?' Ellen squinted in Dee's direction.

'A dog. Cute little curly haired thing.'

'Sounds like a chocolate bar.'

'Again,' Lily interrupted. 'You guys know what you want, or don't want, in this case. Morgan says no, so you say okay I'll get a dog. Am I the only woman on the planet who just doesn't know for sure one way or the other? I blew up my relationship in case I might want one in the future and if I don't then I'll have blown it up for nothing.' She leaned forward on the table, placing her chin in her hand.

Dee nudged Morgan. 'What time is it? Please tell me it's after eleven o'clock.'

'Eleven fifteen. Why?'

'Fuck it. I'm ordering a bottle of wine. This conversation is getting way too intense and this one needs to be cheered up,' Dee said, pointing in Lily's direction. 'I have a rule about drinking before eleven o'clock.'

The waiters were busily clearing away the remains of the breakfast buffet.

'Franco!' Dee called. 'Can we have a bottle of wine, *per favore*? Actually, let me save you a journey. There are five of us so let's be realistic. Make it two.'

Franco shuffled over to the table. '*Buona idea, signora!* You start the party early!'

Dee leaned in towards Lily and whispered. 'I bumped into the one from reception ... what's her name? The wedding-planning woman. Anyway, she said that she has found some minister who was available tomorrow. I don't know the first thing about him, nor do I care. As long as someone shows up to do the job, that's all that matters.'

'Oh, thank God. I'd actually fear for my life if Morgan found out about it. Especially in her current humour.'

'Sweet Jesus, don't mention a word. Don't poke the beast!'

The two bottles of wine rolled right into lunchtime, so the group of five made their way to the pizza restaurant at the pool. A carbohydrate-fuelled lunch sent the girls splintering in different directions, each intent upon a power nap before reconvening at five o'clock on the terrace.

A few short hours later, post-nap and having wrangled with her hair for thirty minutes, Lily arrived at the terrace. Guests had already started to gather and the local Napoletana trio had started playing. As Lily made her way to the pop-up champagne bar, the trio belted out an upbeat rendition of 'Tarantella Napoletana', which instantly had the guests swaying on the spot. Dee and Morgan were holding court dressed in colour-coordinated off-the-shoulder maxi dresses.

'Definitely Morgan's idea,' Lily thought with a smile.

She made her way through the crowd, wearing a blush-pink off-the-shoulder dress by the Australian brand Bronx and Banco. In the six months she had been with Peter she had worked hard to drop a dress size, unconsciously but constantly intimidated by all the overtly skinny New Yorkers who frequented the best New York restaurants but rarely ordered anything other than tuna tartare and overpriced fish dishes. But, tonight, on the terrace of San Montano, she felt like a million dollars. The fabric was a fine textured mesh that was tapered at the waist, with a voluptuous skirt that moved as she did. The four-inch nude sandals forced her to stand straighter and walk slower and she could feel people stare at her as she stepped carefully across the terrace.

'You look stunning!' Dee gushed, greeting her with a kiss on the cheek.

'Thanks,' Lily replied. 'Took a lot of work to fit into this dress!'

'It's amazing. Is that the Aussie one you were telling me about?'

'Yep. You look fab! What colour is that? Charcoal?'

'Yes, good eye, Lily. This is charcoal grey and Morgan's is dusky grey. See ... we're coordinated, but we don't match. *That* would be too sartorially crass, apparently. She got these at Carolina Herrera on Madison Avenue. Probably paid more than a month's salary for them, but hey ... she's happy. Personally, I think we look like a type of cloud, but whatever.' She shrugged nonchalantly.

'You're a good sport, Dee.'

'I pick my battles.' She winked, tipping back her glass of champagne.

Lily felt a tap on her hip. It was Elena.

'Oh, hi, sweetie. Don't you look pretty!' she said, admiring Elena's red dress.

'This is my new dress for the party.'

'You look beautiful. Elena, this is my friend Dee,' Lily replied, introducing her to Dee.

'Where's the bride in the white dress?' Elena asked, looking around.

'Well, that part is tomorrow. Tonight is the party.'

'Oh,' Elena said, looking disappointed. 'Will I see her tomorrow, Lily? The bride?'

Lily looked at Dee who bent down to Elena's height. 'Definitely. I'll make sure that your name is on the list. You have to see the bride, right?'

Elena beamed with pride as Matt wandered up behind her.

'She took off running when she saw you,' he said, smiling at Lily. 'I think you made quite an impression on the boat.' He hesitated before continuing. 'You look stunning.'

Lily blushed. 'Thanks. Elena looks so pretty,' she replied, directing the conversation away from herself.

'Oh, there was a whole conversation this morning about which dress she'd wear to the party. We had to try on several – right, Elena?'

Elena nodded. '*Papà*, I'm going to see the bride tomorrow in her white dress. Tonight is just a party so she won't be wearing her white dress.'

Lily stooped down to her height. 'You look very grown up in that dress, Elena.'

She beamed again, looking down to admire her dress. As Morgan joined the group, Lily explained that she would be the one in the white dress tomorrow. Elena's face lit up in anticipation.

'What's wrong with you?' Dee whispered in Morgan's ear. 'Why are you so jittery?'

'I'm not jittery.'

'Yes, you are. You keep doing that thing with your hands, wringing them out like a dishcloth. You do that when you're anxious.'

'Oh, it's nothing. Probably just nerves,' Morgan said with a dismissive wave of her hand.

'Come on, let's get you a drink,' Dee said, dragging her in the direction of the bar.

'You're staying for dinner, right?' Lily said, turning her attention back to Matt.

'We'll stay for a little while, a slice of pizza at least, but I've got to pack up tonight as I leave tomorrow.'

'Oh, right, you leave tomorrow.'

'Yeah, the worst of the work is done on the villa, the dusty part at least, and it's fit to live in again. I still don't have a finished kitchen, but we have a little summer kitchen outside, so that's all we need, especially this time of year. Anyway, staying here is costing me a fortune and it will be good to get settled back into the house. I've missed having Elena around,' he said, scooping her up in his arms.

'*Papà*, you'll make my dress all wrinkles! Put me down!' she shrieked, flattening her skirt with both hands.

'Okay, okay, sorry,' he said, rolling his eyes as he lowered her back to the ground. 'Are you going to have some pizza before we go back to the room?'

'*Sì!*' Elena exclaimed, clapping her hands. 'Lily, are you coming for pizza too?'

'Definitely. I love pizza.'

'Yeah! *Papà*, Lily is coming too,' she said matter-of-factly.

'Okay, good. We'll have to disappear after a couple of slices of pizza. It will be late for her and well past her usual bedtime. We'll just duck out. She's not big on goodbyes.'

'Okay, I get it. I'm not big on goodbyes either. Hey, you don't have a drink yet,' Lily said, noticing that Matt was empty-handed.

'Yep, got to rectify that. Can I get you another?'

'Do you seriously think I'd answer any way but yes? It's a party, Matt!'

'Sorry, I'm not used to this. I've been a bit of a recluse for the past couple of years. I know more about *PAW Patrol* than I care to admit. Be right back. Elena, I'll get you a *limonata*, okay? Can I leave her with you?'

'Sure, we'll be fine – right, Elena?'

Elena nodded and smiled as she slipped her hand into Lily's and moved closer so that her right shoe was up against Lily's left sandal. She ran her hand down the length of Lily's skirt and beamed up at her in silence. Lily couldn't help but wonder at this adorable child who was so happy and content in herself, and so utterly willing to trust her. She felt an unprompted well of emotion as she gazed down at her, knowing that she had been through so much, and that in the future she would ask the inevitable questions about why Mommy had left. She squeezed her small hand, wanting to take away in advance the pain that she would one day feel when she would try and fail to understand why she had been left behind.

*

An hour later, a gong was sounded, signalling that the guests should make their way to the outdoor pizza restaurant for dinner. Two long tables of twenty had been set to seat the forty guests. White linen tablecloths that fell to the grass billowed in the light breeze and dozens of mismatched off-white candles ran the length of each table, casting a pale-yellow glow on to the vases of white bougainvillea clusters. A canopy had been erected overhead, draping multiple strings of criss-crossed fairy lights, which only added to the magical air. Waiters had been decked out in black-tie for the occasion and bustled about busily between the pop-up wine bar and the serving stations.

The evening flowed mellifluously under the stars with the happy sounds of chatter and laughter ringing out across the hill. Bottles of local Ischian wine were poured for the multiple antipasti and pizza courses. Once Dee had heard that Vigna del Lume, the local white wine, had won the coveted prize of number one white wine in the world at the Vinitaly awards, she had cancelled all plans to serve any other wine.

Once the last of the courses had been cleared, Morgan stood up and clinked her wine glass. She asked for everyone's attention, explaining that she would be far too emotional to make a speech tomorrow and so she had opted to do so tonight instead. Dee turned around, her face registering surprise, as everyone turned to face Morgan.

'Since I was a little girl, I've been a sucker for every fairy tale ever written, but it always stood out to me that they ended in "happy ever after" with a Prince Charming. In *Cinderella*, he picked the poor girl who went to a party in glass slippers; in *Sleeping Beauty*, he woke the damsel from her spellbound sleep; and even *The Frog Prince*, who is under the spell of a wicked fairy, transforms back to a human once kissed by the princess, and once again, they live happily ever after.

'But what if you didn't want a Prince Charming? What happened to your "happy ever after" then? I was an only child who grew up in an affluent, conservative community with a mother who clearly did not approve of who I was becoming. My father was a sweet man who adored me, but he died when I was young. When you've been cast aside by your own mother, it's hard to believe that someone else will love you unconditionally, and so for the longest time, I didn't think it would happen for me because I didn't fit the mould. So, I had a string of disastrous relationships, searching for love in all the wrong places, before eventually kind of giving up and throwing myself into my career.

'Then, at a dinner party one weekend, a friend introduced me to a funny, blunt, gorgeous Irish woman who would change my life. It took me weeks to muster the courage to ask her out, because I think I knew then just how special she was, even before I had really gotten to know her. I was captivated by her exuberant spirit and her can-do attitude, and the fact that she didn't care what other people thought of her was something that I admired hugely. She was very much her own woman, whereas I had spent most of my life afraid to be who I really was.

'I finally asked her out, but she said no, saying that she had only recently moved to America and wasn't ready to get into anything serious. I was devastated and retreated back into my shell, but a couple of weeks later she changed her mind and, in doing so, changed my life. I have never known what it is to be loved like this and I will be forever grateful to the gods who sent her to my country and to that dinner party. Tomorrow I will marry this funny, crazy, sweet, caring Irish woman who taught me what unconditional love feels like and lit up my life in doing so. Tomorrow is my very own fairy tale. Tomorrow . . . is my happy ever after.'

The speech moved half the crowd to tears, including Dee, who for once didn't try to forcibly change the emotion of the conversation, but instead kissed her bride-to-be and dabbed the corners of her eyes with her white linen napkin.

At some point, Matt had disappeared quietly with Elena. The tables had been cleared and the guests lingered over after-dinner drinks. Some danced, barefoot, to the traditional Italian tunes being played, others stood and took in the view, drink in hand, swaying to the music as it drifted past them into the night air.

'Oh my God, that was a gorgeous speech, Morgan. I was sobbing quietly into my napkin,' Lily said later, as she hugged her friend.

The five girls had reconvened in a circle at the head of the table with Dee and Morgan. A waiter moved around them, topping up their glasses of white wine.

'What's the *matter* with you?' Dee asked, turning to face Morgan. 'You're very fidgety.'

'Nothing,' Morgan replied as her phone pinged. She turned away and pulled it out of her bag, tapped furiously at the screen and slid it back out of sight. 'Nothing!'

Dee looked at her suspiciously. 'You look like you've done something bad. I hope you haven't arranged some terrible surprise for me that I'm going to hate. You know I can't tell lies and I'll tell you I hate it and then you'll be all upset.'

Morgan's phone pinged again.

'Okay, I'm not buying it. You're up to something. What is it?'

Morgan tapped on her phone and shoved it back in her bag once again. 'Well, actually, it's not about you. It's got nothing to do with you. Lily . . . ' she said, her voice trailing off as she nodded towards the entryway to the lemon grove.

The four of them turned to look over their shoulders.

Peter stood at the top of the path.

Ellen started to cry quietly.

Lily, Dee and Kitty just stared.

Peter hesitated for a moment and then began to walk slowly towards them through the small, well-dressed crowd, an uncertain look on his face.

'What are you doing here?' Lily asked quietly.

'Hi,' he said, hesitating before taking a step towards her. 'I called Morgan a few days ago to make sure that my showing up like this wasn't going to screw up the wedding. I didn't want to be that guy.'

Dee's jaw dropped and she glared at Morgan. Peter cleared his throat and continued. 'I'm sorry, Lily. I should never have let you go like that. I should have gone after you right away . . . I should have gone after you a thousand times since then. I was an idiot. I'm sorry.'

Lily stared up at him, unsure what to say. Her heart was pounding in her chest. Peter pulled out the chair alongside her and sat down facing her.

'I'm sorry I didn't come after you sooner,' he said quietly. 'I was pissed off and that whole conversation got out of hand. I lost my temper and I'm sorry. I thought I had it all figured out and that I didn't want to have kids and if that was going to come between us then I could let you go. But I was wrong. I can't let you go.' He hesitated momentarily before continuing. 'When Morgan said it was okay if I showed up, I cleared my calendar and got on a plane the next day. I had to see you. I've missed you. Can you forgive me?'

Ellen let out a small involuntary sob.

He reached out and squeezed Lily's hand.

Lily was suddenly conscious of the four girls staring at her, awaiting her response. 'But I don't understand ... I mean ... with everything that happened ... I'm just surprised, that's all.'

'Well ... I guess I was expecting to hear from you, but you just cut me off, and it hurt. I know the guy is supposed to be tough and uncaring ... just, you know, move on ... but I thought the months we had spent together were amazing. Then we had that massive argument and you just disappeared.'

'Right, so then you went and cancelled my flight. That was a really shitty move, Peter. I had to use about a million Amex points to get a flight last minute.'

'What? Lily, I didn't cancel your flight.'

'Well, someone did, Peter, and it wasn't me. I just got an email saying it was cancelled.'

'Lily, I swear. I had my assistant cancel my flight as I figured I'd no longer be welcome at the wedding. I cancelled the whole trip ... oh shit ... I had booked our tickets, hadn't I, so your reservation was linked to mine. She must have thought that I meant to cancel both of them when I told her to cancel the whole trip. Oh God, I'm sorry. I had no idea. Honestly.'

'She never liked me,' Lily mumbled.

'No, it was my mistake. I just told her to cancel the flights in a fit of rage. But honestly, I only meant to cancel my own flight . . . not yours.'

Lily frowned, thinking back to the automated email she had received. Had she overdramatised the whole thing? Had it really been an honest mistake? Peter acting like a jerk made it a lot easier for her to cut him off and believe that she'd made the right choice.

'But you never even tried to get in touch with me once. You just gave up.'

'I was a jerk, yes . . . initially. But I showed up at your place a few days later and there was no answer. I had my assistant do some digging on social media and I saw that you had left earlier than planned for Italy, so I didn't feel I should bother you when you were away with the girls and there was this wedding and all . . . ' He hesitated and smiled a small smile. 'You had blocked me on social media, but I figured you'd still be connected to one of my crew, so I asked a few of the girls to check. You look stunning, by the way.'

He hadn't taken his eyes off her the entire time.

'Oh,' was all she could manage.

'Then you called me that night and you said that you weren't sure if you'd made the right decision . . . that you were confused, and we had that long conversation.'

'Oh,' was all she could muster again.

'I know this might not be the right time. And that you're here with the girls and there's going to be a wedding tomorrow ... and that I let you down and screwed this up royally. Lily, I know all that. But I have to ask you something.'

'Oh, good God,' Ellen said in a muffled voice behind her napkin as Dee's jaw dropped for the second time.

'I know that we're different and we want different things and I know that some of those things drove us apart, but I'm crazy about you. I have been since the first day we met. You're good for me.'

'Peter—'

'No, please – let me finish. You make me happier than I've ever been. I don't take things as seriously any more. I don't stress out as much. I appreciate the little things, like you always say I should do more. I realised all that when you left. Everything felt empty and flat. I missed you.'

He reached out and took her other hand. 'I'm moving back to London. Will you come with me? We can start over. A totally fresh start ...'

'Oh!' Lily said, unable to hide her shock. She had been expecting a different question and wasn't sure if she was disappointed or relieved that she hadn't heard it.

Ellen leaned in towards Dee. 'I thought he was going to ask her to marry him,' she whispered.

'Yeah, I bet she did, too,' Dee replied, her expression deadpan.

'Wow ... that's ... well ... um ... What about your business?'

'I'm putting someone in place to lead the US team, but our biggest opportunities are in Europe right now, so I'm moving back there at the end of the summer. At least say you'll think about it. I know it's a lot to consider and this is not the best time to talk about it. Just think about it . . . please.'

'Okay . . . ' she said slowly.

'Really?' he said, grinning as he threw his arms around her.

'Okay, as in okay, I'll think about it,' she said quietly. 'I don't know. I love New York, and this is all . . . well, sudden, I suppose. I thought you were gone. But what about—'

Peter placed a finger to her lips. 'We don't need to get into all of that now. Plenty of time for that later. God, you look amazing!' he said, planting a kiss on her lips.

A waiter approached and asked if he would like a drink.

'Darling, take these,' Kitty said, placing all five empty glasses on the tray. 'And come back with a full tray *per favore.*'

'Well, ladies, I must say I'm impressed,' Peter said, holding Lily's hand in his. 'This is quite the spot. Morgan, I wouldn't have expected anything less.'

Dee caught Lily's eye and raised both eyebrows.

Lily shrugged, almost imperceptibly in response and mustered a smile. Her head was reeling. She had thought about little else other than Peter for the past two weeks and now here he was telling her it had all been a big mistake, a big misunderstanding. He had seemed genuine enough in his insistence that he hadn't cancelled her flight, so if she had so easily got that wrong and had unfairly blamed him, then what else had she misunderstood? It was all very confusing, and her head was buzzing from the wine.

Peter leaned in closer to her. 'I booked a room at the hotel. I wasn't sure how you'd react to seeing me . . . but I'm hoping that I won't have to use it,' he said, kissing the side of her face. 'You smell good—'

'Peter!' she whispered, turning to face him. 'Stop!'

'Okay, okay,' he whispered into her ear. 'I'll stop mauling you for now, but I'm telling you, Lily Ryan, you've never looked sexier. I don't know . . . something about you is different . . . you look different. This place suits you.'

She knew she looked good tonight. She had worked hard at getting in better shape for months, and she felt great in her new dress, but it was still nice to hear it. She breathed in the smell of his aftershave, so familiar to her, and allowed herself to lean back in to him. He kept his arm around her shoulders, subconsciously grazing her shoulder with his fingers as he chatted with the girls. It felt good to be back in his embrace, to feel wanted. She breathed a deep breath and took a glass of wine from the waiter.

'*Grazie,*' she said with a smile as she gazed up at the stars.

'What's this?' Peter asked, taking a sip of the wine and grimacing.

'It's from Ischia,' Lily replied. 'It's a local wine that—'

'Nah, I need a real drink,' he said, motioning for the waiter to come back. 'Yeah, can I get an Old Fashioned? Actually . . . make it a double. It's been a long day.'

Lily frowned slightly when she heard his brusque command but decided to say nothing – he had come all this way to see her and must be exhausted.

Dee made another attempt to catch her eye, but Lily avoided her gaze. She wasn't ready to have a conversation about Peter turning up and what it all meant, as she didn't have all the answers herself, but for now, it felt good to be back in his arms.

Peter raised his glass and toasted the bride and bride. 'Thank you for letting me crash the party. I packed a suit for tomorrow, so if you've got room for one more then I'd love to witness this spectacular event.'

'Of course,' Dee replied politely, stealing a look at Lily, who appeared determined not to meet her eye.

Half an hour later Antonio approached the group, looking meticulous in a pale grey suit. '*Buona sera*, and how was the party tonight? Everything was okay, no?'

'Yes, Antonio,' Morgan said with a smile. 'It was absolutely fabulous. I can't thank you enough.'

'And you are ready for tomorrow? You have a big day ahead! An exciting day too, no?'

'Yes, and to that end, I'm off to bed. Goodnight everyone. I've got forty years of wear and tear on this face ... I don't need to add black bags from lack of sleep, too.'

'I think I'll have a nightcap,' Kitty said, a slow smile spreading across her face.

'Ah, allow me, *signora*,' Antonio said, signalling to Ambrogio, who was hovering nearby. '*Un po' di Rucolino.*'

'Would you care to join me for one, Antonio?'

'That is very kind of you, Kitty, and I would love to, except ... ' He paused to check his watch. 'Except, it is very late, and my wife would not be too pleased if I was to come home much later.'

'I should have known,' Kitty said with a wry smile. 'Yes, of course, I understand.'

Kitty moved to sit next to Ellen. 'Antonio, you Italian men might be raging flirts, but I have to admire your loyalty at the end of the day. Ah well, I'll have to coerce this

310

one instead,' she said, putting an arm around Ellen. 'Can I talk you into a nightcap, darling?'

'Twist my rubber arm,' Ellen replied with a mischievous grin.

'Then the Rucolino is on me, ladies,' Antonio said gallantly.

Dee and Morgan opted out and made their way back towards the main building. Peter stood up and took Lily's hand, interlacing her fingers with his, before leading her down the narrow path.

'Do I need to pick up my room key?' he asked, pulling her in to him as they walked.

Lily looked up to meet his eyes and shook her head.

Chapter Twenty-Three

Lily quietly closed the door to her room. She could hear Peter singing in the bathroom. Why was it that men had to pee the minute they got back to the room? She placed her forehead against the door and took a deep breath. What did all this mean? Did this automatically mean that they were back together? But he was moving to London. Her head was spinning, and she suddenly felt tired. This was far too much to have to think about right now. She loved New York and her small one-bedroom apartment on the Upper West Side. And what about her green card? She had worked hard to get it and moving back to London could mean that she'd have to relinquish it. She had built a life for herself in New York and the thought of starting all over again in London was exhausting.

But what about Peter? She'd have him in London. What would it mean if she stayed in New York? Could they do long distance? If they were back together again, could they make that work? Surely, he had thought about it. After all, he had travelled all this way to see her. That had to mean something. Peter didn't do grand gestures for the sake of it, but what about their last conversation?

She turned and made her way towards the bed. The turn-down staff had closed the full-length white linen curtains, placed a mint on her pillow and set out her white cotton hotel slippers alongside the bed. She leaned one hand on the bed and went to kick off her heels, but hesitated. Her legs looked great in high heels. Peter had always said so. Her feet ached, but the dress would look weird if she took off her heels. She'd look four inches shorter, for one, and the shape wouldn't be as flattering with her feet flat on the ground.

She wandered over to the window instead, pulling the cord to open the curtains. Directly outside her door was a twelve-by-six-foot plunge pool, illuminated from below by underwater lights and surrounded by a border of burgeoning purple bougainvillea and tall hedgerows of jasmine. Beyond that lay the open sea, silver and still in the moonlight. She pulled back the sliding door and breathed in the heavily scented night air. There was no doubt in her mind that this was the most beautiful place she had ever been. The heady night air was intoxicating. Stepping outside on to the small, private terrace, she closed her eyes and breathed in deeply.

Peter came up behind her and placed his hands on her hips, leaning in to kiss her neck. He pulled her back in towards him, his hands gently tracing the length of her arms before kissing the other side of her neck. Lily moved her head to one side and closed her eyes. Silently, he reached for the zipper on her dress, slowly pulling it down. The blush-pink dress fell to the ground.

Lily angled her leg and stepped provocatively out of the dress, turning to face him. She looked quickly to make sure that none of the neighbouring rooms had a view of her terrace.

'God, I've missed you,' he said, his breath heavy.

He wanted her. She knew it and it felt good. She so rarely felt in charge or in control of her life, but she did at this moment. Peter was here, he had come to win her back and he wanted her. This gorgeous man had travelled halfway across the world for her. He had picked her. That had to mean that they could make it work, no matter what, and that he was willing to do whatever it took.

She wrapped both arms around his neck and kissed him deeply. She unbuttoned his shirt and peeled it off him, letting it drop to the ground.

He reached down and cupped her bottom, pulling her tightly in to him.

'You look good,' he whispered, his hands moving to unhook her strapless bra and fumbling with the clasp.

She could smell the whisky on his breath as he spoke. Stale whisky. She hated the smell of it and turned her face instinctively.

'What's the matter?' he asked, frowning at her.

'Nothing . . . I just . . . I don't know, this is all so . . . weird.'

'Me?'

'No, of course not, it's just that . . . well, two weeks ago we . . .'

'Oh, come on . . . just let it go. We're here now,' he said as he kissed her again. 'I want you back, Lily. I came here for you, for us. Everything was . . . I don't know, empty after you left. I was an idiot. I'll do whatever you want. Can't we forget about all of that and just start over?'

'Whatever I want?' Lily repeated, pulling back from him, a small frown forming on her face.

'Yes, whatever you want. Isn't that what you want? What

do you want me to say? Why are you frowning at me like that? Come on, don't get all worked up.' He put his hands on the sides of her face. 'Come on,' he said, leaning in to kiss her again. 'God, I've missed you. Haven't you missed me?'

'Yes, but Peter . . . wait. It's not "whatever I want". That's the problem. I don't know what I want and maybe I'll never know, but . . . why are you here? I thought that's why you were here. That you were okay with that. Are you not?'

'Not this again,' he sighed. 'Surely this week has shown you that a baby changes everything. You wouldn't be here if you had a baby, Lily. You don't get to live the same life with kids. Trust me, I know. Come to London with me. We'll start over together. We'll get a place in Chelsea or Marylebone . . . a townhouse. We're great together, Lily. You just said it yourself – you don't know what you want, so why throw all this away? I don't want to lose you again, Lily. Come on . . . I promise you, you won't regret it.'

He was offering her everything she thought she had always wanted. Except the one thing she still wasn't sure that she might ever want. They were right back where they had left off in New York. She suddenly felt very naked and exposed.

'I thought you had come here because you had changed your mind, or at least that you were open to the possibility of it,' she said, reaching down and picking up her dress. 'I haven't changed mine, Peter, and yes, I don't know what I want yet . . . and I'm sorry about that. But if we're to do this then it has to be what you want, too.' She pulled the blush-pink dress closer to her.

'So, we're back here again?'

She felt something inside of her sink. That feeling of

being disappointed again. The weight of disappointment tugged at her on the inside and she was powerless
to stop it.

'I'm sorry.' She didn't know what else to say. Her head
hurt. At this point she didn't know if she knew anything for sure.

'Right, I should have known,' he said, under his breath.

'Sorry?'

'Nothing, Lily, it's just that I should have known, that's
all,' he said, with an exaggerated sigh.

'Should have known what?'

'That it was stupid to come here and think you'd be open
to us getting back together,' he said, bending down to pick
up his shirt.

Lily frowned. 'Peter, I'm sorry you came all this way,
but I haven't like had a lobotomy or anything in the past
week. What exactly were you expecting to find when you
arrived here?'

'*You!* I was expecting to find you! The Lily I fell in love
with, who was so much fun and happy and easy-going . . .
the Lily I spent the past six months with, the one who
wasn't preoccupied about whether or not she wanted kids.
I saw the photos of you on Instagram and you looked
happy! You looked happy and you looked sexy, and I
missed you, so I booked a goddamn flight and here I am.
And nothing has changed. You haven't changed. You still
want it all.'

'All? Are you joking? I didn't ask you to come here,
Peter. I left your apartment, remember? You told me
that you were done, and you definitely did not want to
have any more children, so I left. Remember? *I* left *you*!

And now here you are saying "poor me I came all this way" and acting like the massive argument in New York never happened, or that the whole thing just magically went away.'

She wrapped the dress around her as best she could and walked back into the bedroom, swapping out the dress for a hotel dressing gown and pulling off her shoes. She sat on the edge of the bed, deflated. The room was no longer a potential haven of sexual reconnection, and neither was she.

'I thought you had come here because you had changed your mind,' she continued, her head pounding now. 'But you haven't, have you?'

Peter came and stood alongside the bed as he stuck his arms into his shirtsleeves. He cast his eyes down to match each button with the right buttonhole.

'No,' he said quietly.

Lily nodded, taking in the enormity of what he was saying. His answer was a definitive no once again. She didn't need any more proof.

She nodded again. 'Right.'

Peter stood, staring at an indiscriminate corner of the room.

Lily slunk down to the carpet, her head leaning back against the deep mattress, and closed her eyes for a moment. 'I don't know for sure, but I think that a baby might be part of what I want in the future. Or maybe I'm totally wrong, maybe I won't want one at all, but I know that I want the choice,' she said, her head dropping down to her chest. 'You had kids because your ex-wife wanted to have them, and you resented her as a result of it. I don't want you to agree with me now and then resent me later. If I'm to have kids then I want to have them *with* someone, not against them.'

Peter leaned one hand on the corner of the bed and sat down on the carpet alongside her. 'Okay.'

Lily turned to look at him again. 'Okay, what?'

'Okay ... I get it,' he said slowly. 'You're right. I never really wanted kids. My ex-wife did, so we had them. I could have done without it, but she couldn't. Look, there are all sorts of reasons it didn't work out with her, but you're right – you should have the choice. I'm just sorry that I can't give you that.' He turned to face her. 'It's the only thing in the world I can't give you.'

Lily looked down at the ground. 'I know. I'm sorry that you came all this way and—'

'It's okay. I needed a break. It felt good to get out of town.' He shrugged, a small smile forming on his face.

'Peter, twenty-four hours in Italy isn't a break.'

'Yeah, well, that's what you get when you aim high and sign up for the winner's circle. The work doesn't stop,' he said, sighing as he tipped his head back against the mattress. 'Look, I can't change what I want, just the same way you can't change what you want. But I can't go back to having kids, Lily. I'm sorry.'

'I know. Me too.'

'I'm just going to go,' he said, quietly.

'Okay,' Lily replied.

'I wish things were different, but ...'

'I know.'

'I would have given you everything.'

'I know.'

There was nothing more to say. One decision lay between them like a massive chasm and neither of them could breach it. He gave her a small smile and closed the door softly behind him. It was quietest he had ever left a room.

Chapter Twenty-Four

The shrieking of her alarm pulled Lily from a deep sleep. Silencing it, she rolled over on to her back, staring at the ceiling. She had to be in the olive garden in twenty minutes to review the set-up for the afternoon's ceremony with Dee. Padding to the bathroom, she splashed water on her face and tied her hair up into a knot. She pulled on a navy one-piece swimsuit and yanked a full-length blue kaftan from the drawer. Her mouth felt like dry cardboard, but she didn't have enough time for coffee. That would have to wait.

She took a small bottle of San Pellegrino from the mini-bar and downed it in one go, the bubbles helping to satiate her thirst. She bent down to retrieve her dress from the floor at the foot of the bed, shaking her head as the events of the previous night played in her head like a movie preview.

'Disaster,' she mumbled, slipping her feet into her flip-flops and grabbing her room key.

Dee was already in the olive garden, along with Marco and the wedding planner. A pergola had been set up at the end of the garden, with sheer white fabric that rippled in the faint sea breeze. Massive urns overflowing with white hydrangeas stood left and right of it and a wooden platform had been set up in one corner to accommodate the string quartet.

'Hey, where's Peter?' Dee asked, looking over Lily's shoulder. 'I thought he'd be glued to you for the day.'

'He's gone.'

'He's *what*?' Dee shrieked. 'What did you do?'

'Nothing. Well, I don't actually know if he's gone from the resort, but he's gone from me, that's for sure.'

'What the hell ...? I saw him at breakfast briefly, but he disappeared before I got to say hello. I was wondering where you were. What happened?'

'Well, basically, nothing has changed. We ended up having a delayed replay of the same conversation and he hasn't changed his mind about any of it. So, we had a massive argument and he left.'

'Oh, for fuck's sake. I was sure that he had changed his mind when he showed up last night.'

'No, I think he hoped that I might have. I think when he called Morgan to get confirmation that it was okay to show up, he took that as it was okay to pick right up with me again, so he hopped on a plane thinking that we'd just pick up where we left off – without the baby argument. He said the right things initially, but ultimately he hadn't changed his mind about any of it.'

'Son of a bitch!' Dee fumed.

Lily looked down at the ground. 'You know what, Dee? I'm better off knowing now. We could have gone down this road again for God knows how long and I'd have arrived at the exact same spot. He doesn't want to have kids, period. In a fucked-up sort of way, I kind of respect him for having such a strong conviction. At least I know where I stand. He was very decent about the whole thing in the end but we're just not going to be able to get past this.'

'So how do you feel about it all? How did it feel seeing him again?'

'I don't know . . . I mean, it was great to see him, but sort of confusing too, to be honest. I hadn't expected to see him here, so it was all out of context.'

'And what about Matt?'

'What *about* Matt?'

'Well, it's just that you've been spending all this time with him and you two get along really well. Do you think there's anything there?'

'No, he's lovely, but that's way too complicated. He has Elena to think about and to be fair I think she's his priority right now, as she should be.'

'He is kind of hot, though,' Dee said, leaning over to nudge Lily with her elbow.

'He's definitely hot,' Lily agreed, grinning at her friend. 'But his life is a bit of a hot mess and so is mine so . . . ' She shrugged. 'Anyway, why are you here in shorts and T-shirt and not at the spa or the hairdressers or something?'

'I've been dragged to the spa five times this week. There are no more bits of me to rub or moisturise. I'm here to make sure the chairs are in straight lines or I swear to God she'll stop to fix them coming down the aisle.'

Lily laughed despite herself. 'Are you nervous?'

'Yep!' Dee said, taking a deep breath.

'Okay, come on, let's do something to take your mind off it.'

*

For the next hour, Lily and Dee watched the San Montano team stage the olive grove for the wedding ceremony. Once they had left, the two girls fiddled with the rows of chairs, repositioned the urns so they didn't block anyone's view and picked up stray rogue leaves from the pathway that Morgan would soon walk down. They alternated between chatting excitedly to silently dwelling on their own thoughts, and happily passed the time in each other's company.

Just a few hours later, Morgan walked slowly down the centre of the olive grove to the strains of Pachelbel's Canon in D, performed on two violins, a viola and a cello. She was resplendent in a custom Oscar de la Renta off-the-shoulder gown with a billowing full skirt, her hair tied in an elegant chignon at the nape of her neck, a cream-coloured rosebud tucked in at the side.

Her bride stood awaiting her under the pergola in a tai-lored ivory Tom Ford tuxedo. Dee even wore nude heels for the occasion and beamed with pride as she watched Morgan walk down the aisle.

Lily thought it was the happiest that she had ever seen them look and her eyes welled up with tears of happiness for her two friends. She was determined to put last night out of her head and not let it get in the way of such a happy day. Ellen stood on her right, already overcome with emotion and dabbing her eyes with a tissue. Lily caught her eye and smiled, thinking that she had never looked prettier. She looked tall and slim in a long satin navy dress, her hair piled up in a knot and secured by two pearl clips. On her left, Kitty looked almost regal in a striking orange gown, and in her four-inch heels she towered a foot over Ellen.

'You look *stunning*!' Ellen whispered loudly to Kitty.

'So do you, darling. Navy is your colour. Now, switch places with me, will you?'

'Why?' Ellen asked, shuffling to her left.

'Have you seen Morgan's cousin? He only arrived this morning. Divine creature and apparently single. Time is limited, darling, so I want to make sure I'm highly visible,' Kitty replied, smiling across the aisle at Morgan's American cousin.

The ceremony lasted just under twenty minutes, which was a far stretch from the original conversation they had had with the events team at San Montano. The bride kissed the bride and the crowd erupted in applause and cheers. Lily spotted Marco and Antonio applauding at the back of the olive grove, on hand to ensure that everything went according to plan, but equally, she guessed, to witness and share in the outpouring of love, happiness and hope that filled the ancient olive grove.

The crowd dispersed, taking it in turns to congratulate the brides as the string quartet played all the wedding classics. The first of many bottles of champagne was popped, the sound of the cork popping attracting another cheer from those nearby. Laughter, chatter, happy cheers, the clinking of glass and the strains of the string quartet were all that could be heard for the next hour as the chairs were quietly removed and the guests milled about under the early evening sun.

'So ... how did I do?' Dee asked, hugging Lily as she congratulated her.

'Fabulous! I was very proud of you,' Lily beamed. She turned to hug Morgan. 'You look spectacular! The dress is incredible!'

'Thank you. I won't want to take it off. This is all like

a dream,' Morgan said, her face radiant with happiness. She placed one hand on Lily's arm. 'Dee told me what happened. I'm so sorry, Lily. When he called to ask if he could come, I really thought—'

'Morgan, forget it. He came, he tried . . . it's over,' Lily said, taking a deep breath. 'Honestly, it's okay. I'm fine. It's for the best.' The three of them took champagne glasses from a passing tray. 'Here's to one day finding the kind of happiness that you two were lucky enough to find. And what an absolutely spectacular way to celebrate it, here in this magical place. *Salute!*'

'*Salute,*' they both replied, clinking the three glasses together.

An hour later, at the sound of a gong, the group began to make their way towards the restaurant. Lily caught up with Dee, who was standing on the terrace, a cocktail glass in her hand.

'What's that?'

'One of Ambrogio's My-gronis. I can only take so much champagne. I needed a real drink. Fancy one?'

'Sure!' Lily replied, waving at Ambrogio.

Ambrogio gave her the thumbs-up sign and appeared two minutes later with a My-groni on a silver tray. '*Ecco,* Signora LeeLee. *Salute!*'

'Where's your bride?' Lily asked, looking around the terrace.

'Bathroom. I have to wait for her here as apparently it takes two people to get her and that skirt down the stairs!'

'Oh right,' Lily said. Her eyes darted left and right across the terrace.

'What's up with you?' Dee asked.

'Nothing,' Lily replied with a shrug. 'I just thought he'd come, that's all.'

'I saw him earlier, just before the wedding, but I think he left. I spoke to him briefly at reception. He was pretty decent, actually. Congratulated me and all that. He said he was spending the night at a hotel in Naples and flying back to New York in the morning.'

'New York? Oh, right . . . ' Lily said haltingly.

'Ah . . . ' Dee said slowly. 'You meant Matt.'

Lily blushed instantly. 'I—'

'For God's sake, Lily, what's stopping you?' Dee interjected. 'It's clear that you're attracted to him. You're like a dimmer switch, for Christ's sake, lighting up whenever he's around and going dark again when he leaves.'

'Dee, it's complicated. I have to get back to New York and get stuck into this new business, so I don't have time for any distractions. Plus, I have to figure out if I'm going to stay in my apartment or if I can even afford it right now and I probably need to get a part-time job while I figure it all out because I blew my salary for the last six months on heels that I'll never wear again and fancy matching underwear. And that's just *me*! Matt's life is a whole other bucket of complicated. My head is full of all kinds of shit right now.'

'Well, then empty it out! You might have some explaining to do after he saw you with Peter last night, but nothing really happened, right?'

'He saw me with Peter?' Lily asked, suddenly aghast.

'Yeah, he left to hand Elena off to the babysitter and then came back down.'

'Shit, I didn't see him.'

'No, because you were like adhesive on Peter. But nothing really happened last night, did it?'

'No, I even managed to screw up the make-up sex. I should have had sex first and then argued with him. I can't even get that right,' she said, rolling her eyes.

'Who are we talking about? And how do you screw up having sex? Sounds like a bit of a contradiction in terms, if you ask me,' Kitty said, as she and Ellen came to stand alongside them. 'Is this a private My-groni party or can anyone join? Ambrogio!' She gestured for another round.

'Am I interrupting something?'

Matt walked up to the group holding Elena by the hand. He was dressed in a navy suit and white shirt, and she in a navy linen dress with a stitched-on white belt, and navy patent shoes. 'Good evening, ladies. Dee, congratulations! Sorry we're late. I watched the ceremony from the back of the olive garden but there was some confusion about Elena getting here so I had to duck out and collect her. It was very tense all the way back here, making sure we got here in time to see the bride – right, Elena?'

Elena nodded furiously. 'Yes! I didn't want to miss her!'

'Hi Matt, I'm just glad you made it. Hi, Elena,' Dee said, crouching down to say hello.

'How come you're not wearing a white dress?' Elena asked, looking directly at Dee.

'Oh, don't worry, there is a bride in a very large white dress around here somewhere,' Dee said. 'It's hard to miss her.'

Matt frowned as his phone rang. 'Sorry, excuse me. This is my contractor again. It's the fifth call this afternoon. I have to take this. Do you mind keeping an eye on her for a minute?'

'Sure, no problem,' Lily replied.

'Are you a lesbian?' Elena asked, turning to Dee.

Dee stifled a laugh. 'Yes, I am, as a matter of fact. Why do you ask?'

'Because you're marrying another woman. My mommy's a lesbian,' Elena replied matter-of-factly.

'No wonder he has commitment issues,' Kitty murmured behind her cocktail glass. 'Exactly how many lesbians are on property, do you think?' she asked no one in particular. 'I'm beginning to feel outnumbered.'

'Oh, right,' Dee replied, still face to face with Elena. 'That makes sense. Where's your mommy now?'

'In Portland . . . that's in Oregon.'

'Sounds about right,' Dee said with a shrug of her shoulders. 'Lesbian capital of the world – one of my favourite cities to visit, in fact.'

'She lives there now. She's in charge of Nike. That's where their biggest office is. It's their headquarters.'

'She's what?' Lily asked.

Elena sighed exaggeratedly. 'She's in charge of all the money, and she has to live in Portland because that's where they keep the money . . . in the headquarters office.'

'Actually,' Dee said, slowly standing back up again, 'the CFO of Nike *is* a lesbian.'

'See! I told you,' Elena said nodding furiously.

Lily turned to Dee. 'How do you know that?'

'I actually know her, and she's a pretty cool woman to be honest.'

'Are you seriously telling me that you know Matt's ex-wife?'

'Elena, is your mommy's name Roberta?' Dee asked.

'Yes,' she said. 'You smell nice.'

Dee smiled. 'Thanks, so do you.'

'I know,' Elena said with a shy smile. 'Do you know my mommy?'

'Yes, I met her once in Portland. We had a good chat. I like her.'

'Me too. But she's my mommy, so I guess everyone likes their mommy.' She shrugged.

'Do you see her very often?' Lily asked.

'Of course I do. She's my mommy. You have to see your mommy a lot. But I live in New York with my daddy because she's so busy at work,' she said, twisting her ponytail in her right hand. 'I'm getting a new bike for Christmas.'

'A new bike? That's cool. What colour?' Lily asked, stooping down to the same level as Elena.

'Red. It's my favourite colour. Guess what, Lily,' Elena said, her eyes lighting up with excitement. 'I'm staying at the hotel again tonight because our house isn't fixed.'

'Oh, lucky you!' Lily replied as Elena chatted on about her hotel room.

'Okay, I'm going to go check on my bride,' Dee said. 'She may have got stuck somewhere in that dress. See you downstairs.'

Matt returned with two glasses of champagne and one *limonata*. 'Be careful you don't spill that on your dress,' he said, handing Elena her drink.

'*Papà*, I'm *four* now,' she replied indignantly.

'What's going on with the house?' Lily asked as they moved to one of the wrought-iron tables in the garden.

Matt rolled his eyes. 'Oh, the tiler was finishing up today

and cut one of the main water pipes coming into the house. So the plumber had to be called to fix the leak. It's a bit of a mess, so we're going to wait until tomorrow to move back in. Just the usual last-minute hiccups, I guess.'

'Are you always this patient about everything?'

'No, definitely not, but when you spend enough time in Italy you just learn to accept delays as par for the course. Especially on an island. It's like this place has its own time zone.'

'Am I going to see the bride soon?' Elena asked, slurping the end of her lemonade noisily through her straw.

'Yes. Why don't we head down towards the restaurant? She'll definitely be down there,' Lily said, standing up from the table.

Matt reached over and put a hand on Lily's arm.

'I heard about what happened with that guy . . . the guy from New York, your ex-boyfriend? I saw you with him last night when I came back down and it looked like . . . well, I didn't want to interrupt.'

'Yeah,' Lily said, pretending to pick something off of her dress. 'It was . . . I'm not sure what it was really – an optical illusion maybe, because it wasn't what it looked like at all.' She turned to face him. 'He's gone.'

'I'm sorry,' he said, his eyes not leaving hers. 'I met Morgan at the bar, and she told me. I'm not sure why, but she said something about having given him permission and having gotten it all wrong. I didn't understand the details to be honest, but I'm sorry it didn't work out.'

'Yeah, thanks. Well, like I told you on the boat, it's complicated but this time it's over for good.'

'Hell, I sure know how that goes. Want to change the subject?'

'Please!' she said with a sigh.

'Okay. Come on, Elenita, let's go find that bride, shall we?'

'I'm going with Lily, *Papà*,' Elena replied, taking Lily's hand.

Matt smiled. 'Don't worry, we're all going down together. Then we'll have to see where our seats are. This is a wedding, remember? So, we'll all have our own special seats.'

'I've never been to a wedding before,' Elena said, looking up at Lily as she skipped alongside her.

'Weddings are fun. First there's dinner and then there's dancing.'

'If you need to go do maid-of-honour stuff, please do. It looks like Elena would happily be stuck to you like a clam for the evening, but don't let that get in the way of whatever you need to do.'

'Are you joking? It's a "title-only" role. I had to practically beat Dee to convince her to have a twenty-minute ceremony in the first place. Trust me, there will be no more duties to be performed. I'm officially retired for the evening,' she said, laughing.

As she got to the door of the restaurant, she paused to glance at the table chart. Scanning the chart, she couldn't help but smile. Someone, and she had a strong suspicion as to who it might be, had clearly done a last-minute seating-chart shuffle. Two of Morgan's cousins had been ousted from Table One and in their place were Matt and Elena.

'Is this a mistake?' Matt asked as he spotted their names at Table One.

'No mistake, Matt,' Morgan said confidently as she walked towards him. 'I'm done with mistakes, so take a seat, honey. I should know better and learn to mind my own goddamn business.'

Elena gasped as she turned around and saw the bride. 'You're beautiful!' she said, both hands clutching her small purse as she stared at Morgan in the white dress. She reached out one hand and hesitated before lightly touching the skirt. 'It's so white.' Her voice was barely a whisper. She pulled her hand back and looked up at Morgan with a smile. 'You look like a princess.'

Morgan stooped down as best she could to reach Elena's level. 'Today, I feel like a princess,' she said, smiling at the earnest face before her. 'It's like this is my very own fairy tale. And you are the most darling little girl I have ever seen in my life. Look at you in that dress! Baby girl, I think we need a photo. What do you say?'

Elena turned around, her eyes wide, in search of Matt. '*Papà!* The bride wants to take a photo with me, *Papà!*' She glanced down at her feet and moved in as far as the big white dress would allow. Standing as close to the bride as she dared, Elena smiled her widest smile as Morgan leaned down and wrapped one arm around her shoulders.

Lily smiled at the little girl's unfiltered joy and turned to Matt. 'Are you okay?' she asked, noticing that his eyes had welled up with tears.

'Yeah, sorry.' He took a deep breath and cleared his throat. 'She's everything to me and to see her so happy like this, after everything she's been through the past couple of years, just . . . '

'I know. Well, I don't, but I can imagine,' Lily replied kindly as she turned back to watch the four-year-old girl and the bride beam for photos.

As they took their seats at the table, Lily turned to whisper in Elena's ear. 'You know, if today is Morgan's fairy tale, then that means you are in it. Have you ever been in a fairy tale before?'

Elena looked up at Lily, her eyes wide as she shook her head. 'No, I've never been in a fairy tale before.'

'Me neither!'

The dinner conversation was light-hearted and fun, and Elena proved to be as delightful as she was adorable. Once dinner was finished and the settings had been cleared, Elena was allowed to pull out her tablet at the table and was soon absorbed in a world of talking pink pigs. Matt moved to the other side of her and sat on the empty seat alongside Lily as the band started to play their first tunes.

'So, you leave for New York tomorrow?'

'Yep, very reluctantly,' Lily said, hanging her head in dismay. 'How much longer are you actually here for?'

'Another four weeks.'

'God, I'm so jealous. Sounds like a dream. Summer in Ischia ... renovating your own villa. Not too shabby.'

Marco appeared at the table and spoke to Matt in Italian.

'Marco's sister Ilaria is going to watch Elena for a while,' Matt explained. 'Elena adores her, and I figured the party might run late and she'd get tired of hanging out with the adults, so she's going to watch *Peppa Pig* in peace back in the room.'

'Everyone knows everyone on the island, I suppose?' Lily asked, as he helped Elena put the tablet back in her bag.

'Pretty much.' He turned his attention back to Elena. 'Okay, Ilaria is waiting for you. I'll be up in a little while, okay? If you need anything just call me.' He kissed her on the forehead.

Kitty wandered by the table and leaned down to Lily. 'Things are looking up! The hot American cousin was struck off of Table One and ended up alongside me. Everything for a reason, darling,' she said with a wink.

Elena skipped off happily holding Marco's hand as Matt sank back into his chair. He ran his hand through his hair, leaving it looking completely dishevelled. Lily tried to hide a smile, her eyes following the strong line of his jaw.

'You look tired,' she said. 'Were you at the house all day?'

'Yeah. I'm not sorry to have all that hard labour behind me. I mean, I had contractors coming and going, but it was a lot more work than I thought it would be trying to keep it all together.'

She nodded, leaning back and wrapping her hands around one knee.

'It's too bad you're leaving tomorrow,' he said, looking directly at her. 'I'd love you to see it.'

'You would?' she asked, her heart giving a jump in her chest.

Every conversation with him was confusing and intoxicating at the same time.

'Yeah, it's small but it's got a nice garden and a great view of the sea. I just don't know the first thing about interiors, so it's going to be pretty basic for a while until I figure out what to do next. The truth is, I—'

His phone rang and he rummaged around in his pocket for it.

The truth is that you what? Lily asked herself, her thoughts suspended as he pulled out his phone.

334

'*Ciao, amore!*' he said, his face lighting up with a smile.

Lily looked at him expectantly.

'She's on her way back down,' he said, with a laugh. 'I wondered how long that might last.'

Moments later Elena rejoined the table, this time with Ilaria in tow. 'Can I stay here, *Papà*? I missed the party.'

Matt laughed. 'Sure! That's a much better idea.'

'Hi, Lily,' she said, waving across the table as she clambered up on to the chair.

'Hi, Elena,' Lily replied, smiling at the happy little face staring back at her.

'Sorry,' Matt said, turning back to face Lily. 'What were we talking about?'

'Oh, you were saying something about the house and—'

'Lily, why aren't you dancing?' Elena asked loudly across the table.

'Pardon?'

'You said that at weddings there is dinner and then dancing, but you're not dancing.'

'Oh right, well, we were just chatting so—'

'*Papà*!' Elena said, a serious frown settling on her face. 'You're not dancing. It's a wedding, *Papà*.'

'You're absolutely right, Elenita,' Matt said, pushing his chair back from the table. He stood up and buttoned the top button of his navy blazer before slowly extending a hand down to Lily. 'Would you like to dance?'

Lily felt her stomach lurch up into her chest as she took his hand and joined the other couples on the dance floor. Matt held her close as they moved with the rhythm of the music. With her face close to his neck, she breathed in his scent and closed her eyes. His body felt warm and strong against hers as he moved her with surprising ease. The fingers of his left hand were entwined with hers, his other arm resting just above the small of her back.

'Maybe when I get back to New York we could meet . . . for dinner or something? I've wanted to ask you that for days, but I didn't know if you'd be open to it,' Matt said, turning ever so slightly so that he could see her face. 'Remember the other day on the boat . . . on the way back from Procida, when Elena fell asleep in your arms? Well, I had a thought . . . I decided that if she could open up and let someone in again, then maybe it was okay for me to do the same.'

Lily wasn't sure if her stomach flipped or her heart jumped, but something went off inside her. Her head reeled as she stared at him, oblivious to everyone else on the dance floor.

'You did?'

He nodded in response, not taking his eyes from hers. There were so many unanswered questions swirling around in her brain and so much that she had yet to figure out. The music and the noise seemed to fade around her as her heart hammered in her chest.

'Look, I don't have all the answers, Lily. In fact, I probably bring more questions to this than anything,' he said, gazing down at her with a smile as they moved slowly with the music. 'I loved Morgan's speech, but I'm not Prince Charming and I'm kind of hoping that you're not Cinderella, because whatever this is, it feels pretty real to me.'

'I'm definitely not the Cinderella type,' Lily said, shaking her head. 'I'm more of a Lara Croft *Tomb Raider* character if you don't mind.'

Matt threw his head back and laughed, pulling her closer to him. 'I stand corrected. Yes, that's far more appropriate' he agreed. 'Man, I'm going to have to get better at this stuff before I ruin Elena for life,' he said, shaking his head. 'She'd do way better with someone like you in her life. A free-spirited, strong female voice in her ear.'

'I don't think you'll ruin her entirely. I think she's already displaying plenty of free-spiritedness of her own. Is that even a word?' Lily asked with a tiny frown.

'Don't ask me. You're the writer,' Matt said with a smile as he released one arm and twirled Lily gently around.

Elena clapped her hands in delight as she watched on with Morgan and Dee. As she spun, Lily could feel herself unfurl. She had a plan, she had hope, she had the promise of a new beginning. Everything felt possible again as Matt turned her around and pulled her gently back into his embrace.

Leaning into him, Lily marvelled at just how much had happened since she'd arrived on this small Italian island a week ago. Now, surrounded by her tribe and with Matt leading her slowly across the dance floor, she wondered if perhaps motherhood wasn't always a decision that you needed to make consciously. Maybe, instead, it showed up when you were least expecting it, in the shape of a four-year-old girl.

Acknowledgements

A very special thanks . . .

To my agent, Hannah Weatherill for your unwavering support and sound advice. I remain indebted to you for plucking me from obscurity and taking a chance.

To my editor Rebecca Roy – I'm so glad I landed with you following that internal reshuffle! It's clear that you love what you do as your enthusiasm is infectious and I hang up the phone (or click off the Zoom call) wanting to try harder and be a better writer, every single time.

To Darcy Nicholson, editorial director, who can weave in and out of all our lives at a moment's notice and still manage to keep all the literary balls in the air.

To Thalia Proctor, for not criticising my repeated abuse of the humble comma but instead presenting all my foibles with grace and humour.

To the entire team at Sphere. I am honestly so grateful to all of you from proofreading to cover art to marketing and publicity and everyone in between – I am still astounded by the number of people it takes to bring a book to life.

To my sisters Martina and Angela, two of the most frank, direct humans one can hope to meet. Thanks once again for being the first draft readers and for stepping briefly out of character and wrapping the initial critique in only kind words. Much appreciated!

To all my sweet friends on the island of Ischia for shoving me off the beaten path and introducing me to the parts and the people that you all love. Now I do too.

To the team at San Montano Resort, Ischia – the most wonderful group of people who exude such pride in what they do and where they live. Yes, it's a real place and yes, it's utterly magical. I only hope that I've done a decent job of describing just how intoxicating a place it really is.

To the Rick O'Shea Book Club in Ireland – huge thanks for the lovely comments, kind social shares and words of encouragement for my first book, *The Italian Escape*. You guys made the daunting task of writing this second book far less terrifying!

To Uncle Ger for changing his lifelong literary habits and ploughing through my first book – I can't tell you how much that meant!

To Tom, The American, for continuing to believe that this is the only path to be on and for being a late-night editor as the first draft came together and I tried to gauge funny or not funny.

And finally, to you, the readers, my sincere thanks, because without you, what is the point?